FEMALE QUIXOTISM

EARLY AMERICAN WOMEN WRITERS

Mrs. Hannah Webster Foster, *The Coquette*
Susanna Rowson, *Charlotte Temple*
Tabitha Gilman Tenney, *Female Quixotism*

FEMALE QUIXOTISM

Exhibited in the Romantic Opinions and
Extravagant Adventures of Dorcasina Sheldon

TABITHA GILMAN TENNEY

Edited with an
Introduction and Notes by
JEAN NIENKAMP AND ANDREA COLLINS

Foreword by
CATHY N. DAVIDSON

New York   Oxford
OXFORD UNIVERSITY PRESS
1992

Oxford University Press

Oxford   New York   Toronto
Delhi   Bombay   Calcutta   Madras   Karachi
Petaling Jaya   Singapore   Hong Kong   Tokyo
Nairobi   Dar es Salaam   Cape Town
Melbourne   Auckland

and associated companies in
Berlin   Ibadan

Introduction, Note on the Text,
Selected Bibliography, and Chronology

First American edition of *Female Quixotism*, 1801

This paperback edition, with new editorial matter, first published
in 1992 by Oxford University Press, Inc.
200 Madison Avenue, New York, New York 10016

Oxford is a registered trademark of Oxford University Press

Library of Congress Cataloging-in-Publication Data
Tenney, Tabitha, 1762-1837.
Female quixotism: exhibited in the romantic opinions and
extravagant adventures of Dorcasina Sheldon/
Tabitha Gilman Tenney; foreword by Cathy N. Davidson;
edited with an introduction and notes by Jean Nienkamp and Andrea Collins.
p.   cm.—(Early American women writers)
Includes bibliographical references.
ISBN 0-19-507414-9 (pbk.)
I. Nienkamp, Jean. II. Collins, Andrea. III. Title. IV. Series.
PS3000.T5F4 1992
813'.2—dc20   91-23398

2 4 6 8 10 9 7 5 3 1

Printed in the United States of America
on acid free paper.

FOREWORD

While doing research on reading in early America at the American Antiquarian Society, I came across the diary of Patty Rogers, a fascinating account of adolescent courtship behavior (i.e., petting) couched in disguised literary and classical allusions applied to various people in the town of Exeter, New Hampshire, in 1785. Not many eighteenth-century diaries mention sexuality at all, and it is especially rare to find a woman's version of the gender rules circumscribing courtship. Indeed, Patty's account of the various "liberties" a young man takes (or tries to take) is so unusual among surviving diaries that hers was originally catalogued as a fantasy. With its abundant allusions to contemporary fictional heroes and heroines, its Sternian exclamatory prose style, its pseudonymous references to men such as "Portius" and "Philam[m]on," the diary does seem more a reflection of literature than of life. But one entry in this diary caught my attention. It mentioned a "Miss T——G-m—," whom Patty describes as "a person peculiarly disagreeable to me—not from any injury she ever did me, but there is a Certain something, in her manner, with which I am ever disgusted." "Miss T—— G-m— was, I interpreted, Tabitha Gilman, a quiet young woman in Patty's busy social circle. After checking genealogical records and family histories to confirm dates and identities, the diary's "code" became clearer as did the account of the love triangle in which Patty played an unhappy role.

Philammon was Dr. Samuel Tenney, a surgeon who, after serving in the Revolutionary War, had come home to Exeter to find himself a suitable wife and start a political career. He was obviously drawn to both the impetuous, novel-loving Patty (the kind of girl with whom a former soldier in his late thirties might take liberties) and the more sober, respectable Tabitha Gilman (the kind of girl who would make a proper wife for a future Congressman). After the marriage, Patty stayed on unmarried in Exeter while Tabitha followed her new husband to Washington where she wrote *Female Quixotism*, the story of the impetuous, novel-reading Dorcasina Sheldon who also loses at love. In Patty Rogers' diary I'd stumbled onto a small part of Tabitha Tenney's biography and possibly even the biographical basis of her novel.

Decoding the diary was hardly a momentous literary event. ("So what?" one of my friends bluntly responded when I communicated my "discovery.") But, on another level, the whole process of and motivation for deciphering Patty Rogers' diary is paradigmatic of early American women's literary historiography. A fragment of a diary becomes significant because, against odds, it has survived. The kind of records—correspondence, journals, drafts of manuscripts—that have been preserved by worshipping progeny for many (but certainly not all) male writers are typically absent for women. Papers are destroyed or lost, records are not kept. Even local historians (not known for modesty about a town's accomplishments) tend to overlook the contributions of female citizens. Tabitha Gilman Tenney has only a few lines in the *History of Exeter* (1888): "Dr. Tenney's wife was Tabitha, daughter of Samuel Gilman, a highly accomplished lady. She was the author of two or more published works, the chief of which was *Female Quixotism* which had much popularity in its time, and went through several editions." How many successful novelists had Exeter produced by 1888? Was there no more to tell about this one?

Similarly, both the Tenney and the Gilman family histories formulaicly discount Tabitha as simply "daughter of," "wife of," and "very accomplished lady." *Female Quixotism* is one of the best novels written in America before 1825. It is a clear counter-example to the tired literary cliché that women wrote only "domestic novels" or "sentimental novels" or—what does this mean?—"women's novels." Patty Rogers' gossipy revelations about Miss T—— G-m— are interesting because, quite simply, there is virtually nothing else. The whole story is an allegory of how the quilt of women's literary history has been made from the smallest of scraps and remnants.

But the best piece of all in this piecing together is the novel itself. By turns boisterous, satirical, biting, sardonic, incisive, ribald, and finally sad, *Female Quixotism* is a remarkable book. It is my great pleasure to present this first modern edition, edited by Jean Nienkamp and Andrea Collins. Textual notes explain references that might not be obvious to contemporary readers, but, as the editors make clear in their Introduction, the book also stands on its own as a singular look at America in 1801, as an important text in the history of American fiction and women's writing in the United States, and, most of all, as a novel that is a pleasure to read, even at this distance of nearly two centuries.

Cathy N. Davidson

ACKNOWLEDGMENTS

We are grateful to the staffs of the American Antiquarian Society, the Boston Public Library, the Dartmouth College Library, the Earl Gregg Swem Library of the College of William and Mary, the New Hampshire Historical Society, the New York Public Library, and the Pattee Library of the Pennsylvania State University for their generous assistance in our research for this edition.

The quotations from the Martha "Patty" Rogers diary and the Tabitha Tenney letter fragment are used through the courtesy of the American Antiquarian Society and the Trustees of the Boston Public Library respectively, to whom we owe additional thanks.

Andrea Collins wishes to thank the Department of English at the Pennsylvania State University for its generous support through the Katey Lehman Fellowship in Poetry and Fiction. The Office of Computer and Information Services of the Pennsylvania State University provided significant support for the ongoing work of this project. Jean Nienkamp wishes to thank the Academic Computing Fellowship program for its very generous assistance throughout her graduate work. We further appreciate the computer assistance provided us by the College of Liberal Arts Center for Computing Assistance, the Center for Academic Computing, and John T. Harwood at the Pennsylvania State University and by Jim Huddle at Old Dominion University.

Many of our colleagues offered us their support of the project from start to finish. We are particularly grateful to Cynthia Miecznikowski Sheard, whose own work introduced us to the novel, and to the members of the Early American Literature seminar of fall, 1987. A useful resource has been Sally Hoople's 1984 dissertation, "Tabitha Tenney: *Female Quixotism*" (Fordham University). For assistance with annotations, we wish to thank Robert D. Hume of the Pennsylvania State University and others who responded to our electronic mail inquiries. For assistance with proofreading, we wish to thank P. A. Nickinson and D. L. Cortner.

Editions like this one owe much to the pathbreaking work of Cathy N. Davidson, whose book *Revolution and the Word: The Rise of the Novel in America* has challenged our deepest assumptions about the study of the American novel. Cathy Davidson's generosity and kind assistance made possible our publication in this series. We have enjoyed working with her; with William Sisler, formerly of the Oxford University Press; and with Linda Robbins of the Oxford University Press.

Finally, Professor Carla J. Mulford suggested this project and provided support and encouragement during our research and through the multiple drafts of our editing and writing. We dedicate this volume to her with affection and respect.

Jean Nienkamp
Andrea Collins

CONTENTS

INTRODUCTION

When *Female Quixotism* was first published in 1801, the United States was engaged in building a national identity. All aspects of life—not just the laws inherited from England—were scrutinized for their suitableness for Americans. What literature, entertainment, and fashions were most appropriate for a people who were distinguishing themselves culturally and commercially from their British roots? What extent and kind of education would promote civic responsibility among men who had never previously had a voice in government and women who would be rearing future generations of the citizenry? What, after all of the wartime rhetoric concerning freedom and natural rights, should America do about its slaves? While *Female Quixotism* addresses all of these concerns, the novel touches on them in the context of its central concern, what books good citizens "should" read.

Particularly at issue was the growing popularity of novels, a genre that troubled the molders of early American society. First, in a nation not too far from its Puritan origins, novels came up against the charge that fiction was immoral because it was tantamount to lying. Readers today usually wouldn't make this observation, because they use other standards of "truth" for judging literature, but the charge carried great moral weight during the eighteenth and nineteenth centuries. Many writers of novels of the period, Tabitha Tenney included, tried to avoid this charge by asserting in their titles or prefaces that their books were "true histories."

Furthermore, people in Federalist America prided themselves on their no-frills practicality, and they often associated entertainments with frivolous European luxuriousness. Many novels were imported or pirated from England, so a patriotic distrust of those works was a natural extension of the boycott of British goods encouraged during the Revolution. Robustly nationalistic works such as Royall Tyler's play, The Contrast (1787), Joel Barlow's poem, *The Vision of Columbus*

(1787), and William Hill Brown's novel, *The Power of Sympathy* (1789), contended that European culture was inappropriate and debilitating for the rigorous necessities of American life.

Particularly important during a time when a majority of the population was quite young was the purported effect of novels on young people. Most of the era's criticism directed against novel reading—criticism in sermons, pamphlets, books, newspapers, and magazines—argued that reading novels impaired the education of the nation's youth. Novels, it was thought, made immoral actions seem more interesting than virtuous ones. By emphasizing romance and adventure, some critics argued, novels gave young people false ideas of life and particularly made women unsuited for and unhappy with the domestic roles for which society destined them. Such are the primary arguments *Female Quixotism* explicitly offers in its criticism of novel reading.

Many authors of novels written during this period attempted to exempt their works from the criticisms directed at novels by criticizing novel reading—of other kinds of novels, of course. William Hill Brown, in *The Power of Sympathy*, argued that American women were harmed by reading English novels just as Charlotte Lennox in *The Female Quixote* (1752) claimed that English women were harmed by reading French romances. Tabitha Gilman Tenney attempted to distinguish *Female Quixotism* from the romances it criticized in a much more thoroughgoing way. While most of the novels deploring novel reading had sentimental, if not romantic, endings, *Female Quixotism* was consistently anti-romantic to the very end. Instead of portraying the ultimate marriage of the central characters who go off to live "happily ever after," instead of concluding with a sentimental death scene in which a woman dies while still young and beautiful with a crowd of relatives, friends, and her true love mourning her, *Female Quixotism* follows its protagonist, Dorcas Sheldon, to her unmarried old age, to physical deterioration, disillusionment, and ultimate loneliness.

But this ironic denouement is not the only difference between *Female Quixotism* and its contemporaries. Like *Don Quixote*, and unlike the sentimental novels written by Tenney's contemporaries, *Female Quixotism* is a comic, boisterous anti-romance. The novel's cutting wit spares hardly any segment of society: droll servants, earnest merchants, scheming scholars, and self-deluding gentry all get their fair share of ribbing.

Female Quixotism takes place in the isolated village of L——, Pennsylvania, up the Delaware River from Philadelphia. The central character, Dorcas Sheldon, restyles herself "Dorcasina" to accord better with the romantic notions she has acquired from her naive reading of too many romances. These romantic notions occasion a series of misadventures as Dorcasina searches in vain for the passionate love portrayed in her beloved books. After rejecting the honorable advances of her first suitor, "Lysander," who fails to act or write like the heroes of her favorite novels, Dorcasina has a number of hairsbreadth escapes from unscrupulous men who want to marry her only for her money.

The first of these escapades involves the Irishman O'Connor, portrayed as a rascal who easily captures Dorcasina's heart by imitating the romantic language of novels. O'Connor, having forged letters of introduction to insinuate himself into the Sheldon household, is discovered and run out of town by Dorcasina's father, Mr. Sheldon. Dorcasina becomes convinced of O'Connor's villainy only after she sees him in the pillory on felony charges. Dorcasina shifts her attentions to the wounded Captain Barry, who is recuperating from a war injury in the Sheldon household. But Dorcasina's marriage plans are foiled again. After a nighttime elopement, she discovers her beau is actually the Captain's servant, James. Mr. Sheldon provides a more "suitable" suitor to his now forty-five-year-old daughter in the person of the merchant Mr. Cumberland, but for once Dorcasina's romantic notions serve her well as Mr. Cumberland also turns out to be more interested in money—any woman's money—than in Dorcasina herself.

After Mr. Sheldon dies, Dorcasina's close neighbors and friends the Stanlys assume the responsibility of preventing Dorcasina from marrying foolishly. Throughout the novel, the Stanlys have served as the counterpoint to Dorcasina's misguided education as they keep their daughter Harriot from reading novels and provide her with the social skills Dorcasina lacks. Their first challenge after Mr. Sheldon's death is to stop Dorcasina from marrying her servant, John Brown, whom she romantically and stubbornly insists is a gentleman in disguise. In rollicking scenes featuring cross-dressing and sexual innuendo, Harriot masquerades as the dashing Captain Montague to woo Dorcasina away from Brown. But even Harriot's combined efforts with Scipio, the Sheldons' faithful and resourceful African-American servant, fail. Finally, kidnapped from L—— by the Stanlys and kept on an isolated farm to separate her from both Brown and her novels, Dorcasina almost marries a supposed widower, Seymore, before he is imprisoned as a debtor and reveals to Dorcasina that no one would marry her except for her money.

Amidst all of these escapades, Dorcasina is variously kidnapped, molested, and tricked by both disguise and circumstance in her search for true love. Dorcasina ends up alone at fifty, bereft of her attractiveness and romantic delusions—a singular fate indeed for the "heroine" of a novel, although a far from singular fate for such a "middling" American woman as Dorcasina.

Remarkably, Dorcasina's misadventures seem to be the only upheavals in L——, even though the fifty-year period represented in the novel encompasses the Revolutionary War, its economic precursors, and the subsequent politics of nation-building. Few of these momentous changes agitate or inconvenience the lives of the Sheldons and their neighbors. But not all of the developments evolving on the larger national scene are excluded from this isolated setting. Many of the social issues being debated in public arenas directly affected women's domestic lives, so even the microcosmic world of *Female Quixotism* had to cope with issues of gender, race, and class—issues as volatile then as they are today.

Relations between the sexes during this period were determined by women's economic dependence on men, a dependence completely controlling their lives in the latter half of the eighteenth century. In this pre-industrial age, religious and legal tenets confined most women to domestic duties, either in their own households or (as ill-paid labor) in the homes of others. The low wages and scarcity of suitable work for women continued an economic subjugation that reflected the disadvantageous legal status of women. A woman's legal status at this time depended on her marital status in a system of coverture inherited from British common law. While an unmarried woman—a *feme sole*—lacked political rights such as the right to vote, a married woman, or *feme covert*, was even more constrained by her lack of property rights. Wives could not keep the wages they had earned; they could not own property separately from their husbands—or make wills or sign legal documents or even have custody of their own children.

In this context, the absurd comedy of Dorcasina's search for a husband is a novelistic rendering of an ominous reality. The novel suggests that Dorcasina's fate as a single woman might be preferable to the potential misery of her life with an ill-suited husband. Women's single career choice—who and whether to marry—determined their lifelong felicity and their livelihoods. In practice, *whether* to marry was hardly a matter of choice. Social consensus assumed any marriage was preferable to "spinsterhood," contrary to Mrs. Stanly's position that the single life is a reasonable and positive choice for women. On the other hand, Tenney—careful to portray no "happily-ever-afters"— provides that even the suitable and loving marriage of Dorcasina's neighbor, Harriot Stanly, is punctuated with misfortunes.

Female Quixotism depicts romance novels as pernicious precisely because they incapacitate women for making critical choices about marriage. Dorcasina is educated at home by her father, who allows her to read novels that "fill the heads of artless young girls" with "airy delusions and visionary dreams," "sometimes to their utter ruin," instead of having the benefit of a mother's guidance, which "would have pointed out to her the plain rational path of life" (3). Mrs. Stanly, on the other hand, sends Harriot to Philadelphia for her education, admonishing Harriot's governess not to allow the child to read novels.

Tenney's case against novel reading seems to concur with that of many advocates of education for women. No doubt, Tenney would have agreed with educators like Benjamin Rush and even Judith Sargent Murray, who argued that women must be trained in subjects that would allow them to conduct the primary education of their children (both male and female) and to converse intelligently in polite society. This attitude was far from universal, as the narrator of *Female Quixotism* suggests in the condemnation of those "enemies to female improvement" who "thought a woman had no business with any book but the bible, or perhaps the art of cookery; believing that every thing beyond these served only to disqualify her for the duties of domestic life" (13). On the contrary, *Female Quixotism* portrays no necessary conflict between learning for women and the fulfillment of domestic duties.

Women are not the only socially disadvantaged group limned in

Female Quixotism. The novel offers a depiction of the ambiguous social relations between African-Americans and the ruling white elite during the period when the northern states began the gradual emancipation of their slaves. Representative of the changing status of African Americans in the North, Scipio is bought as a young boy by Mr. Sheldon, but he appears to be a free servant late in the novel, when he anticipates having to seek a new position if Dorcasina marries John Brown. Dorcasina's diatribe against slavery early in the novel illustrates the strong feelings raised by the institution from the beginning of the Republic, and it suggests the leading role women played in abolitionism.

A change in the legal status of African-Americans does not, however, bring about an immediate change in the racial attitudes of Anglo-Americans. *Female Quixotism* suggests both the older stereotypes white Americans held and a newer sympathy toward African-Americans. Scipio is an African-American version of the age-old "wise fool" character in literature, a character not unlike the fool in Shakespeare's plays. Although typified as an "African wag" who is frequently described in terms relative to other "persons of his complexion" (210, 238), Scipio is one of the most fully and sympathetically drawn characters in a novel in which many of the servants' antics are pure buffoonery. Furthermore, ambiguous attitudes about race relations emerge in Dorcasina's behavior: Dorcasina pontificates at length about the evils of slavery, but she is scandalized by her own inadvertent "familiarity" one evening with Scipio, "when, with her snowy arms, she encircled Scipio's ebony neck" (58).

Sentiments toward characters of other nationalities are not so ambiguous. Concomitant with the nationalistic fervor gripping the United States after the Revolution was the rejection of anything or anyone foreign. The two nationalities coming in for much of the negative critique in the novel are the Irish and the French. The stereotype of the "Irish rogue"—represented in Book I by O'Connor and the "shrewd Irish servant" who tries to rape Dorcasina—was carried over to the new nation from eighteenth century British novels and culture. Strong anti-French sentiment arose in the United States after the perceived hellish excesses in the name of republicanism during the Reign of Terror. French influence is thus attributed to the moral depravity of Seymore and Mr. M. of the village of L——in Book

II. In general, the novel advocates a morally based isolationism to protect America from corrupting European influences.

In addition to the depiction of gender, ethnic, and international relations, *Female Quixotism* offers a rich portrayal of class structure in the United States at this period. Dorcasina's whole search for romantic love is premised on her status as a wealthy woman: to Dorcasina, marriage is not a necessity of economic survival, because she is of the landed class. But hers is not the only social level portrayed. Class distinctions are evident in the obviously hierarchical relationship between the wealthy Dorcasina and her maid Betty. Even finer detail, though, is achieved in the episode in which Mr. Cumberland courts Dorcasina, while Betty believes he is actually courting her. The distinctions between the landed elite, the *nouveau riche* merchant class, and the lower-class servants provide the source for an abundance of misunderstanding and farcical humor. Later in the novel, when Dorcasina plans to marry John Brown, the kitchen antics of the servants and the friendly guidance of Mrs. Stanly take on a new, urgent tone, as all attempt to restore the threatened social order in the Sheldon household. Tenney brings these issues alive without pretending any panacea is available in this comedic, but realistic, world.

Female Quixotism responded not only to its post-Revolutionary American social setting, but also, parodically, to a literary culture that spanned the Atlantic. Tenney's familiar and sometimes irreverent use of English literature reflects both her support for the reading of literature by women and her critique of naive reading of romance novels. In *Female Quixotism*, Tenney makes direct references to Samuel Richardson's *Sir Charles Grandison* (1753-54) and Tobias Smollett's *Roderick Random* (1748); and she quotes other writers such as Shakespeare, Milton, Dryden, Pope, and Sterne. Given such evidence of Tenney's broad reading and literary interests, it is not surprising to find extensive parodic allusions in her work to other novels popular at the time—even as she condemns many of them for giving women false expectations of life.

The title *Female Quixotism* suggests immediately that Tenney places her novel in the context of Cervantes's *Don Quixote*. The pair consisting of Dorcasina and Betty is one of the more lively echoes of Don Quixote and his servant Sancho Panza among the many literary offshoots of Don *Quixote*. The dependence of the plot on Dorcasina's "novel-mania" is the most striking parallel with Don Quixote, but Dorcasina also exhibits the latter's moments of intelligence and bravery. Each of these novels, too, portrays its protagonists in their growing decrepitude: compare Dorcasina's being "deprived of all the flesh her bones were ever clothed with; and her skin . . . sallow and full of wrinkles . . . her front teeth . . . all gone" (233) with Don Quixote having "little flesh on his bones and a face that was lean and gaunt" [1]

Likewise, Dorcasina's servant Betty is equally a counterpart to Sancho Panza in her superstitions and her propensity for taking the physical abuse stemming from Dorcasina's adventures. Like Sancho Panza, Betty is initially the voice of reason and common sense against Dorcasina's quixotic delusions. But Betty's realism gradually becomes tainted with Dorcasina's illusionary world to the point that Betty imagines romantic possibilities between herself and first Mr. Cumberland (an aspiring man of a higher social class) and then John Brown (a man young enough to be her son). Just as Sancho Panza seems eventually to trade places with Don Quixote in clinging to romantic dreams, Betty attempts to recreate the hope after Dorcasina's disillusionment: "'Oh, never worry about that now, ma'am; you may yet get a good husband, and live as happy as the days are long'" (321).

While Female Quixotism is structured episodically, like Don Quixote and the popular picaresque novels of the mid-eighteenth century, the similarity between individual episodes is limited by the fact that the protagonist in Female Quixotism is a woman: respectable women at this time did not have the kind of footloose mobility characteristic of the picaresque hero. One situation common in the picaresque novel is the use of masquerade by a friend in order to lead the protagonist away from his or her delusions. In Don Quixote, Sanson Carrasco dresses up as the Knight of the Mirrors and then the Knight of the Moon, in order to defeat Don Quixote in battle and require that the old "knight" return to his native village. In Female Quixotism, Harriot dresses as Captain Montague to woo Dorcasina away from her imminent marriage to John Brown, and Harriot collaborates with her father's protective abduction of Dorcasina when milder measures fail. In both Don Quixote and Female Quixotism, the friends' motives are not purely altruistic: Carrasco, as the Knight of the Moon, wants revenge for being defeated by Quixote as the Knight of the Mirrors; and Harriot expects to be amused by her deception.

Other situations in Female Quixotism parody those common to

many eighteenth-century British novels, which were popular in America and available in cheaply pirated or imported editions. The masquerades and cross-dressing practiced with great earnestness in *Pamela, Sir Charles Grandison,* and *Roderick Random* are spoofed in the high-jinks of Philander, Betty, Harriot, Seymore, and the barber Puff. The contrived abduction scenes are likewise evocative of other novels, but self-consciously so:

> The very same accident had formerly happened to Harriot Byron [of
> *Sir Charles Grandison*], though she was, to be sure, rescued in a
> different manner; and Dorcasina's satisfaction would have been
> complete, had O'Connor chanced to have been her deliverer (139).

The contrived nature of the abduction scenes in *Female Quixotism* reduces to an absurdity the abductions in *The Female Quixote, Pamela,* and *Joseph Andrews.* Similarly, Dorcasina's mistaken elopement with James undermines the seriousness of such scenes in *Clarissa* and *Tom Jones.*

The fact that *Female Quixotism* parodies the literary milieu in which it was conceived does not belittle the original twists Tenney gives to each situation, or the broad humor with which she delineates them. Suggesting that the summerhouse scene between Dorcasina and Scipio, O'Connor and Miss Violet is Shakespearian in its use of multiple mistaken identities and twisted romances does not preclude appreciation of its farcical humor and sly hints of miscegenation. On a grimmer note, nothing in all of Pamela's or Clarissa's fainting fits or Sophia Western's night-time peregrinations over England conveys the dread of Harriot's first night-time walk as Captain Montague, or the real threat and disgrace of Dorcasina's attempted rape and its consequences.

A final question about literary influences might be an obvious one, of how much Tenney owes to Charlotte Lennox's *The Female Quixote,* a similar parody published half a century earlier. Certainly, many of the situations are the same: like Lennox's heroine Arabella, Dorcasina lost her mother at an early age and was raised and educated by her father in a secluded setting. They each have a faithful female servant and *confidante*, although Betty is a much more lively and Panza-like foil to the vagaries of her mistress than Arabella's Lucy. They both have genuine, suitable suitors, as well as impostors who are after their wealth; both imagine potential lovers in servants (not to mention almost all men they meet); and both adopt peculiar modes of dress that serve as visible signs of their mental peculiarities. Finally, the understanding of each is "corrupted" through the reading of literature foreign to their own countries: Arabella is obsessed with the French heroic romances of the previous century, while Dorcasina pictures herself the heroine of books like *Sir Charles Grandison* and *Roderick Random*. Thus, they both serve as nationalistic warnings as well as anti-romance warnings.

Otherwise, Tenney has created a very different female Quixote, based on a more thorough anti-romanticism. Lennox, although her basic tenet is to criticize romance reading, creates a romantic heroine who is "conventionally young, well-born, lovely, intelligent, and virtuous" and who ends up marrying her original suitor, Glanville, and living happily ever after, "united . . . in every Virtue and laudable Affection of the Mind."[2] Tenney, in contrast, more realistically portrays Dorcasina as being "a middling kind of person, like the greater part of her countrywomen" (4). The novel follows Dorcasina over a time period of fifty years, during which time her delusions become increasingly absurd and pathetic. Instead of the conventional marriage and happy ending, Dorcasina finds herself a disillusioned old maid, resigned to a life of charity and novel reading. Thus the parodic and hence didactic nature of Tenney's novel is much more consistent than that of Lennox's.

Moreover, Arabella undergoes relatively few adventures and spends a disproportionate amount of time lecturing her cousins (and anyone else she meets) on the romantic precedents for her behavior and expectations. As we have already seen, Tenney sketches most of Dorcasina's life and skips from adventure to adventure. In doing so, she follows the example of Henry Fielding:

> When any extraordinary Scene presents itself, (as we trust will be often the Case) we shall spare no Pains nor Paper to open it at large to our Reader; but if whole Years should pass without producing any thing worthy of his Notice, we shall not be afraid of a Chasm in our History; but shall hasten on to Matters of Consequence, and leave such Periods of Time totally unobserved.[3]

This selective focus is one of the reasons why Tenney's narrative is a much more rollicking, funny tale than Lennox's. Dorcasina's escapades engage the reader in a way that Arabella's monologues cannot possibly. So while Tenney may have derived her original conception from Lennox's *The Female Quixote*, which was available in America (although there is no external evidence Tenney read it), in transmuting her material Tenney creates a portrait of "female quixotism" having all the vitality and slapdash humor of a new nation attempting to find a cultural identity.

Female Quixotism thus provides a window on both the social and literary worlds of the late eighteenth century in America. Popular and timely in its own day, the novel offers today's readers a new perspective on eighteenth century literature and on many of our own social issues. Just as *Female Quixotism* served as an anti-romance for its readership in the early nineteenth century, today it can serve to de-romanticize our notions of the early American republic, which was not only peopled by larger-than-life heroes such as Washington and Jefferson, but by women of all classes and other disadvantaged groups trying to live the best life they could—and vying among themselves in their efforts.

Biographical Sketch

What we need for a discovery of the life of Tabitha Gilman Tenney is a faithful *confidante*, one of whose functions is to relate the history of her companion to all sympathetic inquirers, like Arabella expects of Lucy in *The Female Quixote*:

> To recount all my Words and Actions, even the smallest and most inconsiderable, but also my Thoughts, however instantaneous; relate exactly every Change of my Countenance; number all my Smiles, Half-smiles, Blushes, Turnings pale, Glances, Pauses, Full-stops, Interruptions; the Rise and Falling of my Voice; every Motion of my Eyes; and every Gesture which I have used for these Ten Years past; nor omit the smallest Circumstance that relates to me.[4]

Instead, we have only the formulaic mentions of Samuel Tenney's "highly accomplished" wife; the brief, gossipy details afforded by diarist Patty Rogers and memoirist Elizabeth Dow Leonard; and the imprecise and didactic fables of writers like Evert A. Duyckinck, who claims "her father died in her infancy, and she was left to the sole care of her pious and sensible mother,"[5] even though her father lived until Tabitha was sixteen and had six younger brothers and sisters.[6] Piecing together these sources still leaves a tantalizingly incomplete picture of "a woman," as Elizabeth Dow Leonard says, "who had written a book, punctuated and printed it."[7]

Tabitha Gilman was born on April 7, 1762, in Exeter, New Hampshire, to Samuel Gilman and his second wife, Lydia (Robinson) Giddings Gilman, the eldest of their seven children.[8] According to surviving reports, Tabitha seems to have had the strong maternal role model her novel's heroine lacks. Her mother, "an educated and forceful woman," is said to have raised Tabitha in a "Puritanical, bookish, and secluded" manner.[9] Duyckinck credits Tabitha's interest in literature as providing her with "a facility and correctness of language which gave her noticeable freedom and elegance in conversation," so perhaps "Tabby" Gilman's upbringing was not entirely secluded.[10]

Certainly, in 1785, she was "courted" by Dr. Samuel Tenney, who had served as a surgeon in the Revolutionary War. This is noted by Martha ("Patty") Rogers, another resident of Exeter whose diary for that year has been preserved. Rogers's antipathy to Tabby Gilman— "a person pecularly [sic] disagreeable to me—not from any injury she ever did me, but there is a certain something, in her manner, with which I am ever disgusted"—perhaps stems from the fact that Dr. Tenney seems to have been courting Patty Rogers at the same time he courted Tabitha Gilman. Samuel Tenney walked Rogers home from church, gave her romance novels to read, and took "liberties" with her at her own house.[11] If Tabitha's life bore any similarity to Patty's—an assumption that may not be as safe as it sounds, since Patty seems to have been known as a girl with "too much sensibility" in contrast to the sober Tabitha—then her young adulthood was probably filled with work at the home, frequent visits to friends, meetings on Sundays, and assemblies on Thursday nights.

Tabitha married Samuel Tenney in 1788, when she was 26 and he 40 years old, trading the invisibility of a young single woman for the social and legal invisibility of a wife. We have few facts about Tabitha after her marriage: she evidently published a reader for young women, *The New Pleasing Instructor*, in 1799; she accompanied her husband to Washington on his election to the Senate in 1800; and she published *Female Quixotism* in 1801. This sketchy outline can again be supplemented through anecdotal information from various sources. What a shame it is that we don't have the letters she wrote from Washington, which Duyckinck says "are specimens of her talent at graphic description, as well as illustrative of the fashion and manners of the times."[12]

One window we do have into Tenney's "public" life (that is, after her books were published anonymously) is provided by Elizabeth Dow Leonard. Leonard's reverence for the "real live authoress" does not survive her lively sarcasm, however, and the picture Leonard offers of Tenney verges on the comical:

> She was the lawful wife of Judge Tenney, a brawny, raw-boned and awkward but very good man, with more law in his pocket than in his head. Tabitha affected the dignified and the delicate and sentimental, also the statuesque. Her motions were slow and solemn as of one "who lived apart and reasoned high," and her speech the words of an oracle. "You talk as slowly as Tabby Tenney" was an Exeter proverb.[13]

The reserved nature that was probably the result of Tenney's "Puritan, bookish, and secluded" upbringing, then, is seen by Leonard as an affectation. She supports this accusation with a wonderful "description" of Tenney's reaction to George Washington's death:

> She had a valuable mirror in her hand when she received the terrible news of G.W.'s fate. She walked leisurely across the room, laid the mirror safely down, placed herself in a proper attitude, adjusted her garments like Caesar when he fell, and then fainted away, and so paid her patriotic tribute to the great man's memory and did not sacrifice her looking glass, as a less sensible and discreet woman would have done.[14]

Tenney evidently maintained an extremely proper social front, behind which it is difficult to discern her real feelings. This socially proper reverence for Washington is again reflected in an existing fragment of a letter by Tenney, which appears to be addressed to a younger woman: "You must not broach any of your tory sentiments, for the memory of Washington is greatly venerated here."[15]

Dr. Tenney was at Washington for three terms as a Federalist senator, during which time he opposed on every single vote the election of Jefferson as president. He also voted for the continuation of the Alien and Sedition Act, used to suppress political dissent during the Federalist era. The Tenneys had no children, although they did have in their household during some part of their marriage Anne Gilman, a distant younger cousin of Tabitha's and the daughter of a close friend of Samuel's. After Samuel Tenney's death on February 6, 1816, Tabitha returned to Exeter and is said to have applied herself to needlework. She does not seem to have written for publication after *Female Quixotism*. She died in Exeter on May 2, 1837.

Notes

1. Miguel de Cervantes Saavedra, *The Ingenious Gentleman Don Quixote de la Mancha,* trans. Samuel Putnam (1604; New York: The Modern Library-Random House, 1949) 25.

2. Charlotte Lennox, *The Female Quixote or The Adventures of Arabella,* ed. Margaret Dalziel (1752; London: Oxford Univ. Press, 1970) xiii, 383.

3. Henry Fielding, *The History of Tom Jones,* ed. Martin C. Battestin and Fredson Bowers (1749; Middletown, Conn.: Wesleyan Univ. Press, 1975) 76.

4. Lennox 121-122.

5. Evert A. Duyckinck and George L. Duyckinck, *Cyclopaedia of American Literature,* ed. M. Laird Simons, 2 vols. (Philadelphia: Rutter, 1877) I: 521.

6. C. H. Bell, *History of the Town of Exeter* (Boston, 1888) 383; Martha Jane Tenney, *The Tenney Family* (Boston: American Printing and Engraving, 1891) 57. Arthur Gilman, author of The Gilman Family, does not even say that much about her, but gives almost a full page to her husband, even quoting a letter from him to a different Gilman.

7. Elizabeth Dow Leonard, *A Few Reminiscences of My Exeter Life,* ed. Edward C. Echols (Exeter, N. H.: Two By Four Press, 1972) 47.

8. Arthur Gilman, *The Gilman Family,* (Albany: Joel Munsell, 1869). The Gilman genealogy is confused on the point of how many elder half-siblings she had. On p. 70, it says that Samuel Gilman had 2 children by his first wife, Tabitha Gilman; on pp. 96-97 it names 6 children born prior to his marriage to Lydia.

9. Jessica Hill Bridenbaugh, "Tabitha Gilman Tenney," *Dictionary of American Biography,* ed. Allen Johnson et al. 22 vol. (New York: Scribners, 1928-37) 18: 374.

10. Duyckinck I: 521.

11. Martha "Patty" Rogers, diary for 1785, The American Antiquarian Society, Worchester. Entries of note include the June 20th reference to "Miss T— G-m—"; Rogers begins to give Samuel Tenney the pseudonym "Philammon" on April 21; reference to Philammon courting Miss Gilman, July 13; liberties referred to August 4 and September 21 (the same day he "absolutely denied . . . courting Tabby"). Samuel Tenney must have been quite a gallant at the time: when Patty asked him about Tabitha, he replied "I

like her as well as the rest of you girls and no better." See also Cathy N. Davidson, *Revolution and the Word: The Rise of the Novel in America* (New York: Oxford Univ. Press, 1986) 191-92. The diary had long been of interest to the staff of the American Antiquarian Society, but Cathy Davidson was the first to connect its references to "Miss T—G-m—"and "Tabby" with the author of *Female Quixotism.*

12. Duyckinck I: 521.

13. Leonard 47.

14. Leonard 48.

15. Tabitha Gilman Tenney, letter fragment, date and recipient unknown, Boston Public Library.

NOTE ON THE TEXT

The text is based on the American Antiquarian Society's copy of the first edition, published anonymously by Isaiah Thomas and E. T. Andrews in 1801. *Female Quixotism* went through five editions during the first half of the nineteenth century. The first, two-volume edition was published in 1801 by Isaiah Thomas and E. T. Andrews of Boston. The second (1808) edition was evidently composed of sheets left over from the 1801 edition and rebound with a new title page by Thomas and Whipple. The third and fourth editions were published by J. P. Peaslee of Boston in 1825 and 1829. The fifth, three-volume edition was published by G. Clark of Boston in 1841. The frontispiece facsimile from the 1841 edition appears through the courtesy of the Gardner-Harvey Library at Miami University.

The earliest known attribution of *Female Quixotism* to Tabitha Gilman Tenney is by a contributor to the *Cyclopædia of American Literature* (1855) in an unsigned, undated letter in the Duyckinck Family Collection of the New York Public Library.

Eighteenth-century typography has been modernized: long *ſ* becomes *s* throughout. The only other silent emendations we make involve minor changes in punctuation and spelling for clarity.

Annotations have been provided to the numerous quotations used by Tenney throughout the text, as well as to phrases and words that have changed meaning or are no longer in common usage. The "Notes" section following the text is correlated to the text by page and line number.

SELECTED BIBLIOGRAPHY

Biographical sketches of Tabitha Gilman Tenney may be found in Duyckinck and Duyckinck, *Cyclopaedia of American Literature* (1855), and in *Dictionary of American Biography* (1936), *American Women Writers* (1982), *A Dictionary of British and American Women Writers, 1660-1800* (1985), and *Notable American Women, 1607-1950* (1971).

Treatments of *Female Quixotism* may be found in L. D. Loshe, *The Early American Novel, 1789-1830* (1907), H. R. Brown, *The Sentimental Novel in America, 1789-1860* (1940), and H. Petter, *The Early American Novel* (1971). More recent criticism may be found in Cathy N. Davidson, *Revolution and the Word: The Rise of the Novel in America* (1986), C. K. B. Matzke, "'The Woman Writes as if the Devil was in Her': A Rhetorical Approach to Three Early American Novels" (diss., 1983), and Cynthia Miecznikowski, "The Parodic Mode and the Patriarchal Imperative: Reading the Female Reader(s) in Tabitha Tenney's *Female Quixotism*," *Early America Literature* 25.1 (1990): 34-45. The only full-length study of *Female Quixotism* is the 1984 dissertation by Sally C. Hoople, "Tabitha Tenney: *Female Quixotism*" (Fordham University).

CHRONOLOGY OF
TABITHA GILMAN TENNEY

1762	April 7. Born in Exeter, New Hampshire, to Samuel Gilman and Lydia Robinson Giddings Gilman.
1788	September. Marries Dr. Samuel Tenney, physician.
1799	*The New Pleasing Instructor*, a reader for young women possibly written and compiled by Tabitha Tenney, published anonymously.
1800	Accompanies Samuel Tenney to Washington, D.C., where he serves for three terms as a Federalist Senator representing the state of New Hampshire.
1801	*Female Quixotism* published anonymously.
1816	Tabitha Tenney moves from Washington to Exeter upon the death of her husband.
1837	May 2, death of Tabitha Gilman Tenney.

FEMALE QUIXOTISM

Dorcasina's visit to O'Connor, at the Inn.

TO ALL
Columbian Young Ladies,
Who read Novels *and* Romances.

DEAR GIRLS,

DURING a half a year's residence at Philadelphia, I was frequently diverted with a recital of some particulars of the life of Miss Dorcas Sheldon. These appeared so whimsical and outré that I had a strong inclination to acquire a knowledge of her whole history. With this view, I got introduced to her, at the house of her friend, Mrs. Barry; and, after a few weeks acquaintance, prevailed on her to favour me with a minute account of her adventures, with a generous permission to publish them, if I thought proper, for the advantage of the younger part of her sex.

The work, ladies, now courts your attention; and I hope you will be induced to read it, as well for my sake, who have spent much time in compiling, and cash in publishing it, as for your own, for whose particular use it is designed, and to whom it is most respectfully dedicated.

I am sensible you will find it a very singular and extraordinary piece of biography, and that you may suspect it to be a mere romance, an Hogarthian caricatura, instead of a true picture of real life. But, when you compare it with the most extravagant parts of the authentic history of the celebrated hero of La Mancha, the renowned Don Quixote, I presume you will no longer doubt its being a true uncoloured history of a romantic country girl, whose head had been turned by the unrestrained perusal of Novels and Romances. That, by observing their baneful effects on Miss Sheldon, who was in every other respect a sensible, judicious, and amiable girl, you may avoid the disgraces and disasters that so long rendered her despicable and miserable, is the sincere wish,

My dear young Ladies,
Of your Friend and Admirer,
THE COMPILER.

BOOK I

Chapter I.

ON the beautiful banks of the Delaware, about thirty miles from Philadelphia, dwelt a worthy and venerable man, by the name of Sheldon. In his younger days, he had been a considerable traveller, and had consequently seen much of the world. Some disappointments and mortifications, to which a turn of mind somewhat singular had subjected him, in some European city, had inspired him with a total dislike of all populous places. On his return, therefore, from his last foreign tour, he could not be persuaded to fix his residence in Philadelphia, the place of his nativity; but having married a wife, a necessary ingredient in man's domestic happiness, he purchased an estate near enough to this capital of North America, to enjoy its conveniences and the society of a few of its inhabitants, for whom he had a particular friendship; and devoted himself to agriculture. One daughter was the only fruit of this connexion.—Her history, being filled with incidents of a singular nature, we are now about to give to the public.

At the age of three years, this child had the misfortune to lose an excellent mother, whose advice would have pointed out to her the plain rational path of life; and prevented her imagination from being filled with the airy delusions and visionary dreams of love and raptures, darts, fire and flames, with which the indiscreet writers of that fascinating kind of books, denominated Novels, fill the heads of artless young girls, to their great injury, and sometimes to their utter ruin.

Little Dorcas, for so was our heroine called after her paternal grandmother, was too young to be sensible of the loss she had sustained; but her father lamented their common bereavement with keen and unutterable anguish. It is wisely ordered, by a kind Providence, that time should blunt the edge of the sharpest sorrows. Were it otherwise, and were our grief for the death of a dear friend to be always as lively and keen as in its first days, life would be a burden too heavy to be borne. But, thanks to that benign Power, who kindly "tempers the wind to the shorn lamb," every day usually lessens its poignancy. Thus it was with Mr. Sheldon. By degrees his grief subsided, and his affection for his infant daughter increased, till it engrossed almost every thought of his mind; and his very existence seemed to be bound up in her's. He attended to her education with the utmost care and assiduity; procuring her suitable instructors of every kind, and frequently executing the pleasing office himself, for which his native good sense and various acquirements eminently fitted him. In every branch of her education, Miss Sheldon made great proficiency. She had received from nature a good understanding, a lively fancy, an amiable cheerful temper, and a kind and affectionate heart. What a number of valuable qualities were here blended! But it is a mortifying truth that perfection is not to be found in human nature. With all these engaging endowments, she was unfortunately of a very romantic turn, had a small degree of obstinacy, and a spice too much of vanity.

Now I suppose it will be expected that, in imitation of sister novel writers (for the ladies of late seem to have almost appropriated this department of writing) I should describe her as distinguished by the elegant form, delicately turned limbs, auburn hair, alabaster skin, heavenly languishing eyes, silken eyelashes, rosy cheeks, aquiline nose, ruby lips, dimpled chin, and azure veins, with which almost all our heroines of romance are indiscriminately decorated. In truth she possessed few of those beauties, in any great degree. She was of a middling stature, a little embonpoint, but neither elegant nor clumsy. Her complexion was rather dark; her skin somewhat rough; and features remarkable neither for beauty nor deformity. Her eyes were grey and full of expression, and her whole countenance rather pleasing than otherwise. In short, she was a middling kind of person; like the greater part of her countrywomen; such as no man would be smitten with at first sight, but such as any man might love upon intimate acquaintance.

Mr. Sheldon, as was before observed, had conceived an extreme aversion to cities. He therefore, after the death of his wife, visited Philadelphia but rarely; and still more rarely took his daughter thither. In his neighbourhood were a few genteel families, with whom he associated occasionally; but with one only intimately. He had a fondness for books which he indulged to the utmost extent. History was his favourite reading; and next to that (a singular taste for a man) he delighted in novels. Consequently his library was furnished with the best histories, ancient and modern; and every novel, good, bad and indifferent, which the bookstores of Philadelphia afforded.

Miss Dorcas Sheldon, either from nature or education, possessed nearly the same taste in books as her father, with this difference only, that novels were her study, and history only her amusement. Mr. Sheldon, who himself had experienced nothing but pleasure in the time spent in reading the former, unfortunately indulged his daughter in the full latitude of her inclination; never considering their dangerous tendency to a young inexperienced female mind; nor the false ideas of life and manners, with which they would inspire a fanciful girl, educated in retirement and totally unacquainted with the ways of the world.

One year after another passed away in great harmony and domestic happiness, Dorcas dividing her time between her father, (of whom she was extremely fond) the superintendance of his domestic concerns, and her favourite occupation of reading, till she had reached her eighteenth year. At this time Miss Dorcas became extremely dissatisfied with her unfashionable and unromantic name; but as she could not easily change it, she was determined to alter and give it a romantic termination. She, therefore, one day, after expressing great dislike to it, begged her father, in future, to call her Dorcasina. Mr. Sheldon laughed, at first, at the whim which she had conceived, and endeavoured to rally her out of it; but finding that it was to her a matter of serious importance, and thinking there could be neither harm nor impropriety in granting her request, he acceded to her wishes, and she was ever after called Dorcasina.

About two years after this, a circumstance happened which formed an important era in the life of Miss Dorcasina. Mr. Sheldon, one day, received a letter from an old esteemed friend in Virginia, whom he had not seen for fifteen years, informing him of his intention of making him a visit; adding that he should bring with him his only son, the stay and prop of his declining age, and the darling of his fondest affections. Lysander (by which name we shall call the young gentleman) was about twenty-five. His person was noble and commanding; his countenance open and liberal; and his address manly and pleasing. His understanding was rather solid than brilliant, and much improved by education and travel. His ideas of domestic happiness were just and rational; and he judged from what he had observed, that an agreeable matrimonial connexion was much the happiest state in life. He, therefore, wished to marry; but there happened to be no lady in the circle of his acquaintance, who perfectly both satisfied his judgement, and pleased his fancy.

Miss Dorcasina, on perusing the letter, handed by her father, thought the time was now come, when she should experience the sweet satisfaction of loving and being loved.—The similarity of their circumstances; Lysander an only son and she an only daughter; the old gentleman's coming so far to see her father; his never having done it before; and his bringing his son with him, all served to confirm her in the opinion, that he was the person decreed by the stars to become her husband.—She would, to be sure, have been better pleased, had their acquaintance commenced in a more romantic manner. She wished that, in passing by, his carriage had broken down, and he been brought in wounded; or, that he had accidentally met her scouring the woods on horseback, (an amusement in which she took great delight) and that her horse being unruly, he had arrived just in time to save her from falling; or, which would have been still more to her taste, that some resolute fellow, in love with her to distraction, but who had made no impression on her heart, had carried her off by force to marry her, and that Lysander had rescued her by his gallantry, and conveyed her back in safety to the arms of her distressed parent. But as none of these romantic adventures, with which she had been so delighted in novels, had ever happened to her, she thought she must be satisfied if, at their first interview, he beheld her with raptures of delight; and of this she entertained not a shadow of doubt.

The night previous to the day, on which, with alternate emotions of hope, fear and pleasure, she expected the arrival of Lysander, she returned at her usual hour to her chamber, attended by a female domestic, who, having been brought up in the family from seven years old, had become her confidante and favourite. This she considered indispensable; for it would have been entirely out of character, and setting aside a most essential circumstance in the life of a heroine, not to have had either a friend, to whom she could confide the secret of her love, or a maid who could be bribed by an enamorato, to place a letter in her way, and then confidentially assert that she knew not from whence it came. Both these characters are frequently united in the same person, as was the case in the present instance; for there being no female among her acquaintance in the neighbourhood, whose notions of love were so refined, or, if you please, so romantic, as were those of Miss Dorcasina, she declined all intimacy with them, and preferred Betty to the double capacity of servant and confidante. Betty was a few years older than her mistress: she was a good-hearted, honest creature, possessed of a tolerably good natural understanding; but very ignorant and extremely superstitious.

After Dorcasina had disposed herself in bed, she requested Betty to sit down by the bed-side, saying she had something of consequence to communicate. Betty having seated herself in an attentive posture, Dorcasina began by informing her that it was impressed on her mind, that she and the young gentleman, who was next day expected, should, at first sight, fall violently in love with each other; and that she had not the least doubt but he was the person destined by Heaven to become her husband. Betty remaining silent, (for indeed she was at a loss for a reply) Dorcasina thus continued: "Though I know that love is stronger than death, and that with a beloved object a person may be happy on the top of the Alleghanies, or among the snows of Greenland; yet I must confess I shall feel a sensible pain at quitting my dear and affectionate father, and this delightful spot where I have passed all my life, and to which I feel the strongest attachment. But what gives me the greatest pain, is, that I shall be obliged to live in Virginia, be served by slaves, and be supported by the sweat, toil and blood of that unfortunate and miserable part of mankind." "Perhaps, ma'am," said Betty, "Lysander and his father treat their slaves well, and they live comfortable and happy." "Comfortable they may be," replied Dorcasina, "but slavery and happiness are, in my opinion, totally incompatible; 'disguise thyself as thou wilt, still, slavery, thou art a bitter pill.' They complain of the idle, thievish, unfaithful disposition of their slaves; but let the proprietors in their turn, be degraded to servitude, let them be made prisoners by the Algerines, let them have task-masters set over them, to drive them out to labour in herds, like the beasts of the field; then should we see whether they would be more faithful or more industrious than the wretched Africans: then should we see whether, after a number of years had elapsed, and they knew their servitude would terminate but with life, their minds would not become degraded and vicious with their situation." "I heard your father and another gentleman arguing upon this very point, ma'am, t'other day; and says your father, says he, for I remembers his very words, 'the most judicious among the proprietors of slaves think it is a great evil transmitted them by their forefathers; but an evil they know not how to remedy.'" "Yes, but there is a remedy," replied Dorcasina, with quickness, (who by this time was warmed with the subject, it being one upon which she never could with patience reflect) "it is said, that some whole districts in one of the Southern States, have emancipated their slaves, and pay them wages for their labour; and that they find their account in it; the negroes with a spirit of emulation and gratitude, performing much more service than while held in bondage." "Well ma'am," said Betty, "'tis pity you should make yourself so uneasy beforehand; perhaps you and the young gentleman wont fall so violently in love with each other as you imagine; and perhaps you never will become his wife." "Oh! I have so strong a pre-sentiment, that I am as sure of it as if we were actually married." "If that is the case," said Betty, (who seeing the young lady so fixed in her expectations, declined disputing farther about it) "may be you will prove a blessing to the poor blacks. If you marry Lysander, perhaps you can coax him to set them at liberty, and hire them as you hire white servants." "Who knows but I shall," exclaimed Dorcasina, quite transported with the idea, "and I assure you, Betty, my influence shall be exerted to the utmost in their favour, when I become their mistress." Having no farther occasion for Betty, she dismissed her. She then indulged herself in the agreeable, humane, but romantic idea, that, being the wife of Lysander, she should become the benefactress of his slaves. She even extended her benevolent reveries beyond the plantation of her future husband, and, wrapt in the glow of enthusiasm, saw his neighbours imitating his example, and others imitating them, till the spirit of justice and humanity should extend to the utmost limits of the United States, and all the blacks be emancipated from bondage, from New-Hampshire even to Georgia. By these pleasing illusions, her mind was so soothed and composed that she soon become a fit companion for the drowsy god, who held her fast locked in his embraces till late the next morning.

Chapter II.

WHEN Dorcasina arose, her features were lighted up with an unusual glow; and an uncommon degree of expression sparkled in her eyes. Her father observing it, as they sat at breakfast, told her, that by the pleasure which appeared in her countenance, he fancied her dreams had been agreeable. She blushed extremely at a consciousness of the cause; but made him no reply. The whole of that day she amused herself by forming ideas of the person of Lysander, and his first address when he should be introduced to her.

The long expected hour at length arrived. Just as they were sitting down to tea a carriage drove up to the gate, and Lysander and his father were announced. The two old gentlemen were extremely pleased at meeting again, after so long an absence. They had travelled together upon an intimate footing, in their youth; and had never met but once since, which was in Philadelphia, fifteen years before. Mr. Sheldon received the son of his friend with the greatest satisfaction; who, on his part, was equally pleased with a person whom he had so often heard his father mention in terms of the warmest friendship. Mr. Sheldon then introducing his daughter to the father and son, the latter complimented her in the same style of easy politeness in which he had done her father; no trembling, no emotion, no hesitation in speaking to her. What a thunder-stroke for poor Dorcasina, who had calculated upon piercing him through and through at the very first glance! So great was her chagrin and disappointment, that she appeared to great disadvantage, sitting silent and thoughtful through the tedious hours of evening, which to her had never before appeared so long. Lysander, several times, politely endeavoured to engage her in conversation; but all his attempts proving fruitless, he listened the remainder of the evening to the two old gentlemen, who were talking over the adventures of their youth.

As soon as supper was over, and the gentlemen retired, Dorcasina retreated to her chamber, in a far different state of mind from that in which she had entered it the evening preceding. Disappointed in her sanguine expectations of making an immediate conquest of the heart of Lysander, she felt the same indifference towards him that he had manifested towards her. Her mind being so warped by the false and romantic ideas of love, which she had imbibed from her favourite authors, she never considered that the purest and most lasting affection is founded upon esteem and the amiable qualities of the mind, rather than upon transitory personal attractions. Her understanding was not, however, so entirely perverted as to prevent her seeing that she had, by her coolness and reserve, treated Lysander in a very improper manner. She, therefore, though baulked in her dearest hopes, determined to repair her fault, and to treat him with the same polite attention with which her conduct was marked towards every other person. With this determination she composed herself to rest; not, however, without a sigh at the sudden downfal of the pleasing fabric she had the night before raised.

Lysander, on his part, was much disappointed in Dorcasina, having heard that she was a sensible, agreeable, and amiable girl. Amiable, he knew not but she might be; but she appeared far from agreeable; nor did he discover any striking marks of understanding, either in her looks or conversation.

Dorcasina, the next morning, arose with more composure than she had experienced for some days before. She frequently addressed her discourse to Lysander, resolved to make amends for her last night's deficiency. Her usual intelligence sparkled in her countenance; affability and attention to her guests, and duty and affection to her father, were so eminently conspicuous, that Lysander could hardly persuade himself to believe that she was the same cold, inanimate piece of clay he had attempted to converse with the preceding evening.

The two gentlemen were so well pleased with their visit, that they lengthened it out to almost a month; during which time Lysander became insensibly fond of the company of Dorcasina; he discovered new beauties in her every day; and saw so many proofs of her sweetness of temper, condescension to the servants, and duty and affection to her father, that he thought he never had beheld a lady so well calculated to render a man happy; and, although at first, he thought her ordinary in person, she now, by the force of her many engaging qualities, appeared to his admiring eyes to be almost a beauty. But he was not sensible of the strength of his attachment, till the time arrived to bid her adieu. The reluctance with which he performed it, and the pain he felt at parting, fully convinced him that he had left his heart at L——.

As soon, therefore, as he reached home, he formed a design to address her by letter, on the subject of a connexion. The only reason for not putting it in immediate execution, was the uncertainty of its success. He did not relish the idea of a refusal. She being the only lady to whom he ever thought of making an offer of his hand, he wished at least, to be sensible that he was not wholly indifferent to her. He ran over in his mind every circumstance of her conduct towards him, and recognized in it a great deal of sweetness and politeness; but nothing that indicated any partiality, or preference of him to any other gentleman who was a guest at the house, even for a few hours. After having deliberated for several days and nights, (for so much was his mind engaged in this affair, that it deprived him of a good part of his sleep) he determined to communicate to her the sentiments with which she had inspired him, in the manner before mentioned; wisely considering that such a prize was worth endeavouring to obtain, though he should fail in the attempt. He, therefore, by the next post sent her the following letter:

"WILL the amiable Miss Sheldon be offended at my consulting her on a subject, in which my heart is deeply interested? Before my late visit at L—— I never had seen the woman whom I wished to make my wife; but it was impossible to live under the same roof with you a month, to have daily opportunities of observing your numerous virtues and amiable qualities, and to remain indifferent to you. I knew not how deeply my heart was engaged, until I had quitted your hospitable mansion. I then felt in it a void, which I am confident nothing but your presence can ever fill. We are now no strangers to each other's person, character or situation. I flatter myself, therefore, that you will not judge this an abrupt declaration, or think me presuming when I solicit the happiness of being considered as your lover. From the opinion I have of your goodness, I imagine that you will not take pleasure in inflicting pain, or in keeping in suspense an honest heart, entirely devoted to you. I, therefore, beg the favour of you to grant me a speedy answer. If I find I am not agreeable to you, it will render me extremely unhappy; but if my passions meet your approbation, I shall esteem myself the most fortunate of mankind.

"LYSANDER."

LY.'s letter not like novels

Upon the perusal of this letter, Dorcasina experienced but one
sentiment, and that was mortification. She read it over and over again;
and was, to the last degree, chagrined at its coldness. She compared
it with various letters in her favourite authors; and found it so widely
different in style and sentiment, that she abhorred the idea of a
connexion with a person who could be the author of it. What added
greatly to her disgust was, that he said not a word of her personal
charms, upon which she so much valued herself. Not even the
slightest compliment to her person; nothing of angel or goddess,
raptures or flames, in the whole letter. She determined, therefore,
without much deliberation, to answer it in plain terms, and to give him
a flat refusal; and accordingly wrote as follows:

"Sir,
"I RECEIVED your letter safe by the post, and will answer you
with the same sincerity by which it appears to have been dictated. I
know not the man who possesses a larger share of my esteem. I have
noticed your good qualities, and acknowledge your merit; and your
friendship I should think it an honour to deserve. But my heart is
untouched; and I experienced not that violent emotion, at first sight
of you, which always accompanies genuine love; nor do I think the
passion with which I have inspired you, sufficiently ardent to ensure
my happiness; as your letter was such as I suppose your grandfather
might write, were he, at the age of eighty, to take it into his head to
marry. I hope you will not take amiss the freedom with which I speak
my sentiments, or suppose it the effect of levity; but be assured that
it is from a firm conviction, that we are not destined by Heaven to
make each other happy.
"With sentiments of the highest esteem,
"I wish to remain your friend,
"Dorcasina Sheldon."

Upon the receipt of this curious epistle, Lysander was lost in
astonishment. He could hardly credit the evidence of his own senses,
or believe that the agreeable Miss Sheldon could think and write in so
whimsical and romantic a manner, when, upon every other subject,
she conversed with the greatest good sense and propriety. He at
length concluded that to be her weak side; and endeavoured to
console himself by reflecting that he was fortunate in escaping a

connexion with a woman whose ideas of matrimonial happiness were too exalted ever to be realized; convinced that violent raptures are never lasting, and that the greatest connubial happiness is enjoyed, where the passion on both sides is founded on the solid basis of esteem, and heightened by a knowledge of the good qualities of the beloved object.

Chapter III.

AFTER this affair had passed over, there was nothing of the kind took place to disturb Dorcasina's tranquillity for a long period of time. Although the reputed heiress of a thousand pounds a year, which at that time was considered, in America, as a great fortune, she was not troubled with many admirers. Several concurring causes kept her free from solicitations of this kind; one of which was, that the retired manner in which she lived prevented her from being very extensively known; add to this that some of the gentlemen who were fortunate enough to be of her acquaintance, knew how much of her time was dedicated to novels, and how uneasy she was when a new one appeared, till she could make herself mistress of it; reckoning these books her greatest treasures, and perusing them, her supreme felicity. Those, therefore, who were acquainted with this circumstance, notwithstanding the temptation of her money, and her agreeable person, were too prudent to think of seeking her in marriage; wisely foreseeing the inconveniencies which would result from having a wife whose mind was fraught with ideas of life and manners so widely different from what they appear on trial. Others there were, who understood only that she spent much time in books, without any knowledge of the kind which best pleased her. It was sufficient to keep them at a distance, to know that she read at all. Those enemies to female improvement, thought a woman had no business with any book but the bible, or perhaps the art of cookery; believing that every thing beyond these served only to disqualify her for the duties of domestic life.

Dorcasina passed that part of her life from her twentieth to her twenty-fourth year, between her books, her attendance upon her father, and acts of piety and charity. Let not the youthful reader start at the mention of piety in the catalogue of a young lady's virtues; I can assure them that Miss Sheldon was really pious, but not ostentatious; and the mild, charitable, and liberal complexion of her religion was one of her greatest ornaments. Her mind was also "open as day to melting charity." The fame of this virtue extended far beyond the sphere of her own little neighbourhood. All the poor for many miles round applied to her, and were sure to be relieved; for it was her invariable rule to send none away empty-hand; and the poor and weary traveller was sure to find entertainment and refreshment under this hospitable roof. It is true, she was sometimes imposed on by unworthy objects; but that gave her no uneasiness, as she was frequently heard to say, that she had rather supply the wants of two unworthy objects, than that one worthy one should go away dissatisfied. Some, perhaps, may wonder that her father did not put a check upon her liberality, as age generally renders callous the sweet and fine feeling of benevolence. He had in his youth been as enthusiastically charitable as his daughter, often observing that riches were put into the hands of one part of mankind that they might assist the other; and that it was an incumbent duty upon the rich to impart liberally to their poor brethren. In other respects he was not of an expensive turn; and living considerably within his income, he was highly gratified to have his beloved daughter become his almoner. He, therefore, with pleasure supplied her with whatever money she had occasion for, as well to bestow in acts of charity as for any other purpose.

About this period an event happened in the neighbourhood, which afterwards became to Dorcasina a source of great pleasure. This was no other than the birth of a daughter to a Mrs. Stanly, a very intimate friend and acquaintance. Dorcasina was naturally fond of children; she was, therefore, highly gratified when her most esteemed friend was blessed with a charming little girl; and immediately begged the favour of furnishing it with a name, a favour which the parents cheerfully granted. It was, therefore, agreeably to Dorcasina's request, christened by the names of Harriet Caroline Clementina, being the names of persons, whose history she had taken great delight in reading. An attention to, and fondness for this child, was now added to her other avocations, and she seldom passed a day without seeing it, either at home or at Mr. Stanly's. This, Mrs. Stanly, in the infantine age of her daughter cheerfully permitted: but being a lady of an excellent understanding, and great discretion, she very wisely determined, as soon as she should arrive at a proper age, to send her out of the reach of Dorcasina's influence, who she was sure, would not fail to infect the mind of her young friend with the same poison which had operated so powerfully on her own. And this resolution she put in practice some years after, by sending her to an eminent boarding-school in Philadelphia, with an express injunction to the governess, never to indulge her in perusing novels: so great was her aversion to them, from seeing their effects on a person, who, in other respects, was worthy of being held up as a perfect pattern of goodness, discretion and virtue.

Chapter IV.

THE thirty-fourth year of Dorcasina, was another remarkable era of her life, as at that age she was addressed in a style of love and gallantry exactly adapted to her taste. The year before, there had arrived at Philadelphia, from Europe, a young Irishman, about twenty-one years of age. He was natural son to the steward of an Irish nobleman. During his life time, his father had kept him at school. The boy was likely, impudent, and a good scholar; always at the head of all mischief in every school he attended; and remarkable for having always a pack of cards in his pocket, and for attending every cock-fight and horse-race, within a dozen miles of him. Upon the death of his father, which happened when he was about twenty, being left in a destitute situation, he repaired to London, the general resort of people of all conditions, to try his luck at gambling, or any other kind of villany which would procure him a subsistence.

Upon his first arrival at this metropolis, he chanced to form an acquaintance with a gang of young highway robbers; who, finding him a lad of true spirit and mettle, persuaded him to attach himself to their company. In his first attack, he was bold and successful, receiving fifty guineas for his share of the booty; but being afterwards recognized by the person whom he had robbed, he was apprehended and committed to prison in order to take his trial. Here his reflections were not of the most pleasing nature, as he expected nothing less than to swing for his villany; and he fully determined, in his own mind, that, should he have the good fortune to escape the impending danger, he would forever renounce the business which brought him into it. The day of trial came, and with it an increase of his terrors; but he escaped his expected fate by an error in the indictment. Overjoyed at being once more at liberty, he continued firm in his determination of quitting an employment which had led him into such dangers, in spite of all the remonstrances and even threats of his companions.

He next pitched upon an occupation which he thought would be attended with less hazard, as it was practiced by all ranks from the peer to the beggar. He was for sometime successful and unsuspected; but being elated by his good fortune, he became by degrees, so bold and unguarded in his practices, and was so frequently detected in unfair play, that no person would venture to engage him. He thought it now high time to decamp, and repair to some place, where, being unknown, he might pass unsuspected. He hesitated for some time what part of the world to visit; but becoming accidentally acquainted with a master of a vessel from America, he engaged passage for Philadelphia. The captain, though perfectly acquainted with his character, was induced by the offer of a generous reward, to import him; never considering what mischiefs have been occasioned to this country by its being an asylum to European convicts, fugitives from justice, and other worthless characters.

On our young gentleman's arrival in Philadelphia, he betook himself to his old employment of gambling, and became equally notorious as he had been in London. Finding his credit ruined, he formed the resolution of travelling over this extensive continent, to seek his fortune and get money by whatever means he could. The first night of his peregrination, he happened to stop at L—— on the banks of the Delaware, the place of residence of Dorcasina. Being a young fellow of genteel and engaging appearance, he was complimented with the best room in the inn at which he put up. Before he reached it, he passed the house of Mr. Sheldon, which being the best in the village, raised his curiosity to know something of the owner: accordingly, when the landlord appeared, he requested to know to whom it belonged. The landlord being of a communicative disposition, informed him of every particular respecting the inhabitants, not forgetting Dorcasina's affair with Lysander, which had been long publickly known, as well as her motives for refusing him. Our hero

immediately perceived the weak side of her character, and thought he
might avail himself of the discovery to obtain possession of her person
and future fortune.

Filled with these exhilerating ideas, he closed not his eyes during
the whole night; but ruminating on the most probable means of
engaging the affections of his future dulcinea. Being informed by the
loquacious landlord, that she often walked alone in a beautiful grove
behind her father's house, upon the banks of the Delaware, revolving
the plan many times in his mind, he determined upon meeting her as
if by chance, in this wood.

He was now just turned of twenty-two; his person was tall, well
proportioned and graceful. He had fine black eyes, good features, and
a florid complexion.—In a word, superficial observers would have
called him handsome; but those of more nice discernment would
pretend to discover, by the expression of his countenance, that he
possessed neither a good heart, nor a good temper. Be that as it may,
he valued himself not a little upon his personal beauty, and thought,
to a person of Dorcasina's ignorance of the world, and romantic turn
of mind, he should be wholly irresistible. Possessed with these
flattering ideas, he arose with the sun, and he waited with impatience
for the afternoon, that being the time in which, he was informed, that
Dorcasina generally took her solitary walks.

At four o'clock, on a warm summer's day, he dressed himself to the
greatest advantage; took with him his flute, upon which he played in
a masterly manner; put a book in his pocket, and sallied forth into the
wood, armed at all points for conquest, in the fullest expectation of
making his fortune. He rambled about, upon his first entrance, for
some time, admiring the solitude and beauty of the grove. Indeed,
nature seemed to have expressly formed it a place in which lovers
might breath their sighs, and pledge their mutual vows. At length he
seated himself upon a little knoll, surrounded by venerable elms,
whose wide spreading branches meeting with each other, formed a
beautiful natural arbour, almost impervious to the rays of the sun.
Having rested himself a little, he pulled out his flute and played till the
whole wood resounded with its melody. After every tune he would
stop, listen and look round, to see if he could not discover the divinity
of the place. But no mortal footstep was to be heard; no immortal
goddess to be seen.

After having almost exhausted his breath, he threw aside his flute, and, taking out his book, began to read, apparently with great attention; but his mind was otherwise engaged. He began at length to grow impatient; and feared that he should not meet with the mistress, not of his soul, but what was in his opinion of much more consequence, of a thousand pounds a year. After having turned over the book till he was weary, he again took up his flute; when stopping after a tune to listen, he distinctly heard the sound of distant footsteps. They approach, and his heart palpitates with unusual violence. At length he perceives at a distance among the trees, a number of fine large cows, driven by a chubby-faced boy, "who whistled as he went for want of thought." These were no other than the cows of Mr. Sheldon, going to pour their evening treasure into the pails of the ruddy milk-maids. The disappointment and vexation of O'Connor (for that was the name of this Hibernian fortune-hunter) were almost too great for one of his sanguine temper to bear. It being now after sunset, he almost despaired of seeing his charmer, for that day. He, however, addressing the boy in a very condescending manner, asked where he lived, and to whom belonged all those fine cows. The boy replied, that he lived in the great house yonder, and that the cows belonged to 'squire Sheldon. He then inquired his name, and how old he was; and being answered that his name was Patrick, called him namesake, (Patrick being the christian name of our adventurer) and, giving him a piece of money, dismissed him. All this he did that it might be reported at the house, and possibly reach the ears of Dorcasina. Nor was he deceived in his conjectures. The boy went home quite delighted, telling the milk-maid that he had seen the beautifulest and the kindest gentleman, in the grove that he ever saw in his life; that he was not proud, for he called him namesake, and gave him some money, which he shewed her; and finally, that he made the woods ring again with his music. This intelligence was communicated by the milk-maid to Betty, and from her it went immediately to the chamber of Dorcasina, where she was confined by a cold taken a few evenings before, by walking too late in the grove, and which had prevented her on this day from making her appearance there.

Her imagination was immediately at work in conjecturing who this fine stranger could be. It was no uncommon thing for the people in the vicinity to amuse themselves by walking in the grove; but she had never met a stranger there alone. She asked Betty a thousand questions, which the latter being unable to answer, the boy was called up, and every particular of his form, features, and dress inquired into, with surprising minuteness. The answers given by Patrick served only to inflame her curiosity. His being seated with his flute and book, indicated that he was not a traveller hastening to the end of his journey, but rather pursuing it leisurely, and stopping to enjoy every agreeable situation; or it might be some person, who had come to reside in the country during the intense heat of summer. At any rate, she regretted extremely her having been prevented from taking her accustomed and favourite walk, as there would have been something beautifully romantic in meeting an accomplished stranger, in so retired and charming a spot. The idea of conquest immediately occurred; and she gave her imagination the reins in forming the tender interviews and vows of everlasting love, which she would probably receive, in a place so suited to inspire this passion.

As for O'Connor, he waited with the utmost impatience, until it became quite dark; when, chagrined at his disappointment, in a musing and thoughtful mood, he slowly and reluctantly took his solitary way to his lodgings. He was, however, too enterprising and persevering to give up the pursuit for one disappointment; but went to bed fully determined to haunt the grove every day till he should meet there with the object of his wishes. Accordingly, the next day, he repaired to the spot, dressed in a more elegant manner than before. There he passed the time in reading, walking, and playing on the flute, till near sunset; at which time the snowy robe of an elegant female appearing through the trees, caught his attention. He entertained not the smallest doubt but that he had now met with the object of his wishes. In conformity, however, to the plan he had arranged, pretending not to see her, he took up his flute and exerted all his art to charm her senses, by its most soft and melodious notes. Casting now and then a stolen glance towards her, he observed that she approached; when, all at once, she having come sufficiently near him, he lifted up his eyes and appeared lost in astonishment. His flute dropped from his hands, and he stood, for some minutes, fixed like a statue. This surprise was partly affected and partly real; for the female, who now stood before him, appeared to his ravished senses beautiful beyond any thing he had ever seen. Her form and features were elegant and regular; and by the assistance of paint laid on in the nicest manner, her complexion vied with the lily and the rose, while the hour and the situation heightened every charm.

O'Connor at length addressed her in the following manner: "What angel, what goddess, what celestial charms are these which now bless my admiring eyes? I am lost in transports of love and admiration." Then dropping on one knee, and kissing the hem of her garment, he exclaimed, "Condescend, goddess of beauty, if I am not too presumptious, to inform me whether you are of celestial origin, or a mortal clothed in heavenly charms?" The fair one looking upon him with a bewitching smile, reached out her fair hand, and bidding him rise, told him that he greatly overrated her small portion of beauty; that she was neither angel nor goddess, but a mere mortal, come to seek shelter from the sun's too ardent rays, in that cool and charming retreat. Our hero, seizing with eagerness the proffered hand, almost devoured it with his kisses; and, encouraged by her freedom, he requested her to be seated. Placing himself by her side, one arm thrown round her delicate waist, and one of her hands fast locked in his, he poured forth a torrent of compliments, and expressions of love and raptures; declared that he never before had seen the woman who had made the smallest impression on his heart; and that he could not support existence if she did not lend a favourable ear to his addresses.

Turning upon him, in a languishing manner, a pair of lovely blue eyes, the lady affected to behave with some little shew of propriety; telling him that as they were utter strangers to each other, she should incur the censures of an ill-natured world, should she listen too abruptly to his addresses. But to these remonstrances he objected the violence of his passions, and the impossibility of his living without her; adding, that though their persons were strangers, he was sure their souls were entirely congenial. At length, by repeated protestations of everlasting love, he brought her to confess, that, having observed him for some time before she approached, she did not look upon him with an eye of indifference. He returned her a thousand thanks for this favourable declaration, and immediately renewed his entreaties that she would receive his addresses. "I should like," said she smilingly, "to be acquainted at least with your name, before I consent to receive you as a lover." "My name, my angel," replied he, "is O'Connor; a name celebrated in the annals of Ireland." Then, without entering into further particulars concerning himself, he observed that her name was a matter of perfect indifference to him, since he was so well satisfied with her divine person; and again urged his request that she would lend a favourable ear to his addresses. After a few more trifling objections, which he found no difficulty in removing, the obliging fair one blessed him with her consent.

Every thing thus far succeeding according to his wishes; the facility with which he had gained the most material point, urged him on to push his good fortune as far as it would go. He thought it much the wisest way to secure his prize, if possible, while within his power; fearing that her father would never give his consent to the match, when he should come to inquire into his character and situation. He, therefore, proposed that she should accompany him to his lodgings, and there pass the night; that in the morning they should set off for Philadelphia, and have the indissoluble knot tied, as soon as the law would admit. At this proposal the lady appeared much offended, assuring him that she could not think of being so precipitate, (though in her heart it was the very thing she wished) nor take a step to wound her reputation, which, being a jewel of immense value, had hitherto remained unsullied. Any person of the least degree of modesty would have been repulsed at this reply to so extravagant a request; but, happily, modesty was not in the catalogue of our adventurer's good qualities. He, therefore, urged his request with all the eloquence and address of which he was master; assuring her that she should have an apartment at the inn, which he would not presume to enter; and that at Philadelphia he would procure separate lodgings. The modest fair one, appearing overcome by his importunity, held down her head and answered not a word. Our adventurer, therefore, considering her silence and apparent embarrassment as omens in his favour, seized the propitious moment, saying, "Come my adorable angel, let us despise the censures of an ill-judging world; let us follow the dictates of all-powerful love; let us be united and happy, and bid defiance to its malice." So saying, he raised her from the ground, and hurried her out of the wood, being greatly astonished, with all his confidence, at his unexpected success; and fearing greatly lest she should change her mind, and repent her precipitancy; or, that some unforeseen occurrence should intercept his happiness.

It being now nearly dark, they walked with hurried steps till they reached the inn, which was about a quarter of a mile from the grove. Upon their arrival, he ushered into a room not commonly used by the family, till he should go and bespeak an apartment, where she would be free from all intrusion. Fatigued with her walk, she threw herself into a chair, pulled out her handkerchief, let fall a few tears, which were always at command, and pretended to be greatly affected with the rash step she had taken. This, she observed, it was now too late to remedy; since her accompanying him to his lodgings could not fail of being known, and would irretrievably ruin her reputation, should she now think of retracting. Her lover endeavoured to soothe her to calmness, by the kindest words and most endearing expressions; assuring her that the endeavours of his whole future life should be to repay her condescension; and he trusted, that, with the blessing of Heaven, she would have no reason to repent her choice. Having succeeded in calming her apparent uneasiness, he left her to seek the landlord, and met him standing in a thoughtful posture at the outward door.

Our adventurer and his dulcinea did not enter so suddenly as not to be observed by the landlord. As he was perfectly acquainted with the person and character of the lady, he was determined, immediately, to dislodge her; and stood then hesitating whether to enter the apartment, or wait till O'Connor should come out; which he no sooner did, than the landlord, no longer able to restrain his indignation, thus addressed him: "So, young gentleman, these are fine doings, a'n't they?" O'Connor, fearing the lady should overhear their conversation, said in a low voice, "Hush, for Heaven's sake! be silent, and let her have an apartment for this night only; to-morrow she goes with me to Philadelphia: when I am master of her estate and person, and come to reside among you, you may depend upon my favour, and that I shall be one of your firmest friends." The landlord perplexed and irritated at a reply which he could not understand, answered in a voice not at all softened; "Estate! yes, a fine estate you'll have with a w—— I'll warrant. But you may seek another lodging: she shall go packing directly. I'm not going to have the credit of my house ruined, which for twenty years has been perfectly good, by no such madams, I'll assure you, sir." O'Connor, perplexed and confounded, in his turn, at what he had just heard, answered: "What is it you say? Pray explain yourself. What mean you by calling Miss Sheldon such opprobrious names?" "Ha! ha! ha! very good, excellent, by jingo; and so she has been and palmed herself on you for Miss Sheldon. But she's an impudent baggage, and no more Miss Sheldon than our Moll is." "Who then, for Heaven's sake, is she?" interrogated the astonished Irishman. The landlord then gave him to understand, that she was one of those unhappy females, who are lost to all sense of modesty and virtue; too many of whom are to be found in all our large towns: that,

about a month before, she had come into the village with a young
gentleman from Philadelphia, where she had passed for some time,
for his wife; that, about a week before, they had a violent quarrel, and
parted; that, in his anger he exposed her character, left her, and
returned to Philadelphia; since which time, she had been strolling
about in quest of prey, and it was natural to suppose she would have
no objection to obtaining so handsome a young fellow as O'Connor for
a husband. Our adventurer at this relation lost all patience. He cursed
himself a thousand times for his foolish credulity; and could hardly be
prevented, by the landlord, from kicking out of the house a person
whom he had just before prevailed on, with much apparent reluctance,
to enter it. The landlord then persuaded him to retire to his chamber;
while he went and ordered the lady to decamp; which he did without
any resistance or hesitation.

O'Connor, then calling the landlord into his chamber, inquired
very particularly and minutely about the person of Miss Sheldon, that
he might not again be so egregiously deceived. The landlord who did
not want for penetration, immediately perceived the drift of O'Connor's
inquiries, and was satisfied that he had some design upon Miss
Sheldon; but of what nature, whether honourable or otherwise, he was
not able to determine. He resolved, however, to give her intelligence
of it, that she might be upon her guard against his machinations. He
would even, if necessary, have fought for her to the last drop of his
blood; so much had her goodness, condescension and charity endeared
her to every person in the village. In consequence of his determination,
he, the same evening, sent her the following epistle:

"MADAM,

"THERE is at my house a young gentleman that axes many
questions about you. He is handsom, dreses wel, and seems to have
plenty of money. He walks every afternoon in the groove, and this
evening picked up a drab and brought her home, who he thought
was you; but when he found he had got the rong sow by the ear, was
as mad as a march hare, and would have kicked her out a dores, if I
had not prevented him. I hope you will excuse my boldness in riting,
and be assured it is out of pure friendship, and good wil, and
wilingness to sarve you.

                              "From your humble sarvant,
                                 "JONATHAN GREENOUGH."

Miss Sheldon was surprised and perplexed, but not greatly displeased at this intelligence. There was something mysterious and romantic in the affair, which she impatiently wished to unravel. She compared it with the account the boy gave of the gentleman he had seen in the grove, and justly concluded that it must be the same person. His mistaking a woman of bad fame for her, wounded, indeed, her delicacy; and his carrying her to his lodgings was what she could not account for. His committing the mistake, however, was a plain proof that he was a stranger to her person; so that it could be nobody who had fallen in love with her at sight. She thus tortured her imagination the whole night, without once closing her eyes to sleep; and as her cold was now so much better as to admit of her leaving the house, she determined, at all events, to gratify her inflamed curiosity the next afternoon, by throwing herself purposely in his way. She judged it most proper to take Betty with her, lest he should have some bad design upon her. She waited with the utmost impatience till four o'clock, her usual hour for walking, and then, thus accompanied, set out for the grove.

On entering the borders of this sequestered scene, she requested Betty to remain there, while she went forward to explore the interior, with no other companion than one of her favourite novels. She then sauntered along till she arrived at the very spot, where, upon the tender hooks of impatience, O'Connor had, for three days, waited to get a sight of her, being a little natural arbour, where Dorcasina had passed many happy hours. She had not long been seated, when the persevering O'Connor, determined not to give up the chace, entered the grove; and, coming over against the arbour, perceived it occupied by a female form. Fearful of being again deceived, he walked softly towards her, and critically examined her whole person, which agreed so well with the landlord's description, as to leave no doubt on his mind, that he had at length found the object of his search. Ever fruitful in expedients, he had got a plan ready formed, to have the identity of her person confirmed by her own mouth. Fortified with this resolution, he walked directly up to her, so that she saw him not till he was just before her. Upon lifting up her eyes, and seeing so near her his graceful figure, she started and blushed involuntarily. O'Connor, on his side, with all his confidence, was somewhat awed by her modest and dignified appearance, so widely different from the bold and forward air of the beautiful, but depraved female, he had the day before met there. So great a power has female virtue, though unaided by external charms, over even the most abandoned of men.

O'Connor bowed in a graceful manner, and said, "Your humble servant, madam." "Your servant, sir," returned Dorcasina. A silence of some moments ensued. It was at length broken by O'Connor, who observed, that it was a fine afternoon; and added, fixing his eyes full on the face of Miss Sheldon, that she had chosen a most delightful place in which to enjoy it. "A very charming one indeed, sir," replied she. "No person of taste, sentiment, or feeling could reside near this charming spot, without passing much time here: you live in its vicinity, I presume, madam?" "I do, sir, and here many of my leisure hours are most agreeably spent." "Think me not impertinent, ma'am, if I venture to hazard a conjecture, that the person whom I now have the honour of addressing, is the amiable Miss Sheldon, whom I have so often heard mentioned by my friend Lysander." "My name is Sheldon, sir." "I was very sure of it; no other person could answer the description given by Lysander, who is the most unhappy of men, and has in vain endeavoured to erase your image from his heart. Many times have I attempted to console him, and urged him to make another choice; but all my endeavours were ineffectual; he constantly answered that the world could produce but one Miss Sheldon. I then thought him unreasonable and extravagant; but now, that I have the supreme delight of beholding her, for whom he sighs, I am no longer surprised at his fixed determination of never seeking another connexion." "Lysander, sir, is a man of great merit, and one whom I very highly esteem. When saw you him last?" "About six weeks since," replied our confident adventurer; though before his loquacious landlord had informed him of the particulars of the affair between Lysander and Miss Sheldon, he knew not that such a person existed.

After this, they entered into a conversation of a more general nature; Dorcasina imagining, that if he were the friend of Lysander, she ran no risque in his acquaintance, as she was very sure that none but men of honour and character would be admitted to a place in his friendship. They, therefore, conversed together in an easy and agreeable manner. O'Connor entertained her with an account of the customs and manners of Europe, and of all the British modern authors of the greatest celebrity; but dwelt with peculiar pleasure on the writers of novels, and asserted that they alone described the passion of love in its true and genuine colours. While he was thus haranguing, he would cast such languishing glances upon Dorcasina, from his fine black eyes, and heave such amorous sighs from his apparently enraptured bosom, that she was pierced through and through. In this pleasing delirium she continued chatting with our adventurer, till at length the setting-sun admonished her that it was time to retire, though she was surprised when she observed that luminary sinking into the lap of Thetis; so agreeably and imperceptibly had the moments passed. She, however, retained prudence and resolution sufficient to make a motion to rise, saying, it was time for her to be gone. O'Connor, upon this, sprang lightly from his seat, and offered her his hand, to aid her in rising. She did not decline his proffered assistance, at which he appeared penetrated with joy, and stood for some time, silently and ardently gazing at her, while he pressed her hand in both his. At length, his words, as it were finding utterance, "Must I then lose you?" he said; "must I thus part with you, and never, perhaps, be again favoured with your presence? Oh! forbid it Heaven, I cannot support the idea!" Then dropping her hand, and pretending a degree of confusion for the liberty he had taken, he fell on one knee and exclaimed, "Forgive me, Miss Sheldon! divine excellence, forgive a man so enraptured with your charms that he hardly has the full exercise of his reason." "Rise, sir," said Dorcasina, "I beg of you to rise. I cannot bear to see you in this humble posture." "I never will, I never can rise," replied O'Connor, "till Miss Sheldon will promise that she will not drive me to despair, till she give me some encouragement that she will, as usual, frequent her favourite grove, where I shall daily and nightly wander, like a restless ghost, in expectation of the supreme felicity of again beholding her." Dorcasina, with a gracious smile, replied, that the appearance of a real ghost would hardly deter her from taking her agreeable and accustomed walk. O'Connor, overjoyed with his success, having poured out his thanks for her goodness, arose from his humble posture; and they slowly took their way together out of the grove. Having arrived at the spot where Betty was stationed, who, by this time, had begun to be alarmed for the health of her mistress, on account of the heavy dew which was beginning to fall, they bid each other good night. Dorcasina leaning on the arm of her faithful maid, directed her steps homeward. Not so, our artful adventurer. He fixed himself against the body of a tree, and stood straining his eyes till Dorcasina was out of sight; while she, pleased with this proof of his love, moved slowly onward, and every few steps, desired Betty to look behind and see if he still kept his post. Nor could she avoid frequently turning her own head to have a last look of her charming enamarato.

As soon as they had lost sight of him, Betty inquired who that fine spark was. "Whoever he is," replied Dorcasina, "he is a divine fellow, a perfect Sir Charles Grandison." Betty, surprised to hear her mistress speak in such terms of this stranger, as she never had before heard her speak of any other man, inquired his name, and from whence he came. "To tell the truth," said Dorcasina, "he informed me of neither one nor the other; and it would have been very rude in me to have asked him: but I am certain of his being a gentleman, and a man of character; for he informed me that my old acquaintance, Lysander, was one of his most intimate friends."

At the name of Lysander, Betty fetched a sigh, always having regretted that her mistress refused so suitable a match, and prophesying in her own mind, that she would live to repent it. "I wish," said she, "that he may be half as good a man as Lysander." "Lysander, to be sure," replied Dorcasina, "is a very good man; but how inanimate a lover! Oh! how differently did the charming stranger address me! How ardent and impassioned was his manner! Indeed, his whole soul shone out at his eyes, which were more expressive, if possible, than his words." "What, has he then made love to you, ma'am?" "Yes, indeed, he has, and his sentiments are so congenial to my own, that I am certain we are destined for each other." "So you thought of Lysander, ma'am." "But it was before I saw him, Betty; the moment I beheld him, I was convinced of my mistake; I felt none of that fascination, that enchantment, that inexpressible something, which draws the soul along in spite of all our efforts to resist the bewitching influence." "Well, my mind of him," said Betty, "is, that he is a bold, impudent fellor, to go for to talking about love the first time he seed you; and as he has been walking in the grove for some days, I suspects that he is after no good, and that he is no better than he should be. As to what you say of his warm manner, compared with Lysander's, you never heard him talk of love, he only writ you a letter; perhaps his talk about it would have been as lively as this forward fellor's, who nobody knows." Dorcasina smiled to hear Betty so earnest; and only observed, that were the stranger to address her by letter, she doubted not it would be in a far different style from that which Lysander penned.

By this time they had reached the house. Dorcasina attended her father, in a titillation of spirits, which she had never before experienced; and she exerted herself in an unusual manner to entertain him. She smiled as she spoke to the servants; and her eyes, which had begun to lose something of their brilliancy, sparkled with all the pleasure of renovated youth. When she ascended the stairs to go to bed, her steps were as light as those of a fairy; and her ideas of the most pleasing kind, as she had now acquired a lover exactly to her taste: and after she had fallen a-sleep, her dreams perfectly corresponded with her waking ideas. As for O'Connor, he went strutting to his lodgings, felicitating himself upon his invention and address, and laying plans for the management of the fair domain, of which he had not the least doubt of soon gaining possession.

Chapter V.

THE next day appeared much longer to our impatient lovers than usual. They imagined that father Time, with multiplied years, had loaded his wings with an additional weight of lead. At length, the clock sounded four. O'Connor, dressed in the elegance of fashion, tripping along as light as feathered Mercury, soon arrived at the place of destination.

Dorcasina, on her side, was uncommonly solicitous about her appearance. Her dress was changed three times, before she thought it sufficiently becoming. When the hour of four arrived, her heart bounded, and her feet would willingly have carried her directly to her favourite haunt; but she checked her inclination, judging it best to heighten her lover's impatience, by making him wait for her a while. She, therefore, tarried a full quarter of an hour, looking incessantly at her watch, and thinking that the hands never before moved so slowly. At the expiration of the fifteen minutes, her whole stock of patience being exhausted, she called to Betty, desiring her to follow: and took her way towards the place of meeting.

O'Connor's impatience was equal to her own. He had passed the time since his arrival, in walking up and down the grove. At length, espying the snowy whiteness of her flowing robe through the green foliage, he flew towards her, and seizing her hand, which he pressed

with fervour to his lips, "How kind is this in you, my angel," said he,
"thus to bless me with your presence. What hopes, fears, and tumults
have, by turns, agitated my breast since I parted with you last evening!
Good Heavens! a state of suspense is, of all others, the most miserable!
Will you not, goddess of my soul, bless me with one kind, one
encouraging word?" "Indeed, sir," said Dorcasina, "I know not what
encouragement you ought to expect from me, who am still a stranger
to your name and country; and, till yesterday, had not even seen your
person." "Oh! talk not of an acquaintance of yesterday. Our souls
have been long acquainted; and the time since yesterday has appeared
to me an age. But, my guide, my guardian angel, my better genius, you
shall be immediately satisfied, as to the particulars you mention."
Then leading her into the little arbour, which by this time they had
reached, he seated her on the most elevated part of the turf, and
placing himself in an easy and graceful posture, at her feet, he begun,
with the utmost confidence, in the following manner:

"My name, my charmer, is O'Connor. I am the only son of a
gentleman of large fortune in the north of Ireland. Unfortunately, I
had a female cousin, who was likewise an only child, and heiress to an
immense fortune. Our parents destined us for each other from our
infancy, that the estates might not go out of the family; and that neither
of us might disgrace the uncontaminated blood of the O'Connors, by
matching with families less noble and ancient. They, however, wisely
kept their project from our knowledge; nor were we even admitted to
see each other; being kept at different schools, at distant places, till my
cousin was sixteen, and myself twenty years of age. At that period we
were brought together; still ignorant, however, of the intended
connexion. My cousin, it might be confessed, was a very beautiful girl;
but Heaven had not (though our parents had) destined us for each
other. I beheld her with the most perfect indifference; and contemplated
her as I should a fine picture, or a statue. After having been several
times in her company, my father, one day, informed me that I must
prepare myself for matrimony; for that he and my uncle had resolved
that their children, in one month from that day, should be united. I
was thunder-struck at this intelligence; and the more so, as I knew, that
when my father had once formed a resolution he was immoveable in
it. I kneeled, begged and prayed; urging my total indifference to the
lady, and the little chance I had for happiness in the connexion. But all
was in vain; my father was inexorable; and I left him with a

determination to quit Ireland forever, rather than wed a woman to whom I was wholly indifferent. I, therefore, in a few days, embarked privately for England, where I tarried till I had viewed every thing worthy of a stranger's notice. Impelled, by a restless curiosity, to visit the rising States of America; and charmed by the unrivalled character of the immortal Washington, I embarked for this country. After an agreeable passage, I arrived in Virginia, bringing letters of recommendation to several gentlemen of respectability; among whom was the father of Lysander. The old gentleman invited me to his house, where I passed some weeks. In this time, I contracted an intimacy with his son, to whom I imparted my situation, and the reason for which I left my native country. He approved my conduct, and in return for the confidence I had placed in him, related the particulars of his visit to you, and of his attachment consequent upon it. He, as I had the honour yesterday of informing you, still lives single for your sake. His greatest delight was in talking of you; and in those conversations, he passed such high encomiums on your beauties, graces and virtues, that my imagination was inflamed, and I passionately loved before I saw you.

"As soon, therefore, as I could decently disengage myself, I set out for Philadelphia, fully determined to pay a visit to the dear object who filled my thoughts by day, and my dreams by night. I, however, concealed from Lysander my design, as well as the passion with which he had inspired me; and early, one morning, bid him adieu, telling him that I was impatient to visit the capital of America. After passing a month in that city, I came to your village and took up my quarters at the inn. Solicitous to obtain a thorough knowledge of you, I addressed myself to my loquacious landlord, and from him received every information I wished. He particularly mentioned your frequent walks in this enchanting grove. This circumstance was highly gratifying; for it naturally suggested to my mind the idea of here throwing myself in your way, in order to obtain a glimpse of your divine person. This plan I immediately began to execute. The two first days were spent in vain hopes, and disappointed expectations; but the third, oh! heavens and earth, how propitious! I beheld you! I found you a thousand times more charming than even my imagination had painted you; and my chains are now so fast rivetted, that it is impossible for any thing but death to break them asunder. And now (falling upon his knees, and shedding a torrent of tears) my goddess, my angel, having thus given you a true and faithful account of myself, I implore your pardon, your pity, and, shall I presume to say, your love!"

Dorcasina kept a profound silence, and was variously agitated during this recital. Pleasure, however, bordering on transport, was predominant; and though she wished, through modesty, to conceal her emotions, they were plainly discovered by the artful O'Connor, who now thought himself certain of her heart. After a silence of some minutes, Dorcasina told him she was much obliged by his relation, and the partiality he avowed; but that she thought an acquaintance of two days would hardly justify any concessions in his favour. At the same time, giving him an invitation to the house, she told him she was sure her father would be highly gratified by his company. To this he replied, that none of the gentlemen to whom he had letters in Philadelphia were acquainted with her father; and that he did not think proper to intrude himself into his house, with no other recommendation than his own account of himself; but that if he could be blessed with any hopes from his adorable daughter, he would write to his friends in Philadelphia to procure him letters from some person with whom her father was acquainted.

Thus, our ingenious adventurer, for the present, artfully evaded an introduction to Mr. Sheldon; intending, if possible, to get such a hold of his daughter's affections as to marry her in spite of all the opposition the old gentleman could make, even after he should discover his being an impostor. He, however, with all his rhetoric, could get no farther encouragement from Dorcasina, than a promise to meet him in the grove, at the same hour, the next day. They then parted for the night; he fixing himself in the same posture, to see the last of her, as he had done the night before; and she turning her head as many times, to take a last look at him.

Dorcasina having joined Betty, they walked homeward in a profound silence; the former regaling her imagination with the scenes of the afternoon, and the latter wondering greatly at her mistress's imprudence, in thus going, unaccompanied, avowedly to meet a stranger in so retired a place. Upon their arrival at the house, they found that Mr. Sheldon had gone, much indisposed, to bed. This, at any other time, would have given great pain to the heart of his virtuous and affectionate daughter; but so fully was her mind occupied with her new connexion, that it occasioned her but a momentary uneasiness. She retired immediately to her chamber; Betty still following like her shadow. After securing the door, to prevent any interruption, she unbosomed herself to this faithful maid; giving an account of every thing which had passed between O'Connor and herself; hoping, by this frank relation, to remove the prejudices which Betty had conceived against him. As soon as she had ended, "I hope," said Betty, "he will turn out what he pretends; but I thinks, ma'am, you ought to give Lysander credit for his constancy. Time, it seems, ha'n't cooled his passion; and this appears to me the true sort of love. I thinks you had'n't better have no more to say to this smooth-tongued Irishman; but get your father to write a letter to Lysander's father; tell him you have changed your mind, and will take his son, if he will come and offer himself again." "Good heavens! Betty! would you have me guilty of such a piece of indelicate forwardness? Why, it would be the right method to make the man despise me. Besides, I should rather die than marry a person who was indifferent to me, if I felt no partiality for any other. But this is not my case. The heavenly O'Connor has taken such full possession of my heart, that, were I now to be crossed in my inclination, I never should be able to survive it." "Pho, pho," said Betty, "all this stuff you have got from your books. I thought never any good would come from so much poring. People don't so easily die of love. I have known a great many crosses, but they all got it over in time, married some other person, and lived very happy." "Those are the ideas, Betty, of vulgar minds; they know nothing of that pure refined passion, which, absorbing every faculty of the soul, swallows up all concern except for the beloved object. Two lovers, in this case, are the whole universe to each other; and are well satisfied to live in caves and deserts, and feed upon the earth's spontaneous productions. And such is the sublime nature of my love for O'Connor. I would traverse the whole globe, and, for his sake, brave every danger." "For the sake of a fellor you have known but two days," exclaimed Betty! "I hope you have not told him what you would do for his sake." "No, Betty, I have not been in such haste to let him know my sentiments. It was fit that I should first be made fully acquainted with his, respecting me; and since he has so candidly imparted to me every thing I wished to know, I do not, I assure you, intend to keep him long in suspense." This she uttered in a serious manner; at the same time, informing Betty, that, having no farther service for her, she wished to be left to her repose.

Betty withdrew in silent dejection, convinced that the affections of

her mistress were firmly fixed on O'Connor, and that she was offended
by the liberty she had taken in speaking her sentiments of him. She
was greatly distressed, lest Dorcasina should throw herself away on
a worthless profligate. She had sagacity enough to observe, that her
mistress, already past the prime of youth, and, having never been
remarkable for beauty, was now less an object of love than at the age
of eighteen. She observed, likewise, that O'Connor was apparently
many years younger; that he was handsome, graceful, insinuating,
and a great flatterer. She, therefore, very justly suspected that he was
some needy adventurer, less solicitous about her person than her
property; but she dared not go so far as to hint her suspicions. She was
astonished that a lady, who had hitherto conducted with so much
propriety, should, at this stage of life, be so little solicitous for her
reputation, as to meet, by appointment, in the grove, a person, with
whom, but three days before, she was wholly unacquainted. Filled
with these perplexing ideas, and loving her mistress with a sincere
affection, poor Betty knew not what course she ought to pursue. She
sometimes determined to impart to Mr. Sheldon the whole affair; but
this she feared would offend Dorcasina past forgiveness. Unable to
come to any resolution, she heaved a deep sigh, and hushed her
inquietudes in a profound sleep.

Chapter VI.

NEXT day, at the usual hour, Dorcasina again prepared to meet her
lover in the grove; and again she desired the attendance of Betty, who,
silently and reluctantly followed her. There, firm to his purpose, she
found her Hibernian; who, as soon as he descried her, flew towards
her with all the raptures of an impassioned lover. "Divine charmer,"
cried he, "how shall I ever repay this kind condescension? With what
raptures my heart is filled, only at the sound of your foot-steps! I live,
I breathe, I exist but in your presence. Separated from you, I should
be in a state of annihilation, did not your idea, filling my mind, inform
me that I still have an existence. I hope, my heavenly charmer, life of
my soul, and light of my eyes, that you have now come with a
determination to put an end to the torture of my suspense; for I am well

assured, that so heavenly a form, and so immaculate a mind, can never take pleasure in tormenting the meanest of mankind; much less a person who adores her as I do." Dorcasina was so delighted with this rhapsody, which she thought exceeded all that she had ever read of the most violent love, that she could scarcely refrain from throwing herself into his arms, and confessing a mutual flame. But having some shadow of discretion still left, she checked herself. One mystery hung upon her mind, which she wished to have cleared up before she consented to be his forever. This was, the account given her by his landlord, of his having mistaken a woman of bad fame for herself; and her accompanying him to his lodgings before he discovered his mistake. It did not enter into her imagination how he could have been so grossly deceived; or why, under that belief, he conducted her to the inn. She, therefore, told him there was one circumstance which she wished to have explained before she could give him farther encouragement; and then informed him of her having been apprized of the foregoing incident. O'Connor, with all his confidence, was greatly abashed. He changed colour, and stammered. The attack had come so unexpectedly upon him, that he had not time to exercise his invention in framing a solution. He, however, soon recollected himself; and assuming his wonted easy confidence, made Dorcasina the following relation:

"As I was walking solitarily in this grove," said he, "wishing, longing, and hoping to meet my adorable Miss Sheldon, an elegant female form caught my attention. We immediately made a motion towards each other; we met, and after the first compliments were passed, fell into an easy and familiar conversation. In the course of it, she informed me that her name was Sheldon; and that she lived in the house just by the grove. She requested, in return, to know my name, and from whence I came. And is it possible, thought I, that this should be the lovely Miss Sheldon, whose charms were described by Lysander, in such glowing colours, as to set my heart on fire? I cannot deny but I thought her handsome; yet, how far short did she fall of the idea I had formed of your divine person! an idea, which I have since found so fully realized. I was disgusted, too, by her forwardness and want of delicacy; and my mortification was extreme, when I found that the person, a sight of whom I had taken such pains to gain, disgusted rather than pleased me. Feeling, however, a reverence for the whole sex, I treated her with politeness, and the conversation was prolonged till the shades of evening began to envelope us. Vexed, mortified, and disappointed, I then arose to leave the grove. She, too, arose, saying, it was time, likewise, for her to retire. We walked in silence to the skirt of the wood; when, instead of turning towards what I supposed to be her own home, she said, that so fine an evening induced her to lengthen her walk; and she accordingly took the way to my lodgings. On our arrival, the confident creature, to my utter astonishment, proposed going in and passing the evening. My situation was now embarrassing. I hesitated. At length, however, I led her into the house, seated her, and immediately left the room, fully determined to retire to my chamber and leave her to her own reflections. But, happening in my way to meet my landlord, he soon undeceived me with regard to the character of the lady who had thus graciously accompanied me home. I now lost all patience. The impudence of the creature in daring to assume the name of the most lovely and virtuous of her sex, raised my indignation to the highest pitch; and I should certainly have turned her out of doors, in no very genteel manner, had not the landlord restrained me, and dismissed her himself."

Dorcasina, during this recital, was variously affected. She had once, at church, seen the person in question, and thought her the handsomest woman she had ever beheld. She was, therefore, highly gratified at the preference given by O'Connor to her own beauty. Her indignation was, however, raised, at having her name assumed by so worthless a creature; but it was soon succeeded by the delight she experienced at her lover's resistance of so strong a temptation. By his conduct, in this embarrassing situation, her opinion of him was greatly heightened. She thought him a Scipio in continence, and a perfect model of delicacy and virtue.

Having finished his relation, she cast on him a look of ineffable complacency. As this did not pass unobserved by O'Connor, he determined to improve to his own advantage, the present favourable situation of the mind of his mistress. "Divine perfection," said he, "you are now acquainted with the whole affair. Will my charmer forgive me for being, even for a short time, so egregiously deceived? Will she vouchsafe me her fair hand in token of forgiveness?" "Where there is no fault," said Dorcasina, with an encouraging smile, "there is nothing to be forgiven." "Thanks, a thousand thanks for this goodness," returned O'Connor. "And now permit me to urge the cause upon which depends my happiness, and even my life. Hang there any other doubts upon the mind of the supreme arbitress of my fate? If not, pronounce, I beseech you, my doom. Cast upon me your favourable regards; at least, if you cannot crown me with love, wound me not with cold disdain." Dorcasina, her heart filled with love, and her eyes beaming with affection, replied, "Why, Mr. O'Connor, should you talk of disdain? Do you think I should have consented to meet, in this place, a person whom I disdained?" "Heavens and earth!" exclaimed O'Connor, "what do I hear? Am I not then indifferent to you? Ah! complete your begun goodness, and confirm my happiness. Say, oh! say, you will be mine." With the blush of modesty on her countenance, Miss Sheldon returned, "With the consent of my dear and reverend father, I will not oppose what you so ardently wish; but, unless that can be obtained, I should not be happy, even with the amiable O'Connor."

Our adventurer, upon this, fell on his knees, and pressed her hand in speechless rapture. He then arose, and encircling her in his arms, impressed upon her lips an ardent kiss. "This," cried he, "is the seal of my happiness. How shall I support myself? Teach me, lovely Dorcasina, to bear the weight of bliss; this transport of delight." "I hope, sir," said Dorcasina, "you will meet with nothing to obstruct your happiness; but moderate your transports, and depend upon my constancy. Write to Philadelphia for letters to my father, and I will ensure you a good reception. We will not fail, mean time, of meeting here, till his sanction to our connexion be obtained." "Beautiful as Venus, good as beautiful, and wise as good," cried the enraptured lover, "I will write immediately to my friends, to procure me the wished for introduction. In the mean time, I beseech you not to let one day pass without blessing me with your presence; for should you, but one day, withhold yourself from my enraptured view, it would be the longest and most melancholy of my life." "You may depend on my affection for that," replied Dorcasina, "you would not, I assure you, suffer alone. But it is now almost dark, and time for us to part." So saying, she arose, and they walked arm in arm out of the grove; both perfectly well pleased, but from quite different causes. He, from the prospect of becoming master of a thousand a year; and she, from thinking herself on the point of obtaining a husband equal to her most sanguine expectations.

Chapter VII.

AFTER parting with her lover, at the edge of the wood, Dorcasina, "gracious, mild and good," (her displeasure at Betty's last night's freedom, being entirely swallowed up in the immensity of her present love and happiness) leaning on the faithful creature's arm, gave her a particular account of all that had passed; at the conclusion of which, she said, "And would you believe me, Betty? he downright kissed me; and not my cheek, but my lips!" Poor Betty, uneasy and distressed, remained for some time, thoughtful and silent; while her mistress, totally unmindful of her sadness, ran on, in the most extravagant manner, in the praise of O'Connor, saying, that she had, at last, been so fortunate as to meet with her kindred soul; that he was the most modest, most engaging, and perfect of mankind; that her bliss would be complete in an union with him; and, that nothing on this side heaven would be capable of adding to her felicity, when once she should become his wife. Betty, indignant at hearing her mistress express herself in this enthusiastic manner, at length, broke silence. "Then you mean to marry him, ma'am; and not let your father know nothing at all about it!" "Heaven forbid! Betty, that I should be guilty of such an act of ingratitude to the best and most indulgent of parents. But my dear father cannot possibly have any objection to Mr. O'Connor, when he comes to know him as well as I do. He is waiting only for some letters from Philadelphia, to present himself before him; and I am so far from entertaining any doubt of his consent, that I am certain he will rejoice in his daughter's happy prospects." "Well, ma'am, I hope every thing will turn out to your heart's content; for I am sure, I wishes for your happiness as much as for my own. But there is many a slip between the cup and the lip; and many disappointments in this vale of tears."

Dorcasina was so entirely absorbed in her own agreeable cogitations, that she paid not the least attention to Betty's last speech; and not a word more passed between them, till they reached the house. Dorcasina, upon entering, was roused from this pleasing delirium, by being informed that her father was more indisposed than he had been the night preceding; that he had gone to bed, and desired to see her as soon as she should have returned. She entered his apartment with trembling anxiety, and approached softly to his bed, to see whether he were asleep. Finding him awake, she set down by his bed-side; and taking his hand, inquired, in the tenderest and most affectionate manner, how he found himself. "I am very sick, my dear," answered her father; "but I hope to be better in the morning." Dorcasina, finding his hand hot, and his pulse quick, was greatly alarmed, and begged him instantly to send for a physician; but, there being none within three miles, he replied, that he would try, for that night, to compose himself; and, if he were not better in the morning, he would do as she desired. "But, my dear Dorcasina," said he, "I am less concerned for myself than for you. I am uneasy at your walking, of late, so long in the grove. You know it was but last week, that you caught there, a cold, which confined you, for some days, to the house. I requested, therefore, your attendance here, not so much on my own account, as to beg that you will have more regard to your health, and my happiness, than again to protract your walk to so late an hour." Dorcasina melted to tears at her father's situation, and this proof of his paternal love, promised, without hesitation, that she would, in future, return with the setting sun. Satisfied with this promise, he advised her to retire to bed; but Dorcasina resolving not to leave him, begged him to endeavour to get some sleep; adding, that feeling, at present, no inclination for it herself, she would take a book and sit by him, till she did. Acquiescing in the wish of his beloved daughter, this affectionate parent, somewhat relieved, soon fell asleep. It was not, however, the quiet sleep which nature requires. He started and groaned; appeared disturbed by uneasy dreams, and frequently turned from side to side. He awoke, at length, about midnight, perfectly delirious. Dorcasina, terrified beyond measure, called up Betty, and told her to dispatch a man and horse, immediately, for the doctor. About day-light the doctor came: he found his patient very ill; and the whole house, beside, in the utmost consternation. After prescribing for Mr. Sheldon what he judged to be proper, he ate some breakfast, and endeavoured to prevail on Dorcasina to follow his example; but she refused his solicitations, saying, she was utterly unable to swallow a morsel of food, while her dear father was insensible to her attentions.

About eight o'clock, Mr. Sheldon fell again into broken slumbers; but awoke at twelve, in the same situation as before, his fever and delirium not in the smallest degree abated. Dorcasina, who had watched every breath as he slept, hoping, upon his waking, to find him rational, now almost gave him up to death, and herself to despair; and, when the hour of four arrived, her delirium nearly equalled his. Her distress at the situation of her father, and the disappointment of her lover, who she knew would be waiting for her in the grove, was greater than she could support. She wept, she wrung her hands, and walked about in all the agonies of the bitterest grief. At length, her recollection coming to her aid, she bethought herself of sending Betty, with a message to her lover, informing him of the cause of his present disappointment. Betty, moved at the distress of her mistress, willingly undertook the commission, and found O'Connor walking about, in the greatest impatience, as it was now near five o'clock. He saw, by her looks, as soon as she appeared, that something had happened; and, as impostors live constantly in dread of detection, he was greatly alarmed lest something had happened to blast his expectations. Without, therefore, giving Betty time to speak, he thus accosted her. "Well, my good Betty, how do you do? and how is your lovely mistress? You look sad: Heaven forbid, that any thing has happened to the mistress of my soul." "Miss Dorcasina, sir, is well, but in the greatest trouble imaginable. Her father lies at the point of death; and she sent me here to tell you the reason of her not coming."

O'Connor was revivified at this intelligence; not only because he found himself undetected, but because Mr. Sheldon's death would give him greater pleasure than any other possible event; for, in this case, there would be no obstacle to an union with his daughter, and coming into immediate possession of his estate; whereas, should he marry her in the life time of her father, he would be obliged to wait for his decease, to become master of his possessions. Disguising, however, his pleasure, under the mask of hypocrisy, and assuming a look of extreme dejection, "How kind in my charmer, how considerate, how like herself," said he, "to send, in the midst of her own affliction, to relieve me from a painful suspense. Oh! why do my unhappy stars forbid my going to the dear creature; clasping her to my faithful bosom, and participating in the sorrow with which she is overwhelmed. But tell me, Betty, is there no hope? Is it beyond the skill of the faculty to save the father of my divine Dorcasina?" "He is very bad, sir; but kind Providence, I hope, will bless the means, and spare him to us a little longer." "How old is he, Betty; is he very aged?" "Alas, no sir!

He was born the very same day my mother was, as I have often heard her say; and if she had been alive, she would have been exactly fifty-seven, the twenty-first day of last March."

Here, our adventurer, was again mortified, at not finding Mr. Sheldon so old, by some years, as he had imagined. He begun to think, if he recovered from this sickness, that it would be hardly worth his while to marry Dorcasina, and wait, perhaps, twenty years before he should become master of the property. However, as he had gone thus far, and seeing no prospect of doing better, he concluded to take Dorcasina now, and the property when it should please Heaven to take to itself her father. While he stood, wrapt in these contemplations, Betty had moved to be gone. This waked him from his reverie; when, calling her back, "Tell your angelic mistress," said he, "that my sufferings far exceed her's; and that it will be impossible for me to— But, indeed, Betty, I am so full, I cannot express myself. When I can gain a little composure she shall hear from me again." So saying, he pulled out his handkerchief, and leaning against a tree, began to weep and sigh most bitterly. The kind-hearted Betty, notwithstanding her prejudices against O'Connor, could not help compassionating his distress; and, after saying all she could think of, to comfort him, returned in haste to the house.

The tears from the eyes of O'Connor were dried as soon as she disappeared; and he passed the remainder of the day between a new play, and the hopes of receiving intelligence of the death of Mr. Sheldon. Having finished his play, and no other messenger arriving, he retired to his lodgings, from whence he dispatched the following epistle:

"MY DEAREST LIFE AND LOVE,

"HOW shall I find language to express the keenness of my sufferings? To know that you are in distress, harrows up my soul. Why am I not permitted to fly on the wings of love; assist in your filial duty; and, by participating, lessen your anxiety? My dear, my amiable, my adorable Dorcasina, let me conjure you not to give way too much to grief. Your father will, perhaps, recover; but, if Heaven ordain the contrary, you must consider that he cannot live always; and your faithful lover flatters himself, that you will have too much compassion on him, to injure your health, or endanger your precious life, by giving yourself up to unavailing sorrow; and that you will endeavour to preserve both, to bless with supreme happiness,

> "My angelic Miss Sheldon,
> "Your devoted, ardent, and passionate adorer,
> "Patrick O'Connor."

We will now return to the house of mourning, from which Betty had been dispatched. She had left her mistress in an agony of distress, and Mr. Sheldon raving with unabated delirium. At four o'clock, nature appearing almost exhausted, he fell into a sweet and gentle slumber. After remaining an hour in this situation, he awoke, his fever much abated, and his delirium quite gone. Dorcasina, who, as usual, had been watching every breath he drew, was overjoyed to hear her father once more speak in a rational manner; while the physician pronounced the crisis past, and the danger over. Her mind being thus relieved, she left the chamber of sickness, and retired to her own. Here, with pain mingled with delight, she listened to Betty's relation of the interview in the grove. She was charmed with the proofs of O'Connor's love and sensibility; and pained at the suspense and anxiety he appeared to endure. And, now her mind was relieved, her first wish was to relieve that of her lover. While consulting with Betty on the means of doing it, his letter was put into her hands by the boy, who had first encountered him in the grove. After reading it three times over to herself, she read it again aloud to Betty. Having finished, "You see now, Betty," said she, "the difference between this letter and that of Lysander. How cold, how unimpassioned was that, compared to the warmth, the ardour, the ecstacy of this. The dear O'Connor has a heart susceptible of genuine love. Ah! how impatient I am again to behold him! to see his soul shining out at his fine eyes, and speaking unutterable things! Ah! why do not the tardy messengers with the letters arrive, that I may be speedily united to the most amiable of human beings; to my first, my last, my only love?"

Thus ran on Dorcasina, in more impassioned terms than she had ever before used. Several circumstances concurred to set her into this delirium of joy. She had just been relieved from a greater weight of grief than she had ever before experienced; and her heart was lightened of a burthen which had become almost insupportable. While enjoying this new set of feelings, occasioned by a prospect of her father's recovery, the letter of her lover increased and heightened them. In this joyful and affectionate mood, she sat down, and produced the following letter:

"BE comforted, my O'Connor, for your Dorcasina is relieved. My father is pronounced out of danger; and I long to see you, that we may rejoice together. How painful is an absence of one day from an object who possesses our whole affections! We have, however, one consolation; our pleasure when we meet, will be proportionably great. I have read over your letter again and again; and it is now in my bosom, next to my heart. I shall preserve it with the greatest care, as containing proofs of the purest love that ever warmed a human breast. I esteem myself, in your affection, the happiest of women.
                                                "DORCASINA SHELDON."

"P. S. As soon as my father is well enough to leave, I will give you intelligence of it."

Having dispatched this epistle, Dorcasina returned again to her father; and, finding him still comfortable, she listened to his reiterated supplications, and, retiring to bed, soon fell into a sound sleep.

The next morning, she arose with the sun; and finding her father surprisingly mended, she entertained thoughts of visiting her favourite retreat, and still more favoured lover. Mr. Sheldon, however, appearing in the afternoon a little more indisposed, she restrained her impatience, and determined to defer it till the next day.

Chapter VIII.

UNFORTUNATELY for our lovers, the next two days being rainy, no intercourse took place between them. The subsequent morning being remarkably fine, and Mr. Sheldon quite recovered, Dorcasina dispatched the following billet to her lover, by the boy, Patrick; who, on account of his name, had become a favourite:

"THIS will inform the most faithful and affectionate of lovers, that one, to whom he is very dear, will be at liberty to meet him, this afternoon, at the accustomed place; hoping then, to hear the agreeable intelligence of his having received the expected letters, as her impatience is very great to see together, two persons, dearer to her than the whole world beside."

O'Connor was somewhat perplexed, upon the receipt of this billet, as he had to invent excuses for the non-arrival of letters, for which he had never written. He was also disappointed and chagrined at the unexpected recovery of Mr. Sheldon. It blasted all the fine prospects of becoming immediate master of his property, with which, in his first illness, he had agreeably flattered himself. After revolving the matter, for some time, in his mind, he saw no other way of extricating himself from his present embarrassment, than to pretend impatience that the letters did not arrive; and urge Dorcasina to an immediate marriage. Having formed this resolution, he set out for the place of interview, where he found his mistress had just before arrived. Their meeting was such as might be expected; on his side, feigned raptures; and on her's, real ones ill dissembled. "The ensuing scene can be easily imagined by the feeling heart; and to those devoid of sensibility, the description would be insipid; we, therefore, pass it over in silence," and return to Mr. Sheldon.

Soon after his daughter had left the house, he was, on inquiring for her, informed that she had gone to take her usual walk in the grove. He was pleased with the intelligence, as she had suffered so much anxiety on his account, and had been, for four days, detained at home by his illness. Finding himself so far recovered as to be able to walk, without much difficulty, he thought, as it was a fine afternoon, that the fresh air would contribute to restore his strength. He, therefore, laid a little plan, which he imagined would be an agreeable surprize to his daughter; render her walk more pleasing, and be beneficial to himself. This was no other than to take a walk to the grove, and attend Dorcasina upon her return home. He accordingly set out; but was obliged, in order to recruit his strength, to stop several times on the way, finding himself weaker than he had imagined. Being arrived at the entrance of the wood, he bent his steps slowly and cautiously towards the arbour, in which he expected to find his daughter; and where, indeed, before he got very near, he did discover her; but, good Heavens! how much to his astonishment! O'Connor, at that moment, sat close by her side, one arm thrown round her waist, while with the other hand, he held both her's; and with all the ardour of counterfeited passion, was urging her consent to their immediate union. Dorcasina, pleased with his energy, though not consenting to the measure, beheld him with her face dressed in smiles, and her eyes beaming with affection. They were too much engaged to observe Mr. Sheldon, who could hardly credit the evidence of his own senses. He stood, for some moments, immovably fixed; but, at length, recollecting himself, he retreated immediately out of sight, lost in doubt, wonder, and astonishment, at what he had just observed. He was now no longer at a loss to account for his daughter's late increased attachment to the grove; but who the gentleman could be, or from whence he came, he could form no kind of conjecture. His daughter, too, brought up in such retirement; conducting always with such prudence and delicacy; blessed with a good understanding, and loving him with the most ardent affection; that she should, at this time of life, so far forget what she owed herself and him, as to meet a stranger, in a clandestine manner, and be upon terms with him of so much familiarity, struck him to the very soul. Filled with these distressing reflections, he measured his steps slowly and with difficulty back to the house; where, being overcome by the fatigue of his walk, and the agitation of his mind, he fainted as soon as he had reached the threshold. The whole house was instantly alarmed. Being taken up, and conveyed to his bed, by proper applications, he soon recovered.

The boy, Patrick, being near the door when he arrived, and seeing him fall, concluded he was either dead or dying. Without waiting to know the issue, he, therefore, ran to the grove, where he knew Dorcasina was gone, and interrupted her from a dream of happiness, with the alarming information that her father was dying.

Dorcasina, upon this intelligence, started up, and, without waiting for any assistance from her lover, ran home with all speed. Entering the house, with dismay on her countenance, and meeting Betty in the passage, "O my dear father!" exclaimed she, "where is he? Conduct me to him." Betty prudently stopping her, and begging her to calm her agitated spirits, informed her that he had recovered, and that he had only fainted, from the fatigue of too long a walk. Her fears in regard to him, being thus composed, her next concern was for the situation in which she had left her lover. Turning round, she observed Patrick, who had directly followed her home; giving him a reprimand for so greatly alarming her, she dispatched him back to the grove, with a message to O'Connor, that her father had only fainted, and was now recovered. Our adventurer highly delighted with the former intelligence, remained in the grove to wait the issue; judging by the attention of Dorcasina upon a late similar occasion, that she would not suffer him to remain long in suspense. Seeing Patrick advance, he expected pleasing intelligence; but being, contrary to his wishes, informed that Mr. Sheldon had recovered, he lost all patience; and his usual caution forsaking him, "The devil he is," cried he, "why, what stuff is the old fellow made of? I'll be d——d if he has not as many lives as a cat." The poor astonished boy, who had imagined himself the messenger of joyful tidings, scampered back again as fast as his legs could carry him.

O'Connor, recollecting himself, and thinking he had gone too far, called after him to return; but Patrick had already gotten out of hearing. His own exclamations, however, gave him not half the uneasiness as the intelligence brought by the boy. He knew that his own address, and the blind passion of Dorcasina were such, that he could easily make his peace with her, if they should ever come to her knowledge. But how to get fairly rid of the old gentleman, was a question of difficult solution.

Dorcasina found her father sitting in his easy chair, weak, languid and melancholy. The dejection of his countenance alarmed her. She inquired eagerly how he did; and why, in his present feeble state, he had ventured to leave the house? "Alas! my dear," replied he, "it had, perhaps, been better for me had I not attempted it. I am distressed, greatly distressed, and my relief can come only from you. From you, therefore, I expect it. May I not calculate upon your affection? Have I not been a most indulgent parent to you? And have I not a right to expect, in return, that you will do every thing in your power to ease me of a weight almost too insupportable to be borne?"

Dorcasina was surprised, perplexed, and astonished. Unable to conjecture to what this discourse would tend, she was greatly hurt to find that her father entertained the smallest doubt of her affection. With streaming eyes, therefore, she replied: "What, my dear sir, have I done to forfeit thus your good opinion? Why torture me with doubts of my love, or my obedience? In what respect have I been so unhappy as to fail in my duty to you? Try me, I conjure you, command me. If I know my own heart, I would willingly lay down my life for the sake of my dear and venerable parent." Mr. Sheldon, softened and melted in his turn, could hardly find resolution to distress her by communicating his discovery; but, her reputation and happiness depending on the present moment, he replied: "You have not, indeed, my dear, been deficient in your respect to me; but you have grossly failed in that which every lady owes herself." He then briefly related his intention of surprising her in the grove, his walk thither, and the manner in which he had found her engaged; which, together with the fatigue of his walk, was the cause of his sudden illness. "And now," added he, "if you have any respect for my opinion, or regard for your own character, you will inform me who that person is, with whom you appeared so greatly pleased; how you commenced an acquaintance with him; and upon what footing he stands with you."

Dorcasina was extremely embarrassed by this unexpected discovery; not, however, from a consciousness of any impropriety of conduct; but because her modesty was wounded, by having been seen by her father, in such a situation. Besides, she wished and intended to have agreeably surprised him, by introducing her lover with the testimonials of his merit, which she daily expected. In this situation, she hesitated, blushed, and looked extremely silly. But her pure mind, unused to deceit, disdained, even on this occasion, to equivocate. She, therefore, in as correct a manner as her confusion would admit, gave him a particular account of her first meeting with O'Connor, and of every circumstance which had passed, during the course of their short acquaintance. When she ceased speaking, a profound silence ensued: Dorcasina waiting to know her father's opinion of her lover; and he, lost in astonishment, at the impudence of the fellow, and his daughter's credulity and extreme imprudence. He forbore, however, to wound her feelings by any severity of remark on her conduct; and, after a pause of some minutes, he only mildly observed, that Mr. O'Connor might be what he pretended; but, that it was possible he was an impostor; that, therefore, it would be but prudence to decline meeting him again, till the expected letters should put his character out of question. "An impostor!" exclaimed Dorcasina, in accents of astonishment. "Indeed, sir, it is impossible, absolutely impossible. Were you but as well acquainted with him as I am, you could have as little doubt of the sincerity of his professions. Besides, what inducement can he possibly have to take so much pains to deceive me?" "Inducement, my dear, why, money is an inducement to a great many wicked and dishonourable actions; and every species of deceit is practised by mankind, to obtain it. Born and educated in retirement, you judge of them by the innocence and rectitude of your own unsuspecting heart. I know them experimentally, and have found villany and malice concealed under fair forms and elegant manners, as well as every virtue under a disgusting exterior. This O'Connor, I fear, is of the former class, a needy adventurer; who, knowing you to be the only child of a man of some property, has addressed you in this clandestine manner, to gain possession of your heart, your person, and your father's estate."

The idea of an interested marriage having never entered into Dorcasina's imagination, she was both mortified and surprised, that her father should harbour suspicions so degrading to the pure and ardent passions, which warmed (as she imagined) the breast of her lover. "Indeed, sir," said she, "you judge too hastily of the most sincere and amiable of mankind. I never before knew you so uncharitable. Every expression, every look evinces the sincerity, and integrity of his soul; and so perfectly am I convinced of it, that upon his veracity I should be willing to stake my life." "Well, well, my dear, time will discover whether he is what he pretends to be, or only an impudent impostor. The expected letters will set all right; and if I find him worthy of you, I shall be happy to receive him as a son-in-law; as the only wish I have ungratified, is, to see you united to some worthy man. In the mean time, I have one favour to ask of you, which is, that you will not meet him again in the grove, until the letters in question arrive."

Dorcasina was extremely troubled at this request. It had always been her pleasure to conform, in every instance, to the wishes of her parent, whose mild commands had ever been to her a law. For the first time, she now thought his request unreasonable. Being equally unwilling to disoblige him, or to disappoint her lover, a struggle of some minutes between duty and love ensued. The latter, at length, being triumphant, she begged her father not to insist on her complying with his request; "For, convinced as I am," cried she, "of O'Connor's integrity, I cannot refuse meeting him, at the accustomed place, without accusing myself of injustice and cruelty, since I am certain he will suffer the most exquisite pain at being deprived of my company." "Well, but surely, my dear, some regard is to be had to the opinion of your father, and to your own reputation, as well as to the feelings of a person with whom you have been little more than a week acquainted. Consider the slanderous imputations, to which your thus daily meeting, alone, a stranger, in a sequestered grove, will subject you. Your reputation has hitherto remained unspotted. Preserve, I beseech you, its unsullied purity, by complying with the wishes of a father, who loves you better than his own existence."

Dorcasina was extremely moved at her father's pathetic expostulation; but still she could not resolve to give pain to her lover. "You distress me, deeply, by your tenderness," said she, "and I wish it were possible for me to comply with your desires. But as to the censures of an ill-judging world, I value them not. While conscious of the rectitude of my intentions, and the innocence of my actions, I defy the utmost shafts of malice." "Alas! my daughter, how art thou fallen! You did not use to argue thus. You once thought a woman's reputation a jewel of inestimable value. It is impossible for me to entertain an exalted opinion of the man, who, by an acquaintance of one week, has thus perverted the ideas of propriety, with which, for almost thirty years, I have been furnishing your mind." Cut to the quick, by reproaches so new, and extremely hurt by the sarcasm on her lover, Dorcasina could contest the point no longer; but, bursting into tears, she begged him to say no more; adding, that in compliance with his wishes, and not from any doubts she entertained of her lover, she would deny herself the pleasure of her wonted walks in the grove. She begged him, at the same time, to exonerate O'Connor from the charge of having influenced her sentiments, with regard to the opinion of the world; for no person, she assured him, paid a greater regard to it than he did.

Upon this, she bid her father an abrupt good night, and retired hastily to her chamber, to give free vent to the emotions with which her soul was agitated. There, to add to her vexation, Betty, with great satisfaction, related what had passed in the grove, between Patrick and O'Connor. At this recital, she was, beyond measure, vexed; not that she believed a single word of it; but she thought they had all conspired together to calumniate the beloved of her soul. This opinion, as would naturally be supposed, served only to heighten her attachment; and, had he been present, at that moment, it is probable he would have gained his point, by obtaining her consent to an immediate marriage. As soon as her words could find utterance, she thus poured out her indignation. "It is false, Betty, every syllable of it. O'Connor never uttered such words; it is all a vile forgery of that boy, Patrick; and, had I my will, he should not remain in the house another day. I beg of you, Betty, in future, not to listen to such vile stories."

"Why, what could I do, ma'am? I was busy in the kitchen, when he came in and told Nanny of it. I could not help hearing him, unless I had stopped my ears." "It is very evident, Betty, that you very willingly keep your ears open to hear any thing to the prejudice of O'Connor; but I beg, in future, as you value my favour, that you will no more report to me such infamous fabrications." Betty, effectually checked, withdrew in silence, and left her mistress to her own reflections.

Mr. Sheldon was so much disturbed by what he had seen and heard, that it was impossible for him to compose himself to sleep. His daughter's blindness and infatuation, filled him with astonishment; and he regretted, now it was too late, his having indulged her in perusing those pernicious books, from which she had evidently imbibed the fatal poison, that seemed to have, beyond cure, disordered every faculty of her mind. That O'Connor was an impostor, was evident from the whole tenor of his conduct; and Mr. Sheldon spent the chief of the night, in ruminating on the means of detecting him. He, at last, thought of a method, which must be infallible, and which he determined immediately to put in practice. This was no other, than writing to Lysander to be informed whether or not he knew any thing of O'Connor. If it should appear that he knew no such person, all the rest of O'Connor's pretensions must, necessarily, fall to the ground; and he did not doubt, but that his daughter's natural good sense would easily enable her to overcome a passion for a stranger, so suddenly conceived, and so imprudently cherished. Soothed and calmed by these pleasing expectations, towards morning, he gained the repose which his uncommon agitations rendered so necessary.

Chapter IX.

As soon as the day dawned, Dorcasina arose to pour into the faithful billet her disappointment and sorrow. Sitting down to her bureau, with nothing but a morning gown thrown about her, she penned the following lines to her adored lover:

"IT is with the most poignant anguish, that I inform my amiable O'Connor, that my father, having discovered our mutual attachment, and frequent meetings in the grove, has extorted from me a promise, to meet you there no more, till the arrival of the expected letters from Philadelphia. You may judge of the pangs which rend my heart, by those which you will doubtless suffer. Why do the tardy messengers so long delay their coming? Ah! when shall I again behold the most perfect of mankind?

> "From the most wretched of women,
> "D. SHELDON."

The receipt of this billet threw O'Connor into the utmost perplexity. He cursed the person, whoever it might be, that had informed Mr. Sheldon of his designs upon his daughter; and wished, from his soul, he had died when he was so near it, and not have returned again to life, to blast the fair expectations which he had been so near realizing. This was what he had always feared, as he was sure of meeting with infinitely greater difficulties, in managing a man who knew the world, than in deceiving his fond and credulous daughter. But having gotten into difficulty, he set his wits at work to extricate himself out of it. He had been interrupted in his last interview with Dorcasina, by the report of her father's illness; and he still flattered himself, that, had he opportunity to urge his suit, he should be able to prevail on her to consent to what he so earnestly desired. He, therefore, returned her the following answer:

"MY EVER ADORABLE DORCASINA,

"HOW wounding to my feelings were the contents of your billet! I was not prepared for such a stroke, and have not fortitude to support myself under it; especially as the messenger, by whom my letter was conveyed to Philadelphia, has returned without delivering it; my friend, to whom it was addressed, having set out the week before on a tour to the Eastern States. I shall, therefore, unless my charming mistress will deign to order it otherwise, be obliged to wait an age, another three days; for so long will it take the messenger, (whom I shall instantly dispatch with a letter to another of my friends) to go and return with an answer.

"To live three days without seeing you, is absolutely out of the question. I cannot support the idea. Therefore, as your father required only a promise not to meet me in the grove, you are, I presume, at full liberty to see me elsewhere. I conjure you, then, if you value my peace, my happiness, or my reason, to meet me this evening, in the summer-house, in your father's garden, as soon as the family have all retired. Do not, I beg of you, supreme arbitress of my fate, drive me to despair, by refusing your consent to this interview, so necessary to compose the mind of your most faithful,

"Most ardent,

"And almost distracted lover,

"P. O'Connor."

Dorcasina, softened, convinced and overcome by the pleadings of her lover, supported as they were by those of her own heart, scrupled not to consent to his request. In consequence of this determination, she sent him word, that, at 11 o'clock in the evening, she would meet him at the appointed place.

At any other time, or upon any other occasion, her upright soul would have despised the meanness and duplicity of a conduct so totally unworthy of her character. But to such a degree was she infatuated, by the insinuating addresses of O'Connor, that, by his influence, she now declined from the straight path of rectitude, which, till this time, she had trodden with undeviating steps. She passed the day in impatient expectation of the arrival of the hour, which was to bless her with an interview with the beloved of her soul; and not a word passed between her father and her, upon the incidents of the foregoing day. Transported with the idea of the pleasure she was soon to enjoy, she appeared more cheerful and attentive than usual; while her father, on his part, gratified at seeing her apparently so happy, under the constraint of a promise which he had with so much difficulty obtained, treated her with uncommon marks of tenderness and regard.

Mr. Sheldon had a large garden, and well stocked with every kind of fruit which the season and climate afforded. The servant who had the care of it was a tall stout negro, called Scipio. The boys here, as in every other village, were troublesome and mischievous. Mr. Sheldon frequently gave them fruit; but, not satisfied with this, they would often go in the night and help themselves; trampling down every thing in their way, to the great detriment of the garden, which Scipio valued himself on keeping in excellent order. The night before that upon which our lovers were to meet, the garden had been robbed of some fine melons, and the vines greatly injured. This put the gardener into a great passion, and determined him to watch in the summer-house, at the bottom of the garden, upon this ill-fated night. Having a favourite in the village, of his own colour, he imparted to her his design, and she kindly agreed to keep him company.

Scipio, not happening to mention his plan to any of the family, Dorcasina was, unfortunately, ignorant of it. At the appointed hour, therefore, when she thought the family all asleep, she softly descended the stairs, and opening the door which led to the garden, went directly to the summer-house. Scipio, who had previously taken his station there, had unluckily fallen asleep; and, when Dorcasina arrived, was snoring loud enough to be heard all over the garden. Thinking it to be her lover, and feeling some degree of mortification at the circumstance, she stood a few moments irresolute. But at length, determining not to disturb him, she approached him softly, sat down by his side, and, putting one arm round his neck and resting her cheek against his, resolved to enjoy the sweet satisfaction which this situation afforded her, till he should of himself awake. This liberty, in his waking hours, her modesty would have prevented her from taking; but, with a heart thrilling with transport, she blessed the accident, which, without wounding her delicacy, afforded her such ravishing delight.

While she was thus indulging herself in these blissful sensations, O'Connor and Miss Violet entered the garden at the same time, but at different places; and, both taking their way to the summer-house, encountered each other at a little distance from it. O'Connor, seeing a person in white advancing towards him, thought, naturally enough, that it could be no other than his mistress. As soon, therefore, as he approached her, he dropped on one knee, and poured forth a torrent of words in the usual style, blessing his supposed angelic mistress, for her goodness and condescension, in thus favouring him with an interview. Miss Violet was at first struck with astonishment, and could not divine the meaning of those fine compliments; but, perceiving by his manner and address, that it was a gentleman who thus humbled himself before her, and having a spice of the coquette in her disposition, she had no objection to obtaining a new lover; but, being totally at a loss what to reply to such a profusion of compliments, delivered in a style so new to her, she very prudently remained silent. Thinking her silence occasioned by her fear of being heard in the house, as they were then pretty near it, O'Connor rose from the ground, took her hand, which he kissed and squeezed all the way, and led her in silence to the summer-house.

Scipio and Dorcasina were seated at the back side, and our Hibernian, having placed his sable mistress just at the entrance, began again to pour forth his expressions of gratitude and love. Dorcasina, knowing his voice, was lost in amazement; but she had not time to wonder long; for Scipio, dreaming of thieves, and being waked by the voice of O'Connor, started suddenly up, and, darting towards the door, seized him by the collar, held him fast with one hand, and cuffed him at a most unmerciful rate with the other; bawling all the time, "You dog, take dat; next time come teal our melon. I teach you better manners." O'Connor was greatly enraged at finding himself so roughly handled, but having discretion enough not to expose himself by speaking, he only struggled, in vain, to disengage himself. Poor Dorcasina, overcome by surprise and terror, jumped out of the window at the back side of the summer-house, and fainted upon the turf. Miss Violet sat a silent spectator of the scene; and, after Scipio had taken ample revenge upon the supposed thief, he let him go; telling him at the same time, that if ever he caught him there again, he should not come off so easily. Exasperated beyond measure, but glad to get out of the hands of a fellow so much stronger than himself, our unlucky adventurer sneaked to his lodgings, cursing alternately Mr. Sheldon, his daughter, Scipio, and himself; vowing, if possible, to be revenged on them all, for his disgrace. Not that he suspected his mistress to have had any hand in it; but such was the violence of his temper, when once raised, that every person who came in his way, was sure to feel the effects of it. After he had left the garden, Miss Violet, who could as easily change a white lover for a black, as receive the addresses of a new one, simply told Scipio, upon his interrogating her, that she met a man in the garden, who immediately fell on his knees and began "to talk fine ting" to her, but that she would not listen to him, and took her way directly to the summer-house; whither he followed, close behind her, and had just entered as Scipio attacked him. "Ah! good for noting dog!" said Scipio, "I bang him well; he no come again arter Violet, nor arter melon!" They then made themselves very merry with the reception he had met with.

In the midst of their glee, Dorcasina, who had hitherto been senseless, began to recover; and, listening a few minutes to the conversation of the African lovers, soon discovered how matters were situated. Mortified and disappointed beyond measure, she crept into the house, and got to bed undiscovered; where, between her own personal chagrin, and distress for her lover, she lay the whole night in sleepless agitation. She feared, lest he might suspect that she had some hand in his chastisement; and was extremely solicitous, not only to undeceive him, but to convince him of her concern and tender sympathy. This was by no means an easy task. Her delicate mind could hardly bear to reflect on her familiarity with her father's servant; much less could she endure the idea of its coming to the knowledge of any other person; and least of all, to O'Connor's. Her integrity and regard to veracity would not suffer her to say the thing that was not strictly true; and she was harassed the whole night by a train of the most unpleasing reflections. At length, however, her anxiety for her lover overcoming every other consideration, she wrote him the following letter, which, as soon as she thought him awake, she dispatched:

hypocrisy

"IT seems as if some evil genius took delight in crossing the designs of two faithful lovers. I am informed of the unworthy treatment, which the most worthy of mankind, last night, received. Anxiety for my dearest O'Connor prevented me from closing my eyes, for the whole night; and they are so swoln with weeping, that I can hardly see to guide my pen. I am now sufficiently unhappy; but shall be the most miserable of women, if any fatal consequences shall follow this most unfortunate rencounter. How I lament that tyrant custom, prevents my flying to you, informing myself of your situation, and administering to your every want! I am, at present, in the most painful suspense. I ardently desire, yet dread to hear from you. Heaven grant that I may hear good tidings. Dispatch the messenger as soon as possible to your disconsolate and affectionate
                                            "D. S."

O'Connor had just attempted to open his eyes, as this letter was delivered him. But his face was so swelled that one eye was entirely closed, and the other he could open no farther than just to discern the characters of his mistress. Having, with much difficulty, perused them, he desired the messenger might be called up; who, having approached his bedside, O'Connor spoke to him in the following manner: "Tell your lovely mistress, that my situation is painful and disagreeable, but I hope not dangerous; that I am not, at present, able to write; but that the first use I make of my recovered eye-sight, will be, to thank her for all her goodness." He then kissed the letter, and putting it in his bosom, "Tell her, also," said he, "that this will conduce more to my restoration, than the prescriptions of all the faculty put together." He then dismissed him; and, sending for the hostess, desired her to examine his head, and see if it were necessary to send three miles for a surgeon to mend it. Upon examination, it appeared shockingly swelled and discoloured; but the skin not being broken, she thought, that by proper applications, she could restore his former appearance without the aid of one, though she imagined it would be some time first.

Notwithstanding Dorcasina's late prejudice against the boy, Patrick, he was the person she now employed to carry her letter. She had engaged him to secrecy, when she had sent him with a message to the grove; and, knowing his fidelity, was sure he would not betray her. He was filled with astonishment at the sight of O'Connor; and, on his return, represented him to Dorcasina, as being in the most doleful plight. He then faithfully delivered the tender message sent by O'Connor. Patrick's account filled her with the most unpleasing apprehensions; as she supposed that her lover made the best of his situation, to prevent her being too much alarmed. After dismissing Patrick, she gave herself up to the most violent grief. She beat her breast, and tore her hair; walking about the chamber, at the same time, like a distracted woman.

In this situation she was found by Betty, who now came to summon her to breakfast. The faithful creature, ignorant of what had passed, (for Dorcasina had concealed her intention of meeting O'Connor in the garden, on account of her prejudice against him) was greatly alarmed at seeing her mistress in such a paroxism of grief. Apprehending that some irreparable misfortune had befallen her, she begged to know the cause of her trouble. Dorcasina informed her, in few words, of the situation of her lover, concealing only the place and the person, where and by whom he had been so roughly handled.

Betty was greatly relieved at finding it was nothing worse; and secretly wished he had received ten times as much. Seeing her mistress, however, in such deep distress, she endeavoured to comfort her; telling her, that, probably, he had quarrelled with some person, and found himself overmatched. Such affrays, she said, were very common, and were seldom followed by any serious consequences. Dorcasina refused to be comforted, and sent to her father, requesting him to dispense with her attendance at breakfast; alleging, that she had a violent head-ach, which in fact was the case. As this was a disorder to which she was frequently subject, Mr. Sheldon received the apology, and breakfasted alone. His own health being now nearly re-established, he went out, soon after breakfast, to oversee his labourers, among whom he passed the time till dinner.

In the mean while, Dorcasina had taken her bed, with marks of as great sorrow as ever was experienced for the death of a lap-dog, or favourite parrot; and, refusing all sustenance, she gave herself up to sighs, tears and lamentations. Towards evening, however, a scheme entered her mind, which seemed to afford her a small ray of comfort. This was one of the most extravagant that had ever yet entered the romantic imagination of a love-sick girl, and such as no lady, in her senses, would have attempted to execute, who was not blinded to all sense of propriety, and regard to reputation. She was, however, so far gone with the novel-mania, that it appeared a proper attention to a lover, who had suffered so much for her sake. This was no other than to pay him a visit, in the evening, at his lodgings. After settling the manner of accomplishing it, her mind was calmed, her head ceased to ach, and she arose, and attended her father at tea, with a tolerable degree of composure.

As soon as it was dark, she sent Betty out of the way, on an errand; and, calling Patrick to her, she gave him a piece of money, telling him that she wanted his assistance, in a secret expedition, which he must be sure not to reveal to any living person. She then dressed herself in Betty's clothes; and, to disguise herself the better, she wore a strange old-fashioned bonnet, which had been her mother's; to which she added a veil of black gauze, that entirely concealed her face. Thus equipped, she sallied out, attended by Patrick, and took her way directly to the inn.

Being arrived, she sent Patrick to tell the hostess that Betty wanted to speak with Mr. O'Connor alone; upon which, the landlady went and informed him of it; who desired that she might be immediately shewn up. Dorcasina, then dismissing Patrick, with a new injunction to secrecy, followed the hostess, in silence, to the chamber of O'Connor. Our adventurer was sitting in an arm-chair, wrapped in a gown; his head was swathed with so many bandages, that only one eye, his nose and mouth were visible; and his whole head was swelled to an enormous size. Dorcasina could hardly persuade herself that it was her identical handsome lover. Her affection was not, however, in the least degree abated, at seeing him in this disgusting situation. It was rather increased, by being mingled with sentiments of pity and kind concern.

She advanced directly up to him, before she discovered herself by throwing back her veil. His surprise was equal to his pleasure, at this unexpected visit. He reached out his hand, and poured forth his acknowledgments with so much volubility, as shewed, that in his late disaster, his tongue at least had received no injury. Dorcasina, on her side, was so overcome, by seeing him in such a situation, that she could not utter a single word; but taking her place, in a chair beside him, she vented her grief in a torrent of tears. Our artful adventurer, seeing her mind thus softened by his situation, thought it a good opportunity to urge his favourite point, an immediate marriage. He began his attack by endeavouring to console her. "My dearest life," said he, "give not way, I beseech you, to such immoderate sorrow. Be calmed, my angel; and believe me, that one of your precious tears causes me more pain than all the blows I received. If, however, they were tears of joy, instead of grief, they would afford me the most exquisite pleasure, since they add so much to the splendour of your beauty, and heighten, in so great a degree, those irresistible charms, of which I flatter myself, with, one day, being the envied possessor." He then made use of all his eloquence, to persuade her not to wait the tardy messengers, and the dilatoriness of his friends, whom he supposed too deeply immersed in business to be able to pay that ready attention to his request, which the impatience of his love demanded. He even went so far, encouraged by the imprudent step she had taken, as to propose to her, not to return again to her father's house; but to take an apartment in the inn, have the banns published the next Sunday; and to go to Philadelphia and have the nuptial knot tied, with all practicable dispatch. This business performed, he proposed to get the proper recommendations to her father, and then return, and, throwing themselves at his feet, humbly implore his forgiveness.

Dorcasina listened to him in silent pleasure. This manner of proceeding was so conformable to many instances which she had read in her favourite authors, that she was upon the point of giving her consent. But, happily for her, the idea of her father, who had not yet recovered his strength, since his late indisposition, grieved at her having quitted his house, and taken a step of such importance without his knowledge, presented itself to her imagination. She reflected also, that a few days could make but little difference, either to herself or her lover. These ideas, fortunately, gave her resolution enough to resist his importunity; and all he could obtain of her, in this interview, was, a solemn promise never to marry any other man. He, on his side, voluntarily swore, calling heaven and earth to witness, that, as she was the first woman he could ever love, she should be the only one; and that, if he could not obtain her in marriage, he would, thenceforth, for her sake, lead a life of celibacy.

O'Connor was so engaged with the idea of urging her to consent to his plan, that he never once thought of inquiring how his disaster of the preceding night had happened, or how it came to the knowledge of his mistress. This omission she regarded as a lucky circumstance, as it relieved her from the disagreeable necessity of either owning the truth, or swerving from it.

After an hour's rapturous conversation, our lovers parted for the night, with vows of unshaken constancy and everlasting love.

Chapter X.

THERE had arrived, that day, at the inn, a gentleman from Philadelphia, attended by a shrewd Irish servant, possessed of as much impudence as his countryman, O'Connor. Unfortunately for Dorcasina, he was standing in the entry, when she arrived. Seeing a woman of such a strange appearance, his curiosity was excited, and he determined to watch her closely. Consequent upon this determination, he heard the message delivered to the hostess by Patrick, and saw the former shew Dorcasina the way to O'Connor's chamber. Resolved to see the end of the adventure, he waited patiently, at the bottom of the stairs, till, after an hour's absence, he saw her descend them.

Thinking that he might insult with impunity, one, who had been so long alone with a man, in a chamber of a public house, he followed her out, and, catching her round the waist, addressed her in the most indecent terms. Dorcasina, wholly unused to such treatment, and fearing to cry out, lest she should be discovered, found herself in a more disagreeable situation than even that she had been in the night before, when, with her snowy arms, she encircled Scipio's ebony neck.

Her fright and terror were indeed extreme; and she struggled, with all her strength, to disengage herself. This rencounter, attracting the attention of a number of small boys, who were at play at a little distance, they advanced, to see more distinctly what was going forward. The fellow, upon their approach, quitted his hold; but, at the same time, set upon her the whole gang of boys, (as a poor timid hare is beset by the hunters) telling them that she was some person in disguise, who had come thither with no good design. Dorcasina rejoiced to find herself free from the rude attacks of this unmannerly stranger, sat out immediately upon the run, with all the boys in her train, halloing, and endeavouring with all their might to overtake her. Not being so well accustomed to the exercise as they were, she was soon obliged to slacken her pace, upon which they overtook her; and, one seizing her gown, another her handkerchief, and a third her bonnet, they stript her in an instant of the two latter, and left her only some tattered remains of the former. To add to the disasters of this unlucky night, in running through some mud, she lost both her shoes. In this forlorn condition, she reached the house of her friend, Mrs. Stanly, with her impertinent attendants close at her heels. No sooner had she opened the door, than, overcome by fatigue, mortification and terror, she fell senseless upon the floor. The noise of her fall, bringing Mrs. Stanly to the door, the boys thought proper to retreat, throwing into the entry the fragments of her dress. Mrs. Stanly, seeing a woman all in tatters, lying upon the floor, supposed her to be a person intoxicated with liquor; and, being a woman of great humanity, as well as resolution, she called to the servants to come to her assistance; and stood by with a candle while they raised the unfortunate object from her prostrate posture.—But what was her astonishment, when, on looking in her face, she found it to be her friend, Dorcasina Sheldon! Observing her without life or motion, she presently comprehended that she was in a fainting fit; and, ordering the servants to bear her gently in, and lay her on a sofa, by proper applications, she soon restored her. Upon her first recovery, she looked round in astonishment, not immediately comprehending how she had been conveyed thither. But, casting her eyes upon her tattered dishabille, she presently recollected every circumstance of the evening's adventure, and was covered with confusion at the painful idea of its disastrous termination.

Mrs. Stanly was the first to break silence; being impatient to know how Miss Sheldon came to be so roughly handled, and why she, who had always been so loved and esteemed in the village, should have received treatment so wholly unworthy the respect due to her character. Dorcasina remained for some time in a profound reverie, wholly at a loss for answers to the inquiries of her friend. At length, she determined to impart to her every circumstance of her connexion with O'Connor, from the commencement of their acquaintance to the present moment. This she did, in as concise a manner as the subject would admit. When she had ended, Mrs. Stanly, in her turn, was silent from surprise and astonishment. She well knew, that Dorcasina had imbibed from the books she had perused, a most romantic turn; but she had no idea that she could have been led so widely astray from the path prescribed by reason and prudence.   And, while she inwardly deplored her infatuation, she felicitated herself on having placed her own daughter out of the reach of such pernicious books and examples. After a little reflection, she thought it would be acting the part of a friend, to speak her sentiments to Dorcasina, with all the freedom which friendship would warrant.   Requesting her, therefore, to listen without interruption, and take what she had to say, in good part, she expiated largely on the extreme imprudence of her connexion with O'Connor, who, as was evident from all his conduct, was an arrant impostor. She, in the strongest terms, expressed her disapprobation of her folly and rashness, in paying him a visit; which, if known, however unsullied her reputation had hitherto been, would infallibly throw a stain upon it, which it would be no easy matter to remove. Dorcasina listened to her, with the attention she had required; and, when she had finished, replied, that she was totally mistaken in her suspicions of O'Connor; that she was so fully persuaded of the truth of all his assertions, that the whole world united, would not be able either to stagger her confidence, or diminish her affection; and that a very few days would convince her friends that she had not made an unworthy choice. At the same time, she confessed that the visit she had recently made him, was an imprudent step; and, since she had suffered so severely in consequence of it, she had no great inclination to repeat it.

After this, she requested Mrs. Stanly to lend her some clothes; and, tying up the fragments of Betty's to be sent by a servant, she made the best of her way home, where she arrived without any further molestation.

Rumour, at length, began to be busy with the conduct of Dorcasina. She had been twice observed coming out of the grove with O'Connor;

Mr. Stanly's servants spread the report of her falling in at the door, in the plight above mentioned; and the boys knew that she had come from the inn where O'Connor lodged. Various reports were accordingly spread concerning the affair. Some said, that she went in disguise, to run away with a stranger; and others, that, having appointed a meeting in the grove, and not finding him there, she went to his lodgings in pursuit of him: while the few, who understood O'Connor's situation, rightly conjectured that she went to pay him a visit, in his confinement. All, however, joined in wondering at, and in condemning her conduct. One of those busy bodies, who delight in telling news, was officious enough to inform Mr. Sheldon of the reports in circulation, respecting his daughter. Too well assured of her attachment to O'Connor, he gave credit to part of what he heard; but totally disbelieved the tale of her having visited him at his lodgings. He was deeply concerned that any part of her conduct should be subject to such animadversions. Being informed, again and again, of the visit, which had caused Dorcasina such severe mortification, he began to be alarmed; and determined to inquire of Mrs. Stanly whether the adventure, above related to have happened at her house, was a fact or a fabrication. She could not deny but that Dorcasina, terrified in the street, by a party of boys, had taken shelter in her house, and immediately fainted. Mr. Sheldon perceiving that she hesitated and appeared unwilling to tell him all, conjured her, if she had any regard to his happiness or the reputation of his daughter, to conceal nothing from him, that he might take proper measures to check the growing evil. Mrs. Stanly thus urged, complied with his request, and related every circumstance of that disastrous evening.

Mr. Sheldon listened to her, with extreme anguish; and, though a man of great firmness, could not refrain from shedding tears, at the recital. In the midst of his sorrow, Mr. Stanly, for whose worth he felt the highest esteem, entered the room. His wife, from a delicate regard to the character of her friend, had at first concealed from him this unlucky adventure; but, being soon after informed of it, by some of his neighbours, as coming from his own servants, he inquired of his wife concerning the report: and, grieved to the soul at finding it was no secret, she had communicated to him whatever she knew. Mr. Sheldon, supposing him to be acquainted with the adventure, did not endeavour to conceal his emotions; but requesting his friendly advice in the affair, the three consulted together upon the means of breaking up so dangerous a connection. It was Mr. Stanly's advice that Mr. Sheldon should endeavour to obtain Dorcasina's promise, that she would never marry, without his consent; and that he should, moreover, write immediately to Lysander, to know if he were acquainted with such a person as O'Connor. If, by Lysander's testimony, O'Connor should prove to be the person he pretended, they thought there could be no reasonable objection to the match; but, if he should disclaim any knowledge of him, it would clearly prove him to be an impostor; and they concluded that it would be impossible for Dorcasina to withstand such clear proofs of his villany.

Mr. Sheldon approved this advice, as it coincided with his own intentions. He, therefore, went directly home with a view of sounding Dorcasina immediately. She had just been reading a letter from O'Connor, in which he informed her of his being much recovered. This intelligence had put new life into her: so that, when her father entered, he found her in better spirits than she had been since the adventure of the summer-house. He began by observing that he was rejoiced to see that tranquillity of mind and serenity of countenance again restored, which it had been the delight of his life to promote and to observe, and which of late had been so greatly interrupted. "I hope," continued he, "that the cause of your uneasiness is entirely removed; and that you never, in future, will have the least intercourse with that artful O'Connor." "Speak not of him in such injurious terms, I beseech you, sir," said Dorcasina; "did you but know him, you would confess the wrong you do him. Be assured, sir, that he is all that is great, generous and noble; and worthy your highest regard. My connection with him is so far from giving me uneasiness, that it is the happiness of my life: but we must participate the pains, as well as the pleasures of a beloved object. My late uneasiness arose from an unfortunate accident, which has, for nearly a week confined him to his chamber; and my present happiness from being informed that he is almost recovered." "Alas, my dear! I pray Heaven that you are not deceived. But tell me what are your intentions? He has been talking of letters of recommendation; but they do not yet appear. This is a suspicious circumstance; and you surely cannot think of marrying him, without knowing his character, from some person well acquainted with him." "As to that, sir, I am in no haste to marry; but I am impatient to introduce him to you, that my choice may be sanctioned by your approbation." "You must acknowledge, my dear, that I am older, and know more of mankind than you do; and you ought to be so well convinced of my affection as to believe I wish for nothing more ardently than your happiness." "I confess your superior experience, sir; and it has hitherto been the pride of my life to think I enjoy the kindest affection of the best of fathers. And it has been no less my delight to render him happy by my attentions." "Well then, my dear, as a further proof of my affection, I promise you that my sanction to your choice shall not be wanting, if the recommendation of O'Connor's friends coincide with his own pretensions. I am about to write to Lysander, on the subject, and I will abide by his single testimony. In the mean time, I must insist upon your giving me your word that, if he prove an impostor, and unworthy of you, you will immediately dismiss him." "That I will, sir, with the greatest readiness; in the fullest confidence of obtaining your consent, the moment you become acquainted with him." "Then you promise me, without hesitation or mental reservation, that you never will marry him without my consent." "I do, most solemnly." "Very well, I am satisfied; and you may depend upon it, that the man upon whom my daughter has placed her affections, will meet from me a welcome reception whenever he presents himself properly recommended." "I thank you, sir; this is of a piece with the rest of your goodness." After this they separated for the night, both well satisfied with what they had obtained of each other. Mr. Sheldon did not think proper to mention, in this conversation, the intelligence he had received of her visit to O'Connor; nor the publicity of the fact; deeming his daughter already sufficiently mortified, and well convinced, from the account of Mrs. Stanly, that she would have no inclination to repeat it. After retiring to his closet, he employed himself in writing to Lysander in the following manner.

"SIR,

"THERE came to this place, about a fortnight since, a young gentleman who calls himself O'Connor. The account he gives of himself is, that he is son to an Irish gentleman of fortune; that he left his country to avoid a match, which his father had concluded for him; but which was disagreeable to himself. He says, further, that he had letters to several gentlemen in Virginia, where he arrived about three months since; and amongst the rest, delivered one to your father, with whom he passed a month; and that he informed you of the cause of his quitting his country. As he has become a candidate for the favour of my daughter, you will perceive how deeply I am interested in the truth of his assertions. You will, therefore, greatly oblige me, by informing me, as soon as possible, all you know respecting him.

"Remember me with the warmest affection to your father: tell him that the month which he and you spent with us, I reckon among the happiest days of my life; and that I flatter myself with again enjoying the same pleasure.

"I am, sir,

"With sentiments of the highest esteem,

"Your obedient humble servant,

"JAMES SHELDON."

Dorcasina, on her part, retired to her chamber and employed herself in writing to her beloved O'Connor. It was now a week since she had seen him; but Patrick had, every day, passed backward and forward with letters filled with the most tender and ardent expressions of real and pretended affection. Nay, so much did her lover employ her thoughts, that, not content with writing once a day, she often imagined she had omitted something in her letter of the morning, and, frequently, in the afternoon, sent another. The contents of that, which she now dispatched were as follows:

"YOUR letter of this evening has filled me with unspeakable pleasure. You say that, in two days at farthest, you shall be able to come abroad. What ecstatic delight to behold again the dearest and most engaging of men, after being deprived of his company an age, a whole week. You will, I trust, by that time, receive the expected letters; and I shall have the supreme felicity of introducing you to my beloved parent. He is going to write Lysander for your character; so that I shall have the pleasure of seeing you doubly recommended.

Adieu, mon cher ami,

D. S."

This letter, as was naturally to be expected, threw our adventurer into the greatest perplexity. He saw all his splendid expectations ready to be blasted. He cursed his ill stars for having led him into the summer-house adventure, which, by preventing his daily intercourse with his mistress, had deprived him of the opportunity of urging the point he had so much at heart, and in which he flattered himself, notwithstanding her positive refusal, that, by dint of address, management, and perseverance, he should finally have succeeded. He saw no other way to prevent the total disappointment of all his hopes, than by striking a bold stroke, and forging a letter from some person of note in Philadelphia; which would at least prove an antidote to the expected one from Lysander; and possibly enable him to prevail on Dorcasina to have the nuptial knot tied before Lysander's answer could arrive.

Chapter XI.

ON the third day after forming this resolution, O'Connor was perfectly recovered from his bruises. He, therefore, informed Dorcasina, that having received the long expected letter, he was coming, with joyful haste, to throw himself upon the mercy of her father. He then dressed himself in an elegant manner, and boldly presented himself, for the first time, at the door of Mr. Sheldon, with a forged letter in his hand. It was in the name of Mr. W. of Philadelphia, recommending the bearer to Mr. Sheldon, in the warmest terms. Though Mr. Sheldon did not personally know Mr. W. he was well acquainted with his character; and therefore scrupled not to receive O'Connor in the politest manner. The latter had not, now, to deal with the credulous and lovesick Dorcasina; but with a man of judgment and penetration, and one who knew mankind.

Mr. Sheldon viewed the man of his daughter's choice, with a scrutinizing eye. He could not but acknowledge him to be a man of a handsome person and genteel address; but the expression of his countenance made him tremble for the happiness of his daughter, when it should be confided to the keeping of a person, the bad qualities of whose mind were written in such legible characters in the lineaments of his face. His flattery, too, to Mr. Sheldon was exceedingly fulsome and disgusting: but the joy of Dorcasina could hardly be restrained within proper limits. Her happiness was extreme, in contemplating her father, her lover, and herself assembled under the same roof. She had not, now, to fear mistaking Scipio in the dark, for O'Connor; or being hooted and insulted in the street, by rude and lawless boys. She could now converse whole hours with her lover, without shame or apprehension. But, as no happiness is without its alloy, to her extreme disappointment and mortification, her father did not think proper to invite him to take up his residence at his house. On the contrary, when O'Connor, after passing the afternoon and evening, without having been for a minute left alone with Dorcasina, arose to depart, Mr. Sheldon only paid him the usual compliment of asking him to favour them with his visits as long as he should continue in the village. This was quite an unexpected stroke to our adventurer; as he had calculated upon being made one of the family, and of having hourly opportunities of urging his suit, both with Mr. Sheldon and his daughter. He had not, however, at this visit, mentioned the matter, lest the discerning Mr. Sheldon should judge him precipitate.

The next morning, as early as decency would admit, he renewed his visit, and requesting to speak with Mr. Sheldon alone, opened to him the purport of it. He informed him of his first meeting Dorcasina in the grove; the favourable impression she had made upon him, which was strengthened by the report of her many amiable qualities; that he had some reason to flatter himself that he was not wholly indifferent to her; that he should not thus long have deferred waiting on him, had he not wished, at his first interview, to present the letter he had the honor of delivering yesterday, and which he flattered himself had convinced Mr. Sheldon, that in family, fortune and character, he was not wholly unworthy his favourable notice. He concluded by begging Mr. Sheldon to make him the happiest of mankind, by consenting to his connection with the only woman he had ever wished to make his wife.

Mr. Sheldon, but half pleased with this address, answered him with politeness, but not with that ready acquiescence in his wishes, which O'Connor had hoped. He thanked him, in polite terms, for the honor he intended his daughter; at the same time observing, that as their acquaintance was but of yesterday, he saw no occasion for being precipitate, and thought, that before they engaged themselves unalterably, they had better be further acquainted with each other's dispositions, and that for want of such previous and necessary knowledge, many a couple had been rendered completely wretched. He thus politely evaded a positive answer; and, as some doubts, in spite of himself, still hung upon his mind, which the expected letter from Lysander would either confirm or dispel, he wished to give O'Connor no further encouragement till it should come to hand. O'Connor, though inwardly fretted, durst not object to the reasonableness of this proposition. Just at this juncture Mr. Sheldon was called to some person, with whom he had business. O'Connor, being left alone, traversed the room with hasty strides, muttering his dissatisfaction at every step. "D——d cautious! A cunning old fox! Would it had pleased the Lord to have taken him to himself! But I'll match him. I will, if possible, outwit him, and have his estate incumbered with his daughter, about whom he makes such a fuss, in spite of him."

While these things were passing below, Dorcasina was traversing her chamber above, in no less fermentation. She had been informed that O'Connor had arrived; that he had requested to speak with her father, and that they were actually in close conference. This intelligence threw her into such a tremor of delight, that it was impossible for her to be composed. She first took up her work; but pricking her finger at every stitch, she threw it aside, and replaced it with a book. Here she succeeded no better; her eyes, it is true, ran over the page, but she was unconscious of a single idea it contained. She then went below, and tried a tune on her forte piano; but here, again, all was wrong, and nothing was produced but jarring discords. She finally abandoned herself to walking her chamber, entirely occupied with what was passing below, and totally conscious where she was, or how she was employed.

Betty, at this juncture, happening to enter the chamber, was struck with the quickness of her motions, and the wildness of her air. "What will you be pleased to order for dinner to day, ma'am?" No answer being given, nor the least attention paid to the interrogation, Betty repeated the question. Her mistress continuing still silent, and still in rapid motion, she began to be alarmed for her intellects. She thought, however, she would make one more effort to draw her attention: "Mr. O'Connor is below in the parlour, alone, ma'am." This had the desired effect. "Alone, do you say Betty? Where is my father?" "He has just been called out, ma'am."

Dorcasina, upon this intelligence, hastily descended the stairs, leaving Betty to cook the dinner as she pleased. Opening the door upon her lover rather suddenly, he had hardly time to smooth his brow to that complacency, which, in her presence, he always wished to wear; and though he affected to smile and caught her hand as she entered, the skirt of the cloud, which had so recently overspread his features, did not escape her observation. She augured ill of the proposal to her father, and her countenance instantly changed. "Why this gloom upon your features?" said she, as he led her to a seat. "My father surely does not oppose himself to our happiness?" "The father of my Dorcasina cannot intentionally err," replied O'Connor. "All his measures are dictated by prudence. But, in this instance, give me leave to say, it is the prudence of frozen age, and but ill accords with the warmth and impatience of my love. He has not absolutely rejected my suit, nor has he blessed it with his full approbation. He recommends a longer acquaintance, that we may be better known to each other; as if I wanted any further proofs of the immaculate goodness of my adorable Dorcasina." "O! if that be all," returned she, "and he permit you to visit us, I am perfectly well satisfied and very happy; confident, as I am, that the more my amiable O'Connor is known the more estimable will he, in every respect appear." "Thank you, my angel, for thus expressing your opinion. But think of my unequalled love; my impatience to call you mine; my fear lest some unforeseen accident should deprive me of my treasure, my crown, my happiness. Deign, sovereign mistress of my enraptured soul, to become yourself my advocate. Plead with your father in my behalf. Urge him to shorten the days of my probation, and to make me the happiest of mankind, by giving to my arms his incomparable daughter."

This speech, accompanied with a look of extreme tenderness, entered the very soul of Dorcasina, and infused into her a real portion of that enthusiasm, which he so well knew how to counterfeit. She looked at him for some moments, in speechless rapture; "I will," at length cried she, "I will be your advocate. Who would not plead for such exalted love? Happy above women shall I esteem myself, in possessing such a husband; a husband, whom kind heaven has formed the very counterpart of myself."

After an hour, passed in such interesting conversation, O'Connor took his leave, and Dorcasina, her eyes sparkling with love and transport, went immediately to urge her father on the important topic. After seeking him, for some time, she found him in his study, sitting in a musing, thoughtful posture. This sight brought her to her senses. She feared lest some anxiety disturbed him. She was embarrassed at the idea of the business she came upon; and not knowing how to begin, stood for some time irresolute and in a most awkward situation. Her father seeing her embarrassment, and conjecturing she had something to communicate, inquired if she wanted him, or any particular book out of his library. This hint relieved her; and she went immediately to taking down books, and replacing them, till she could gain sufficient composure to begin upon the interesting subject.

Mr. Sheldon himself led the way. "I suppose, my dear," said he, "Mr. O'Connor has informed you that he has requested my permission to form with you a matrimonial connection." "He has, sir." "I hope you are not in such haste to change your situation, as not to be willing to obtain a further knowledge of his disposition, by a longer acquaintance; and that you are not disposed to rush headlong into a state which will determine your happiness or misery through life?" "As to myself, sir, I am by no means in haste to be married. I have not, however, on my mind the shadow of a doubt respecting the perfect goodness of Mr. O'Connor's disposition; or of his possessing every other virtue, which can adorn humanity. But his passion is as violent as it is tender. He is impatient to have the indissoluble knot tied, that we may never, in this world, be again separated. On his account, therefore, and at his request (for who can resist when he pleads) permit me, sir, earnestly to solicit your consent to our immediate union."

"I have ever found you, my dear, willing to listen to reason; and I hope your passion for O'Connor has not so far misled you, as that, at this crisis of your fate, you will refuse to yield to its dictates? You know I have written to Lysander on the subject. Wait only till I receive an answer from him, which will be at farthest in a week; and I give you my word that, if his account agree with O'Connor's, I will no longer oppose your union, though I must, at the same time, confess, that as your acquaintance is of so recent a date, it would better accord with my ideas of propriety to have it deferred to a more distant period." Tolerably well pleased with what she had gained, Dorcasina thanked her father, and quitted the study.

In the afternoon, O'Connor, impatient to know how his mistress had succeeded, renewed his visit. She received him with a smiling countenance, and related what had passed at the interview in the study; adding, that for her own part, she was perfectly pleased with what her father had granted; and hoped that her dear O'Connor would have no reason to be dissatisfied. But here she was disappointed. O'Connor was greatly chagrined, and having now no reason for concealment, the emotions of his mind were instantly painted on his countenance. An indifferent spectator would have there read illnature and vexation; but Dorcasina saw nothing but tender sorrow, occasioned by the excess of his love, and his unexpected disappointment. She exerted herself to soothe his melancholy; observing that a few days, or a week, could make no essential difference, since they could now pass as much time in each other's company as they pleased, without fear of censure or reproach. But, alas! simple maid! she knew not what cause for disquiet the expected letter had for her lover; who, notwithstanding all her endeavours, remained gloomy and thoughtful, during the whole visit. Upon his leaving her, she experienced a mingled sensation of pain and delight. She was distressed at seeing him so sad; but when she reflected on the cause of his dejection, which she supposed to be the immensity of his love, she was soothed into a calm and delicious pleasure.

The next day O'Connor appeared more cheerful. Mr. Sheldon himself received him and invited him to dine. The conversation turned on indifferent subjects; the manners and customs of Europe, and the present situation of America. Nor was the field of literature unexplored. On all these subjects, O'Connor appeared to advantage; for having always retained the taste for books, which he had acquired at school, where, as was before observed, he was allowed to be a lad of parts and a good scholar, as well as a most mischievous fellow, he was not deficient in information, and possessed the natural eloquence of his nation. Mr. Sheldon, in spite of his prejudices, began to be pleased with him, and, as he found Dorcasina's affections so firmly fixed upon him, he secretly wished that Lysander's account might be in his favour. Dorcasina, observing the favourable impression, which he made upon her father, was all life, joy and ecstacy. It was the happiest day she had ever known. Nothing remained on her mind to occasion her the least uneasiness. Her expressions of pleasure were as simple and artless as those of a girl of fifteen; and the presence of her father hardly restrained her from discovering marks of tenderness for her lover.

Some days passed away in this agreeable manner, O'Connor assuming a tolerable degree of cheerfulness, while at Mr. Sheldon's, where he passed great part of his time; but, when left to himself, he was a prey to the uneasy reflections, ever attendant on a depraved and vicious heart. He revolved many plans, in his mind, to counteract the effects, which he was sensible Lysander's answer would produce. But not being able to form one to his satisfaction, he determined to trust to his invention, when the emergency should arrive.

At length Lysander's answer reached Mr. Sheldon, couched in the following terms.

> "SIR,
>
> "I am ever happy when I have it in my power to render any service to Mr. Sheldon, or his amiable daughter. In compliance with your request, I, therefore, inform you, that I know no such person as you describe in your letter; and that no gentleman of the name of O'Connor has ever done us the honor of a visit. Most probably he is an impostor from Europe; too many of whom, I am sorry to say, are found in this country.
>
> My father returns his grateful and affectionate remembrance. Be pleased to present my respectful compliments to Miss Sheldon,
>
> > "And believe me to be, dear sir,
> >
> > "With sentiments of the highest esteem,
> >
> > > "Your humble servant,
> > >
> > > "LYSANDER."

Since the favourable impression made by our adventurer on Mr. Sheldon, this intelligence was not altogether so welcome as it would have been, while his prejudices remained in full force. He had began to wish for ground to think well of O'Connor. It was, therefore, rather an unpleasant circumstance to have his opinion entirely changed; and all his former suspicions so fully confirmed. He was, however, thankful to heaven for having enabled him to detect the impostor before it was too late, and the doom of his daughter irrevocably fixed. He was now led to believe that the letter from Mr. W. was forged; and he determined to consult his friend, Mr. Stanly, who was a man of the world, and personally acquainted with that gentleman, on the best means of ascertaining it.

Mr. Sheldon received the letter late in the evening, after Dorcasina, who had passed most of the day in her lover's company, had retired to bed, not suspecting the storm, which was so soon to burst upon them. Early in the morning, he requested her company in his study. Holding a letter in his hand, which he told her, as she entered, was from Lysander, and assuming a serious and impressive manner, "this letter," said he, "contains full proof of O'Connor's worthlessness. Lysander affirms that he knows no such person. I flatter myself that you possess too much good sense and discretion to encourage, a moment longer, the addresses of a person, who is totally unworthy of you; and who, lured by the property you will one day possess, has clandestinely, and in an artful manner, insinuated himself into your good graces."

Dorcasina was, at first, thunderstruck with this intelligence; but a moment's reflection restored her to herself. She did not believe a single syllable of the villany of her adored O'Connor; being confident that there must be some mistake in the matter. She answered her father, however, only by tears, which flowed spontaneously at his imagining her lover capable of so much deceit. After waiting some time for a reply, Mr. Sheldon put the letter into her hands, and went out to oversee the labours of the field; judging it most prudent to leave her, for a while, to her own reflections.

Dorcasina, as soon as he had left her, perused the letter; but her opinion of O'Connor was too firmly established to be capable of being shaken by such an incident; and, recollecting what he had told her of Lysander's still retaining his passion for her in its full force, she instantly concluded that he was determined, if possible, to prevent her giving her hand to any other person, and had taken this method to effect his purpose. But she was resolved that his artifice should not avail; and, for the first time, wished for a speedy marriage, that she might thereby punish his disingenuity, and frustrate all his expectations. The more she pondered, the more was she confirmed in this idea; and being impatient to communicate the letter and her opinion to O'Connor, she was just about dispatching Patrick after him, when his arrival saved her the trouble.

O'Connor, observing that she had been in tears, mistrusted the real cause, as it was always uppermost in his mind. Taking her hand, and assuming the most tender and passionate air, "what has happened," cried he, "to cloud the brow of the most lovely woman in the universe? Tell me, I beseech you, my love; impart your sorrows to your faithful O'Connor, that he may lessen them by participation." Smiling upon him through her tears, with ineffable sweetness, and, at the same time giving him the letter, "there," cried she, "see to what lengths a disappointed lover is capable of going. Lysander, unsuccessful in his own suit, is determined to keep every other person at a distance."

O'Connor, having cast an eye over the letter, was greatly and evidently disturbed; but felt much indebted to the blind credulity of Dorcasina for having, in part, extricated him from the present embarrassment. He immediately laid hold of the idea as the most fortunate one that, in the present emergency, could possibly have been started. Pretending, however, to be greatly astonished, "is it possible!" cried he, "am I awake? or do I dream? Can Lysander, the man whom I would implicitly have trusted with my life and fortune, be guilty of so base and treacherous an action? But a consideration of his motives lessens my indignation. Alas! I know but too well the keenness of his sufferings by what I should myself have experienced, had I been equally unsuccessful. Almighty love! how great is thy power, and what mischiefs dost thou not occasion! I pity him from my soul; and since he has not alienated the affections of my beloved Dorcasina, I can forgive him. Had he succeeded, I would not have sat down contented with the loss; but would have pursued him round the world, and forced him to retract the base falsehood, or vengeance should have been his portion. But what says your father to the letter." "Alas, you have now touched the string of my sorrow! It has succeeded with him but too well: and I am grieved to the soul that he should entertain so unfavourable an opinion of the most amiable of mankind." "What shall we do, my love, to regain his good opinion? which, next to yours, I value beyond that of any other person whoever." "He has no suspicion of the cause of Lysander's enmity to you," replied Dorcasina. "I will represent the matter in its true light, and I doubt not but that, when he is informed, he will acquiesce in our opinion, and no longer oppose himself to our happiness." "Pray heaven it may be so," said O'Connor; but he expected other things from Mr. Sheldon, whose consent he now despaired of ever obtaining; and built his whole hopes of success on the fondness and promise of Dorcasina, that she would never marry any other person. He, however, thought it would be most conducive to his success to let her make the attempt; and should she be convinced of the impossibility of gaining his consent, he depended on obtaining her's without it: not knowing that she was equally bound to her father never to marry without his permission.

Our lovers, after passing the whole morning in the accustomed manner, parted, with as sanguine expectations of being united, as before the letter was received.

After Mr. Sheldon had given the necessary directions to his labourers, he went immediately to Mr. Stanly, and related to him the contents of Lysander's letter. They agreed perfectly in the opinion that the letter, in the name of Mr. W. was a piece of forgery; and were equally astonished at the unparalleled impudence and artifice of O'Connor. To put the matter beyond a doubt, Mr. Stanly proposed writing on the subject to Mr. W. Mr. Sheldon thanked him for the proposal, and begged him to execute it immediately; as he wished to obtain every possible proof of O'Connor's imposition, that his daughter might be able, the more easily, to dislodge him from her affections.

As soon as the two friends had settled this matter between them, Mr. Sheldon hastened home to observe what effects the letter had upon Dorcasina. She received him with her usual cheerfulness, and they dined together in great harmony. Mr. Sheldon was at a great loss to account for this tranquillity. It was impossible she could doubt the truth of Lysander's assertions, whose merit she had ever been ready to acknowledge; and, if she believed them, she must be greatly mortified at such an egregious imposition; he also thought it must cost her much pain to efface from her heart the image of a person, on whom she had so fondly doated. She had ever been too artless and open to disguise her feelings; her present conduct, therefore, apparently free from all anxiety, was a riddle, which he could not solve.

After they had dined, a maid servant, who had been cleaning the room, where she and her lover had passed the morning, brought a pocket handkerchief and gave it to Dorcasina. "Here ma'am," said she, "is Mr. O'Connor's handkerchief, which he left, this morning, in the back parlour." It was of cambrick, with his name marked at full length. She received it with a smile of pleasure, and, after having examined the name, folded it carefully and put it in her pocket.

This little incident was not unobserved by Sheldon; and the apparent satisfaction it afforded Dorcasina occasioned him great uneasiness. As soon as the servant, who attended them at dinner, was withdrawn, Dorcasina, eager to exculpate her lover, and restore him to her father's good graces, began a conversation, which Mr. Sheldon as eagerly wished for. "Who could have thought, sir," said she, "that Lysander would have been guilty of the meanness of denying any knowledge of his friend?" Mr. Sheldon, in accents of surprise, asked, "What, is it possible that you should think Lysander guilty of such baseness? You certainly wrong him. His sentiments are much too elevated to allow him to descend to such conduct. Besides, what motive could he possibly have in deceiving us, for whom he professed the warmest friendship; and for you a passion still stronger?" "That very passion was the cause, sir. You may remember I informed you that, at my first acquaintance with O'Connor, he told me that Lysander still ardently loved me, and that the constant praises he bestowed on me inspired him with the first design of visiting me. Now to me nothing can be more evident than that he has done it from pure jealousy, and to ruin O'Connor in my opinion." "Alas, my dear! I grieve to see you thus infatuated. Will you persist in giving less credit to one of your own countrymen, whose character for probity is well known and acknowledged, than to a foreigner, whom nobody knows, and who has nothing to recommend him but his own bare assertions?" "Hold, I beseech you, sir," cried Dorcasina; "wrong him not by such an injurious suggestion. He is sufficiently recommended by his own shining virtues, and deserves your highest admiration. Did he not also bring a letter from Mr. W. one of the most respectable merchants in Philadelphia, recommending him to your friendship in the warmest terms? You certainly injure him by intimating that we have only his own word to depend upon." "That letter is a vile forgery, believe me," said Mr. Sheldon. "Mr. W. never wrote it; it was an invention of O'Connor's own imagination." "Say not so, I beseech you, sir," cried Dorcasina, bursting into tears. "It is impossible that O'Connor should be guilty of so infamous an action, and I cannot endure to hear him so greatly abused." "That matter," said Mr. Sheldon, "will soon be ascertained. Mr. Stanly is well acquainted with Mr. W. and will write immediately respecting O'Connor and the letter in question." "I rejoice to hear it with all my soul," replied Dorcasina; "Mr. W. has not the same motive for disclaiming his acquaintance that Lysander had. O'Connor will come out of the furnace purer than gold seven times tried." "Well, we shall see," replied her father. "In the mean time, I hope you have not forgotten the promise you made me never to marry him without my consent?" "I have not sir, and I hold myself inviolably bound by it. On the other hand, I am equally bound by one I made him of never marrying any other person; and I am determined never to break either of them."

Mr Sheldon was confounded at this information; but his chagrin was somewhat lessened at her determination not to break either promise; for he thought it an evil of much less magnitude for her to remain single during life, than to throw away herself and fortune upon a worthless adventurer. He observed, however, that it was a very rash promise; and he feared she would have reason to repent having made it. "It is the least of my fear," said she; "for, should you be so cruel as to refuse your consent to our union, and should he depart and leave me to mourn, though seas might roll, or mountains rise between us, still, so deeply is his beloved image engraven on my heart, his idea so twisted with its cords, that it would be impossible for me to think of another love; and it would be my choice and my pleasure, for his sake, to lead a single life." "What! would you voluntarily lead a life of celibacy for the sake of a fellow, who proves so totally unworthy of you? Your notions my dear are strangely extravagant; and I trust that a little reflection upon their absurdity will lead you to renounce them." "What! renounce my darling, my favourite ideas of everlasting love and eternal constancy, upon which I build all my hopes of worldly happiness? No, Sir; depend on it, I shall never be guilty of such inconstancy, such impiety in love. I could almost as easily renounce my religion, upon which I build my hopes of happiness in a future life."

Mr. Sheldon, grieved to the soul at finding the pernicious effect produced by the books he had injudiciously indulged her in making her chief amusement, did not think proper to argue the matter any longer; but employed the means necessary to prevent her seeing O'Connor, till Mr. Stanly should receive an answer from Philadelphia. "Be that as it may," said he, "I hope you will oblige me so much as not to have any farther intercourse with O'Connor, till we know the result of the letter to Mr. W." "Pardon me, sir, but I must say I think that an unreasonable request; especially as you have countenanced his visits, and appeared perfectly satisfied with him." "You mistake, my dear; I never was perfectly satisfied with him; and, however I might wish that, for your sake, he would prove to be a man of honor, I always had doubts and suspicions, which all his address was not able entirely to remove: and as it was for your sake that I received and treated him with politeness, I think I may require a little sacrifice of you, in return, without appearing either unjust or unreasonable."

He touched the right string. In mentioning his tenderness for her, he awakened all her's towards him. Regard for her lover was for the moment swallowed up in love for her father. She then, without further opposition, promised what he required.

Chapter XII.

As soon as Dorcasina had made this sacrifice of her inclination to her duty, she retired to her chamber and gave free vent to the emotions with which she was oppressed. She now experienced the fallacy and uncertainty of all sublunary felicity. Yesterday, she was the happiest of human beings: to-day, she experienced a sad reverse. Her grief was bitter and severe; but it did not carry her to despair. Her faith in the integrity of O'Connor being still unshaken, she flattered herself that the letter from Mr. W. would cause another revolution, in the mind of her father, which would be altogether in his favour. But alas! she was now debarred the pleasure of seeing him; and of having her sorrows soothed and composed by the magic voice of love and sympathy. She was also distressed at the thoughts of what her lover would suffer by this separation, and she wished to communicate to him her promise. But fearing the shock would be too great for him, she was willing to delay it as long as possible.

While Dorcasina remained thus distressed, Betty, who had seen her leave her father in tears, came into the chamber in the design, if possible, to sooth and comfort her. At her entrance, she found her on the bed drowned in tears, and sobbing, as if her heart would break. The kind creature placed herself by her side, and inquired, in an affectionate manner, what had happened to cause her so much sorrow. "Alas, Betty! I am the most unfortunate woman in the world. Could you have believed that, after my father had received and treated O'Connor with so much attention, he would now turn against him, calling him an impostor, an adventurer, a fortune hunter, and many other opprobrious names. Oh, Betty! my soul is vexed at hearing the most perfect of mankind so grossly abused." "I suppose, ma'am, your father has some reason for changing his mind." "He thinks he has, Betty; but he is imposed upon. If he would but listen to reason, and not suffer himself to be so blinded by prejudice, I could easily convince him of his error." "Well, ma'am, isn't it as likely you should be deceived as your father? He is older than you, and ought therefore to know more." "In most affairs, I grant it, Betty, but not in this. He is not sufficiently acquainted with O'Connor to appreciate his merit; he has not had my opportunities of knowing how much his soul abhors deceit, and how incapable he is of dissimulation or falsehood." "Perhaps, ma'am, he has found him out to be a papish, and does not wish you to marry a man of that religion, for fear he should not make a good husband." "My father is too liberal, in his sentiments, to make that an objection, Betty, even if he knew it to be the case. He has taught me to believe that the good and virtuous, and sincere, of all religions, will be accepted of God, and that he is not displeased with the variety of forms in which he is worshipped." "These are new-fashioned notions, I believe, ma'am; and I cannot fully enter into them. My mother, heaven rest her soul, was as good and pious a christian as ever lived, and she said that the Pope was Antichrist, and papishes miserable sinners."

Dorcasina now demanded of Betty, pen, ink, and paper. "I must rise," said she, " and inform O'Connor of the promise my father has exacted of me, and desire him, alas! to visit me, at present, no more." She then, with streaming eyes and aching heart, wrote as follows:

"WERE ever two faithful and tender lovers persecuted as we are? My father is deeply prejudiced against you, and has obtained from me another promise that I will not see you, till Mr. Stanly receives an answer to a letter he has written to Mr. W. You will therefore comprehend that your further visits here must, for a while, be suspended. I will not speak of my own sorrow, because I wish to comfort you, who, I am not ashamed to confess, are the dearest part of myself. Be not, I beseech you, too much afflicted. The time cannot be long before we shall receive proofs of your innocence, which, I trust, in spite of Lysander's base attempt, will be satisfactory to my father.

From your afflicted   D. S."

Upon the receipt of this billet, O'Connor retired to his chamber to read it. "Curse on my ill stars," cried he in a rage, as soon as he had perused it. "Here is a pretty piece of work. I shall now be completely blasted. But I'll persevere, if it be only to plague that old fox, and obtain his fond, silly, sickening daughter in spite of him." After having thus vented his indignation he composed himself to answer her letter, in the usual style.

> "HOW superlatively miserable am I that the father of my adorable mistress should think me capable of conduct which, were I guilty, would rank me with the basest of mankind. I am hurt, deeply hurt, my angel, at having become the object of such injurious suspicions. From any other person I would not tamely bear them. But when I consider them as coming from the author of my Dorcasina's being, I check my resentment, and suffer in silence. "How blessings brighten as they take their flight." I live in imagination on the blisful hours passed in your company, of which I am now unjustly deprived. Heaven give me patience to bear this privation: It is almost too much for my weak philosophy. I trust to your affection for never giving such another promise, and am your unhappy adorer.
>
> O'CONNOR."

After reading this letter Dorcasina retired to her closet; and turning over her favourite authors, she found numerous instances of persecuted lovers, cruel parents, and tyrannical guardians. To find herself precisely in the situation of many sister heroines afforded her more consolation than, in the present juncture, she could have derived from any other source. She became calm by degrees, and determined, since there was no alternative, to wait with patience for the letter which was to decide her fate.

Her father seeing her calmness, hoped that she began to view O'Connor in his proper light; and that her reason would finally get the better of this most sudden, violent, and foolish passion: he, therefore, carefully avoided every thing which might lead to the subject, and awaken disagreeable ideas in her mind.

Thus elapsed nearly a week, of which, however, no day passed, without some tender intercourse by letter, between Dorcasina and her pretended adorer. The latter, as may well be imagined, was far from being at ease. On the contrary, he was perpetually casting about for expedients to counteract the effects which Mr. W's expected letter might produce on Dorcasina. He, at length, fell on one that will appear in due season; and which, though an insult to her understanding, was nevertheless greedily swallowed.

As to Mr. Sheldon, O'Connor, knowing himself to be ruined in his opinion, and indignant at being thus detected and exposed, was determined to give himself no farther trouble about him; but to build all his hopes of success on the attachment of his daughter; whom he was now more eager than ever to obtain, in order to be revenged for the affronts given him by her father.

Mr. Stanly at length received the expected letter from Philadelphia. Mr. W. informed him therein that the letter presented, in his name, to Mr. Sheldon, was a base forgery; and that he had no personal knowledge of any such man as O'Connor. He, however, added, that Mr. Stanly's letter had raised his indignation to such a pitch, that he could not avoid shewing it to a master of a vessel he had lately taken into his service, who happened to be present. On perusing it, he instantly recognised in the description of O'Connor, an old acquaintance. "He then informed me," continued Mr. W. "that he had brought him from England in his last voyage, totally destitute of friends, fortune, and character; that he had been tried for his life at the Old Bailey, for a highway robbery, and escaped the gallows only by an error in the writ: that, while in Philadelphia, he subsisted by gambling; and finally, that he was a most worthless and abandoned profligate."

Mr. Sheldon, as he read this account, shuddered with horror; and thanked heaven for having put it in his power to save his darling child from the effects of her own credulity, and O'Connor's villany. He hesitated, at first, on the manner in which he should convey this intelligence to her; but thinking that the letter needed no comments, and being willing to spare her the confusion his presence must necessarily occasion, at the discovery of such a scene of iniquity, he sent the letter to her by Betty; and immediately went to consult Mr. Stanly on the best means of freeing the village from such a nuisance.

On entering her mistress' chamber, with the letter, Betty found her deeply engaged, and apparently greatly delighted, in reading one, which she had just received from O'Connor, expressed in the most extravagantly fond and romantic terms. Betty, entering unperceived, set herself down, in a corner, to wait till her mistress should have finished one letter before she delivered her another. But this was not very quickly done; Dorcasina was so transported with the expressions, which she thought more animated, more tender and more charming than any she had yet received, that one, two, or three readings could not suffice her; and after every perusal, she kissed it as many times, and with as much ardour as ever O'Connor had done her hand, in the strongest paroxysms of transport.

At length, after the fourth reading, she put it into her bosom, exclaiming, at the same time, with an air of rapture, "dear, divine youth! Best beloved of my soul! What balm, what sweet consolation do your letters afford me! What pure, sublime, disinterested love is here displayed! Surely cupid himself must have guided your pen, and dictated every sentence. How strongly do I experience the truth of the poet's assertion,

"Heav'n first taught letters for some wretch's aid,
"Some banish'd lover, or some captive maid:
"They live, they speak, they breathe what love inspires,
"Warm from the soul, and faithful to its fires;
"The virgin's wish without her fears impart,
"Excuse the blush, and pour out all the heart;
"Speed the soft intercourse from soul to soul,
"And waft a sigh from Indus to the pole."

As soon as she had pronounced these lines, Betty stepped up and presenting her the letter, with which she was charged, and being ignorant of the contents, said she hoped it would afford her as much satisfaction as the one she had just been reading. But, good heavens! what a contrast. She trembled; she turned pale; her eyes were cast upwards, her hands clasped, and her bosom heaved, as if her heart would burst its enclosure. Betty, greatly alarmed, and fearing Dorcasina would have a fit, rang the bell violently for assistance; and then, unpinning her clothes, held a smelling bottle with one hand, and fanned her with the other. The violent ringing of the bell brought up together all the females of the family. Betty, desiring them to fetch some water quickly, they all as suddenly made their exit, running against, and jostling each other, in their eagerness to assist a person, whom they all so dearly loved. One of them, more nimble than the rest, having arrived with the water, Betty rubbed her temples, sprinkled her face, and put some to her mouth, begging her, at the same time, for heaven's sake, to endeavor to swallow. But a more powerful remedy than either salts, water, or air, came to her assistance. This was a sudden and violent torrent of tears, which, bursting forth all at once, called back her spirit, which seemed for some time struggling to take its flight. Betty, overjoyed at this mark of returning sensation, told the women she had no farther need of their assistance, and set herself quietly down by the bedside, to wait till Dorcasina had relieved her full heart of the load which oppressed it. Her tears flowed long and copiously.

At length, in words interrupted by groans and sobs, she thus poured out her troubled soul. "Ah, Betty! they have at length succeeded: They have accomplished their purpose. With the malice of fiends, they have conjured up a thousand falsehoods against one who never injured them; and have, I fear, ruined him forever in the opinion of my father. How many difficulties has true love to surmount! My dearest O'Connor will now have to prove their malice before he will be able to obtain my hand. So many embarrassments would discourage a common love: but that of the dear injured man is proof against all opposition; and how much ought mine to be increased, Betty (if it were possible to add to it) by his unremitting perseverance? Some enemy in disguise, or some rival of O'Connor, has set himself at work to blast our happiness. But heaven, I trust, will never suffer such abominable falsehood to remain undiscovered; and my father will yet be convinced of my O'Connor's worth, notwithstanding appearances are at present so much against him. That vile captain, to invent such a story; who is he, and what could be his motives? I shall have a worse opinion of mankind, on account of this vile slanderer, as long as I live."

"What captain do you mean ma'am, and what have they said about Mr. O'Connor, that troubles you so much?"

"A Captain who pretends he brought him over from London. Oh! he has thrown upon his spotless character the blackest aspersions. They are too bad; I cannot repeat them. But depend upon it, Betty, Mr. O'Connor will prove them all to be false, groundless, and malicious." "But suppose he shou'd'nt be able to, ma'am, what wou'd you do then? You woud'n't marry a man of bad character, wou'd you?" "What vile suppositions, Betty! But I am not concerned. I will stake my life he is innocent of the crimes laid to his charge as the unborn babe: But I must see him. I am now no longer bound. My promise was only to remain in force till this letter should arrive. I will myself inform him how injuriously he is treated; he shall have the consolation of knowing, from my own mouth, that it has not lessened him in my opinion; and that I believe every syllable of it to be false." "But I should think, ma'am, you had better see what he says first. If you tell him right off hand, you don't believe it, and all that, you may be sure he'll say it is not true." "Never fear, Betty, I believe I know how to manage such delicate matters quite as well as you do."

She then desired Betty to call Patrick, while she employed herself in writing a billet to O'Connor, in which she desired him to come to her that evening at 11 o'clock; adding that the letter from Philadelphia had arrived; and that she had many things of importance to communicate. Having dispatched it she became more calm, consoling herself with the idea of again seeing her adored, after so long and painful an absence.

Mr. Sheldon having consulted with Mr. Stanly on the means of ridding himself and the village of O'Connor, it was agreed that Mr. Stanly should by letter desire him to give up all thoughts of Miss Sheldon, and inform him at the same time, that her father would never give his consent to the connection they had contemplated. Accordingly Mr. Stanly wrote O'Connor the following letter.

> "SIR,
> "MY friend, Mr. Sheldon, after a thorough investigation of your character, having formed a determination never to consent to your marrying his daughter, has requested me to give you the information; and at the same time, to assure you that all attempts to gain her will be fruitless. If, therefore, you wish to save him any further uneasiness, and to prevent all trouble to yourself, you will immediately quit the village.
>
> THOMAS STANLY."

"D——d concise," exclaimed O'Connor, as soon as he had read it; "not even your humble servant at the bottom. I shall take my own time to quit the village, and I'll be d——d if I am not revenged first. Who cares for his consent? I would not ask it now if I knew I could obtain it. No, no, I'll marry the old maid without it; and then let him help himself as he can."

In the midst of this soliloquy Dorcasina's billet was delivered him by Patrick. "So, my feathered mercury," said he, "you have brought me something from your mistress, that will give me pleasure I hope. It has arrived in good time; for I have received d——d ungentlemanly treatment from her father. Go below, my good lad, and wait till I see if it require an answer." O'Connor sent Patrick down that he need not be further witness to his ill humour, which it was impossible for him to controul. "Well, now let us see what sickening stuff this contains?"

This billet being penned in Dorcasina's usual tender style, O'Connor found he need not apprehend a change of her sentiments towards him, and he was highly gratified by the prospect of being again admitted to see her. He thanked her a thousand times for this indulgence, and assured her that he should wait, with the utmost impatience, for the hour to arrive, when he should be once more superlatively blessed in an opportunity of throwing himself at the feet of the goddess of beauty, and divine mistress of his affections.

At Mr. Sheldon's return home, he found his daughter calm but dejected; and observed she had been in tears. His tenderness was, if possible, increased. He pitied from his soul the struggles she had made; and his voice was that of soothing and paternal love. He however, was careful not to touch "the string upon which vibrated all her sorrows." He exerted himself to entertain her with indifferent subjects, and her gratitude being awakened by this delicate attention, he succeeded beyond his expectations. They passed together the whole afternoon and part of the evening. At eight o'clock Dorcasina, pretending a head ache, retired to her chamber, hoping thereby to induce her father to seek his at an early hour.

Mr. Sheldon was too little at his ease to feel any inclination to sleep. Therefore, soon after his daughter had quitted him, he retired to his study, to relieve his mind of the anxieties he had felt during the day, by interesting himself in some entertaining and elegant author: all blessings light upon the memory of the inventor of letters, whoever he might be: How often is the weary and troubled mind comforted and consoled, by availing itself of their friendly aid! How often is the keenest sorrow suspended or forgotten, while one is perusing the entertaining or instructive page.

Dorcasina's heart beat with pleasure, when she heard her father ascend the stairs. She supposed he was retiring to rest; and waited for the interesting hour of eleven with extreme impatience. Going softly down, and planting Betty in the entry to stand centinel, she waited, in an adjoining room, the coming of her lover. O'Connor, arrived punctually at the hour; and was introduced by Betty to the presence of her mistress. It would require the pen of a Richardson to describe the ecstacy, and raptures of this meeting: but as mine pretends to no such powers, they shall be passed over in silence.

Her first transports being somewhat abated, "You can have no idea my dear O'Connor," said Dorcasina, "how vilely you are slandered and abused. Mr. W. disclaims your acquaintance; and the master of a vessel, who pretends he brought you over, has invented a thousand falsehoods, and I fear they have been but too successful in prejudicing my father against you. But, thank heaven, I am not so credulous. My faith in my O'Connor's integrity remains unshaken, and my love undiminished." "Thanks, a thousand thanks, my angel. This is no more than what I expected, from the most exalted of women; and believe me, Dorcasina, my confidence in you had been equally unbounded had our situations been reversed. But you were deceived, my love, in supposing me ignorant of the calumnies invented against me. I have had the fullest information from a faithful friend in Philadelphia; and he has enabled me to discover the cause. Lysander, who is intimately connected with Mr. W. has been there; and, by his address, has prevailed on him to conduct himself in the same base manner towards me that he has done himself. Between them they have invented the falsehoods transmitted to your father. Thus all can be traced to your fatal charms, which it is impossible for any man to behold, without becoming your slave. And these divine charms, are they not destined to make me some compensation for the injuries, which, on your account, I have suffered? I think myself extremely unfortunate in having, through the malice of my enemies, lost your father's good opinion: but as they have not succeeded in ruining me, in the opinion of my charming, my destined bride, fulfil your promise; bless me; make me the happiest of mankind; let us wait no longer for a consent, which perhaps will never be obtained, and which we ought no longer to wait for. Are we not in fact bound to each other by the most solemn promises? Yes you are mine; our vows are registered in heaven; and no power on earth shall ever tear me from you. Let us fly; let us improve the present moment. I will place you with a reputable family, till the knot is tied, which will bind us forever."

O'Connor uttered this speech, with great vehemence, and had actually forced Dorcasina to rise, and drawn her some steps towards the door. Overcome by his pleasing violence, she had not power to make any resistance. But, as he stopped to open the door, she had time for recollection, when, withdrawing her hand, regaining precipitately her seat, she suddenly exclaimed, "whither, beloved of my soul, Oh whither would you draw me? Know I can never be your's without my father's sanction. I am bound, by a solemn promise, never to marry you without his free and full consent."

This was to O'Connor like an unexpected stroke of thunder: for he thought himself sure of conquest, and upon the eve of realizing all his wishes. His assurance now left him; with folded arms he, for some moments, stood motionless and silent. At length he exclaimed, "Alas, what have you done? you have rendered me the most wretched of mankind." Then throwing himself at her feet and shedding a torrent of tears: "Oh, cast me not off but have compassion on me; for I cannot exist without you. As you have taught me to believe that, in blessing me you would render yourself happy, let not any promise, which your father may have extorted from you, drive me to despair and ruin me forever."

Dorcasina, greatly overcome by the words, the looks, the attitude of her lover, was unable to articulate a single sentence; but throwing herself upon her knees before him, and putting her arms round his neck, and her cheek to his, their tears in copious streams mingled and flowed together. The whole of O'Connor's address having been uncommonly animated, and his voice raised to a pretty high pitch, Mr. Sheldon, as he was musing in his study (for he had laid aside his book) thought he heard the sound of a man's voice, in the room directly under him, and which contained our lovers. He became uneasy, without knowing why, and took the resolution of going down into the kitchen, to inquire who was in the house, at that unseasonable hour. In the kitchen he found Betty alone, and, in a stern voice, demanded to know who was with her mistress. The faithful girl, though she highly condemned the imprudence of Dorcasina, always wished to conceal it from her father. She was, therefore much disconcerted at this unexpected question. But being too honest to invent a falsehood at any time, and now taken by surprise, she confessed, in a confused and hesitating manner, that it was Mr. O'Connor.

Mr. Sheldon had never, since the days of his youth, had his temper so much ruffled as upon this occasion. He therefore immediately entered the room, and, to his further astonishment, beheld our lovers, in the situation before described, kneeling, bathed in tears, and clasped in each other's arms.

A ghost from the infernal shades, could not have alarmed them more than did this sudden and unexpected appearance of Mr. Sheldon. They sprung up instantly from their kneeling posture; and stood, fixed in mute astonishment, before him; while Mr. Sheldon, anger flashing in his eyes, first addressing himself to his daughter, "I cannot sufficiently express my surprise and indignation at your infatuation in thus clandestinely meeting a man, who, upon full proof, has come out an accomplished villain; I command you, as you value my favour and affection, never to see him again." "And you, sir," turning to O'Connor, "there is the door; be pleased to walk out. And I charge you, on the regard you have to your own corporeal feelings, never again to give me an occasion to repeat this indignity." O'Connor, completely disconcerted at this sudden attack, thought proper to make a precipitate retreat, while Dorcasina, terrified at so new a sight as her father in a passion, and overcome with grief at seeing her lover turned out of the house, in so disgraceful a manner, fainted away and fell senseless upon the floor.

At this sight Mr. Sheldon's anger entirely subsided. He called aloud for Betty, and, with all their endeavours, it was a long time before Dorcasina's senses returned. She was then, between her father and Betty, supported to her chamber; and this tender parent, first assuring himself that there was no danger of a relapse, and recommending it to Betty to sit up with her mistress, left them and retired to his chamber, with his heart torn by a variety of the most distressing reflections.

Chapter XIII.

DORCASINA did not go to bed; but passed the night in walking the chamber; in sighs, in tears, and in groans, bemoaning her unhappy fate: while Betty, who never left her, endeavoured in vain to console her. Towards morning, she brought a glass of wine, which she persuaded her to drink; and afterwards, by much entreaty, prevailed on her to lie down in her clothes. Nature, being at length wearied out, she fell into a gentle slumber; while Betty nodded in the easy chair by her bed-side.

Mr. Sheldon was not so happy; he closed not his eyes for the whole night. Never had he passed one, since the death of his beloved wife, in so painful a manner. His daughter's fainting, the strength of her attachment to an abandoned profligate, and their clandestine meeting, caused him the most painful apprehensions. He revolved, in his mind, her virtue, her prudence, her filial affection, the ready obedience of her whole life; and found that she had given him more cause for uneasiness, since her short acquaintance with O'Connor, than during her whole life before. He groaned, in bitterness of spirit, for having suffered her imagination to be so filled with descriptions of such scenes as those he had recently witnessed; and was upon the point of committing to the flames every novel within his daughter's reach. But recollecting that he could not get admittance to her closet, where most of them were kept, without passing through her chamber, he, for the present, abandoned his design, and endeavoured to form some probable conjecture on the future line of her conduct. He was, on one hand, not without some apprehensions, that notwithstanding her promise, O'Connor had gotten such hold of her affections, that he would find means to persuade her to become his wife. This event he viewed with horror. On the other hand, he feared that, were she to remain bound by her promise, her health would be the sacrifice.

Tormented with these reflections, he rose with the sun; and after listening at Dorcasina's chamber door to find that all was still within, he left the house, in order, by a walk, to compose the troubles of his agitated breast. He had not walked far before he met, in a violent rage, the innkeeper, O'Connor's landlord.

This honest fellow, knowing the connection that had subsisted between O'Connor and Dorcasina, and that her father was much opposed to it, very rationally concluded that what chagrined himself would give Mr. Sheldon pleasure. He, therefore, thus addressed him "you need not give yourself no more trouble about O'Connor. The scoundrel has gone off without remembering to pay me a farthing for his board." "Gone off!" exclaimed Mr. Sheldon, with pleasure and surprise. "When did he go, and where is he gone?" "He went last night, in the middle of the night, a mean soul'd puppy; but the d——l knows where he has gone to as well as I do. Would to the Lord I knew, I'd soon have him in jail, and there keep him till he had paid me the last penny; a pretty son of a b——h to call for the best my house afforded; the best chamber; the best provisions, and the dearest wines that could be got; and then, there is, beside, his washing, which was no small matter. A fine kettle of fish I have made of it, to be sure. I am going now to send an advertisement to Philadelphia to try if I cannot catch the rascal."

Mr. Sheldon was so rejoiced, at his flight, that he told the landlord, if he would drop the pursuit, and let him go, he would himself pay the bills, provided he would conceal the circumstance; and let it be known that O'Connor went off without discharging them. The landlord, as much overjoyed at the prospect of being indemnified for his loss, as Mr. Sheldon was at our adventurer's flight, readily promised every thing required; and they both parted, with much lighter hearts than they had met.

We will now return to O'Connor; who, in his solitary walk, the night before, from Mr. Sheldon's to his lodgings, pondered, in silent sadness, on his present situation; and the little prospect he had of success. His money, of which he had been very liberal for every purpose but the right, being nearly exhausted; he concluded that it would be his wisest way to decamp, while he had sufficient left to carry him away from this scene of mortification; and to enable him to lay and execute some new plan for making his fortune. Thus determined he reached his lodgings, where he found the family in bed; but the door unfastened, and a light burning, as he had desired, in his chamber. Full of resentment at Mr. Sheldon's cavalier treatment, he determined to be revenged on him, by keeping his daughter, if possible, single. He therefore wrote her a letter and left it on his table. Then packing up his clothes in his portmanteau, he softly descended, took his horse from the stable, and leaving the village, took his way towards New York.

The letter which he left behind, was couched in the following terms.

"IN an agitation of mind bordering on distraction, I fly from all that can make life desirable, from my angelic Dorcasina; I am driven from your presence by the cruelty of your father. The wide world is before me; and I wander, I neither know nor care whither. Your image indelibly impressed on my heart, will be my constant companion. Henceforth all womenkind will to me be alike indifferent: for never, no never shall I meet with another Miss Sheldon. Oh! my Dorcasina, adored, celestial, divine mistress of my soul; you cannot conceive half the pangs I now suffer. Adieu, dearest, loveliest of women. Condescend to think sometimes on the wretched

O'CONNOR."

This letter was found by the landlord's wife, who went first into his chamber in the morning, upon suspicion of his absence. Finding that he had carried off every thing which belonged to him, she took the letter and run to seek her husband, to inform him of her lodger's flight, shewing him at the same time the letter he had left behind. But being enraged and agitated at his loss, he paid but little attention to it, and, in fact, by the time he met Mr. Sheldon, had entirely forgotten it. Returning home, with a countenance totally different from that, with which he had set out, he informed his wife of his good luck, and added that now O'Connor might go to the d——l for what he cared, since Mr. Sheldon had promised to make him whole. "We are very lucky, to be sure," said the wife; "but I pities Miss Dorcasina with all my soul. She is so good, and kind, and free with every body, 'tis pity she should die for love. Mr. O'Connor sartainly was a handsome and a genteel man. Poor, dear soul! how she will take on, when she knows he has gone. Here is the letter he left for her, I will go myself and carry it, that I may find out how she stands affected." "Don't go, now, for to blab that Mr. Sheldon is going to pay us. I promised not to let it be known; only tell her he went away without paying us a farding." "Never fear, husband, I guess I can *keep a secret*, if I *am* a woman."

So saying, she hurried away with the letter, and going into Mr. Sheldon's kitchen, saw Betty, who, finding her mistress greatly agitated in mind, and very feverish, had just persuaded her to go to bed. The hostess whispering Betty that she had got a letter for Dorcasina, which she wished to deliver herself, she readily conducted her up stairs, hoping that a letter from O'Connor would compose her mistress better than all the nostrums in the world. They found her calm, but in the deepest dejection of spirits; and so entirely absorbed in melancholy contemplations that she did not observe their entrance. Betty approaching the bed, said, "here comes one, that, I hope, brings you comfort, ma'am." Dorcasina, upon this, raised her languid eyes, and no sooner did she perceive the hostess, than a ray of pleasure beamed on her woebegone countenance. "Here is a letter from Mr. O'Connor, ma'am." "A letter! thank heaven, I am once more permitted to peruse the well known characters from his dear hand." Then, hastily opening it, and running her eye over the contents, "Oh heavens!" she exclaimed, "I am ruined and undone; the most wretched mortal that exists. He has gone Betty; driven by my father's cruelty, from all he holds dear; these are his words. Oh, that it would please heaven to take me out of the world! deprived of him who to me was existence, nothing remains for me but despair and death."

"Sure ma'am, you know not what you say," said Betty. "Can you then wish to die, and leave your dear father and poor Betty; and all this for nobody knows who? This is not acting the part of a good christian, nor bearing up under trouble, as I have often and often heard you advise other people to do."

"Common griefs, I confess, may be borne, and time blunts their poignancy: But to be deprived of such a lover, whose equal is not to be found among the sons of men; and to lose him, in such a manner! Ah, Betty, how can I wish to live, after being deprived of him, who alone could render life desirable? But tell me, landlady, when did he go, and how did he look?" "He went last night ma'am; but how he looked, I know not, for he took a French leave; he went off in the night, and never paid us a farding for his board." "The manner of his going agrees exactly with the distraction of mind painted in his letter. Night or day, it was all one to him: and as to his bill it was impossible he should think of it, distracted as he was at the thoughts of losing me. But give yourself no uneasiness on that score, you shall not lose a penny by him: bring me his bill, and I will discharge it with pleasure."

The hostess thanked her for her goodness, courtsied, and hurried home to inform her husband of what had passed, and to consult whether they ought to take pay from Mr. Sheldon and his daughter both. The landlord and his wife were what the world call honest people. They would not do any thing, which the laws forbid, though it could be done with the utmost privacy; but when an opportunity offered of getting money in a lawful way, they were as willing to embrace it as other people. They, therefore, soon settled it, that, as Mr. Sheldon had desired them not to mention his paying O'Connor's bill, they had a right to receive it again from the daughter; especially as Mr. Sheldon was too rich to feel so trifling a sum.

Dorcasina not appearing at breakfast as usual, her father learnt, upon inquiry from Betty, that she was quite indisposed. This he imputed to the right cause; and hoping that a few days would restore her health and tranquillity, he forbore visiting her for the present, fearing that the conversation might take a turn, which would only increase her trouble.

In the mean time, the unhappy Dorcasina was a prey to the most violent grief. In vain did Betty urge her to take a little breakfast; she rejected food, and wept and sighed continually, calling herself the most wretched of women. Betty, in hopes of soothing her sorrow, begged her to read some of the books, in which she had formerly taken such delight. "Alas! no, Betty; even these cannot now give me pleasure. My sorrow is too deep and well founded; a perusal of the happiness painted by some of those authors, of which at present I am deprived, would only be an aggravation; and pictures of *distressed* lovers would heighten my present suffering. But take the key of my bureau, and bring me the letters of the divine youth; *they* may possibly afford me some consolation."

Betty readily did as she was desired, and unlocking the bureau, handed her mistress a packet, which she would not have exchanged for all the treasures of Peru. She had got them arranged in perfect order, tied with a silken string, and wrapped in a cover, upon which was written these words, *Letters from my dearest O'Connor before marriage.* Taking the first in order she kissed the seal, and the superscription; then, after opening it, and pressing the inside upon her heart, she read it three times over. This done, she folded it up again and laid it in her bosom, with that she had received in the morning. In the same manner and with the same ceremonies, she went on till she had got through the whole file; then pressing them altogether against her bosom, with as much ardour, as if they had been the writer himself, she exclaimed, "Oh incontestable proofs of the purest and most exalted passion, that ever warmed a human breast! Ah! Betty, how much do I prize them! They shall be my inseparable companions. These alone shall by my comfort, my consolation, till I again behold him, from whom I received them: There is yet one thing more, Betty, in which I can take delight. Open that drawer and hand me the handkerchief he one day left in the parlour."

Betty did as she was desired, and Dorcasina, taking and kissing it, thus continued; "See here, Betty, see the enchanting name, P. O'Connor. What would I give to know the happy female, who, with her needle, marked this name, so dear to my heart; how greatly should I envy her." Her tenderness and her sorrow found here a romantic consolation, in complaining to the handkerchief of the absence of its owner, his exile, and her fears for his health: Betty surprised at scenes so new, and to her comprehension so foolish, exclaimed, "Lord, ma'am, just as if that handkerchief can understand what you say." "Ah, Betty, you know not what love is, if you did, you would know how to appreciate and personify whatever had once belonged to a lover. These letters, and this handkerchief, will be all my consolation; and while thus caressing, and thus complaining to them, I will indulge the pleasing hope that my lover will one day be again restored."

Mr. Sheldon hoped that his daughter would be sufficiently composed to appear at dinner, but he was disappointed. On inquiry after her he was informed that she was yet in bed, and had not tasted food for the day.

Uncertain whether a visit from him would be acceptable, he sent word after dinner that, if it were agreeable, he would pass an hour with her in her chamber. "The company of my father can never be otherwise than agreeable," was the answer. Upon his entering and approaching the bed, he was struck with the fever, which burned in her cheeks, and the extreme dejection of her whole countenance. The moment she beheld him the sluices of her eyes were again opened; and again the tears descended in the most copious streams. He set himself down by her bed-side, took and gently pressed her hand; and waited, in silence, till the storm should subside.

When he found she was a little composed, he thus, in the most soothing and tender voice addressed her; "I am sorry, my dear, to see you thus give way to grief, for an event, which I view as the most fortunate of your life. Why will you thus injure your health for a vile fellow, who, had you married him, would have rendered your life miserable? for miserable you must have been. Your moral principles have been carefully formed, and your conduct has ever been a model of the purest virtue: what then would have been your distress to have found yourself allied to vice, profligacy, and meanness?" "Oh, my father! spare me. Do not thus add affliction to the afflicted. It grieves me to see you thus blinded, by prejudice, to the merits of one, whose ardent affection and faultless conduct surely deserved a better return." "My regret is equal to your's, my dear. But it is you, who are prejudiced; it is you, who are blinded by a foolish passion for an unworthy object." "Forebear, sir, if you please; and since we shall never agree in sentiment, with regard to Mr. O'Connor, we will drop the subject forever; unless providence, in kindness and justice to such merit, should dispel the clouds of calumny, with which it has been obscured, and lead you to form a more just opinion of him."

"I most willingly agree to it; and if I am ever convinced that I have wronged him, I will as willingly acknowledge it. But I hope, my dear, you will, for my sake, make an effort to forget him; throw off this gloom, and resume your wonted cheerfulness. You have fretted yourself into a fever already; and the physician's assistance will be of no avail, while you thus indulge in fruitless sorrow. Consider, too, what the world will say; and have some little regard to its censures; for they are not always unfounded. Come, cheer up, and let me have the pleasure of drinking tea with you, in your chamber, this afternoon." "To forget him, sir, is impossible; neither do I wish it; for the contemplation of his love, his merit, his graces, will be the sweetest consolation I shall ever experience. As to what the world will say, I heed it not; but for your sake, sir, I will make an exertion to rise, and have the pleasure of receiving you to tea." "Thank you, my dear, you are now again my daughter. I will leave you, for the present, and hope at my return to find this ugly fever entirely abated." So saying, he left her to her own reflections.

As soon as he was gone, "what an affectionate father he is," said Dorcasina to Betty. "I shall ever revere him, though he is the cause of my present unhappiness. But no, I retract, he is not the primary cause. It is Lysander, who is at the bottom of all the mischief. He, it is, that has injured my beloved, and prejudiced my father; and it was these charms, these fatal charms, which influenced him." "Well, ma'am, if that's the case, you can't blame Lysander so much, I should think you ought to pity him a little." "I could have forgiven him any thing else, Betty, but robbing me of my lover; and I must endeavour with a christian spirit to forgive him even that. But, no more of him at present; bring my clothes and help me to rise."

She then, with Betty's assistance, arose and dressed; but was so weak that she sat down, in an easy chair, almost exhausted. At the appointed hour her father again visited the chamber, and was greatly pleased to find her up; though her fever did not appear, in the least abated, and she could scarcely get down one cup of tea. He, however, hoped a night's rest would restore her; if it did not, he was fully determined to send for a physician in the morning.

Dorcasina rested much better this night than she had done the night preceding. In the morning, her fever had left her; but she was still weak and languid. Her father visited her early, and was happy to find her so much recovered. He avoided the tender subject, as they had the day before agreed; and so cordially congratulated her upon her present favourable symptoms, that she exerted herself to appear cheerful, and sincerely wished, for his sake, that her indisposition might be of short duration. After he had quitted her, and during the course of the day, she relapsed, several times into paroxysms of melancholy, shedding torrents of tears, and bewailing her lover, to her faithful Betty; who, finding the sight of the letters a never failing cordial, recommended them frequently to her perusal. Her melancholy and weakness did not immediately leave her. She was confined a fortnight to her chamber, during which her father passed with her all the time he could spare from his usual occupations; and exerted himself, in every possible way, to dispel her chagrin.

Chapter XIV.

THE inhabitants of this village, like those of all other small places, were too apt to busy themselves, with the affairs of their neighbours. The recent love adventure of the first lady in it now became the topic of conversation, in every circle. Few had the right of the story; and a thousand circumstances were added, as destitute of truth as of probability. "Who would have thought," said one, "that Dorcasina Sheldon could have wished to run away, and leave her father's house, to follow a stranger, an outlandish man, to the old countries?" "Sure enough," cried another, "and so good a father too; no wonder he shut her up. He served her very right, for wishing to leave him." "I am not of your mind," said a third. "I think Mr. Sheldon, though in the main a good man, was very cruel to cross his only child in love. If the poor lady should die or go distracted, he would dearly repent his cruelty."

By degrees, the subject of their speculation gained strength, and, in three weeks, was able, for the first time, since her lover's departure, to pay a visit to the grove. This was an enjoyment, for which she had most earnestly wished. She longed, with a mingled sensation of pain and pleasure, to revisit the spot, where she had first beheld the adored youth, in order to recal the rapturous moments she had passed in company with one, who had taken such full possession of her heart. Before she set out upon this visit, an idea occurred to her, which employed all her thoughts; and from which she flattered herself with drawing much pleasure. Being alone with Betty in the morning she unfolded to her her plan. "It is a charming morning, Betty; I feel quite recovered, and I am determined, this afternoon, to visit the spot, where I first beheld the lord of my affections. But it is in your power, Betty, to render the visit a thousand times more agreeable than it would be without your assistance; I hope you will not refuse me a trifling favour." "I am sorry, ma'am, you should doubt my willingness to oblige you. I'm sure I don't know as ever I gave you reason to." "Well, then, Betty, you must know I have taken a fancy to dress myself exactly as I was the day I first beheld my lover; to place myself in the arbour, as I did then; and to have you dress yourself in a suit of my father's clothes, and then come and personate O'Connor." "Lord, ma'am, what a strange vagary! I protest, I begin to think you are a little addled, a little love crack'd. _I_ dress myself in your father's clothes, I act O'Connor! Why I shou'dn't know a word to say; for you well know I have had the misfortune never to have had a sweetheart since I was born!"

Dorcasina was visibly hurt and chagrined to find that Betty so little relished her plan; and, with a cold air, said, "this then is your readiness to oblige me, Betty. I find your professions are very hallow." "Why, ma'am, if it was to do any thing that ever was heard of before, I'm sure I wou'dn't want to be asked twice; but to dress in men's clothes is, I believe, what never was wanted of a maid by any lady before. And, besides, I think it would be quite indecent to go out in the day-time, in that manner." "It is very well, Betty," returned her mistress; "I shall know, in future, what you mean by a willingness to oblige me."

Betty seeing her seriously offended, and considering her late trouble, and consequent weakness of mind, began to waver in her resolution; and, at last, thought there could be no harm in gratifying her in the whim she had taken. "Why, if it will give you as much pleasure as you say, ma'am, I will do as you desire." "Now you say something to the purpose, Betty. My father, you know, has gone some miles from home, and will not be back till late in the evening. We can go, therefore, to his chamber, and you can dress yourself in a suit of his best clothes. I will go first, and be seated in the arbour, and you must follow, soon after." "But, what must I say, ma'am, when I get there?" "Say? why you must call me angel, goddess, and your divine Dorcasina. Tell me how miserable you have been since you saw me; and that my presence inspires you with new life, and pleasure. Tell me how charmingly I look, squeeze my hand, and appear in raptures." "Well,

ma'am, I will do my best to please you." "Thank you, Betty; this proof
of your readiness to oblige me, shall not, I assure you, go unrewarded."

They then separated till the afternoon; when Dorcasina, eager to
put in execution a plan, from which she expected to reap so much
satisfaction, went first to her own chamber, where she dressed herself
as before mentioned, and then with Betty to her father's; where, taking
from a trunk, a rufled shirt, a superfine cloth coat, handsome waistcoat,
black satin small clothes, and silk stockings, she desired Betty to equip
herself in them, without delay.

Betty now repented of the promise she had made; but it was too late
to retract. With the utmost reluctance she pulled off her own clothes,
and dressed herself in those of Mr. Sheldon, in which she made a most
grotesque appearance. Mr. Sheldon was a large man, and taller than
Betty by at least a whole head. Although she was none of the thinest,
the clothes hung upon her, like a blanket upon a post. The small
clothes reached half way down her legs, and the waistcoat half way
down them. As to the coat, it reached almost to her heels. Dorcasina
observed, that the clothes, to be sure, did not suit quite so well as if they
had been made for her; but that this was of little consequence, as she
was only to wear them occasionally. She then left the chamber and
took her way to the grove, telling Betty to be sure and follow her, in half
an hour.

Poor Betty, being left alone, examined herself in the glass, and was
ready to die with shame and vexation, at the ridiculous figure she
made; and understanding, by Dorcasina's last speech, that she intended
repeating the frolic, she vowed to herself it should be the only time she
would ever be caught in such a scrape; and, if her mistress would
indulge in such ridiculous whims, she might get somebody else to
play the fool for her. She then listened in the passage, to find if the coast
was clear; and, observing nobody in the way, she went softly down the
back stairs, into the garden, jumped over the fence, and, with all
possible speed, took the back way to the grove. Arrived at the arbour,
she found her mistress seated, waiting to receive her. She first made
a most ridiculous bow, and then seizing Dorcasina's hand, which she
purposely griped hard enough to give her pain, thus delivered herself:
"Dear soul, intosticating charmer, celestial deity; Mars, Junos, and
Venis; my very marrow is burnt up from the fire of your dazzling eyes.
I have gone about, since I saw you, like a roaring lion; there has been
neither sleep to my eyes, nor slumber to my eyelids." Here she was

interrupted, by Dorcasina, who, quite disappointed, and vexed, said, "why, Betty, this is nothing to the purpose; it is more like the incoherent ravings of a madman, than the address of an ardent lover. Do begin again, and try if you cannot make a speech more to the purpose, and more like my dear absent lover; and, for heaven's sake, do not squeeze my hand so hard."

Betty, determined to act her part, in the worst manner possible, that she need not again be forced into so disagreeable a situation, began another speech more outré, if possible, than the former; but she was interrupted, in the very beginning, by the sudden appearance of Scipio, the gardener, Patrick, the boy, a white servant, and two or three labourers from the field.

The cause of their unexpected appearance, was as follows. When Betty left the house, she was not quite so unobserved as she imagined. One of the maids, who was at work in the kitchen, saw her pass hastily through the garden, jump over the fence, and run toward the grove. She knew, at sight, that the clothes belonged to Mr. Sheldon; and her first idea was, that some evil minded person had got into his chamber, unobserved, and dressed himself in these clothes, with a design to make off with them. Possessed with this idea, she ran to the field, and told the workmen, among whom were the servants of the family, that there had been a thief in Mr. Sheldon's chamber, who had dressed himself in his clothes, and made off towards the grove, as fast as his legs would carry him. Upon this, they all left their work, and joined in the pursuit, entering the grove by different paths, and meeting near the centre, which was the place of the arbour.

Dorcasina, being within, was not at first observed by them; but they immediately discovered the supposed thief, in their master's clothes. "Dare he be—dare de tief; catch him, hole him," cried Scipio; while they all advanced in full speed. But before they had quite reached the spot, to their great astonishment, they beheld Dorcasina. The noise they made occasioning Betty to turn her head, the posse immediately recognized her; and, in spite of the presence of their mistress, could not refrain from bursting out into an immoderate fit of laughter, which continued for some time; while the mortified object of their mirth, sinking with shame and vexation, endeavoured to conceal herself from their view, by skulking behind her mistress. Dorcasina herself was not a little chagrined, at her disappointment and detection. Assuming, however, a serious tone, she desired the servants to leave their idle mirth, and go about their work. Out of respect to her, they immediately complied; but it was a subject of speculation for them, for that afternoon, and for a long time after, as they were unable to comprehend what Betty or her mistress could mean by such a frolic.

As soon as they were gone, Dorcasina desired Betty to come forward and begin her speech again, which, she said, the ill mannered servants had so rudely interrupted. But Betty, now proving refractory, declared positively that she would not again attempt to be a fool, and that no person should again have an opportunity of seeing her, in her present ridiculous plight. So saying, she immediately began to climb one of the trees, of which the arbour was composed; and having, with much difficulty, gained the branches, she got among the thickest of them and sat down, on a large bough, entirely concealed from view. Her mistress the whole time she was ascending, begged her to desist, and to perform the part she had come thither to act. But, deaf to all her entreaties, Betty answered not a word. Seeing her resolute, and safely lodged in the tree, Dorcasina, at length, gave over her importunity, and employed herself, the remainder of the afternoon, in carving the name of her absent lover, upon the bark of every tree in the arbour; and in repeating it to the winds, as, with gentle breath they whispered through the branches.

At length, the approach of night alarming Betty for the health of her mistress, she broke silence, for the first time, since she had gained her retreat, where, like a bear, she had sat growling at her own, and her mistress' folly; and begged her to retire before the unwholesome dews should begin to fall. "Are you not going with me, Betty," said Dorcasina. "Not I, indeed, ma'am, I've no notion of having all the men in the field, halloing and staring after me." "Why, you surely do not intend passing the night here?" "Good heavens, pass the night here! that I wou'dn't for all the world, I should expect to be carried off by robbers, before morning. But, pray ma'am, do you go home, and leave me to take care of myself. I shall skulk home in the dusk, as soon as I can do it, without being observed by them develish workmen." "Well, well, Betty; don't be in a passion, and I will contrive to have them out of the way, when you arrive." So saying, she left the arbour, and made the best of her way to the house.

No sooner had she quitted the grove on one side, than Betty heard the clattering of a number of female tongues on the other. These were three or four of the village maidens; who, having spun their accustomed number of skeins, had set aside their wheels, and come to enjoy, in the grove, the cool breezes of evening, after a warm summer's day. They were true children of nature, unacquainted with art, and as innocent and cheerful as the birds that fluttered over their heads, and chanted their vespers among the boughs. Taking their way directly to the arbour, they seated themselves, without perceiving any person to be near them. Here they indulged themselves, in talking over the news of the village, and joking each other about their favourite swains.

Betty, mean time, from her elevated situation, perceived black clouds arising in the west; and the lightning beginning to flash, indicated the approach of a thunder shower. Terrified at this appearance, as well as at the approaching darkness, which was either unobserved or disregarded by the lasses below, her situation became extremely irksome; for being naturally timid, and particularly much afraid of thunder, she could neither bear the idea of tarrying there any longer, nor of going home in the dark. She waited with the utmost impatience, for the girls to retire; till the wind, rising, and bringing the clouds rapidly over, caused a sudden darkness, which alarmed the girls themselves; and they were just making a motion to depart, when a loud clap of thunder, attended with a heavy dash of rain, determined them to stay, in their present shelter, till the shower should abate.

Poor Betty was now so terrified that she could keep her seat no longer; and, endeavouring to get down, she unluckily slipped, and one of the skirts of her coat, hitching in a branch, she, for a moment, hung suspended in the air; till, the skirt giving way, she came down upon her feet in the centre of this group of girls. This sudden and unexpected appearance of a man, falling from the trees among them, frightened them more than wind, thunder, and rain together. They screamed, they jumped, they run, and made their way to the nearest house, to which any of them belonged; thinking neither of the thunder, rain, nor lightning; but of the man, who, they supposed, was all the way at their heels. Betty, terrified, beyond measure, at finding herself alone in the grove, in the midst of darkness and a thunderstorm, which became every moment more violent, ran off, as fast, in a contrary direction. Having got about half way out of the grove, she imagined she heard somebody behind her; and, looking round, she beheld a creature, all in white, with saucer eyes flashing fire, like a very d——l. This sight greatly increased both her terror and the rapidity of her flight. But frightened as she was, she could not help, now and then, looking round to see if the creature gained upon her. The second time she looked, it had increased to the bigness of a calf; and the third time, to that of a large horse. It was happy for her that she was now near the house, as she thought it was the evil one himself, come to take her off bodily. Being arrived she hastily opened the door, and wholly regardless of her strange appearance, rushed into the kitchen among workmen and servants, with the strongest marks of horror depicted on her countenance.

The men servants had, just before, been relating to the maids that they had found the supposed thief to be no other than Betty, in their master's clothes; describing the strange appearance she made in them. They, at first, made themselves very merry at her expense; but as they all loved her, for the goodness of her heart, they finally began to grow very uneasy at her nonappearance. Their inquietude was not a little heightened by that of Dorcasina's, who had been three times in the kitchen to know if she had returned. When she rushed in among them, in the situation before described, every voice vociferated at once, "what ails you, and what is the matter?" "Mercy on me!" cried Betty, throwing herself into a chair, "how thankful I am to be once more at home, among my friends, who, I was afraid, I never should see again." "Why, what was the matter? were you afraid of being killed by the thunder?" "I should have thought," replied Betty, "that the thunder, and lightning, and darkness, and rain, was enough at once to terrify a body; but, besides all these, I have seen a ghost, or the devil; who run after me till I got into the house. Mercy on me! how frightened I was! I thought I should have died." "A spirit?" cried one, "the devil?" cried another. "How did he look? pray tell us." "Oh, it was all in white, with flaming eyes; and kept growing bigger and bigger, till it got as big as a horse." They were all credulous, superstitious, and terrified, except Scipio: who, under an ebony skin, had more understanding than all the rest, and laughed at the idea of ghosts, and apparitions, like a philosopher. "Fiddletick," cried he, "you only see birch tree, and, in de dark, tink him debil." At the same time, espying under the table, a large white, strange cat, he exclaimed, "what cat dat, where he come from?" And then, bursting into a laugh, immediately added, "Dare, dare de debil; dare de ghos; all de ghos Betty see." Then catching the cat, and finding her to be wet, he was confirmed in the idea.

In fact, Scipio was in the right; for the poor cat, straying in the grove, had followed Betty home, probably to get a shelter from the rain; and her imagination had swelled it, by degrees, to the size of a horse. But she could not be made to believe that it was only a cat she had seen; and thinks, to this day, it was a real ghost.

"But, what debil put him in your head, Betty, to dress in masser croase, and go in de grobe?" This question, as her terror was now somewhat abated, revived all her shame; and, without answering a single word, she took a candle, and retreated hastily up stairs, to pull off those clothes which had been the source of so much mortification, vexation, and terror.

She had no sooner disappeared than Dorcasina again entered the kitchen, and inquired whether she had arrived. Being answered in the affirmative, and informed that she had gone up stairs, she immediately followed her, greatly rejoiced at being relieved from the anxiety she had suffered on her account. She found her in Mr. Sheldon's chamber, stripping herself of her wet masculine habit. "Why, Betty," cried Dorcasina, as soon as she entered, "I could not imagine what had become of you. Why did you tarry so long, and give me so much uneasiness?" "I am sorry you were uneasy, ma'am; but I'm sure I had something worse than uneasiness for my share. This shall be the last time, while I have my senses, that I'll ever put on breeches, or stay in the grove, after it's dark again, I'll warrant." "Why, what is the matter? what has happened to you, Betty?" She then, in as concise a manner as her agitation would admit, gave an account of every thing which happened after her mistress left the grove; dwelling most upon what her imagination was most filled with, the great white monster, with the fiery eyes.

As soon as she had ended, "I am sorry, Betty," said Dorcasina, "that you should be so foolish as to think you saw any thing supernatural. You may depend on it, there is no such things as ghosts or spirits; and the way, in which all such stories are fabricated, is, that people will not examine the object of their terror." "Because, ma'am, you never happen'd to see one, you think there is none; but, if you'd only seen what I have this evening, you'd be convinc'd, I'm sartain!" "Well, well, I find we are not either of us likely to convince the other; so make haste and change your dress." In a few minutes, Betty, to her unspeakable satisfaction, was again dressed in her own clothes, which she would not, at that moment, have exchanged for all Mr. Sheldon's wardrobe.

In hanging the coat up to dry, they now found that part of a skirt of it was lost. This caused Dorcasina a good deal of perplexity, as it was one of her father's best coats, and almost new. She knew not how she could bring herself off, when he should come to make inquiries about the damage it had received. She could not resolve to tell him the truth; and was still more unwilling to descend to a falsehood. This, however, not being a matter of immediate concern, she had the clothes hung up in her own closet, and trusted to her ingenuity to extricate her from the embarrassment, when it should become more pressing.

Early the next morning, Betty was dispatched to the grove in quest of the part of the coat which was missing. She found it hanging on the limb of the tree, from which she had, the night before, in such haste descended.

Chapter XV.

MEANTIME, the four girls, whom Betty had caused to scamper off in such consternation, began, after they had got safely home, to query who the person could be, that had appeared so suddenly among them from the tree. One supposed it to be some man, who, caught as they were in the shower, had climbed the tree for a better shelter, and jumped down on purpose to frighten them: another, that it was a robber, who had concealed himself there; or a person with a still worse design. But one of them, more sagacious than the rest, said she would wager any thing that Mr. O'Connor kept himself hid there, on purpose to meet Miss Dorcasina, when she walked in the grove. This opinion was immediately adopted by the other three; and it was soon noised over the village that O'Connor had frequently been seen, in the grove, since his abrupt departure from his lodgings.

About the time that he had disappeared, a young fellow had been hired to keep the village school; a native of Connecticut, that hot-bed of American genius. He had received his eduction at New Haven college; had just graduated, and was about nineteen years old. He was an excellent scholar, a genius, and a wag. Without being vicious, he loved fun to excess; and was noted for the many tricks he had played his tutors. At the time of his arrival at L—— the topic of every conversation was the love adventure, in which Dorcasina had been recently engaged. He, consequently, was soon acquainted with every particular of the affair, as well as with the character of Dorcasina; the peculiarities of which exceedingly diverted him, and strongly excited his curiosity to become acquainted with her. But as she had been confined, ever since he had been in the village, he had found no opportunity of gratifying it. Being an early riser, he, every pleasant morning, indulged himself with a walk, in Mr. Sheldon's grove; the beauties of which, combined with the melody of a multitude of birds of various kinds, beyond measure delighted him.

Going to take his customary morning's ramble, a few days after the above related adventure of Dorcasina, and strolling into the arbour, the first thing that attracted his attention, was the name of O'Connor, at full length, on a number of trees. He had no difficulty in guessing by whose hand it was carved; and the whim instantly took him to place the name of Dorcasina, on all the trees directly under that of O'Connor. This done, he returned to his lodgings.

By this time, the reports circulating in the village, of O'Connor's having been frequently seen in the grove, had reached Dorcasina. She, at first, wholly disregarded them: but hearing every day some new story; she at length began to think that it might possibly be true. She was convinced that his love for her was so fervent, that he would live upon the spontaneous productions of the earth, with the hard ground for his bed, and the sky for his covering, if he could thereby have the smallest chance of meeting her. But, in this case, there was no need of trusting to nature for a subsistence, as it was an easy matter, by the aid of some faithful person in the village, to have his food conveyed to him. She further considered that she had visited the grove but once since his departure; and that he might then have been in some distant part of it. In short, she worked up her imagination to such a pitch, that she fully believed the grove to have been his residence, ever since he quitted his lodgings.

The idea of his being so near her, filled her soul with a tumult of delight; and, the moment dinner was over, with pleasure sparkling in her countenance, she desired Betty to follow her to the grove; telling her by the way, that having duly considered the matter, she was convinced, almost to a certainty, that her lover had there taken up his habitation. "Dear ma'am," said Betty, "how fast you walk! I declare I am quite out of breath. I think you need'n't be in such a hurry; for I don't believe Mr. O'Connor is there any more than I am at this moment. Why it makes me shudder to think of any person's passing the time there in thunder, and rain, cloudy days, and dismal nights. And such dreadful sights, too, as he must have seen, if he has been there all this time! But it cannot be; for he would starve for want of victuals."

"As to the dreadful sights, Betty, with which your imagination is so filled, they are seen only by the eye of superstition. All the rest is very trifling, compared with the absence of those we love. I have read of all this, and much more, being endured for the sake of a beloved object."

By this time, they had gained the skirt of the wood, and Dorcasina, in an audible voice, immediately pronounced the name of her lover, in order that, if he were within hearing, he might know that she was present. And this she continued to repeat, in a "louder and yet louder strain," till she reached the arbour.

Quite exhausted with having so often and so loudly vociferated the name of O'Connor, she threw herself upon the grass, to recover her breath; when, casting her eyes upon the trees, she suddenly started up again, and in a transport of delight, exclaimed, "see here, Betty; see my name on each of these trees just under my adored O'Connor's. Oh he is here! I shall again see him; again behold all that my heart holds dear."

Thus saying, she darted out of the arbour, and flew round the grove in such a delirium of joy, as wholly to exclude all sense of fatigue; calling loudly again upon the name of her lover. As she was thus running, and thus repeating the name of O'Connor, she chanced to meet Mr. Greenough, his late landlord. As soon as she beheld him, the idea occurred to her that he was in the secret, and supplied her lover with food. She therefore exclaimed, "where is he? landlord. When did you see him? Direct me to him instantly, and I shall be under eternal obligations to you." "Where's who?" replied the landlord. "What do you mean, ma'am?" "I mean Mr. O'Connor, who you know well enough has been concealed in this grove, ever since he left your house; and I entreat you to conduct me to him instantly." "Indeed, ma'am, I don't know, nor don't believe no such thing. And, I protest I know no more where he is than the man in the moon."

Frustrated in her expectations of information from the landlord, she quitted him and pursued her way, still calling incessantly upon O'Connor. Having at length wandered over almost the whole extent of the grove, she rejoined Betty, in the arbour, fatigued, disappointed and chagrined. "Has he not been here in my absence, Betty?" demanded Dorcasina. "No ma'am," returned Betty, "nor do I believe he is within twenty miles of us." "Who then could trace those characters? No hand surely but that of my beloved, and, if he is not in the grove now, I am convinced he has lately paid a visit here, and perhaps will soon make another." Thus saying, she took out of her pocket book a piece of paper and a pencil, and wrote as follows:

IF the supreme lord of my affections, my dearest O'Connor, should again visit this consecrated spot, this will inform him that the heart of his Dorcasina still remains unchanged and inviolably his; that she sickens at the daylight, and has no other pleasure than thinking of him. It will, likewise, inform him that she will be here again to-morrow, precisely at three o'clock.

This paper she carefully placed on the limb of a tree, in such a situation, that it might readily be seen; while at the same time the leaves would shelter it from the dews of the night. Then, leaning upon Betty's arm, she took her way slowly to the house, with her mind strangely agitated between hope, joy, and apprehension.

The next morning, being a very fine one, the scholar failed not to walk in the grove, and visit the arbour, as usual. Discovering the paper which Dorcasina had left there the day before, he took it from the tree, where it had been so carefully deposited; and, finding it unsealed, eagerly examined the contents. Consequences so unexpected from his carving the name of Dorcasina upon the trees, at his last visit, delighted this merry son of Momus not a little; and he was determined to draw as much amusement from the adventure, as it was capable of affording. He, accordingly, took pencil and paper from his pocket, and wrote as follows.

"NOT the high-born and superlatively happy O'Connor has visited this blessed spot: but a youth, of birth obscure, and humble fortune, wanders here, that he may enjoy the supreme felicity of treading in the same steps, and of sitting in the same seat, with the beauteous, the all accomplished, the too charming Miss Sheldon. Without knowing it, she has robbed me of my repose. I saw her but once; I gazed and was undone. I could not have the presumption to aspire to her hand, did I even know her heart to be disengaged.

Situated as I am, every comfort I enjoy is in this spot; which I know Miss Sheldon frequently blesses with her presence: and here I frequently wander while others sleep. I dare not ask her love; but her pity I am confident will not be denied me. The lines, traced by her delicate fingers, I shall presume to keep as my greatest treasures. O happy O'Connor! wretched, wretched Philander!"

This love letter, Philander (that being the name by which we shall in future designate him) carefully placed on the same tree, though not in the same spot, from whence he had taken Dorcasina's; and then retired, extremely well pleased with his morning's adventure.

The afternoon, and the hour of three being arrived, Dorcasina, with a heart palpitating between hope and fear of disappointment, hastened, attended by Betty, to the place of assignation. Finding no person there, and a still and solemn silence reigning around, her heart almost died within her. But thinking it possible that some accident might have prevented O'Connor's coming at the appointed hour, she determined to enter the arbour, and wait the issue. The removal of what she first thought to be her own billet, instantly caught her attention. Taking it down, and finding it to be a different paper, her eye eagerly glanced over the contents, in full expectation of its having come from O'Connor. But how great was her astonishment, when she found it was from a person wholly unknown to her, but who appeared so deeply wounded by one glance of her person. She was far from being displeased with the discovery; her vanity was gratified with this new proof of the power of her charms; and she burned with curiosity to become acquainted with the person, in whose heart she had unwillingly made such ravages. She read the paper to Betty, requesting to know if she could form any conjecture of its author; but Betty was quite as much in the dark as herself.

"It is no common passion, Betty, with which I have inspired this enamoured youth. His language is in the true style of genuine love. Observe, he says he wanders here while others sleep, that he may sit in my seat and tread in my footsteps; and that my billet will be his greatest treasure. All this is indicative of a pure and ardent affection. What an engaging modesty he discovers too! I declare I think, if I had never seen O'Connor, I should have loved him without knowing him. But, alas, poor youth! he must sigh in vain: I have not now a heart to bestow; and it is well for the young man that he is sensible of it. He might otherwise nourish a hopeless passion, which would in time destroy him. My pity, however, he is justly entitled to; this I do not wish to withhold, and he shall have the satisfaction of knowing that it is not denied him." She then wrote as follows.

"MISS SHELDON would inform the unknown youth, who has painted his passion in such glowing colours, that she sincerely sympathises in the pains, which, on her account he appears to suffer; and, that she rejoices, for his sake, at his being sensible that to return love for love is not in her power. She, therefore, as a friend, advises him to endeavour to forget her. And as she finds him susceptible of the purest flame, she sincerely wishes that his next passion may be so fortunately placed as to meet a due return."

Having deposited this billet, in the same place with the former, she seated herself in the arbour; hoping that the love stricken Philander would soon appear, and gratify her ardent curiosity of being made acquainted with his person.

This new love adventure, so entirely occupied her, that she almost, for a time, forgot O'Connor and her recent disappointment. "Betty," said she, "I do, from my soul, pity this young man; but I think I have nothing to reproach myself with; especially since I have confessed my love for another, and advised him to forget me." "Why, no, ma'am," replied Betty; "I don't see how you can help it, if the men will fall in love with you upon sight." "I never will, Betty, sport with the heart, that is devoted to me: and how many soever it may be my lot to inspire with the tender passion, they shall have no reason to complain of being deceived. I despise the man or woman, who gives encouragement, without intending any return. Such conduct, in my opinion, is highly criminal; and whoever is guilty of it ought forever to be debarred the pleasure of connubial love."

As it was now beginning to grow dark, Betty's imagination began to be filled with the idea of spectres and ghosts; and, thinking more of what she saw, when last in the grove in the dark, than of her mistress' last speech, when it was ended, she abruptly exclaimed, "I have not the least doubt but they have, many times, been seen to walk here, by other folks beside myself." Dorcasina, not suspecting what Betty's imagination run upon, and thinking it was her unknown lover, who had been seen to walk there, eagerly asked, "Why did you not inform me that you had seen him walking here?" "Why, so I did, ma'am, as soon as ever I got home; but you wou'dn't believe a word of it, and said it was all a notion." "Pho! Betty, you are dreaming. I certainly never heard a syllable of it before. But, pray tell me, how did he look? Was he handsome, with a dejected air?" "Handsome! mercy on me! no, ma'am. Why, he looked enough to frighten a body out of their seven senses. As I told you before, he grow'd as big as a horse, with saucer eyes flaming fire, and"—"I find, Betty, we are crossing questions," interrupted Dorcasina. "Your head is filled with ridiculous notions of ghosts and spirits; and mine with good substantial flesh and blood, in the form of lovers, sighing at my feet. But I find it is time for us to be gone, or your fears will presently conjure up a host, from the infernal shades." Thus saying, she returned directly to the house, where Dorcasina received a gentle reprimand from her father, for hazarding her health, by staying so late in the grove.

The next morning, Philander hastened to the arbour, with the early lark, impelled by an eager curiosity to know the success of his billet. All he heard of the extravagantly romantic turn of Dorcasina's mind was now fully confirmed, by her answer. It exceeded his most sanguine expectations; and convinced him there were no professions too palpably absurd or gross for her to believe. Determined still further to amuse himself at her expense, he deposited the following billet.

"Superlative Excellence,

"YOUR unexpected condescension, in noticing and answering my poor scrawl, has caused me such a delirium of joy, that I hardly know how to support it; and it has so raised me, in my own esteem, that, were I admitted to your heavenly presence, I should certainly presume to kiss the hem of your garment, or be guilty of some other action equally extravagant. Your angelic goodness has almost inspired me with sufficient confidence to ask a favour. Ah! no, I dare not presume; my heart palpitates, the pen trembles in my fingers, at the bare idea of possessing so invaluable a treasure. But, have I not reason to expect every indulgence from such heavenly goodness and benevolence? Yes, I will trust them. Will you then, amiable perfection, honor me so much as to deposit, in this place, one lock, one small

lock, of your jetty hair? Pardon my boldness, and believe that
nothing but the most ardent love, that ever animated a human breast,
could have induced me to make the request.

PHILANDER."

Dorcasina was charmed with the style of this epistle, which she said
equalled, if it did not exceed, that of her dear O'Connor. The manner,
too, of its being conveyed, had something in it so romantic, so out of
the common way, and so much to her taste, that her curiosity, to know
who could be the author, was raised to the highest pitch; and she
determined to lay some little plan to come at the secret.

Kindly condescending to grant him the favour he had desired,
Dorcasina, taking her scissors from her pocket, cut off a "jetty lock,"
and carefully picking out a few white hairs, with which time had
prematurely sprinkled her head, wrapped the remainder in a piece of
clean white paper, and left it in the usual place.

As Mr. Sheldon was, luckily, to be absent, the whole of the next day,
Dorcasina was able to dispose of the boy Patrick, as she pleased, and
have no questions asked. She, therefore, told him that there was a
person frequented the arbour, whose name she had a great desire to
know; and added, that if he would conceal himself, in one of the
thickest trees, and carefully observe every person who should enter
the arbour, through the day, particularly one that would take a paper
from a certain tree, he should be liberally rewarded. To this the boy
cheerfully consented; it being quite as agreeable to sit at his ease upon
a tree, as to labour, all day, in the field. Betty having stuffed his pockets
with bread and cheese, after an early breakfast, he went whistling to
his station. But he watched in vain. Philander had, according to
custom, visited the arbour, at an early hour, and eagerly seized the
paper. He was extremely diverted at finding the lock requested; but
a little disappointed at its being unaccompanied by a billet. He,
however, pocketed the hair, and marched home to contrive some new
plan to impose on the credulity of Dorcasina, and procure amusement
to himself.

Patrick, faithful to his post, never quitted it, till it began to grow
dark. He then thought it time to return home. As soon as he arrived,
Dorcasina called him into the parlour, and eagerly questioned him
whom he had seen. "Not a living soul, ma'am, but myself." "What,
has no body taken the paper then?" "I looked all about for the paper

ma'am, but not a grain of a paper was there, no more than there is in my eye."

Dorcasina was much disappointed and perplexed that she could not come at the knowledge of this new adorer. After revolving the affair, for some time, in her mind, she concluded that he must frequent the grove in the night, as he had intimated that he wandered there while others slept. She now feared her curiosity would never be gratified; and this idea, to a person of her turn of mind, was not a little mortifying.

This new lover occupied her mind so fully, that her grief for the absence of O'Connor was greatly lessened; though she still loved him, with the warmest affection. The next day, she could not resist the inclination she felt of visiting the grove, in hopes that some new light would be thrown upon the affair. Upon entering the arbour she immediately discovered a folded paper, deposited in the usual place, which she eagerly opened and read as follows:

"HOW shall I express the transports, which thrilled my soul, when with eager, yet fearful eye, I discovered the deposited treasure. Since I have been possessed of it, I have kissed every single hair a thousand times over. But alas! I fear you will have reason to repent your heavenly condescension when you are informed that I am thereby emboldened to ask a still greater favour. I hardly dare to proceed; but my happiness, my reason, and my very life depend upon your granting it. May I indulge the transporting idea that you will grant me one interview, in this delightful retreat, that I may lay open my whole soul to the lady, who occasions me, at the same time, the bitterest pangs and the sweetest joys? I do assure you, divine Miss Sheldon, that it shall be the last favour I will ever ask, and that, after this meeting, my sorrow will be assuaged, and my soul composed. If you grant me this inestimable favour, I beg that it may be in the dusk of evening, lest my weak optics should be overpowered by the splendor of your dazzling beauty. If you deny me this one, this last request, you may expect to see me hanging on the same tree that bears your refusal.

PHILANDER."

Dorcasina read this letter over thrice, pondering on its contents and weighing them maturely in her mind. She hesitated, at first whether she should comply; and considered in what light such a step would be viewed by her dear absent lover. Having persuaded herself that when he should be informed that the life of a poor love-stricken youth depended upon it, he would approve her humanity, she, at length, determined to grant his request; especially as she would thus gratify her curiosity, while she was performing an act of charity.

Having taken her resolution, she communicated to Betty the contents of the letter. "I hope ma'am," said Betty, "you don't intend to be so unwise as to give this saucy jackanapes a meeting." "Why Betty, you surely would not have me so barbarous as to occasion the death of a fellow creature? What a shocking sight it would be to see the poor young man hanging upon one of these trees! a sight surely which would be equally distressing to us both." Betty, from the extravagant pitch to which the matter was carried, and the occular demonstration she had that her mistress was far from being beautiful, suspected the whole to be a trick, and could not conceal her indignation. "Hang himself! a likely story, truly," cried she. "I wish my head may never ache till I see that sight. An impudent rabscallion, with all his fine haranguers. I wish I had the cooking of him; he should have a ducking in the river, that would cool his love for him, I'll warrant."

"I thought, Betty, that you had more humanity. However, as it is impossible that you, who never felt the passion of love, nor read any of those affecting descriptions of it, over which I have shed so many tears, can form any idea of its force and power, or the fatal effects it sometimes produces, I shall not consider you as qualified to give advice, and shall therefore follow my own opinion and risque the consequences." This speech was uttered in so positive and serious a manner, that Betty did not think proper to reply; but sighed inwardly at this new instance of imprudence in her infatuated mistress.

Dorcasina then deposited in the tree a billet, informing her unknown enamorato that she would grant him the favour he asked, on condition that he would not repeat the request; and appointed the evening of the following day for the time of their meeting.

The next day, as evening approached, Dorcasina desired Betty to attend her to the grove. Betty, being on many accounts unwilling to go, on her knees, entreated her mistress to give up the project. But, finding her resolutely bent on fulfilling her engagement, the faithful creature, in spite of her aversion to the adventure, and of her apprehensions of ghosts and goblins, could not bear the idea that her mistress should go to the wood, at that hour, unaccompanied. She therefore followed her footsteps, in silent trepidation.

Being arrived at the arbour they seated themselves on the turf. They had not sat long, when, instead of the expected lover, a female entered, and placing herself by the side of Dorcasina, accosted her in the following manner. "You will, perhaps, be surprised," said she, "when I inform you that I know you did not come here with the expectation of meeting a woman. Philander was the person, whom you expected to see; but know, abhorred rival, that I have effectually prevented his meeting you this night, and am now come to enjoy your disappointment. I would have you to know, you witch! you sorceress! that you have robbed me of the heart of my lover; and I am determined to be revenged."

Dorcasina, as might naturally be expected, was astonished at this address; and remained, for some moments, in a profound silence. At length, she attempted to justify herself, by saying, that she was sorry to be the cause of pain to any one; that, from her own experience, she knew too well the power of love, not to commiserate any person who nourished a hopeless passion; that she had never yet seen Philander, to her knowledge; that this interview was none of her seeking; and that she had consented to it, at his earnest entreaty, on the express condition that it should never be repeated. She concluded by declaring that, as she now found he had been false to another, she would immediately retire, and hold no further intercourse with him.

This mildness served, in appearance, but to irritate the supposed female. "I know your arts too well," cried she, raising her voice, "to believe a syllable of what you say. It is all mere pretence, and you will consent to meet him again the very first opportunity. But you shall not go on thus practicing your devilish arts, with impunity. Your basilisk glance shall not thus rob every man of his heart, and every woman of her lover or husband. Those bewitching eyes, that cause mischief, wherever they are seen, I will tear them from their orbits." Thus saying, she laid violent hands on the terrified Dorcasina; tore off her hat; pulled her hair; and was proceeding to tear off her handkerchief, when Betty, seeing her mistress so roughly handled, started up in her defence, and attacking the stranger with great fury, compelled her to quit Dorcasina in order to defend herself. Dorcasina, thus liberated, darted out of the grove and fled towards the house with all speed, leaving Betty to sustain the combat alone. Finding herself deserted, and her antagonist much her superior in strength, Betty endeavoured likewise to make her escape; but her attempt was unsuccessful. She was held, cuffed, pulled by the hair, twirled round and round like a top, shaken, and pushed up against the trees, without mercy; the person, who thus roughly handled her, exclaiming, all the time, "you ugly old witch, I'll teach you to carry letters, and contrive meetings between your mistress and my lover; you pander, you go-between, you s—t!" Poor Betty begged for mercy, in the most moving terms, protesting that she had said every thing to dissuade her mistress from this meeting; but the enraged virago would not suffer her to go, till she had stripped off her upper garments (her gown being a short one, and of no great value) torn them to rags, and scattered them about the arbour. She then suffered her to depart, telling her, at the same time, that, if ever she caught her engaged in the same business again, she would not only divest her of her clothes, but strip off her old wrinkled hide.

Betty, though more frightened than hurt (for the stranger had taken care not to do her any real injury) thinking herself happy to escape with life, darted homeward, with as much speed as she had done when pursued by the white monster. On the way, she was met by Scipio, whom Dorcasina had dispatched to her assistance, informing him, in great agitation, that she did not know but Betty would be murdered, in the arbour, if he did not hasten to her rescue. Scipio, alarmed at this intelligence, ran with all speed, till he met Betty endeavouring to gain the house. "Who go dere?" cried Scipio as soon as he saw her. "Top. Is it you, Betty?" "Yes," answered Betty, "what there is left of me." "Gor bressa my soul! where you gown, you cap, you hanker, you eberyting?" "The old nick, in the form of a woman, has got them," said Betty. "Where be dis she debil? if I catch her, I trim her well." "I left her in the arbour," replied Betty. "Well, you go home; and I go pay dis debil, for scare you and misse so." Betty, who did not want to be twice desired to go home, instantly trudged off; while Scipio searched the arbour and scoured the woods in vain. The devil had disappeared.

On her arrival at the house, Betty went immediately and presented herself before her mistress, in the same forlorn plight, in which she had left the grove. "I hope you are satisfied now ma'am," said she, "and won't think of visiting that confounded arbour, to meet any more of them impudent, ill-manner'd, low-liv'd fellors, who make such a fuss, and pretend to be dying for love, and are only brewing mischief all the time." "Why you surely cannot suppose, Betty, that Philander had any hand in this mischief, any further than leaving the woman he had once pretended to love: pretended, I say; for if it had been a real passion, he could not so soon have forgotten her."

"Well, I knows what I knows. That was no woman, that handled me so. It was either a very strong man, or the old nick himself. I knows I am none of the weakest; but heaven help me! I was no more in his hands than an infant. Why, I was thump'd, and cuff'd, and bounc'd, and shook, and twirl'd, and had my clothes stripp'd off, and tore to tatters, as if I had been nothing at all. Besides, what I shall not soon forget, in a grum and angry voice, that was no woman's, he call'd me old, and ugly; go between, and strum, and a great many other hard names, which, in my fright, I forgot; Oh! I expect that vile Philander is at the bottom of it all, a good-for-nothing cur, with his pretensions of love and hanging; I declare I shou'dn't desire any better sport than to see him strung up."

"Hush! Betty; you are in a passion and know not what you say: I am extremely sorry that you were so rudely treated; but it is unjust to impute it to Philander. I dare say the poor youth is well nigh distracted at his disappointment. As to the strength exerted by the girl, it was nothing strange; for, if disappointed love does not sink into despair, it drives its victim to rage and madness; and you well know that a person bereft of reason, is, at intervals, much stronger than in the full possession of it. But go, compose yourself, and put on some clothes; and when the servants inquire about the affair, tell them no further than that, as we were sitting peaceably in the arbour, a woman distracted, or in a violent passion, entered and treated us very roughly."

Chapter XVI.

WE will now return to the mischief loving scholar, who, as the reader must have conjectured, was the identical person in woman's clothes, that had so terrified her whom he had pretended so passionately to love. He returned to his lodgings extremely well pleased with his evening's adventure; and set his brain immediately at work to invent some new plan, which would afford him equal amusement.

There had lately come into the village, and set up his trade, a little barber from Philadelphia. He was pert, conceited, foppish and talkative. Philander, being one of his customers, and hearing him often brag of the conquests he had made in the city, took it into his head to render him subservient to his designs upon Dorcasina. Accordingly, the next morning after the adventure in the arbour, going, as usual, to the shop of the barber to be dressed, and finding him alone, he called him a lucky dog, and congratulated him upon his good fortune. The barber stared and desired to know what he meant. "Mean," said Philander, "Oh I could tear out all my beard for madness, to think how much more successful you are with the ladies than I am. Why, the first lady in this village, Miss Dorcasina Sheldon, heiress to a thousand pounds a year, has fallen violently in love with you. You may now give up your shop, and your business; for you will soon ride in your coach." "How can it be?" returned the astonished barber, "I never saw her but once, in my life, and that was last Sunday at church." "The very place in which she lost her heart. You engaged her attention much more than the preacher; and she has been dying, ever since, to have an interview with you." "This is good luck, by Jupiter. I shall forever bless my stars for conducting me to this village. But how came you to be informed of it?" "Why, the truth is, I have made some advances to her myself; but she told me plainly that her friendship was all she could bestow, and was pleased to say that she should be gratified, if I would accept of that, and grant her mine, in return. With this I was forced, for the present, to be satisfied, hoping in time to gain her heart. But, last evening, she sent for me, and made me the confidant of the passion with which you had inspired her; and, at the same time, begged me, if possible, to procure her an interview. She, moreover, sent you this lock of hair, which she begs you to accept, as a token of her love."

"Gad, I don't know what the ladies see in me; but I'm a devilish lucky fellow. Tell the dear creature I will meet her, with the greatest pleasure, at any time she will please to appoint." "There is an arbour, in a grove, near her father's house," said Philander, "which Miss Sheldon frequently visits; and there I imagine she would chuse to meet you. When I have an opportunity, I will consult her, upon the time, and give you information." "What prevents you from going immediately, my lad, and letting her know that I will return her passion? What signifies letting her languish, in suspense, when she may be so easily relieved from it?"

"These delicate matters must be managed with address," replied Philander. "Her father is commonly with her, and I may visit her several times before I shall find a chance to communicate your answer. But make yourself easy; you may depend on my friendship, and best endeavours to serve you both." "Gad, my dear, you are a clever fellow; and, when I am in possession of the thousand a year, you may depend on my good offices in return."

Another customer now entered the shop and desired to be dressed; but our tippee barber, by the scholar's conversation, had been set quite above his business, and almost out of his wits. "Gad, sir," said he, "you may do your own drudgery, I'm not going to comb filthy heads, nor mow grizzly beards any longer. It's a dirty business, and I'm quite sick of it." "You are Mr. Puff?" returned the man, who happened to be of an irritable temper. "What the devil did you come here to solicit custom, and hoist your pole, on purpose to impose on us? But I'll not bear this insolence; I say you shall shave me, or I'll kick your shop down hill and throw you down after it." "Gad, sir, I advise you to take care what you say, or you may have cause to repent it. There is the door, I beg you'd walk out, sir, without giving me the trouble to put you out."

This insult raising the indignation of the choleric man to the highest pitch, he seized Puff by the collar, and, being a match for two of him, would soon have caused him to repent of his foolish vanity, had not the scholar interferred. Seeing matters begin to grow serious, and being conscious that he was the sole cause of the dispute, he begged the angry man to be calm, and then prevailed on the barber to do his duty. As soon as the man was gone, the scholar (who, though he wanted some diversion with Puff, did not wish to injure him in his business) advised him to attend to his customers as usual; intimating at the same time, that, though the lady herself was so deeply enamoured with him, there was no certainty that the match would be equally agreeable to her father; and therefore he might possibly remain a barber all his life. This piece of advice lowered, a little, the towering hopes of the barber; and the next customer, who came, he dressed without difficulty.

It now remained for the scholar to gain the consent of Dorcasina to another interview. To effect this, he contrived, after some delay, to have a letter privately conveyed to her, in which, in the most pathetic terms, he lamented his recent disappointment; representing that the lady, by whom she had been insulted, had greatly injured him; that he was not apt to boast of any favourable regards from the sex, but that, in his own justification, he was now obliged to do it. He, therefore, took the liberty to say, that the lady in question had cast upon him a favourable eye, and had made considerable advances towards an acquaintance; but that he had resolutely discouraged and rejected them all, the fair Dorcasina being the sole object of his love and affection; that, by some means or other, this had come to the lady's knowledge, as well as the honor she (Dorcasina) intended him of meeting him in the grove; that, her temper being naturally none of the mildest, this information had raised it to a tempest; that, before she went to the grove, she attacked, and abused him with her tongue, in the most outrageous manner; and then flew off, telling him that he should not meet her rival without a witness, for she was determined to keep possession of the arbour till midnight; and that, out of pure regard to the reputation of the idol of his soul, supposing she would not chuse to have a witness of their meeting, he had refrained going thither, though it had almost cost him his reason. He then conjured her, by all the powers above, to appoint him another meeting, and deposit her answer in the tree, as usual.

Dorcasina, who had suffered a good deal of uneasiness at Philander's supposed disappointment, and some mortification at not having been able to gratify her own eager curiosity respecting his person, was highly pleased at the receipt of this letter; and, without hesitation, determined to comply with his request. Having formed her resolution, she called Betty and communicated to her its contents; reminding her, at the same time, of her want of charity, in imputing the rough treatment they had met with to Philander. "Well, well, ma'am," said Betty, "be it who it wou'd, that abused me so, I hope you a'n't a going for to think of meeting him there again." "Indeed, I shall, Betty; I think I owe him this piece of complaisance, to make him some amends for his former disappointment." "Well, ma'am, if you will go, I cannot help it; but I hope that you won't insist upon my going with you?" "Indeed, I shall do that too, Betty. But, to remove your fears, I now inform you, that I intend it shall be in the day time; for I think it was rather imprudent to consent to meet a stranger in the evening; not that I am under any apprehensions, from a person so devoted to me; but because, were it known, my reputation, as he has hinted, might suffer by it."

Betty, being sensible that all she could say would be of no avail, in turning her mistress from a resolution she had once taken, especially in an affair of the heart, was somewhat relieved at hearing that she should not again have the spirits of darkness to encounter. She was, however, far from approving of her mistress' consenting to another meeting; especially as her suspicions of Philander's being the author of the mischief, which had befallen herself, were by no means removed. But, feeling no great apprehension of any similar treatment, by day light, she did not think fit to urge her remonstrances.

It being now Saturday, Dorcasina went herself and carried her answer, appointing the Monday following, at five o'clock in the afternoon, for their interview.

As soon as Philander had possessed himself of this answer, he communicated it to the barber; telling him that Miss Sheldon would meet him at the abovementioned time and place, and advising him, by no means, to let the lady wait, as she would think him insensible of his good fortune. "Never fear, my dear," replied the delighted barber; "I never yet made a lady wait for me; and I should be unpardonable to do it, now there is such a fortune depending."

Monday being come, the barber, arrayed in his Sunday clothes, with his hair as white as powder could make it, sat out, at four o'clock, for the arbour, which had been pointed out to him by Philander; who, previous to this time, judging that Puff would arrive at an early hour, had taken possession of a thick tree, to enjoy, unobserved, the coming scene. The barber found the hour of waiting very tedious. He sung, he whistled, and listened attentively to every passing noise; when, at length, his ears were saluted by the sound of female voices, which were no other than those of Dorcasina and her attendant. "Betty," said the former, "you may seat yourself, with your knitting work, without the arbour, and at a small distance from it; for it would not be treating the young man with delicacy, to admit a third person to witness his passion." Betty did as she was desired; and the little barber no sooner discovered Dorcasina approaching the arbour, than, stepping forward, and taking her hand, he addressed her with the utmost familiarity. "Gad, my dear, I began to be very impatient, and was afraid you had changed your mind; but I am very glad to see you at last; pray, my dear, be seated."

This familiar address, so different from what Dorcasina had been led to expect, and from what she had been accustomed to from O'Connor, so totally disconcerted her, that she was unable to answer a single word. She, however, did mechanically as she was desired, and seated herself upon the turf in silence. The barber, placing himself by her, and still holding the hand which she had not attempted to withdraw, pitied her, for what he thought her country timidity, and kindly endeavoured to encourage her. "I suppose, my dear, you feel a little bashful or so; but don't be afraid to confess your love. Be assured you will meet with a suitable return; and that I shall be ever grateful and kind, for being thus distinguished." Dorcasina still more confounded by this strange speech, and wholly unable to comprehend its meaning, continued silent. The barber, after waiting some moments in vain for a reply, again began. "Why gad, my dear, if you don't intend to speak, you might as well have staid at home. Pray now afford me a little of your sweet conversation, if it is but just to say how much you love me."

Here Dorcasina could contain herself no longer. "I had thought sir," said she, hesitating, "I had expected from your professions, a quite different reception from this." "Did you indeed? Gad, my dear, you are in the right." Upon this, he threw his arms round her neck, and almost stifled her with kisses. The astonished Dorcasina endeavoured to disengage herself, but in vain; for the enraptured barber continued his caresses, only at intervals exclaiming, "gad, my dear, how happy we shall be when we are married. I shall love you infinitely, I am sure." Dorcasina, at length, finding breath, in a loud and angry tone, exclaimed, "let me go this moment; unhand me, sir; I will not endure to be thus treated."

Betty, who had hitherto sat quietly knitting upon a stump, hearing the angry voice of her mistress, darted towards the arbour, and instantly recognized little Puff, who had been once or twice at the house (though unseen by Dorcasina) to dress Mr. Sheldon, and whom she had observed to be a pretty, spruce, young fellow. Her indignation being raised at his treatment of her mistress, she sprung upon him before he was aware of it, and gave him, with her large heavy hand, a rousing box on the ear; exclaiming, at the same time, in a tone of great contempt, "the little barber! as I hope to live, ma'am."

This unexpected blow had the desired effect. Puff, surprised in his turn, instantly released the mistress, and turning about to the maid, desired to know what the d——l she meant. Betty did not deign to answer him, but "stood collected in her might." Recollecting, with indignation, the treatment she had so lately received in this very spot, of which she now supposed him to be the instigator, and incensed at his unpardonable insolence to her mistress, she now rejoiced in an opportunity of taking an ample revenge, in kind, for all the affronts they had both received. Rudely grasping him therefore, under one arm (for though naturally mild, she was a virago when exasperated) "You pitiful little scoundrel," she cried, "what is it you mean by thus insulting Miss Sheldon? You pretend for to inspire* to love her, and decoy her here, on purpose to be impudent to her; besides setting some impudent varlet, in women's clothes, to insult me, t'other night." Thus saying, she boxed his ears with great fury, till the terrified barber bawled to her to desist; which she did not do till she was heartily tired.

Meanwhile, the wicked scholar, perched on the tree (determined if matters should come to extremity to descend and take the part of Puff) enjoyed the scene with the highest relish; being obliged to stuff the corner of his gown into his mouth, to prevent laughing aloud and spoiling the sport.

Betty now stood for some moments holding the culprit, as if at a loss what further punishment to inflict; when, luckily for her, there passed by at that moment in her way through the grove, a girl, to whom Puff, on his first arrival at L——, had been very gallant; but whom, since he had entertained the idea of obtaining Dorcasina, he had treated with neglect, and even contempt. "Here, Hannah," said Betty, as soon as she saw her, "come and help me punish this fellor, as he deserves." Hannah, without comprehending the cause of Betty's anger against him, and instigated solely by her own fancied wrongs, readily stepped up and did as she was desired. Betty then drew from her work-bag some skeins of yarn, with one of which they tied his hands behind him, and, with two others, bound him fast to the body of a small tree. While they were executing this part of their revenge, the fears of the barber were greatly alarmed, and he begged, for heaven's sake, to know what they intended to do. "We intend to teach you, Mr. Jackanapes," said Betty, "to mind your business in future, and not go for to making sport with ladies so much above you; and hiring persons to bang, and thump, and ill treat their maids."

*She probably meant aspire [Tenney's note].

The poor barber asserted his innocence, in the strongest terms; declaring he never ill treated any maid, or thought of making sport with any lady; that, had he not had reason to think that Miss Sheldon beheld him with a favourable eye, and appointed him this meeting, he never should have attempted such familiarities.

The two angry females, having thus taken ample revenge, quitted the arbour, and retired each to her own home. While the barber, finding himself left alone, in so retired a spot, and forlorn a situation, was bewailing his fate, in the most piteous manner; the scholar, composing his features as well as he could, jumped suddenly from the tree, and stood before him with every mark of the most violent rage on his countenance. Without giving Puff time to express either his pleasure or surprise, at this unexpected appearance, he began abusing the whole sex, in the most virulent manner; calling them a parcel of proud, deceitful, cunning, mischief-loving furies; protesting he could not have thought it possible that a lady of Miss Sheldon's character would have stooped to such mean arts, to deceive a poor innocent, inoffensive barber. He concluded by declaring that he here renounced her acquaintance, and would never, in future, hold any sort of conversation with her.

By this artful discourse, he turned the barber's suspicions from himself, and fixed all his resentment upon Dorcasina. "Why the d——l," said he, "did you not appear for my relief, when you saw me so abused by that storming virago, from whom I expected nothing less than immediate death?" "Why, to tell the truth," said Philander, "I should have been a little ashamed to have her know I was listening; but, in future, I'll keep no measures with her, I am resolved; for she has made fools of us both."

He then set himself to unbind the barber, blasting Dorcasina and her maid at every breath. This effected, he desired him not to mention the adventure, which had befallen him, but to leave the management of it to him. "I'll lay a plan," said he, "to be revenged on both mistress and maid." "Gad, my dear, that will rejoice my heart. Pray set about it immediately, for I am impatient to be revenged for treatment, which I believe no gentleman ever before experienced." "All in good time," answered the scholar; "I shall be as impatient as you are; but we must wait a proper opportunity, that our satisfaction may be compleat." Thus saying, he and the disappointed barber retired to their respective homes.

Betty, having, as beforementioned, left the arbour, trudged home, very well pleased with the satisfaction she had extorted from her supposed enemy. As soon as she saw Dorcasina, "well, ma'am, " cried she, "I have given it to him. I have made the insolent, little, cut-beard pay pretty well for his insurance."[*] "I hope you have not hurt him, Betty; for though I am angry with myself for being so imposed on, I think him too contemptible an object to excite much indignation." "He may be for you, ma'am, but not for me; and without hurting him much, what with cuffing him soundly, scolding him roundly, and leaving him tied fast to a tree, I have vented indignation enough for us both." "Tied him to a tree? Betty; why, how could you do that?" "Oh I did it ma'am; and he's there fast, and that's sufficient."

"But how long do you intend keeping him there? You certainly will not leave him, in that situation, all night?"

"I shall, at least, make him think that I intend it, ma'am, that his punishment may be the more severer; but I intends to get Scipio to go and untie him before bedtime."

"Besure, Betty, you do not let him know that I was concerned in the affair, for, to confess the truth, I am very much mortified and heartily ashamed of it." "I told you so, ma'am, and beseech'd you not to go. I hope, in future, that you will think I *do* know something." "In this affair I confess, Betty, you judged better than I did; but still there is a mystery hangs about it. I cannot believe that little insignificant barber ever composed those delightful letters which I received, as whoever wrote them must have known, by experience, the full force of the tender passion. But that little saucy fellow's language and address were as distant from it, as the antipodes from each other, I think he must have employed some person to compose them for him. They are so in the style of my dear absent O'Connor's, that I would not value the mortification of having met the barber in the grove, had I, by that means, found out their author." "I wou'dn't give a fig," said Betty, "to know any better than I do."

About nine o'clock Betty told Scipio that happening in the afternoon to meet the little barber in the grove, he had been impudent to her; and that to punish him, she had tied him to a tree. "But I suppose by this time," said she, "he is nearly frightened out of his seven senses. So I wish, Scipio, you would go and release him." Scipio very readily

* Probably assurance [Tenney's note].

consented, and went immediately to the spot; but the bird was flown. He, however, discerned the yarn, by its whiteness, lying on the ground, and carrying it home delivered it to Betty, saying, "here you yarn, Betty; but no barber dare; he get loose, and go off fore I come."

Chapter XVII.

AFTER this adventure, Dorcasina tarried at home, unmolested, a whole month; during which term, she never once visited her favourite retreat. In the interim, her mind had become tolerably composed, and her time was divided between her father, her domestic duties, and her novels. Her thoughts, however, dwelt much upon her absent lover; and his letters, the pledges of his love, were daily read over and daily caressed. She, likewise, often reflected upon the strange behaviour of the barber, and puzzled herself in conjecturing who, in the village, was capable of writing the letters, which she supposed had been by him deposited in the tree.

One evening, in the latter part of August, as she was sitting and revolving all these things in her mind, her father being absent at Philadelphia on business, a man on horseback, wrapped up in a great coat, rode up to the door, and delivering a letter directed to Miss Dorcasina Sheldon, immediately rode off again; nor did any person in the family know who he was, or whence he came. On looking at the superscription, she immediately knew it to be in the same hand with those she had taken from the tree. Her heart fluttered, with a kind of pleasure, at this discovery; for expressions of love so ardent, so similar to her own ideas, and so like those of O'Connor, could not fail of affording her some satisfaction, let them come from whom they would. With eager haste, therefore, she broke the seal, and with great delight read as follows.

"DIVINE ARBITRESS OF MY FATE,
"WHAT an eternity of tortures have I endured, since, from the friendly tree, I took the paper which designed me so much happiness. I went home, in transports almost too great for endurance. I passed a sleepless night, dwelling, in imagination, on the unspeakable bliss

you were about to confer on me. The morning found me feverish and delirious, in which situation I remained a whole week; during which time I raved, as I have since been informed, continually of you. In that time, an accursed barber was sent for to shave me. Collecting from my discourse the happiness I expected, and finding in my pocket, which he had the impudence to search, your last billet, he had the presumption to meet you at the time appointed in my stead. The punishment he suffered for his temerity was much too light. Would to heaven every bone in his skin had been broken. After the ill success of his enterprise, being touched, as he said, with remorse for having thus taken advantage of a man in a delirium, he came, on my recovery, and made a full confession of his guilt; and in the most submissive manner begged my pardon. This threw me into such a paroxysm of anger, that I certainly should have sacrificed him on the spot, had my strength been equal to my passion. But alas! being too feeble to do him any injury, his entreaties, tears and promises finally disarmed me: and prevailed on me to forgive him, upon condition that he should, on his knees, ask your pardon.

"This, divine Miss Sheldon, being my situation, I presume so far on your goodness as once more to beg you will appoint me another meeting; after which I shall, as soon as I recover sufficient strength, bid this village an eternal adieu; for I can no longer breathe the same atmosphere with her, for whom I languish in total despair. The long desired interview, too lovely Miss Sheldon, will do more towards restoring my health, than the skill of all the sons of Galen and Hippocrates combined. You alone can speak peace to my troubled soul, without which my body must continue to languish. Do not then, angelic goodness refuse me this one, this last satisfaction. I shall haunt the grove, for an answer, and I cannot say what will be the consequences of a refusal."

As soon as Dorcasina had ran over this letter, she called Betty, and in a kind of triumph, with an audible voice, read it again. "Did I not tell you, Betty, that there was something mysterious in the affair, and that the barber could not be the author of those interesting letters?" "Mysterious! sure enough," replied Betty, with great indignation. "Excuse me, ma'am; but to speak my mind of the matter freely, I believe some good-for-nothing villain writes all these letters, and plays all these pranks on purpose to plague us."

"How is it possible you can entertain so preposterous an idea, Betty? I am sure, to me it all appears perfectly natural; and the accidents (though I confess somewhat singular) such as might well happen to an amiable young man so deeply enamoured." "Why, in the first place, ma'am, it appears very strange that he shou'd go crazy for love, upon seeing you only once. But such matters I won't pretend for to dispute with you, as you say I am so ignorant about them. In the second place, it is strange they shou'd send for a barber to shave a man, out of his senses; and further, what shou'd the barber go to poking in his pockets for, unless indeed he is a thief and expected to find money there? And lastly, what cou'd he expect to get by meeting you in the grove, instead of t'other fellor?"

"Your objections, Betty, to the reality of Philander's passion are very trifling and very easily removed. Perhaps Philander himself, in his delirium, might take a fancy to be shaved and dressed, possessed with the idea that he was going to meet me. And as he says, in his letter, he raved continually of me, I think it very likely to have been the case. What the barber's inducement was for feeling in his pockets, I cannot take upon me to determine; but it might nevertheless be an honest one. Perhaps he wanted a piece of paper, on which to wipe his razor. I cannot, I confess, so easily account for his meeting me in Philander's room; but the fact is, he did do it, be his motives what they would."

Betty, judging by this speech, that her mistress was fully determined to comply with the request in the letter, sat, for some minutes, silent and sorrowful. At length, unable to contain herself any longer, she said: "well, if you wish ma'am to meet with affronts, and insults, clapperclawing, and smuggling, I would advise you to seek for them in the grove; for I'm sure you found them in plenty in your last visits there; though, to be sure, you escap'd with a whole skin; and poor I had to bear the brunt of both the battles." "Well I am sure you ought not to complain, Betty, since, in the last, you came off with flying colours. But, say no more; for I am resolved to go this once, and am likewise determined it shall be the last time: for I do not think it consistent with my engagements to O'Connor, to do any thing which can be construed into encouragement to another. And I wish to meet him this once but to satisfy the eager curiosity I feel of knowing who he is, and to assure him, with my own mouth, that his passion is hopeless."

The next morning but one the scholar rambled early to the grove, and found, to his great satisfaction, upon the friendly tree, Dorcasina's consent to grant his request.

He had told her the simple truth, when he informed her that he was about to quit the village; for he had performed his engagements, and was now at full liberty to put his mischievous plan in execution. As soon as he had breakfasted, he went to the barber, and told him that the time was now come, when he might obtain ample revenge, for the affront he had received from Dorcasina, and the abuse he had suffered from her maid. Then, unfolding to him his whole plan, he desired him to be at the arbour, in women's clothes, about the dusk of evening; to which the barber most joyfully consented.

Philander next paid a visit to a young farmer of a merry turn, who lived about two miles from Mr. Sheldon's, on a cross, unfrequented road; and with whom he had become acquainted in some of his long and frequent rambles. Being pleased with the humour of the man, so congenial to his own, he had rested frequently at his house, and they had contracted a considerable degree of intimacy. He now took him aside, and told him he wanted his assistance, to be revenged on a girl who had jilted him; that on his first coming to the village, he had been introduced to her, and was so much pleased with her that he had paid her his addresses, and was at first favourably received; but that, falling in company with a young coxcomb from Philadelphia, she had entirely discarded him. He then acquainted him more particularly with the plan of his pretended revenge, and desired him to be at the arbour, in Mr. Sheldon's grove, in the dusk of evening, with the little covered cart, in which he carried his produce to market. The farmer relished the joke, and promised to be punctual at the time and place appointed.

We will now return to Dorcasina, who was almost as impatient, from curiosity, for the hour of assignation, as she had formerly been, from love, when she was to meet O'Connor. The afternoon being warm, she dressed herself in an elegant dishabille, and repaired, at the usual hour to the grove. Calling to mind the delicious moments she had spent there in company with one whom her soul loved, she passed the time till six (the hour of assignation) in wandering pensively about the place.

She, at length, retired to the arbour, and seated herself to receive her new enamorato; while Betty stood a little without, leaning in a melancholy mood against a tree, waiting, with no small degree of apprehension, for the arrival of she knew not whom.

It was now near sunset, when a young man genteelly dressed, of a middling stature, pale complexion, pleasing countenance, with eyes full of fire and expression, made his appearance. As soon as he perceived Dorcasina he stopped, and bowing most respectfully, said, "Am I at length permitted, O sun of beauty, and sum of all perfection, after such repeated disappointments, to approach your adorable presence?" "I know not sir," replied she, "but I am guilty of an impropriety, in permitting it; but your letters, while they demonstrated you to be every way amiable and worthy, moved me so much that I could not find in my heart to deny your request." The scholar then, falling on his knees, exclaimed, "what shall I do to render myself worthy of such goodness and heavenly condescension? Such praise from your lips is almost too much to be borne. You must not look thus kindly, thus sweetly upon me; I shall be tempted to forget the distance there is between us, and to flatter myself with the fascinating idea of supplanting my happy rival, in your affections."

"I should repent having seen you, sir, should you take this advantage of my generosity, in consenting to meet you; and, to prevent your entertaining any ideas of the kind, I must tell you that my affections are unalterably placed, and my solemn promise given to their dear object, never to unite myself with any other man." "O wretch that I am," exclaimed Philander; "must I then, banished from your presence, far from her who is dearer than life itself, drag out the remnant of my life in misery and despair?" "I fear, sir, you will make me repent my indulgence," replied Dorcasina. "As you intimated that one interview would ease your troubled heart, I expected that, after having spent a short time in my company, you would have departed in peace." "Alas!" said the scholar, "when I wrote the letter, I was of the same opinion; but I was deceived: I am now a thousand times more your slave than ever, and I find it will be impossible for me to live without you. Have pity on my sufferings, then; drive me not from your presence to distraction or death. Mr. O'Connor (Oh the detestable name) is absent, perhaps he will never return. Endeavour, then, to transfer that affection for one, who by a voluntary absence has shewn himself unworthy of so much bliss, to a present, a despairing, a dying lover." To this Dorcasina replied: "You greatly injure Mr. O'Connor, sir; I cannot suffer any person to cast a reflection upon him. I applaud him for leaving me; he had the strongest reasons for doing it. But, being bound by his affection, as well as his vows, when he can do it with propriety he will undoubtedly return. But, if I were sure never to see him again, I must repeat it, sir, I am no less bound by affection than promises, and never, never will this heart admit another love. I pity you, sir, from my soul; and will confess that you appear so amiable, that had not my affections been unalterably fixed on another, before I had the pleasure of knowing you, your violent passion would have pleaded strongly in your favour. But, as there is now no hope for you, I applaud your resolution of quitting me forever. Time and absence may effect your cure; and, if your heart should ever admit a second flame, may the object of it be unengaged, sensible of your merit, and return your love with equal ardour. And now, sir, wishing that you may be soon cured of a hopeless passion, and find that happiness with another fair, which it is out of my power to bestow, I bid you adieu." Thus saying, she rose to depart, the sun being sunk beneath the horizon, and the shades of evening fast approaching. The mischievous scholar, however, took both her hands, and with a gentle sort of violence detaining her, besought her not to leave him; but, as it was the last time he should have the happiness of conversing with her, to suffer him to protract that happiness as long as possible.

While she stood irresolute, listening to his extravagant professions, endeavouring frequently to go, and he as often preventing her, the barber, as had been concerted, suddenly rushed, in women's clothes, into the arbour. "So perfidious!" exclaimed he; "have I caught you in the very act of paying your vows to my detested rival?" So saying, he flew at the affrighted Dorcasina, apparently with a design of committing some violent action. But the scholar protected her, by placing himself between them; begging him for heaven's sake to consider what he was about, and not to molest an innocent angelic lady, who had never injured him. "Never injured me?" cried the pretended forsaken one. "Have I not at this moment occular demonstration of the most cutting of all injuries, her meeting you at such a place, and at such an hour?"

The scholar was about to reply, when he was interrupted by the arrival of the farmer, in his covered cart; who, as soon as he had stopped his horse, made up to Betty, and with the assistance of the barber, who now left the arbour and joined him, bound up her mouth with a handkerchief, and with a line tied her hands fast behind her. But this they did not accomplish without a powerful resistance; for, as has been before observed, she was blessed with a larger portion of bodily strength than usually falls to the lot of women; and on this occasion she exerted it, most manfully, in struggling, kicking, pushing, and twisting; so that, had not the farmer been an uncommonly stout man, he must entirely have given over the enterprise. While the farmer and barber were thus employed without, upon the maid, the scholar was treating the mistress within in the same manner. He drew a silk handkerchief from his pocket, which, in spite of her resistance he tied round her mouth; then taking out another, he with less difficulty secured her hands. In the mean while, he begged her not to be alarmed, assuring her, that no harm was intended her; but declared his passion was such that he could not live without her, and that, having no prospect of her yielding to his addresses, he had taken the only method left him, which was to carry her off by force.

He then, with ease carried her in his arms to the cart, where he stood waiting a moment for assistance to put her in. Betty being secured, the barber now came up to the cart, and pretending ignorance of the scholar's design, inquired what he meant by thus binding his rival. "What, ingrate, is your design? if you mean her any ill, I rejoice at it, and will assist you with all my heart." "My present intention," replied the scholar, "is to get her into this cart;" upon which they both took hold, and seated her in it, without much difficulty. The femalized barber then jumped in, and taking his seat beside her, vowed that she should not think to go off so with her lover, for he was determined to follow and see the end of it, if it were only to punish him for his inconstancy.

The farmer now approached with Betty in his arms; for as she refused to budge a single step, he was obliged to clasp her round the waist, and thus to lug her along with her feet dragging on the ground, till they reached the cart, where the scholar stood ready to assist in hoisting her in. In this part of the business, they expected much difficulty; but the faithful creature, finding how her mistress was disposed of, and not being able to endure the idea of leaving her in this distress, suffered herself to be placed in the cart, without further opposition. She was followed by the scholar, and the whole four were, thus cooped up together in this rural carriage; while the farmer walked by the side of the horse, which, with his heavy load, moved slowly out of the wood.

The suddenness of this transaction surprised, rather than terrified Dorcasina. There was something so charmingly romantic in thus being carried off by force, that while she thought only of herself, she was by no means displeased. But, when she reflected upon the distress and anguish it would occasion her father at his return from Philadelphia, her whole soul was dissolved in grief; and she began to weep and sigh most bitterly. Philander, observing her situation, endeavoured to alleviate her distress. He begged pardon for this seemingly rough treatment, alleging the immensity of his love in excuse; and assured her that, after he had conveyed her to a place of safety, it would be his supreme delight to prevent her every wish. "Believe him not," exclaimed the barber; "he will be false and ungrateful, as he has been to me; and the first new face he sees, that has any pretensions to beauty, will estrange him from you entirely."

Then addressing himself to Betty, who sat in the most disconsolate manner, attending to the conversation, "you" said he, "you ugly, fat, beef eating virago, you vile go-between, that faithless youth would never have gone such lengths with your mistress, if you had not encouraged and assisted him. I dare say your greasy palms were crossed by many a piece of silver for decoying her into the grove. Oh! I could pluck every hair from your head, and almost tear your eyes out." Thus saying, he laid violent hands upon her, pulled her hair, shook her, pinched her, and mauled her; but did not do either, with so much violence as he would, with a very good will have done, had he not been restrained by a promise Philander had obtained from him, not to do her any real injury: "for," observed the scholar, "it would be acting too dastardly a part to retaliate her former abuse, when she has no chance of defending herself. When she has the use of her hands, you may engage her, in as close combat as you please, and I will not interfere."

Dorcasina was seriously distressed at hearing Betty so unjustly accused, and so roughly treated; which the scholar perceiving, whispered her not to be under any apprehension; for, if that virago did not presently desist, he would throw her, head foremost, out of the cart. Having now got into the bye road, which led to the farmer's house, he began to whistle as had been previously concerted; upon which the scholar, unperceived by the barber, reached his arms round Betty, and in an instant disengaged her hands, and the next minute took the handkerchief from the mouth of her mistress. Betty, overjoyed at finding her hands once more at liberty, immediately untied the handkerchief and loosed her tongue also. Determined not to lose a moment's use of them, she assailed the poor barber with both, in the most furious manner; who, supposing she had, by her own exertions liberated them, endeavoured manfully to defend himself. The contest was furious, but short; for in a few minutes Betty pitched her antagonist fairly out of the cart. Finding himself very well upon his feet, the poor barber did not attempt to remount it, but walked along behind, contenting himself with abusing Betty, with the hardest names, and most opprobrious language; while Betty, satisfied with her triumph, sat silently listening to the conversation within, and let him rail on totally unheeded.

"What can you propose to yourself," said Dorcasina to Philander, "in thus forcibly carrying me away? A heart I have not to bestow; and even were I to consent to give you my hand, I cannot suppose you would wish to receive the latter unaccompanied by the former." "You judge me very justly, too lovely Miss Sheldon. I should be more wretched, if possible, than I have been for months past, were I master of your person, while your heart belonged to another. But I intend, by my obsequiousness, my tenderness, my unwearied attention and unabated affection, to force you, in spite of yourself, to forget that hateful O'Connor, and to bestow those regards upon me, of which he has rendered himself so totally unworthy." "You flatter yourself with vain expectations," returned Dorcasina. "I have repeated to you so often that my heart is incapable of change, that I hoped, by this time, you were fully convinced of it; but I find I must again make the same declaration. Know then, sir, once for all, that all the tenderness, affection and assiduity you can possibly show me, will never be able, for a single moment, to estrange my affection from my dearest O'Connor. So, pray, sir, release me, and let me return home before my father arrives. My heart bleeds when I think what his sufferings will be, when he comes home and finds me gone, nobody knows whither."

> "None without hope e'er lov'd the brightest fair;
> "But love can hope, where reason wou'd despair,"

repeated Philander. "I shall, at least, make trial of gaining your affections. And, if after years spent in the closest attendance, I should not succeed in supplanting my rival, I shall at least have the satisfaction of reflecting that I did every thing that man could do to move you. Meantime, make yourself easy, loveliest and most adorable of women, with respect to your father. We shall soon stop for the night, and then you may write him what you please; and depend on its being safely conveyed to him, as soon as we have gotten sufficiently out of his reach."

Betty, who sat listening in silence, began now to think that there was no trick in it, but that Philander was seriously in love with her mistress, and really determined to carry her off. Philander, weary of racking his invention for extravagant speeches, now, for the first time since they had mounted the cart, remained silent. Dorcasina sat in a half pleased; half pensive mood; reflecting now upon her father's distress, and now upon her own curious situation. In this mood, and in this manner, they arrived about nine o'clock at the house of the farmer. Dorcasina and her maid were shewn into a small room by themselves, in which was a bed. Soon after some supper was prepared and set before them, but neither of them discovering any inclination to eat, the victuals was removed untouched.

Philander, now entering the room with pen, ink and paper, "Here, charming Miss Sheldon," said he, "here are materials for informing your father of whatever you wish him to know. After you have written, I will dispose of the letter, so that he will receive it immediately on his return." "O! sir," replied Dorcasina, to whom the idea of being parted from her father became now very painful; "dismiss me, send me back, restore me to that disconsolate parent, I beseech you. Do this, and return with me to the village, and I here solemnly promise that you shall have free access to me; that you shall have quite as good opportunities of urging your suit as you can possibly have by retaining me a prisoner." "My dearest angel," replied Philander, "I am sorry to see you thus distressed; but my resolution is taken and I cannot recede. Be calm, and composed; cheer up your spirits, and I will contrive some method of conveying letters frequently between you and your father." Thus saying, he left the room; while Dorcasina, with streaming eyes, sat down to give her father an account of her situation.

> "Honored and Dear Sir,
> "HOW shall I find words to express the anguish I feel, at being torn from the best and tenderest parent that ever lived? Yet, be assured that my distress, on my own account, falls far short of what I suffer on yours. For your better comprehending this strange adventure, I must acquaint you with some particulars, of which you are at present entirely ignorant. About six weeks since, as I was musing in my favourite arbour, I espied my name, cut in various places, on the bark of the trees. A few days after, I found a paper, on one of the trees, addressed to me, from an unknown adorer containing expressions of the most fervent and despairing love that ever were penned. I soon after received another in the same way, supplicating

me, in the most earnest manner, to deposit for him, in the tree, a small lock of my hair. In compassion to his sufferings, I complied with his request; and immediately after I received another letter, begging me, in the most moving terms, to grant him one interview in the grove; which, he said, would serve greatly to compose and soothe his sufferings; declaring, at the same time, it should be the last favour he would ask; and that if I did not condescend to grant it, he would hang himself, on the same tree which bore my refusal. What could I do, my dear sir? I could not support the idea of causing the death of a fellow creature. I therefore consented to meet him. Several causes, too tedious to relate, repeatedly prevented our concerted interview. But, the third time, there entered the arbour a genteel, agreeable young man, whom I had never before seen, and to whose real name I am yet a stranger. He was transported at the sight of me, and urged his passion in as strong, though it must be confessed, not in quite as humble terms as he had done in his letters. He insisted on my forgetting O'Connor and transferring my affections to him. As well might he have insisted that the loadstone should no longer attract the needle, as that the graces and virtues of O'Connor should cease to attract my fondest affections! I urged my solemn promise, and inviolable attachment; and that his hopes and expectations would be all vain. It grew dark, and I made several attempts to retire; but he still detained me, urging his passion, till a man arrived with a vehicle to convey us out of the wood. They then immediately (with the help of a woman who appears to be distracted, one minute execrating, and the next assisting him) confined the mouth and hands of Betty and myself, and conducted us to the house where I now write with the situation of which I am entirely unacquainted. By the time, however, which it took to bring us here, I judge it to be four or five miles distant from the grove. Whither I am to be carried from hence I know not; but the young man promises me all the tenderness and attention possible, by which means he vainly hopes to rob O'Connor of my heart. But the promise, which affords me the greatest consolation is, that I shall frequently be permitted to write to, and receive letters from my dearest father. And now, sir, I beg of you to be comforted, and trust to the goodness of heaven that it will in due time permit us to meet again, in peace and happiness.

"From your affectionate,
"and afflicted daughter,
"D. Sheldon."

"P. S. Notwithstanding your prejudice against O'Connor, I hope, Sir, if we are permitted to correspond, and you should receive any intelligence of that much injured youth, you will have the goodness to give me information of it."

Dorcasina, having finished the letter, sent Betty out for a wafer, who immediately returned, accompanied by Philander and the femalized barber. The former, addressing himself to Dorcasina, said, "I must see the contents of your letter, Miss Sheldon. You are my prisoner, and the laws of war do not permit any paper to pass without inspection. But my principal motive for desiring it is the pleasure, with which my soul is filled, on perusing whatever is penned by your fair hand. Madame Sevignie herself never wrote with half the ease, grace, and elegance, which are conspicuous in the billets of my fair enslaver."

Dorcasina, soothed and gratified by this compliment, immediately gave him the letter; saying, at the same time, "I have not the least objection to your seeing it, sir. It contains nothing private, nothing new, nothing but what I have repeatedly told you."

Philander took the letter, and walked into the other room, where he laughed, till his sides were ready to burst, at this new instance of the vanity and credulity of Dorcasina.

Meantime, the barber, who had been left in the room with the mistress and her maid, again began to rave in a frightful manner at being deprived of the heart of Philander. When, all at once, becoming calm, he walked about in a musing posture, as if something had just occurred to his mind. Then, after having opened the window, and put out his head, as if to examine something, he went to the door and turned a button which made it fast. These manoeuvers somewhat alarmed Dorcasina; though Betty, knowing, by what passed in the cart, that she was more than a match for him, discovered no signs of uneasiness. However, he was more disposed to be their friend than they expected. Agreeably to the plan concerted between him and Philander, he addressed Dorcasina in the following terms: "Though I abhor you more than I can express, for having robbed me of the heart of my lover, yet I am now inclined to do you a piece of service. But think not, proud beauty, it is you alone I mean to assist; no, in serving you I shall serve myself; and, at the same time, disappoint the faithless Philander, by separating you I hope forever. If you will promise me never to hold any further correspondence with my perjured lover, either by writing or conversation, I promise, on my part, to conduct you back this night in safety to your father's house."

Dorcasina, sufficiently gratified with the attempt at carrying her off, most joyfully consented to the proposal of the barber, and readily made the promise required. "You have nothing to do then," said he, "but to get out at this window, and go through the fields, into the road. Philander is now busily employed in reading your letter, after which he will go to supper, and perhaps to bed; so that, probably, he will not miss you till morning. I am well acquainted with every step of the way, and will be your guide till I see you safe home. Come, follow me, and fear nothing." So saying, he sprung out of the window; Dorcasina and Betty following his example. Then, leading them a long way through fields and over fences, he brought them at last to the road. The two females, alarmed at every leaf that stirred, and looking behind them at every step, fearing they were pursued, had hitherto walked very fast. But, being now much fatigued, they were obliged, in spite of their fear, to slacken their pace. Having, by this means, gained a little breath, Dorcasina thus addressed her supposed female companion. "You have no reason, I assure you Miss, for being so greatly my enemy. This evening is the first time I ever saw Philander; and, you may depend upon it would have been the last, though the business had not terminated in this unexpected way. To convince you of my sincerity, I will now inform you that I am engaged to another gentleman, far superior to him in every grace and accomplishment; and with him alone I expect happiness: and further, if it is in my power to assist you in regaining the heart of your lover, there is nothing I would not do to serve you."

The barber, apparently molified by this frankness and generosity, but in reality only the more irritated at her, for endeavouring to make a fool of him, while under engagements to another, replied, "If the case be really as you say, I forgive you, with all my heart; especially since, having succeeded in getting you out of his power, I may hope to be restored to the happiness of which you deprived me." "Very well," said Dorcasina, "we will forget what is past, and in future be friends. I will thank you, Miss, to inform me of Philander's real name; where he belongs, and whither you suppose he would have carried me." "His name," replied the barber, "I am under a solemn promise not to reveal; for, notwithstanding his inconstancy, my love for him is so great, that his influence over me is unbounded. He belongs to

Connecticut, and would most probably have carried you thither." "To Connecticut!" exclaimed Betty, "mercy upon me; what among the savage Indians? How thankful I am that we have escaped. We should, most likely, have been scalped, or, perhaps, roasted alive." "There are christian people, undoubtedly, in the place that Philander came from," replied the barber; "but how you would have faired, in case of a war with the natives, I cannot tell." Dorcasina smiled at the ignorance of both; but did not think it worth while to undeceive them.

Dorcasina, unused to longer walks than what the grove afforded her, was by this time excessively wearied, and stopping frequently, declared she could go no farther. But the revengeful barber as often encouraged her, saying she had now but little way to go, and would soon reach her father's house. In this manner he led them a round about way five miles, the direct one being but two. This was entirely a plan of his own; as he thought thereby to retaliate, both on mistress and maid, the disgraceful treatment he had received from them. At length, about one o'clock, they reached Mr. Sheldon's, Dorcasina so exhausted with fatigue that she could not get up stairs without assistance. The barber, wishing them a good night, at the door, went home fully satisfied with the revenge he had taken.

The servants of the house were overjoyed at their arrival. They had began to be alarmed by ten o'clock, at their staying so much later in the grove than usual; and Scipio with a white servant, had gone thither in quest of them. Not finding them there, they concluded that Dorcasina had gone to pass the evening at Mr. Stanly's and had taken Betty with her.

The clock having struck eleven, and Dorcasina not appearing, the servants again sallied forth and went in pursuit of her to Mr. Stanly's; but finding the family all in bed, they retired without disturbing them. They then went to every house, where she ever visited, with no better success. One of the maids then suggested an idea that she might have taken the opportunity of her father's absence to leave his house, and go to O'Connor, with a design of being married: upon this, they all mounted in a body to her chamber, but, finding every article of her clothing (which was not locked up) remaining, except what she had on, they quickly abandoned their last opinion, and remained in doubt and consternation, till their arrival at the hour beforementioned.

As Dorcasina retired immediately to bed, the servants all gathered round Betty, to know where they had come from, so late and so fatigued. "Lord help me," cried Betty, "let me sit down and take a little breath; for I declare I never was so tired before, since I was born." After a short respite, she gave the following account of their evening's adventure.

"In the first place you must know," said she, "there is a young gentleman violently in love with Miss Dorcasina, who has been teasing and teasing her by letters to meet him in the grove. But I argufied against it with all my might; for I had a notion that it was only somebody did it to impose on her. However, she had such a curiosity to know who the spark was, that writ her letters, which she said beat O'Connor's, though he didn't put his name to 'em, that she would go, this afternoon, to meet him, and wou'd make me go with her. She seated herself in the arbour and I stood outside, worried enough, heaven knows, for fear no good was intended us. Presently comes the spark, who had writ the letters, and goes into the arbour and makes a great many fine speeches to Miss Dorcasina. Then comes one of the devil's daughters, I do verily believe, flying into the arbour, and would, I do believe, have torn out Miss Dorcasina's eyes, if the young gentleman hadn't kept her off. She was in a monstrous passion, declaring as how that the gentleman was her sweetheart, and Miss Dorcasina had got him away, and she would be revenged, and all that. Well, would you believe it, next comes a great stout man, driving a horse-cart. He attacked me, and the woman helped him. I screamed, and he tied my mouth up with a handkerchief. I sit, and kick'd, and pull'd his hair, and he then tied my hands behind me with a rope. He then dragg'd me along, (for I was resolved not to budge a foot) to the cart, into which the gentleman had put Miss Dorcasina, bound and gagg'd just as I was. Seeing the poor dear lady thus cooped up, I cou'dn't bear the thoughts of leaving her; so I let 'em put me into the cart too. Then jumped in that torment of a woman, vowing she would follow us to the world's end; and being all four seated, the man driv away. My evil spirit, the woman, then begun for to pinch and to punch me, and pull my hair, and jamm me up against the side of the cart, as if she was possessed, saying that it was I who had contriv'd the meeting between her sweetheart and Miss Dorcasina; while, heaven knows, I said all I cou'd against it. But my mouth and hands was tied, so I was forc'd to grin and bear it. But presently the young gentleman, seeing how I was buffeted, reached round and loosed my hands, and, I fackens, I no sooner found them at liberty, than I gave her as good as she sent, and push'd her fairly out of the cart; and she follow'd on scolding and calling me all manner of names. But I didn't mind her, and so we went on, till we stop't at the house of the cartman. The gentleman, palarvering up Miss Dorcasina, now told her she might write to her father; and the woman, that had plagu'd us so much, brought some supper; but we cou'dn't eat a bit. Bye and bye, she all at once turned our friend, and said, tho' she hated Miss Dorcasina worse than a serpent, she would help us to get away, if it was only to plague her sweetheart; so she straddled out of the window, when there was nobody in the room but us three, and we follow'd; and I believe in my heart we have come full twenty miles!"

Here Betty ceased speaking, and the servants were all in astonishment, declaring they never, in all their lives, heard any thing so strange.

Betty being weary, and the rest of the servants having their curiosity gratified, they betook themselves to rest; and, buried in sleep, equally forgot the anxieties of the evening, and the toils of the day.

Next morning, Dorcasina was so stiff that she could hardly turn herself in bed. She did not, therefore, attempt to rise till near eleven o'clock; but lay ruminating on the preceding night's adventure with no small degree of satisfaction. The very same accident had formerly happened to Harriot Byron, though she was, to be sure, rescued in a different manner; and Dorcasina's satisfaction would have been complete, had O'Connor chanced to have been her deliverer. Her vanity, which before needed no addition, was now raised to the highest pitch; and she began to think, if she thus killed people, at a glance, it would be her duty, whenever she appeared in public, to veil her charms. In the midst of her reverie, she sighed with compassion for the unhappy youth, who had thus become her slave; and wondered greatly how he would bear his disappointment, and whether she should see, or hear from him again.

The scholar, on his part was so amused with the character of Dorcasina, and so delighted with the success of his plan (respecting which he hoped she would never be undeceived) that he scarcely closed his eyes the whole night; and, early in the morning, he left the village, to return to the place of his nativity in Connecticut.

Chapter XVIII.

DURING these transactions at L——, Mr. Sheldon had fortunately made a discovery, at Philadelphia, which he flattered himself would enable him to cure his daughter of her foolish passion for O'Connor. Going one day into the court of judicature, which was then sitting, he observed at the bar a prisoner, in whom he instantly recognized that abandoned villain. The night he left L——, in the manner before related, he rode towards New York, to which city he at first intended going. Stopping in the morning at an inn on the road, he called for some breakfast, and afterwards for a bed, upon which he threw himself and slept till noon. During dinner, he observed in a cupboard, a number of silver spoons, a pair of canns, and some other small pieces of plate. His money being nearly exhausted, it struck his fancy to convert the silver he saw to his own use. He, therefore, passed the afternoon at the same place, which he employed in observing the house and the stable. He was much pleased, at finding that all the family slept above stairs, and that the chamber alloted him was directly over the treasure he had set his heart on filching. At midnight, when the family were buried in sleep, he stole softly down stairs, and, forcing the lock of the cupboard, he appropriated to himself the canns and the other articles, and left the house undiscovered. Then taking his horse from the stable, he altered his rout, and retraced his steps towards Philadelphia; intending to continue his tour into the southern states. He rode till noon, next day, without stopping for a moment, and had nearly reached the city; when being spent with fatigue and want of food, his horse also refusing to go any farther, he stopped again at an inn; and, after having dined, went directly to bed; intending, in the evening, to reach Philadelphia.

Meantime, his host of the preceding night, who was a very early riser, discovered, on going into the room where O'Connor had supped, that he had been robbed. Having no suspicions of O'Connor, who had so much the manners and appearance of a gentleman, and no other stranger having lodged there, he supposed his plate must have been carried off by some evil minded person who had entered the house during the night. But finding our gentleman's horse missing from the stable, and his person from his chamber, he had no hesitation in fixing the theft upon his Hibernian lodger.

Upon this discovery, he instantly raised his family and some of his neighbours, and dispatching some one way, some another, he himself took the road to Philadelphia. Inquiring of every person he met, if they had seen such a one as O'Connor, whom he minutely described, he found, before noon, that he had got upon the right track, as such a person had been seen by several people spurring his horse, and driving on in a most jehu-like manner. Towards night he arrived at the very inn where our adventurer, buried in sleep, did not so much as dream of the mischief which was so soon to befal him. Upon entering his chamber, with a warrant, the things were found in a portmanteau, and he was immediately conveyed to the city, and safely lodged in the new prison, to take his trial at the next session of the Supreme Court; which fortunately happened while Mr. Sheldon was in the city. So many circumstances appearing against our unlucky adventurer, he was condemned to receive a public whipping, and to be imprisoned for three months.

As soon as Mr. Sheldon heard this sentence pronounced, he hastened to his lodgings; and, taking aside the lady of the house, a Mrs. G. who was a very discreet woman, and a great friend to him and his daughter, he briefly informed her, that an Irishman, some time since, by a pleasing exterior, and pretending to be a man of family and fortune, had ingratiated himself into Dorcasina's affections; that he had soon discovered him to be a worthless adventurer; but that his daughter was so blinded by her prejudices in his favour, that she was not to be persuaded of the falsehood of his pretensions; that upon his refusing to consent to the match, the Irishman had abruptly left the village, carrying with him the affections of his daughter; that, having just been in the court, he had seen him a prisoner at the bar, and heard him sentenced to be whipped and imprisoned for theft; thinking this a favourable opportunity of convincing his daughter that she had placed her love on one of the vilest of mankind, he was determined to return home immediately and bring her to be a witness of his punishment. Mrs. G. approving his resolution, he set out immediately for L——, and arriving the day but one after the last famous adventure of the grove. Dorcasina, who always rejoiced at her father's return, was now uncommonly pleased, as he came sooner, by some days, than she had expected him, and because she burned with impatience to communicate to him the particulars of her late adventure.

"You have surprised me agreeably, sir, by returning so soon." "My stay will be short, my dear. I shall only rummage up some papers necessary for settling the business I have in hand, and return to Philadelphia tomorrow, to put an end to it. What say you to bearing me company? It is a long time since you have visited the city, and Mrs. G. wishes much to see you." "Nothing can afford me more satisfaction sir," said Dorcasina, "and I cordially thank you for the invitation." Dorcasina consented so much the more readily to this journey, as she entertained a secret hope of meeting in the city her beloved O'Connor. And so fully did this idea take possession of her mind, that she lay awake the greater part of the night, feasting her imagination on the transports of their meeting, and framing arguments to convince her father of his innocence.

Next morning, as soon as breakfast was over, Mr. Sheldon and his daughter sat out in their coach for the metropolis. The latter, thinking this a good opportunity for unburthening her mind, began and related every circumstance of her acquaintance with Philander, from his carving her name on the trees to his audacious attempt to carry her off.

Mr. Sheldon listened in silence with mingled sensations of indignation and astonishment: indignant at the impudence and duplicity of Philander, and astonished to the last degree, at the blindness and credulity of his daughter. When she had made an end of her relation, he thus addressed her: "Was it possible, then, that you could think Philander serious in his pretensions? Why, the very extravagance of them carries the demonstration of their falsehood. You may depend upon it, he did it only to divert himself and impose upon you; and your being attacked in the grove, by the woman and the barber, was of a piece with the rest of his plan, as well as your escape from the house to which he conveyed you. He had carried the joke as far as he intended, and then suffered you to make your escape. Oh! he is an impudent scoundrel; and if I can but discover who he is, I will make him pay dear for his unpardonable insolence."

"Indeed, sir," replied Dorcasina, "you quite mistake the matter. Never was a poor youth more violently smitten; and, had you but seen and heard him, you would have been convinced of it to a demonstration. His attempt to carry me away was but the natural consequence of his despair. And, beside, it was no new thing; for I have frequently read of ladies being forcibly carried off by resolute lovers." "Oh! those poisonous, those fatal novels!" exclaimed Mr. Sheldon; "how have they warped your judgment, and perverted your understanding. Would to heaven people could find some better employment, than thus turning the heads of inexperienced females! Would to heaven I could have foreseen the fatal consequences of allowing you a free access to them! But it is now too late, and the evil I fear is irreparable."

Dorcasina, surprised in her turn, at hearing her father express himself in so unusual and passionate a manner, and finding it vain to endeavour to bring him into her sentiments, dropped the subject and was silent; but was totally at a loss to conceive what could have happened, so suddenly to excite her father's indignation against those delightful books, from which they had both reaped so much amusement.

They had a pleasant journey to Philadelphia, where they arrived about the middle of the afternoon. Mrs. G. not having seen Dorcasina for ten years, received her with great politeness, and real satisfaction.

The next morning at ten o'clock, was the hour appointed for O'Connor to receive his punishment. After breakfast, therefore, Mr. Sheldon proposed to his daughter to get into a chaise, and ride with him round the city, in order to observe the alterations that had taken place since her last visit. She consented, with great cheerfulness, and he contrived to be on the spot at the moment they were tying up the criminal. Naturally of a compassionate make, and averse from exhibitions of cruelty of any kind, Dorcasina turned away her head, and begged her father to hasten from the scene. This was the moment for the exertion of all his fortitude. The remedy was painful even to himself; but he hoped it would be effectual to his daughter. Instead, therefore, of hastening, as Dorcasina had requested, he stopped the chaise, and desired her to look but for a moment, and tell him whether that was not one of their acquaintance, or whether he was deceived. She did as she was desired, and beheld O'Connor. They gave him the first stroke and she went into a strong hysteric fit.

Mr. Sheldon, greatly alarmed, fearing he had gone too far, hastily drove off, holding his daughter in the chaise with one hand, and stopped at a small distance, at the house of an acquaintance. Here, with the assistance of another gentleman, he carried her in and laid her upon a bed; where it required some strength to confine her, till the arrival of a physician; and then it was a long time before she recovered.

When her senses first returned, she looked round with surprise, being unable to comprehend where she was, or how she came thither. Mr. Sheldon, reading her thoughts, briefly informed her that she was taken with a fit in the street, and that he had brought her into the house of his friend Mr. D. whom with his lady he now introduced to her. The mention of the street bringing to her recollection the dreadful scene to which she had been witness, the sluices of her eyes were immediately opened, and she wept most bitterly. The Doctor, observing that tears would afford her more relief than all his medicines, took his leave; while Mrs. D. supposing them to be the consequence of her disorder, sat silent, and patiently waited to see her more composed.

Their wishes were at length gratified. By degrees she grew calm, and begged her father to carry her back to Mr. G's. In attempting to rise she found herself so weak she could hardly stand. Mrs. D. with great kindness, urged her to tarry till she should have recovered her strength; and her father joined in the request. She, however, declined their proffered civility; and thanking them for their politeness, with the assistance of her father and Mr. D. she reascended the chaise and returned to Mr. G's. During the ride, although Mr. Sheldon made several observations upon indifferent subjects, Dorcasina made no reply. Being arrived, she informed Mrs. G. that, having had a fit in the street, she wished to retire to her chamber, and to be there left alone and undisturbed. Mrs. G. conjecturing the cause, thought best to indulge her without opposition; and after she and Mr. Sheldon had led her to her chamber, they both retired and left her to her own reflections.

"I have had a painful task," said Mr. Sheldon, as soon as they were seated. "The expedient was a disagreeable, but I trust it will be a successful one." He then briefly related all that had happened; at the same time, requesting Mrs. G. to take no notice of it to his daughter, and to let her have her own way as long as she should remain her guest. Mrs. G. promised to comply with his request in every instance, and said she hoped his plan would have the desired effect.

We will now return to Dorcasina, who, alone and disconsolate in her chamber, gave way to the most violent grief. She was at a loss to comprehend the meaning of what she had seen. O'Connor in so disgraceful a situation was a mystery she could not unravel. The account of the captain, who brought him over crossed her mind; and for a moment, her faith in the integrity of her lover was shaken. But suspicion was so disagreeable and unwelcome a guest, that she soon banished it; while compassion for the sufferings of her lover, and indignation at the supposed injustice done him, alternately occupied its place in her bosom. She had now no one to whom she could unbosom her sorrows; and felt, for the first time, in the most sensible manner, the want of her faithful and affectionate Betty; who, though far from approving many parts of her conduct, participated in all her sorrows, and endeavoured to afford her consolation in all her distresses. But most of all, she longed to have an interview with O'Connor himself. But after having long revolved in her mind, the means of accomplishing her desire, she gave up the design for the present, as impracticable; but hoped that, before she left Philadelphia, fortune would favour her so much as to throw him in her way.

All that day and the next, she kept her chamber, being really too ill to see any company. On the third, her father having finished his business, informed her that nothing detained him in Philadelphia but her indisposition. She had now nearly recovered, but knowing O'Connor to be in the city, she could not bear the idea of quitting it, without having a tête à tête with him. She therefore, in spite of the terrible accident which had befallen her, in her first ride round the city, proposed to her father to take her again the same rout, to ascertain whether her strength were sufficiently restored to enable her to bear the journey home. This was her ostensible reason; but her secret one, and what lay nearest her heart, was the hope that she should again meet with her beloved O'Connor, even though it might be in the same painful and mortifying situation as before; in which case she was determined to solicit her father to interfere, and rescue him, if possible, from the hands of his tormentors. But alike vain were her hopes and her fears. They rode through almost every street of the city; but no O'Connor appeared; and she returned home disappointed, dejected and melancholy.

Dorcasina being somewhat fatigued with the length of her ride, her father concluded to defer his departure, till the day but one after. As she was then pretty well recovered, and unwilling to give her reason for wishing to protract her visit, knowing likewise that her father's business required his presence at L——, she took leave of Mr. and Mrs. G., threw herself into the coach, drew up the glasses, and bid adieu, as she then thought, to all earthly happiness.

Mr. Sheldon, observing Dorcasina's dejection, was extremely desirous of knowing what impression the recent transaction had made upon her, and whether it had not altered her opinion of O'Connor. An unwillingness to begin with her, upon so delicate a subject, for some time prevented his entering upon it. But finding that she kept a profound and melancholy silence, he at length interrupted it, by observing that he thought her happening to be a witness to the punishment of O'Connor a very fortunate circumstance, as he was sure it must convince her that his aversion to him was not without foundation. The mention of this name roused Dorcasina from the profound reverie in which she had been absorbed; her eyes overflowed with tears, and she thus replied. "You are deceived, sir, in thinking I have changed my opinion of O'Connor. Appearances, I acknowledge, are at present against him, and the malice of his enemies is unwearied in persecuting him. Be kind enough to inform me, sir, who were the authors of the barbarous treatment he has so recently received." Mr. Sheldon rejoiced at the request, related every particular of the robbery, which, he said, he himself heard so incontestibly proved in court, that it was impossible not to believe it, the things being found in his possession. "Besides," added he, "for my own satisfaction, and to be certain that I did not condemn him unjustly, I have conversed with Mr. W. a man as well noted for integrity as any in the city, and with the master of the vessel, for whose veracity Mr. W. pledged himself, and they both persist in the former declaration; Mr. W. that he never knew any such person as O'Connor, and that the letter in his name (which I had with me and produced) was a vile forgery; and the captain that he brought him over, (to his shame he confesses it) and that he knew him to be, in England, an abandoned villain, a gambler, and highway robber."

Conviction, now for the first time, flashed in the mind of Dorcasina. She could no longer resist the concurring testimony of so many witnesses. "Alas! Sir," said she, "who could have thought there was so much deceit in mankind!" Mr. Sheldon, more rejoiced at this one short sentence, than at any he had ever before heard her utter, as he was thereby convinced that her eyes were at length opened to the worthlessness of O'Connor, mildly replied, "I have before, my dear, had occasion to observe to you, that your retired manner of life, and almost total ignorance of the world, led you to judge other people by your own virtuous and unsuspecting heart. You have now learnt a lesson, which I hope you will ever remember, and in future put less confidence in external appearances and empty professions." Dorcasina, extremely hurt and mortified at having been the dupe of such an arrant impostor, answered not a word; and her father, perfectly satisfied with the complete success of his little plan, was content to drop the subject. Nor did he think fit to interrupt her meditations, till they arrived, towards sunset, in safety and silence, at their mansion on the banks of the Delaware.

Betty's joy at the return of her mistress was unfeigned, nor was that of the latter, at seeing again her faithful confidant, less sincere. She no sooner entered the house, than retiring to her chamber and desiring the attendance of one who participated in all her afflictions, she poured into her faithful bosom her griefs, her trials, her mortifications; relating, in a minute manner, every thing which had happened in her absence.

When she had made an end of her relation, "could you have thought Betty," said she, "that so much deceit and falsehood could be concealed under so fair an exterior?" "Why ma'am, you knows I never liked him from the first. I always thought he look'd cross and proud; he never, to my notion, was half as handsome as Lysander. I thought all the time what he was after; and that he cared more about your father's money than he did about you. But I was afraid to tell you so. I rejoice to think you found out the creature before it was too late: what a dreadful thing it would have been ma'am, if you had married him first, and found him out afterwards, to be a gambler, a thief, and a robber!" "I desire Betty, to be grateful to a kind providence, who knows much better what is best for us than we do ourselves, for saving me from the snare so artfully spread for me, but still it is a mortifying thing to find the object upon whom we set our first and warmest affections, so totally unworthy of them."

"So I should think ma'am," replied Betty; "and I should think too that, the next time you intend to fall in love with a stranger, you wou'd first find out what sort of a man he is." Dorcasina, notwithstanding her melancholy, could not help smiling at Betty's simplicity and total ignorance of the operations of the mischievous little deity. "Why, surely," said she, "you do not think people can fall in love by design, or when and with whom they please?" "Why, I don't know ma'am what I thinks; but I desire to be thankful that I don't know what this love is that you have read so much about: and I hope ma'am, you have done with it as to O'Connor; and don't intend for to worry, and cry, and make yourself sick any more about him." "Alas, Betty!" replied

Dorcasina, "you speak the truth, when you say you are unacquainted
with the tender passion. You know not the struggles, and the time it
will cost me to erase, from my heart, an image so deeply engraved
there; but as it is now impossible that I should ever be his, I am
determined to set about it and endeavour to accomplish it."

Mr. Sheldon, having succeeded in convincing his daughter of the
unworthiness of one of her lovers, was determined to make a thorough
business of it, and to discover, if possible, who the other was, that had
so ungenerously sported with her credulity and compassion. With
this view, he one day, soon after his return from Philadelphia, sent to
the barber who had acted so conspicuous a part in the farce, desiring
he would come and dress him. The barber readily obeying the
summons, Mr. Sheldon took him into a retired room, and gave orders
to the servants not to interrupt him while the barber should remain.

As soon as Puff had done his office, Mr. Sheldon told him, with a
severe look and manner, that he was fully acquainted with every
circumstance of the treatment his daughter had received in the grove,
as well as with her being forced into a cart and carried away; "and if
you do not immediately inform me," said he, "who was the contriver
of those villanous plots, and acted the principal character in them, you
shall feel the utmost effects of my just indignation."

The poor barber, terrified at these threats, begged Mr. Sheldon to
forgive him; saying that he never should have thought of such a thing,
if he had not been set on by another; and if Miss Dorcasina had not first
ill treated him. "My daughter ill treat you? in what manner pray? I
do not believe it; she never ill treated any person." "Why sir," said the
affrighted barber, "I don't know, I don't suppose she meant to treat me
ill; she only meant to divert herself." "But how was it? If you expect
my forgiveness, tell me every circumstance, just as it happened." The
barber, then, in as concise a manner as his fear and agitation would
admit, informed Mr. Sheldon of every particular, as has been before
related, from the time that Mr. Smith (for that was the name of the
mischief loving scholar) told him that Dorcasina had taken a fancy to
him, to his conducting her home, dressed in women's clothes, on that
memorable night of the adventure of the cart.

Mr. Sheldon listened in silence to the recital; and, when it was
ended, felt no longer any emotions of anger towards the barber,
perceiving he had been the sport and the dupe of Smith, equally with
Dorcasina. After continuing for some minutes silent and thoughtful,

he rang the bell with great violence; and upon the entrance of a servant, ordered him, in a more severe and peremptory manner than usual, to call Dorcasina. Upon her coming into the room, the sight of the little barber, and the recollection of the scene in the grove, made her redden with shame and indignation. "Sit down Dorcasina," said her father, "and hear how scandalously you have been imposed upon." He then requested the barber to repeat his story, that his daughter might be fully undeceived in the opinion she had formed of her pretended admirer. The barber did as he was desired, Dorcasina turning alternately from red to white, and from pale to red, and fidgetting in her chair, as if she had been upon a seat of thorns. At length, when the barber had ended his recital, she burst into tears; and, without uttering a single word, precipitately left the room. Mr. Sheldon, too feelingly sympathizing with her, in her extreme humiliation, suffered her quietly to depart.

He then, after traversing the room for some moments, in much agitation, threw himself silent and thoughtful upon a chair. He, one moment determined to follow Smith, and call him to an account, for his conduct; and, the next, to let him remain unmolested; wisely considering that a prosecution would render the affair public, and subject Dorcasina to the laugh of the world. After thus revolving it for some time in his mind he concluded to let the matter rest, and bury it, if possible, in silence and oblivion. He then turned to the barber and demanded if his business in the village answered his expectation. Being answered in the negative, "I will," said he, "not only forgive, but give you fifty dollars, in hand, if you will leave the place and seek employment elsewhere; provided you give me your solemn promise never to mention a syllable of the affair of Smith and my daughter. But keep it in mind," added he, "that you will be still liable to punishment; and, if ever I hear of your divulging it, I will prosecute you to the utmost extent of the law."

The barber, who would have thought himself well off with a severe reprimand, was overjoyed at the prospect of receiving so much money; and readily promised, in the most solemn manner, whatever was required of him. Mr. Sheldon then, counting out to him the money, dismissed him, with an injunction never to let him see his face again.

Dorcasina, whose mortification was extreme, could not endure to inform Betty of the tricks that had been practiced on her, nor to undeceive her with respect to Philander. She also wrote a billet to her father, conjuring him never to name to her again either of her pretended lovers. After these eclaircissements, she confined herself pretty much to the house, for several years; employing her time, as usual, in the duties of the family, and in promoting the happiness of the best of fathers; endeavouring, by her attention, her cares, and her affection, to banish from his mind, as well as her own, that she had ever known such persons as Philander and O'Connor.

END OF THE FIRST VOLUME.

BOOK II

FELIX QUEM FACIUNT ALIENA PERICULA CAUTUM.
In plain English—
LEARN TO BE WISE BY OTHERS HARM,
AND YOU SHALL DO FULL WELL.

Chapter I.

THE serenity thus restored to the lately agitated family of Mr. Sheldon suffered no material interruption for a number of years. Believing his daughter to be radically cured of her romantic turn of mind, he thanked heaven most fervently for so great a favour; and formed the most agreeable expectations concerning the propriety of her future behaviour. But in this the good man was entirely disappointed. The warmth of Dorcasina's affections was not extinguished by disappointment, nor abated by age. It only lay dormant for want of a proper object to excite it.

In the year 1791, famous for the defeat of St. Clair by the Indians, Dorcasina being then in the forty first year of her age, an incident happened, which renewed all her romantic and extravagant fondness. A young officer from New England, about twenty four years of age, who had been severely wounded in this action, after remaining in garrison till his wounds were so far healed as to permit him to travel, obtained a furlough, in order to perfect a cure among his friends. He was proceeding slowly homeward, attended by a servant, when, upon reaching L——, the residence of Mr. Sheldon, his wounds broke out afresh, and he found it impossible to proceed. It was a dark stormy evening, about the last of January, when, traversing the village in quest of an inn, Capt. Barry was suddenly seized with such violent pains, just against the house of Mr. Sheldon, as compelled him to send in his servant to represent his situation, and to solicit the hospitality of the owner. Mr. Sheldon, whose door, heart, and purse, were ever open to the unfortunate, was no sooner informed of the situation of the suffering officer, than he went directly out, helped him to alight, assisted him into the house; and, in the kind and consoling accents of compassion, regretted his misfortune, and desired him to look upon that as his home, till he should be able, without difficulty or danger, to return to his friends.

Penetrated with gratitude for so hospitable a reception, Capt. Barry thanked him, in a manner, which shewed how sensible he was of his kindness; but in so feeble a voice that Mr. Sheldon begged him to be silent. Then dispatching a messenger for a surgeon, he assisted in putting his guest into a warm and comfortable bed.

Dorcasina having been the night before afflicted with a violent tooth ache, which prevented her sleeping, had, on this memorable evening, retired to bed at an early hour. Being waked out of a slumber, by an unusual noise in the house below, she dispatched Betty, who was nodding by the fire in her chamber, to inquire into the occasion of it. Betty quickly returned with all the particulars, and added, that she just had a glimpse of the young man, as they were helping him up stairs; that he looked deadly pale, and groaned so that it went to her heart to hear him; and she was sure them there savage Indians ought to be driven off the face of the earth. To the latter part of her speech, Dorcasina at that time, paid but little attention. Her imagination was immediately fired, and her heart beat high with expectation. A young officer wounded, coming at that time of night, for relief and entertainment, had something in it so charming, so romantic, and so singular, that she directly concluded he was sent by heaven to become her husband. "Poor young man, he is not mortally wounded, I hope, Betty. How did he look? very handsome, I dare say." "Why, as to that matter ma'am, I don't know how he would look when he was well; but he appear'd so distress'd, I cou'dn't tell whether he was handsome or not." "Well strange things happen sometimes, Betty. I have a strong presentiment that this apparently accidental and painful affair will, in the end be productive of the most consummate happiness to him and to me." Betty, who did not readily comprehend her meaning, replied: "why as to that, ma'am, he does look miserable enough to consume any body's happiness, especially a person's so kind-hearted as you are. But I hope the doctor, when he comes, will subscribe something to cure him." "I find," answered Dorcasina, "that you do not understand me; I must be more explicit. Know, then, that I have not a doubt but the gentleman will recover, because I think him decreed by my stars to become my husband, and thereby to complete my happiness." "Lord, ma'am, what a strange notion! Why, only consider; you're old enough to be his mother." "What a foolish mortal you are, Betty! But when I consider your total ignorance of these delicate matters, I cannot find in my heart to be angry with you. Who, pray, ever read or heard of a few years, one way or the other, being an insurmountable obstacle, when the passion was sincere? Can you imagine that such an incident as this would happen without producing some important consequences? No, depend upon it, Betty, we are designed for each other, and shall be mutually pleased as soon as we become acquainted."

Betty, now comprehending the full meaning and design of her mistress, rolled her eyes toward heaven and sent forth a deep sigh; but remained profoundly silent. She had sagacity enough to perceive that Dorcasina's head was again turned with the idea of a new lover, and was fearful of her acting over again all her former extravagances. After a silence of some time, Dorcasina told her she might go to bed; but first charged her to be stirring early in the morning, and to go immediately to the chamber of Capt. Barry, and with her compliments, inform him that she had sent her to assist his servant in rendering him every service he might have occasion for; "and be sure," added she, "come immediately and report the state, in which you find him, and how he receives the offers you make him."

Betty, having slept as little the night before as Dorcasina, immediately availed herself of the permission to retire, and in a few minutes was buried in a profound sleep. Not so her enamoured mistress. She lay, great part of the night, in a pleasing delirium; in building castles of airy felicity, which she was on the point of enjoying, in a union with a brave and accomplished officer; in figuring to herself his looks, his manners, his address; in contemplating the passion he would conceive for her, and his impatience to behold her, and in contriving how she should first present herself to him, and what dress would most become her on the occasion. After repeatedly revolving all these things in her mind, she fell, towards morning, into a delicious slumber, her dreams being as pleasing as her waking ideas.

Mr. Sheldon was employed in a far different manner, in watching by the bedside of his distressed guest; and waiting impatiently for the surgeon. About midnight he arrived and examined his wounds. After dressing them with skill and tenderness, he gave his patient a dose of laudanum, which soon procured for him the rest he so much wanted. Mr. Sheldon and the surgeon then retired to bed, as did likewise the officer's servant. For Mr. Sheldon, observing that he appeared greatly fatigued, desired him to do it; ordering, at the same time, one of his own servants to watch by the captain, during the remainder of the night.

In the morning, Betty, according to her orders, rose with the sun. Listening at the door of the sick man's chamber, and finding all still within, she thought best not to disturb him; and went down stairs to assist in preparing breakfast. About nine o'clock the servant, who had watched with captain Barry, entered the kitchen, and said that being very thirsty he wished to drink a little coffee. Betty, who had a coffee pot boiling at the fire, thought this a good opportunity to execute the commands of her mistress, as well as to gratify her own curiosity; which was all alive to take a nearer survey of the unfortunate stranger. A bowl of coffee being soon prepared, she insisted upon carrying it with her own hands. Being arrived at the bedside of the invalid, she first dropped a courtesy, and then told him she had brought the coffee, which he had requested. The languid hero, raising himself on his elbow, took the bowl, and tasting the coffee, "this is excellent," said he, " you understand making it, I find, and with dispatch too. I did not expect to see it so soon." "Why, as to that, sir," said Betty, "I have made enough in my life time to know how to make it good; and the reason of your having it so quick, was, that I had it already prepared for breakfast. Miss Dorcasina never drinks nothing but coffee for breakfast, and I drinks it too; though her father always has a dish of tea." "Miss Dorcasina," said captain Barry, "pray who is she?" "Mr. Sheldon's only child sir, and as good, and pitiful, and kind hearted a lady as ever lived. Why, sir, the whole village adores her, especially the poor. They almost worships her, she is so good, and kind, and charitable. She it was that sent me here, sir, with her compliments to you, and if you wants any thing I can do, I am entirely at your service."

"Miss Sheldon is extremely kind," said the captain. "I have, I find, fallen into most hospitable hands. Give my compliments to her, and tell her I know not how to express my gratitude to her and her father for their goodness to me; and you, what shall I call your name?" "Betty Boyd, sir, at your service." "I am extremely obliged to you, Betty, and shall have occasion sometimes for your assistance." "You are heartily welcome to any thing I can do for you sir; how do you find yourself this morning? Don't you feel a little better than you did last night?" "My pain is not quite so severe, Betty; but I am extremely weak, dry, and feverish; but I hope, after I get over the fatigue of riding, that I shall speedily recruit again; especially now I am in such good hands." Betty, now hearing Dorcasina's bell, said she must go and attend her mistress.

Being left to himself, the imagination of our hero having caught a small spark of that fire, which had set Dorcasina's in a blaze, he very naturally associated with the goodness described by Betty, all the charms of youth and beauty. The only daughter of so respectable a man as Mr. Sheldon he thought must possess a thousand attractions. His heart not being engaged to any other object, he was impatient to behold a lady so "gracious, kind, and good," to thank her in person for her attention to him, and her offers of service by her maid.

In the midst of these reflections entered Mr. Sheldon and the surgeon. The former, on observing the weak and feverish state of the patient, requested of the latter that he would not leave him in his present critical situation; to which the surgeon, having no other patient requiring his immediate attention, readily assented.

Chapter II.

"WELL, Betty," said Dorcasina, as soon as she entered the chamber, "have you seen the wounded officer this morning? How is he? Better I hope. And what did he say to the message I sent him?" "Yes, ma'am, I have seen him," replied Betty, "and he is a gentleman every inch of him; none of your proud upstarts, that think themselves too good to speak to a poor person. He was so gentle, and so kind, and so free! He sent his compliments to you ma'am, and he asked me my name, and praised the coffee I carried him. He said he had fellen into such horsepitiable hands that he could not express his thanks." "But you have not told me how he is, this morning, Betty." "Why, ma'am, he said he was dry and feverish; but he hoped to recruit again after he had got over the fatigue of his journey." "How did he look and speak, when you mentioned my name?" "He look'd pale, and ask'd me who you was; and you may be sure, ma'am, I wasn't backward in giving you your due." "Well, what then? What did he say then? Did not love and pleasure sparkle in his fine eyes?" "I didn't see any sparkles in his eyes, ma'am. I thought they look'd rather dull, owing to his weakness I spose; but he sent his compliments, and said he did not know how to thank you."

This conversation was carried on while Dorcasina was dressing, who asked Betty so many questions of the same nature, that she was quite at a loss for answers.

Capt. Barry slept the greater part of the day, in consequence of the opium he had taken the preceding night; and not discovering any inclination to be gotten up, the surgeon thought best not to have him disturbed. Dorcasina could not, with any degree of propriety, think of making him a visit that day, but she frequently in the course of it, passed his chamber door, and would sometimes stop and listen to endeavour to catch the sound of his voice.

The next night our soldier slept well, and on the second morning was so much better as to be able, for a short time, to sit up. After dressing his wounds and finding them in a good way, the surgeon left him, promising to visit him again, as soon as he thought it necessary.

While the patient was sitting in an easy chair, Betty brought him Miss Dorcasina's compliments, with some nice preserves; "which," said Betty, "she prepared with her own hands, and hopes you will relish them. She moreover desires to know how you does to day." "What an excellent young lady," said the captain. "Thank her, Betty, a thousand times for me; tell her I feel in a new world; and that the interest she takes in my welfare will greatly accelerate my recovery." Betty having reported to Dorcasina these gallant and grateful expressions of the captain, she now insisted on preparing all his food herself; and charged Betty constantly to inform him of it. This attention produced new expressions of gratitude on the part of the captain, and new emotions of delight in the breast of Dorcasina. She even did not regret that they could not immediately see each other, as this way of carrying on a correspondence was infinitely pleasing to her, being in her opinion extremely delicate, tender and romantic. This intercourse was continued for two days longer, till they seemed mutually acquainted with, and felt a mutual desire of seeing each other. This desire was so strongly expressed by the captain, who was now able to sit up the greater part of the day, that Dorcasina determined no longer to withhold from him and herself the pleasure of a visit. Had she been going to be presented, for the first time, at the court of the greatest monarch in Europe, she would not have thought it a matter of more consequence. Nor was captain Barry without his emotions, occasioned by curiosity and gratitude.

The fashionable female dress at that time, was the little trig silk jacket and muslin skirt. Dorcasina was all the morning examining her clothes, and considering what colour would best become her. She first tried a white lustring jacket; then a purple satin; then a blue, and lastly a pink. But she finally rejected them all, concluding, as she was going to visit a sick chamber, that a plain white robe would be more proper than any of them. At length, about eleven o'clock, Betty being sent forward to announce her, with trembling steps and a palpitating heart, she approached the chamber of the invalid. He stood up out of respect, at her entrance; but the moment he beheld her, he sunk again involuntarily into his chair. A thin, plain woman, near fifty (as he thought her) was so different an object from the young and lovely female he was prepared to behold, that it was impossible for him to conceal his surprise at the disappointment. Dorcasina, on her part, notwithstanding her matronly age and appearance, being a woman of real delicacy, was, at this first interview, a good deal embarrassed. She blushed, and sitting down in a chair, with downcast eyes, and a confused air waited for the silence to be broken by the gentleman. Recovering at length, and ashamed of his want of politeness, the captain began by thanking her for her attention, since he had been in the house, and the honor she now did him by her visit. Dorcasina, who, notwithstanding her embarrassment, had noticed the first surprise of the captain, imputing it wholly to the force and splendor of her charms, now ventured to turn upon him her languishing eyes, and to reply, that she blessed the occasion which had thrown him in her way; that it was with pleasure she administered to the wants of a brave officer, suffering in the cause of his country, and that she hoped he had not wanted for any thing since he had been in the house. "No madam," said he, "thanks to the humanity of you and your father, I could not have been treated with more tenderness in the house of my parents." "You have parents living then, sir?" "I hope so, madam; they were both living three months ago." "How must they be distressed at what you have suffered. They have been informed, I suppose, of your misfortune." "I fear they have, madam, and I was hurrying home to relieve their anxiety, when the breaking out of my wounds afresh brought me into this hospitable mansion." "Have you written to inform them of your present situation, or do you wish to write?" "I made it a point to write, madam, as soon as I was able to hold a pen, and my letter was dispatched by the post this morning." "It must afford them great satisfaction to receive a letter from you." "They are affectionate parents, and it will no doubt give them pleasure madam."

After this they conversed of the Indians, and the battle, of which she requested a particular account, especially of the part he had performed in it. During his narration, she cast upon him such languishing looks, and tender glances; her countenance so beamed with pleasure, while he was in safety, and her eyes so instantly overflowed, when he was wounded, that the poor man was almost too much embarrassed to proceed in the recital.

After an hour and a half passed in varied conversation, Dorcasina took her leave, giving him a thousand charges to be careful of his health, not to sit up too long, nor, by taking cold, expose himself to a relapse. The moment she was alone with Betty, she declared he was the most modest, the most charming, and the most interesting man she had ever seen. "And it has turned out just as I wished and expected; he is violently in love with me, Betty; that is sufficiently evident. My attentions gained his heart before he saw me, precisely the thing I intended and hoped. Did you not observe his delicate embarrassment on my entrance? the graceful manner of his sinking into his chair? his tender and languishing glances? I admire his modesty in not declaring his passion at once: It is a proof that his love is pure and unfeigned. A true lover is always diffident in the presence of the mistress of his affections."

"I am glad, ma'am, he likes you so well," said Betty; "he is another guess sort of a lover than that impudent O'Connor, or that crazy headed fellor that carried us off in the cart." "Oh, name them not, Betty. I am sick, when I think of them. They were both shameless impostors. I never before had a real lover. I now see the difference between true genuine affection, and that which is counterfeited. One is forward, bold, impetuous, and assuming; and the other tender, gentle, diffident and apprehensive. What a charming affectionate husband I shall have Betty! and how will my father be pleased with the connection."

Thus did this poor lady run on, delighted with her prospect of connubial felicity; while the captain, left to his own reflections, was at a loss to account for the strangeness of her conduct. Her conversation, at the interview, had been generally animated and agreeable; but she let fall some such soft expressions, turned her eyes so lovingly, so frequently, and so languishingly upon him, that he must have been blind, not to have perceived that she *pretended* an affection for him; for, considering that this was the first time she had ever seen him, and being totally unacquainted with the peculiarity of her character, that she really *felt* one never entered his mind.

The next day, Dorcasina failed not to pay another visit to the captain, who now engrossed all her thoughts, and reigned with uncontrolled sway over her susceptible heart. After a half an hour's conversation, the captain began to grow so weary of the proofs of a regard, which he felt he never should be able to return, that in order to be left alone he pretended to be suddenly seized with a violent head ache. This policy, however, did not avail, but had quite a contrary effect, to what he intended; for Dorcasina, out of her great love and tenderness, insisted on bathing his forehead in vinegar, in doing which, she more than once accidentally pressed his head against her bosom. This was a tedious process for the poor captain, as Dorcasina was in no hurry to desist. She so frequently asked him, in the mean time, if he did not feel relieved, that in order to be freed from her officiousness, he was obliged to confess that he did. She then, with a cambrick handkerchief, bound up his head, and insisted on his lying down before she quitted the chamber.

In a conference soon after with her confidant Betty, Dorcasina told her of the ecstatic pleasure she had enjoyed, in rubbing her fingers over the polished forehead of her dear lover. "A thrill of pleasure, Betty, ran from my hand, directly to my heart, which beat with such violence that I thought it would have burst its bounds; and once, when I gently pressed his head against my handkerchief, the dear youth seemed to feel a portion of the same emotion. Oh, how sweet is this interchange of delicious sensations; when, without speaking a single word, two tender and faithful lovers may read every sentiment of each other's souls." "Well, but it seems to me, ma'am," said Betty, "I shou'd rather a man would tell me, in so many words, how much he regarded me, than to do nothing but cast sheep's eyes at me all the time. I declare I wou'dn't give the snap of my finger for a man that was afraid to speak his mind." "I can only repeat, Betty, what I have an hundred times told you before, that, being totally unacquainted with the tender passion, you are not capable of forming a judgment upon it. I tell you again, that being fully convinced by his conduct that he feels for me the most ardent passion, I admire his delicacy in so carefully concealing it; and I dare say that as soon as he thinks he can do it with propriety, he will make a satisfactory declaration of it."

This belief and this expectation had taken so full possession of Dorcasina's mind, that in order to remove his diffidence, and encourage him to speak his mind with freedom, she frequently threw out kind hints; and, by her assiduity and attentions, gave him strong proofs of the affection she had conceived for him. As to captain Barry, he found himself in a most disagreeable dilemma. On one hand, the kindness and hospitality he had received from the family, called for his warmest gratitude, and this he ardently wished to demonstrate; on the other, the fondess, which Dorcasina so plainly evinced for him, demanded a return of a tenderer nature, which he felt it was impossible for him to make, and of which, therefore, he thought himself bound to make no indications. He was fearful of expressing even the esteem he felt for her, lest she should construe it into what he did not mean; and if he discovered no regard for her, nor pleasure at seeing her, he was apprehensive of appearing ungrateful, and insensible of the favours with which he was loaded. Thus circumstanced he was really distressed; and after every visit from Dorcasina, he found that the conflicts of his mind raised a temporary fever, and greatly retarded his recovery. This did not escape the notice of James, his servant, who was as remarkable for his sagacity, as for his fidelity to, and affection for his master. He, therefore, one day, after Dorcasina had paid her accustomed visit, and discovered new marks of an unbounded affection, besought his master, who was uncommonly agitated, to take some methods to prevent her frequent visits: "For, sir," said he, "I observe that after every visit you are much worse; and at this rate we shall never see New England." "It is not possible, James," said the captain, "that I should avoid seeing her. After the kind treatment I have received from the family, my refusing to receive her visits would appear the height of ingratitude, the bare suspicion of which I can never consent to incur."

"Give me but your permission, sir," said James, "and I will engage to rid you of the trouble of her assiduities." "I must know first, James, by what means you will effect it; and whether there be nothing disingenuous nor dishonourable in them." "Nothing in the least dishonourable, sir. As to the disingenuousness of the thing, I don't understand such niceties; but I value myself very much upon the honor of a soldier." "Well, let us hear your plan, James." "Why, it is only for you, sir, to obtain liberty to see Miss Sheldon in her chamber in the evening, and, after you are in bed, to suffer me to put on your gown, and go in your stead. Let me manage the matter in this way, and she shall trouble you with no more of her officious visits, I warrant you." "I can never consent to this plan," said the captain, "it would be a scandalous and gross imposition, which I never can sanction." "Why, sir, if I can make her like me as well as she does you, I do not see any harm in it." "Your ideas of honor and mine are widely different, James. It appears to me so dishonourable a thing, that my mind revolts at the idea; so think no more of it, for I shall never agree to it." James urged it no farther at that time; but he had a strong wish to personate his master, as much for his own amusement, as to contribute to the captain's recovery.

At Dorcasina's next visit, at which James was designedly present, she acted a thousand extravagancies. She insisted upon combing the captain's hair, the leg which was wounded she obliged him to lay in her lap, and observing that his linen was dirty, she desired James to give her a shirt, which she said she would take to her own chamber, and see that it was well aired. After some preliminary conversation upon the topic of love, a subject to which she always led, "I desire your opinion," said she, "captain Barry, on the propriety of a lady's making the first advances, when she has reason to believe that diffidence alone withholds the gentleman." At this request the poor captain almost gasped for breath. Expecting nothing less than an immediate declaration of love, he cast his eyes upon James in a supplicating manner, as if to beseech him, at any rate, to liberate him from his present embarrassment. At length, with much hesitation, he made out to answer, that never having thought much upon the subject, he did not feel himself qualified to give an opinion.

Most men would have been amused with Dorcasina's foibles; but captain Barry was extremely modest, and consequently easily embarrassed. What presence of mind he ever possessed was almost entirely destroyed by the weakness, pain, and fatigue he had so recently undergone. An unusual flush now glowed in his cheeks, and he immediately requested of James some drink, to allay the fever which Dorcasina's unexpected question had raised.

As soon as she had withdrawn, James importuned him in a much more earnest manner than on the preceding day, to suffer him to put his plan in execution, "for it is plain, sir," said he, "as long as she thus haunts, and sticks to you like a burr, you never will recover your strength." "The thing is impracticable, James, even if I should agree to it; as she would immediately discover you, and resent, as well she might, the imposition I had put upon her." "Trust me for that, sir; you know I was allowed to be the best mimic in the whole regiment; and even if she should discover me, I think I have wit enough to bring you off." The captain's firmness now began to stagger; which being observed by his cunning servant, he used so many arguments to gain his point, that, at last, he brought him completely over; and it was agreed that the assignation should be requested at the next interview, provided that James would solemnly promise that he would in no wise treat her in a disrespectful, or unbecoming manner; and to this, upon the honor of a soldier, he readily agreed. Thus was this gentleman, in his weak state of body and mind, prevailed upon to consent to an action altogether unjustifiable, and which, had he been in health, never would have received his sanction.

At his next interview with Dorcasina, after observing, in a low voice, and hesitating manner, that they were subject to frequent interruptions in his chamber, he requested permission to see her that evening, for a few minutes, alone, in her's. At this request Dorcasina's whole frame was agitated; but it was the agitation, not of confusion, but of pleasure, as the eclaircissement she had so long wished for and expected was now, she thought, to take place. She, however, at first hesitated, and did not give an immediate answer, being doubtful whether such a procedure would be consistent with the rules of propriety. But after considering that he was unable to go below, and that, as he had observed, they were subject to continual interruptions in his chamber, in the day time, it would be better to see him in her own, in the evening, she gave a joyful and ready assent; and immediately quitted him to express her transports to her faithful confidant.

"Give me joy, Betty," said she, as soon as she saw her; "all suspense is at an end; I shall be the happiest of women. The charming captain has requested a private interview this evening in my chamber, where I shall have the supreme felicity of hearing his vows and protestations, free from interruption, and without fear of my father's displeasure. I charge you, Betty, not to suffer any person, while he is with me, to enter my chamber." "Never fear, ma'am, you shan't be interrupted," replied Betty, almost as much delighted as her mistress; for, as was before observed, she had discovered a strong partiality for the captain, from the time she first saw him. The captain likewise desired to be left alone that evening, saying he felt inclined to sleep.

Dorcasina, dressed with the utmost care, and with such a profusion of ornaments, as made her appear like an actress prepared for the stage, impatiently waited for the shades of evening.

Evening at length arrived. James, after disposing his master in bed, threw on the captain's gown, being about his stature. He was a fellow of address, and had been well educated. After receiving a thousand charges to treat Dorcasina with respect, and not to say a word about marriage, he took a cane in his hand and limped to the chamber of appointment. It was a bold, rash, and thoughtless step; and if fortune had not peculiarly favoured him, he would certainly have been discovered, at this first interview. The weather happened that evening to be very moderate, so that there were only a few coals in the chamber, which afforded but a faint light. There were, however, two large candles, directly opposite to which Dorcasina had seated herself, to shew her person and dress to the greatest advantage. Luckily for James, the curtains of the bed intervened betwixt him, and such a blaze of light, as must otherwise have betrayed him, at his first entrance. The first thing he did was to hobble boldly up to the candles, with his back to Dorcasina, and to extinguish them both. At this action she was surprised and rather displeased; as the pains she had bestowed on her dress were now lost. But, before she had time to express her disapprobation, James was by her side; and taking one of her hands, "forgive me, lovely Dorcasina," said he, in a low voice, and imitating his master, "for taking the liberty of extinguishing the candles; my eyes are very weak, and cannot bear their light. Besides, I can love you as ardently by the glimmering light of those coals, as by the blaze of a thousand tapers." He then expressed his happiness for this opportunity of declaring the passion, with which she had inspired him, and his hopes that she would look upon him with a favourable eye, and not refuse to accept him as a lover, which, he said, would render him perfectly miserable.

Dorcasina, in her answer, gave him as much encouragement as the most sanguine lover could desire; avowing the passion, with which he had inspired her, from his first coming to the house, even before she had the pleasure of seeing him, and declaring that the moment she heard of his arrival, she thought him directed there on purpose to become her husband.

It was then agreed between them that she should visit him but seldom in his chamber, and that those visits should be very short; "for," observed he, "that James is as cunning and observing as the d——l, and nothing escapes him. But, in this chamber, we can meet each evening unobserved, and uninterrupted." He, moreover, desired her never to have much light in the room, as it was very injurious, he said, to his eyes. After preliminaries were thus settled, and James had tarried as long as he dared, he quitted her undiscovered, and went to communicate his success to his master.

As for Dorcasina her heart dilated with pleasure. It was many years since she had enjoyed such happiness; a happiness which was greatly augmented by the consideration, that, as her father had become extremely fond of captain Barry, the connection would have his entire approbation. She was already impatient to have him acquainted with it; and as soon as James had left her, was upon the point of going to communicate it. But recollecting herself she thought it would be more proper for her lover to do it, and at the same time to solicit his consent to their union.

After James had retired to bed, he could not shut his eyes to sleep for thinking of the adventure, in which he had engaged. The d——l, who never sleeps, or some other evil spirit, took this opportunity to put it into his head, that it would be a charming thing to wean Dorcasina's affections from his master, and fix them on himself, and that to marry the heiress to an estate of a thousand pounds a year, would render him the most happy man in existence. To accomplish these objects he was sensible would require great management and address; but as he thought himself not deficient in either, he by no means despaired of succeeding. With this view he took frequent opportunities, the next evening, of mentioning himself to Dorcasina, observing, in the character of his master, that James was an excellent fellow, that he loved him almost like a brother; that he was of a respectable family, and had received a good education; but that, having been unsuccessful in business, he was obliged, by pecuniary embarrassments, to enlist as a soldier. He concluded by begging her, if she really valued himself, to esteem James for his sake.

In consequence of this information, and this request, Dorcasina the next day took every opportunity of speaking to James, asking him numberless questions about his friends, his country, and the reason of his enlisting; all which he answered in so artful a manner, as to confirm every thing he had told her the preceding evening. Dorcasina thought she discerned in him the manners of a gentleman, and from that time forward treated him with great consideration. He, on his part, delighted with his success, continued his visits every evening; his master constantly desiring to be left alone, under pretence of wishing to sleep.

It was not long before Dorcasina, observing that he said nothing of applying to her father in the affair, proposed, in plain terms, that he should ask his consent, adding that there was not the least doubt but he would grant it with the utmost readiness and satisfaction. Upon this proposal, James pretended to be very thoughtful; sighed deeply, and even pretended to let fall some tears. Dorcasina, alarmed at a melancholy she had never observed in him before, inquired anxiously the cause. It was some time before he make her a reply, being choaked as it were with his grief. At length, in a mournful voice, he said; "there is one obstacle to our union, beautiful Dorcasina, with which I have not yet acquainted you. Know, then, that my parents are so doatingly fond of me, and so interested and particular in the choice I shall make of a wife, that they extorted a promise of me, before I left them, that I should not engage myself to any woman whosoever without their first being acquainted with her, and approving my choice. Thus circumstanced, you see I cannot with propriety apply for your father's consent, without first being sure of their approbation."

This intelligence was a thunderclap to Dorcasina, and she regretted the circumstance in the most passionate terms. "But my dear captain," said she, "we must hit upon some method of removing this obstacle; for we shall both of us be infallibly miserable for life, if we be not united." "I am perfectly sensible of that, my love," returned he; "the idea of being separated from you would drive me distracted; but we will not distress ourselves by anticipating evil. My charming girl, you will, you must be mine; there is not the shadow of a doubt, but that my parents, when they shall once behold you, will applaud and confirm my choice. The only difficulty is to bring you acquainted with each other. I must contrive some means of removing it. I will consider of it, and acquaint you with my plan, at our next meeting." Thus saying, he begged her not to be uneasy, but to rely on his love and invention for extricating them from their present embarrassment. He then wished her good night, and left her for the first time, since their happy meetings, somewhat depressed in spirits.

James, who long before had got his plan all arranged, told her, at their next meeting, that they were in a delicate and embarrassed situation; that he had revolved the matter in his mind, ever since he had quitted her the preceding evening; that there was one method and one only, which he could think of to extricate them, and this he was almost afraid to mention, lest it should not meet her approbation. "Spare yourself this unnecessary fear," said Dorcasina; "if there be nothing dishonourable in your plan, you will find from me no unnecessary scruples." "Thank you, generous Dorcasina; can you consent then to elope, in the night, from your father's house, and trusting yourself to my protection, go with me to New England, to the house of my parents, who I am confident will glory in my choice, and receive you with open arms as a daughter?"

Dorcasina started at this proposal, and was for some moments silent. At length, "what is the necessity," said she, "for all this privacy, all this mystery? I think we had much better lay the whole affair before my father, painting to him our mutual passion, and the difficulties which lie in our way. He will doubtless esteem you the more, for adhering so scrupulously to the promise given your parents, and make not the least objection to my paying them a visit. Perhaps he will even accompany us himself." "Ah no! my dear girl," replied James; "believe me, that will never do. Old people do not view things in the same light with the young. They look upon them through the cold medium of prudence, propriety, and what not. But we, animated with an ardent passion, can overleap small obstacles, and, by constancy and perseverance, remove great ones. Condescend then, charming Dorcasina, to accede to my proposal, without consulting your father. It is true he may be alarmed at the step you take, but you need not keep him long in suspense. You can dispatch a letter from the first place we stop at, informing him where you are gone, and giving him the reasons of your quitting him, without his knowledge and approbation. You have always flattered me with the idea that he would be pleased with the connection we contemplate; and his paternal tenderness and indulgence leave you no room to doubt his forgiveness for the apparent undutifulness of your conduct, when he shall become acquainted with the grounds of it."

Dorcasina began to be moved and to give way to the arguments of her lover. She recollected that she had read of numberless young ladies, who had taken a trip to Scotland, when their parents were opposed to their union with a favoured lover. She began to be pleased with the air of romance and adventure, which her eloping would have, and this more than any other consideration reconciled her to the step. After a few more objections, which she thought it became her to make, she finally agreed to leave her father, her house, and home, for his sake.

Chapter III.

WE will now, for a while, leave these happy lovers to settle the manner of their escape, and return to other scenes less interesting, but more amusing.

Before James conceived the idea of aspiring to the hand of Dorcasina, he had honoured with his particular notice, one of the maids, whose name was Nanny. She was a likely buxom country girl; and as much delighted with the cockade, the uniform, and the attention of James, as Miss Dorcasina was with those of his master. He had made her a number of little presents, and had even gone so far as to talk of marriage. Of late he had strangely neglected her, hardly deigning to speak when he met her. Formerly he used to pass whole evenings in the kitchen; and many a time, by his accounts of ambuscades, battles and defeats of Indians, tomahawks and scalping, he made them contract their circle round the fire. But latterly he was never seen there in the evening, except while eating his supper, and then he was generally silent and stately. Nanny was totally at a loss how to account for this great and sudden change in his conduct, and wished much to come to an explanation; but he avoided her, with so much care, that it was impossible to get an opportunity. As her temper was none of the mildest, she felt no less irritated than mortified at such studied neglect; and those feelings were heightened by the jeers of the other servants, particularly by those of some of the females, who formerly envied her James' attentions.

Not being of a temper to endure such slights, and the mortifications occasioned by them, she determined to watch him narrowly, and, if possible, to find out how and with whom he passed his evenings. At length, partly by her own observations, and partly by hints she obtained by continually pumping Betty, she thought she had discovered that he constantly took his master's place in bed, while he passed the evenings with Dorcasina in her chamber.

Delighted with this discovery, she was determined to go, the first leisure evening, and upbraid him with his inconstancy. This happened to be the same evening upon which James acquainted Dorcasina with his plan of elopement.

Having entered the chamber where captain Barry lay, she softly approached the bed; and sitting down upon its side, repeatedly pronounced the name of James, raising her voice every time, in order to awaken him, as, from his not answering the first time, she supposed him to be fast asleep. Captain Barry, who suffered considerable uneasiness for the imposition practiced on Dorcasina, and was perpetually alarmed lest she should discover it, finding himself mistaken for James, by a female, with whose voice he was unacquainted, determined to lie still and give her no answer. Nanny, unable to rouse him by speaking, first gently jogged him, and not succeeding in this way, she shook him so violently by the shoulder as almost to dislocate it. Finding that he neither spoke nor moved, and suspecting that he only pretended sleep to avoid coming to an explanation, her wrath was raised to the highest pitch, and, attacking him with her fists, she aimed at him blows which would almost have felled an ox, some of which fell on his face, and some on his pillow. The poor unlucky captain still had sufficient command of himself to keep a profound silence; but unwilling to be thus mauled, he seized the virago by both hands, and held her at a distance; while she, endeavouring to disengage herself, poured forth a torrent of abuse, and honoured him with every vile and scandalous epithet, which her indignation could suggest.

Mr. Sheldon, who was sitting still and silent in the room directly under them, hearing an unusual noise and high words in captain Barry's chamber, took a light in his hand and went directly up to discover the cause. He had got near the chamber door, when the captain hearing a step approaching, and observing a light through the keyhole, let go his hold. Nanny, making the same discovery at the same time, ashamed to be caught in such a situation, turned down the bed clothes, and jumping in behind the captain, covered herself up, hoping to remain undiscovered. The captain, indignant at being caught with such a bed fellow, set both his feet against her; and making a strong effort, notwithstanding the wound in his leg kicked her fairly on to the floor. She had just time to exclaim, "mean soul'd puppy," and creep under the bed, as Mr. Sheldon entered the room. She did not, however, so effectually conceal herself as she imagined; for a corner of her gown still remained in sight. This Mr. Sheldon immediately discovered, and setting his foot firmly upon it, inquired of the captain the occasion of the noise, which, he said, had interrupted his study. "Indeed I cannot tell you sir," replied Barry. "You mean you do not chuse to inform me," said Mr. Sheldon; "for surely you cannot be ignorant of it." "Upon my honor, I am totally ignorant of the cause, sir." Mr. Sheldon, having good reason to suppose that the captain equivocated, and that he was guilty of some dishonourable practices, was moved even to anger; and laying hold of Nanny's gown, which was of a strong texture, he dragged her, more dead than alive, from under the bed. "The cause is obvious, notwithstanding you pretend to be so very ignorant of it, sir," said he, in a tone that sufficiently indicated his displeasure.

Captain Barry, extremely hurt that he should entertain so unworthy an opinion of him, begged him to listen with patience and candor, and he would declare all he knew of the affair. Mr. Sheldon, being silent, the captain informed him, that *that* girl, whom he had hardly ever seen before since he had been in the house, entering the chamber softly, in the dark, repeatedly called James; that, upon his making her no answer, she first jogged and then shook him violently, and at last attacked him with her tongue and heavy fists, the truth of which last assertion his bleeding nose would amply testify. "Thus you see, sir, I spoke nothing but truth when I asserted I knew not the cause of the noise that brought you up, and let her deny a syllable of this if she can."

Mr. Sheldon then turned to Nanny, who still sat on the floor, astonished and confounded at finding it to be the captain: her face covered with her hands and her anger converted into shame. "What have you to answer to these charges?" said he, in a stern voice, "speak; answer directly, and without equivocation."

Nanny, finding herself so closely interrogated, thought it best to declare the truth. "I ax pardon, sir," said she, "I thought it was James." Mr. Sheldon thinking this only a pretence grew still more angry. "Do not make the matter worse hussey, by telling a thousand falsehoods; it is no such thing; you could not think it was James, when you knew that this was captain Barry's chamber and bed; and that he was every evening confined to both." "Pray sir, forgive me, sir; I did think it was James, and that the captain was in Miss Dorcasina's chamber." This insinuation was only adding fuel to the flame. "Audacious wretch," said Mr. Sheldon; "how dare you suppose any such thing?" Nanny, terrified almost out of her wits, still begging to be forgiven, said that Betty had told her that the captain went in the evening to Miss Dorcasina's chamber, and that James took his place in the bed; that he having treated her ill, she came up to expostulate with him upon it; but that finding him obstinately silent, she was provoked to give him a good thumping. This story agreeing with the captain's, especially with his saying that she called him James, his wrath towards her began to abate; and in the same proportion it kindled against Betty, by whom he thought his daughter was shamefully belied.

Being determined to go to the bottom of the affair, Mr. Sheldon ordered Nanny to follow him to the chamber of Dorcasina. Poor Barry, in an agony of distress, lest the whole imposture should now be detected, wished James in the middle of the Delaware for suggesting such a plot, and himself there with him for consenting to it.

James and Dorcasina, who sat laying plans of future happiness, were alarmed by the unexpected approach of Mr. Sheldon, whom they heard, in a loud and angry tone, scolding at poor Nanny, for causing such a disturbance. James immediately started up in as great consternation as if the house had been attacked by a thousand Indians, supposing that Mr. Sheldon had discovered him, and was coming to punish him for the deceit he had practised. "There is your father," exclaimed he, "save me; hide me, Dorcasina, under the bed; in this closet; any where; so that he may not discover me."

Dorcasina, conscious of no deceit, was not equally terrified at the prospect of facing her father; though, to be sure, it was rather mortifying to have him surprise her, with the captain in her chamber, in the dark; especially as he knew nothing of their mutual affection and mutual engagements. To avoid so disagreeable a situation, and in compliance with the earnest request of the terrified James, she opened the door of a large closet at the side of the chimney, into which James darted quicker than lightning; and she had just time to turn the key upon him, and seat herself apparently in a composed manner, before a few coals, which were glimmering upon the hearth, when Mr. Sheldon and Nanny entered the chamber. "Where is Betty?" said the former, in an angry manner, as soon as he entered. "I believe she is below in the kitchen, sir; what is your pleasure with her?" "She is accused, by the girl here, of defaming you, Dorcasina, in a scandalous manner." "Of defaming me, sir? I can never believe it. Betty is too good, and too honest, and too much attached to me. There must be some mistake in it. Pray, Nanny, what did she say?" "Speak, girl," said Mr. Sheldon, "and conceal nothing." "Why she said, ma'am, as how that the captain comed to see you here almost every evening; and that Mr. James took his place in his bed."

Dorcasina was somewhat abashed at hearing what she thought the truth, in so abrupt and unqualified a manner; and felt not a little angry at Betty, for her imprudence in betraying her. After considering for some moments in what manner she should act upon this unexpected emergency, she determined that, as truth had always been her guide, it would be her best way to follow it now. She therefore told her father, that, if he would let Nanny withdraw, she would clear up to him the whole mystery.

Nanny, accordingly, at a nod from Mr. Sheldon, made a precipitate retreat, overjoyed at coming off so easily, and hastened down stairs. Dorcasina, after requesting her father to be seated, informed him of what she said she was sorry for having so long concealed from him; that she and captain Barry had conceived a violent affection for each other, at their first interview; that, finding he had no opportunity of declaring his passion in his own chamber, on account of the continual interruptions to which they were subject, he had requested liberty to see her in her own, in the evening; that as his indisposition prevented his going below, she saw no impropriety in granting his request; that he had frequently repeated his visits since, and had uniformly behaved to her in the most respectful, tender, and affectionate manner.

Mr. Sheldon remained for some time silent, after Dorcasina had ceased speaking, not knowing what to think of the account she had given him. He did not indeed scruple her veracity, but considering the disproportion in the ages of the parties, the great strength of Barry's affection appeared to him rather problematical. The affair of Smith and the barber forced itself into his mind; but there was such an appearance of honesty and integrity in the whole of the captain's conversation, that he could not believe he would, like them, sport with Dorcasina's credulity merely for his amusement; much less that he would repay the hospitality, with which he had been treated, with so much ingratitude. Upon the whole he concluded that, tempted by the property to which his daughter was presumtive heiress, he had gained her affections with a view of becoming master of it; and, considering Dorcasina's extreme credulity, her romantic imagination, and the narrow escape she formerly had, he judged that it would be far better to bestow her on so worthy a man as captain Barry appeared to be, than to leave her any longer exposed to the arts and addresses of worthless adventurers.

Having revolved these things in his mind, his features regained their wonted calmness, and he mildly observed, that before going so far with her, he thought captain Barry might have consulted him upon the subject. "He has his reasons for not doing it at present, Sir," said Dorcasina; "and reasons that you would yourself approve, could you be made acquainted with them. But you may rely upon it, Sir, that as soon as he can do it with propriety, he will take an opportunity of laying the matter before you." "Well, well," said Mr. Sheldon, "we will settle it another time. I believe supper waits; come, let us go down and eat it." So saying, he led the way, and Dorcasina followed, intending to send Betty to release James, who, locked up in the closet, had overheard all their discourse. He at first perspired with agony, expecting every moment to be detected; but finding how cleverly Dorcasina had brought him off, he felt happy enough to pass the night there.

Betty having arrived and released him, he went directly to the chamber of his master, whom he found greatly agitated by the incidents of the evening. "James," said he, "I am weary of this imposture, I tremble to think how narrowly we have this evening escaped detection. To what does it all tend, and what do you promise yourself by thus continuing in it?" "Why, sir," replied James, "you know that I engaged in it merely to rid you of Miss Dorcasina's importunity." "Upon what terms are you, and how stand matters between you now?" said the captain. "Can you get off with decency?" "Nothing more easy, sir," replied the artful James. "I praise her beauty, and that gratifies her vanity; I tell her I admire her, and that makes her admire me; but nothing serious has passed between us, and I can discontinue my visits without any kind of difficulty; but as I cannot shake her off all at once, it must be done by degrees." "Well then, I charge you to set about it immediately. As I find that my strength increases daily, and my wounds are nearly healed, I intend going below tomorrow, and hope to be able, in a week or ten days at farthest, to continue my journey."

By promising immediately to comply with the captain's request, James relieved his master's mind of a load, which had long oppressed it: but he had in reality no such intention. It is true after his last narrow escape of detection he had no desire of visiting Dorcasina so frequently as he had hitherto done; but he intended, at the next interview, to request her to be in readiness to depart, at the time mentioned by the captain. His plan was to set out with his master, and go with him as far as he would travel the first day, and take a French leave of him at night; then to return to Mr. Sheldon's, take Dorcasina into a sleigh in the night, and carry her as far from home as he could by the morning; and trust to his good fortune and good address, for effecting a reconciliation, when daylight should discover the imposture. He was, indeed, sanguine enough to suppose that, when she should find out that he was the person in whose company she had passed so many happy hours, and upon whom she had bestowed so many proofs of her tenderness and affection, she would not be inexorable, but after a little pouting, accept the man instead of the master.

When Dorcasina, after supper, returned to her chamber, she first acquainted Betty with what had happened, and then added, "how could you be so imprudent Betty, as to tell Nanny that the captain passed his evenings here?" "La, ma'am," said Betty, "she was so jealous of James, who used to flirt a little with her, when he first come, and kept always teazing me so to know why he didn't go into the kitchen, in the evening as he used to, that supposing you would soon be married, I thought it would be no harm to let her have an inkling of the matter." "But what possessed her, Betty, to go to my father with the story?" "That's what I doesn't know ma'am, but I'll make her tell me."

"You must not in future, Betty, be so indiscreet, and I charge you to say nothing more about my love affairs to any person living. In answer to any future inquiries, tell them that our affairs are best known to ourselves, and that you are not let into our secrets."

The next day Betty attacked Nanny. "I desires to know," said she, "how you come for to go to blabbing to Mr. Sheldon what I told you about the captain and Miss Dorcasina." Nanny, excessively mortified with the termination of her adventure, and not wishing the rest of the servants to become acquainted with it, replied, "I didn't mean Miss

Dorcasina no harm, and I hope she will forgive me. I didn't tell of it till it was dragg'd out of me. So Betty, don't ax me no more questions, for I can't tell you any more about it." With this answer, Betty, as well as her mistress, was forced to be satisfied, and there was no other notice taken of it.

Chapter IV.

THE next morning, the cunning James, as soon as he saw Dorcasina, took the opportunity of presenting his master's compliments, and of informing her that he felt so well that he intended doing himself the pleasure of dining below. This agreeable piece of intelligence set Dorcasina all into a flutter. She had not been in the chamber of the invalid for more than a week, consequently she had not seen him in all that time, although she fancied she had passed almost every evening in his company. She was now transported with joy, at his being so far recovered, that she could have the pleasure of seeing him below, in the day time, in company with her father. She went immediately, her countenance beaming with satisfaction, to communicate to him the joyful intelligence; after which, she added, "this ought to be a day of jubilee, and I think on such an occasion, we should call in our friends to rejoice with us. Suppose we invite Mr. and Mrs. Stanly, and Harriot, to dine with us." "With all my heart, my dear," replied Mr. Sheldon, "I shall be very happy to see them." A servant was accordingly dispatched with an invitation.

Mr. Stanly had frequently visited captain Barry in his confinement, but his wife and daughter had never been in his company. The latter had just been taken from a boarding school in Philadelphia, from which she had returned, at the age of seventeen, an elegant, accomplished girl. She was of a tall stature, with large limbs; but well formed and finely proportioned. Her complexion was a dark brunette, accompanied with black hair, and large, black, sparkling eyes; her features were not very regular; her nose was rather large, with the Roman contour; her mouth small, cheeks red, and teeth white as ivory. Without being handsome, however, she had something in her appearance peculiarly striking. Her disposition was gay and lively;

and her manners easy, sprightly, and unaffected. She had been at home but four days, consequently had seen neither Mr. Sheldon nor his daughter since her return. As soon as the servant from Mr. Sheldon's had delivered the message, "Oh, pray, mama," said she, "let us go; I want to see Miss Sheldon very much; and the wounded officer too, to whom, they say she is very attentive." Mr. Stanly being consulted, they soon agreed to accept the invitation.

Mr. Sheldon's house was now all in a bustle. Dorcasina was in the kitchen herself, great part of the morning. Every delicacy that the house afforded, or that could be collected in the village was brought forward on the occasion; and orders were given for the table to be spread with unusual elegance.

About twelve, Dorcasina retired to dress; and so particular was she in chusing what she thought would most become her, that the business of the toilet was not over till near two. Her jacket was of blue sattin, trimmed with silver fringe; her skirt of white sattin with the same trimming, over which was one of delicate, embroidered, India muslin. So far her dress was very proper, according to the fashion of the day. But in the choice of her head dress she was most unfortunate. Harriot Stanly had brought from Philadelphia that most unbecoming fashion of wearing the turban bound across the forehead. She had appeared at meeting with this head dress, which looked so strange as to make the whole congregation stare at her entrance. Betty, who had been that day at meeting, endeavoured to describe to Dorcasina the "frightful thing" Harriot Stanly had worn. "Why, she looked, for all the world, ma'am, as if her head was bound for the headache."

"You may depend upon it, Betty," replied Dorcasina, "that it is the newest fashion in Philadelphia, and I am determined to wear my turban in the same manner; for you know, that being dressed in the fashion, Betty, heightens one's beauty very greatly; and I am sure the captain will admire me the more for it." "Why, according to my notion, ma'am, I thinks that folks ought to consult their age a little, and not dress out in every new fashion that comes, looking all the while like the greatest frights." "You know no more about dress, Betty," said Dorcasina, "than you do about love. Why, in large towns you can form no estimate of a woman's age by her dress; for they make no distinction between sixteen and sixty. But supposing they did, Betty, I should not think of altering mine these ten years yet; especially as I am now upon the point of becoming a bride." Upon this memorable day, therefore,

Betty was desired to give a more particular description of Miss Stanly's turban, and to assist in fixing one like it upon the head of Dorcasina. Betty did the best she could, and it looked like a caricature of a fashionable head dress. As Dorcasina had for many years seen but little company, her hair had grown to a length very inconvenient for dressing. She, however, had it papered and pinched till Betty's arms ached again. It was then snarled up into two large bunches above her ears, almost half as big as her head, and loaded with powder; and a muslin handkerchief bound tight across her forehead.

Mr. Stanly's family arriving before she was ready to receive them, were entertained till that time by her father. At length she descended, charming in her own opinion as the goddess of beauty; but so outree was her appearance, that Harriot Stanly dared not venture to pronounce a single word in answer to her compliments, for fear of laughing in her face; she only curtsied in silence, and it was with the greatest difficulty she preserved any tolerable degree of gravity.

Dinner being at length announced, the captain was requested to come down, which he did not choose to do before. While he was descending the stairs, which took up some time, on account of his lameness, Dorcasina practised a thousand ridiculous airs. She first ran to the glass to adjust her head; then bridled up, and forced back her shoulders; then sat down, and the next moment got up again, standing, as she thought, in a graceful attitude to receive her lover. The formidable hero, at last made his appearance, and she giggled aloud. Mr. Sheldon having introduced him to Mrs. and Miss Stanly, they sat down to table; not, however, without some difficulty. Dorcasina, being at the head of it next the fire, had fixed a lolling chair for the captain on her left hand, having previously seated Mrs. Stanly at her right. The captain very modestly declined taking that seat; but she insisted upon it with so much earnestness, that, in order to prevent the dinner from spoiling before it was eaten, he was obliged to submit.

During dinner, after the other guests were once helped round, her attention was directed almost wholly to him. "Shall I help you to a small slice more of this ham? Cannot you eat a morsel more of that turkey? Do take another piece of this pudding, or this tart; they are very good, I assure you, for I made them myself." And then she would cast upon him such significant glances, as much as to say, I know you will think them the better for being of my making, that poor Barry was quite confounded, and wished her a thousand miles off.

The two other gentlemen had entered pretty deeply into the politics of the day, so that they did not observe Dorcasina's marked attention to him; but none of it was lost by the female guests, especially by Miss Harriot; who could hardly swallow her dinner without choaking, for the violent efforts she made to contain her laughter. Captain Barry was very much struck with her appearance, and could not help observing the contrast between her and Dorcasina; but whenever he attempted to address himself to her he was perpetually interrupted by the officiousness of the latter.

Dinner being over, Dorcasina contrived still to be at the side of her beloved officer, attentive to his every look and motion. While the company sat conversing, there ran into the room, a great ugly Newfoundland dog, which the captain had brought with him from the army. This dog, when his master was wounded and left for dead on the field of battle, never quitted him till the Indians had retired. He then went to the fort, and by his apparent uneasiness and unusual noises, induced some of the soldiers to follow his steps to the spot where he had left him. Captain Barry having by this time recovered his senses, (for he had been knocked on the head, as well as otherwise wounded) they brought him back in safety. He was thus indebted for his life to the attachment and fidelity of this dog. It may well be supposed, therefore, that he was a great favourite of Dorcasina's. She had, indeed, loved, fed and caressed him, ever since she had been informed of the service he had rendered his master.

The ground being at this time very muddy, the dog, which had just entered the house, was very dirty, and left the print of his feet, at every step, upon the carpet. The captain immediately ordered him out of the room; but Dorcasina insisted upon it that he should be allowed to stay. She called him to her, he wagged his tail and licked her hands; and at length put his two fore paws into her lap. The captain endeavoured to drive him down; but she checked him, and hugging the dog in her arms, declared aloud that, as he had been the means of saving his precious life, he was infinitely dear to her, and that she should make it her business to recount his fidelity, and to treat him as long as he lived with the attention he deserved.

This speech was uttered in the most serious manner, while Dorcasina's eyes, full of tenderness, were fixed on the captain. Mr. Sheldon bit his lip to hear his daughter thus expose herself. Mrs. Stanly looked serious, Mr. Stanly stared, and Harriot, in spite of all her endeavours to the contrary, burst into a laugh. This was too much for poor Barry to bear. He reddened up to the very ears, and rising, begged the company to excuse him, saying that his leg pained him and he must retire to his chamber. But here, instead of extricating himself from difficulty, he involved himself afresh; for Dorcasina, putting down the dog, insisted upon helping him up stairs; which she did, in spite of his entreaties to the contrary, begging him at every step to lean more upon her, and to spare his leg. Being arrived at the chamber, she fixed his pillow, and insisting on his lying down, she covered him up with great care; saying, with tears in her eyes, "I am afraid, my dear captain, that the exertion has been too much for you; pray compose yourself, and I will sit and watch by your side." "Pray madam," said the captain, who almost wished himself annihilated, "go down to the company, and not give yourself the trouble to stay with me. I feel inclined to sleep and your presence will only prevent me." This consideration induced his enamoured dulcinea to leave him, saying she would return when he awoke and see how he found himself.

She then went to her own chamber, and sent Betty down to desire the two ladies to walk up. They very readily obeyed the summons, and being seated, "you may perhaps wonder, madam," said Dorcasina, addressing herself to Mrs. Stanly, "to see me so attentive to captain Barry. But I assure you he deserves all the tenderness I can bestow upon him, and besides, he is shortly to become my husband."

The two ladies looked first upon each other, and then upon Dorcasina, with strong marks of incredulity; for they thought the captain exhibited much stronger signs of disgust than of affection. They, however, being totally at a loss what to reply, were silent; and Dorcasina continued, "you may perhaps be surprised at this information, considering the recent date of our acquaintance; but when two souls are congenial, and cast in the same mould, a short time is sufficient to convince their possessors, that they were born for each other. This, madam, is the case with the captain and myself, and the power who rules over the affairs of men, directed his steps hither, as here, meeting with his kindred soul, he was to bless and to be blessed." She then expatiated largely upon the felicity of mutual love, and said she hoped that Miss Harriot would soon likewise experience its delights. Harriot was silent from astonishment; and her mother observed, that she was quite too young to think of entering into the matrimonial state at present; that, although, when a prudent choice was made, and the parties were sincerely attached, it was productive of much happiness; yet, that no state in life was without its cares, its duties and its sorrows; and that a young lady was or ought to be as happy in her father's house, beloved by her parents, and free from anxieties, as in any other situation whatever.

Dorcasina wondered greatly to hear such sentiments proceed from a lady, whom she knew to be beloved by her husband, and revered by her children; but she made no answer. For thinking it time for the captain to awake, she said she must go and see if he was any better. She went and opened gently the door, and stepping cautiously round the bed, observed that he was to all appearance in a sweet sleep. The fact was, that he was too much vexed to sleep, and lay impatiently wishing for the time when he should be able to quit the family; and thinking that he deserved this persecution from Dorcasina, for the deceit he had suffered to be practised upon her; when, hearing her coming into the chamber, and knowing her step, he pretended to be asleep to avoid her inquiries. She stood looking at him, for some time, in silent admiration, when thinking best not to disturb him, she gently left the chamber, and returned to the ladies.

After another half hour's conversation they were summoned down to tea; soon after which, Mr. Stanly's family took their leave. Dorcasina did not urge their longer stay, as she was impatient to visit the chamber of her dear indisposed lover.

As soon as Mrs. Stanly was alone with Harriot, "Well, mama," said she, "such a ludicrous scene I never witnessed. I really pitied the captain. And did you ever see any body so ridiculous as Dorcasina? I would not be an old maid for all the world." "All single women are not thus ridiculous, Harriot," said Mrs. Stanly; "and I desire that you would speak of them with a little more respect. I know several worthy and amiable women of that class, who live single rather than marry barely for the sake of having a husband. They are, in my opinion, much more respectable than women, who, merely to avoid the imputation of being old maids, will marry the first man that offers himself." "Well, mama, I don't know but they are; but did Dorcasina always treat her lovers in that manner; or is this the first she ever had?" "I never spoke to you, my dear," said Mrs. Stanly, "of Dorcasina's weakness; because I intended, if ever an opportunity presented, that you should have occular demonstration of it, to convince you, in a forcible manner, of the pernicious effects of reading novels. Miss

Sheldon is possessed of an amiable disposition, and an excellent heart; and, on every subject but one, her understanding is strong, and her judgment good; and in her youth her person was tolerably pleasing. But having that propensity so common to youth, to peruse every novel she could lay hands on, and unfortunately obtaining as many as she wished, her head has been, for many years, completely turned; and she has been by turns the dupe of knaves and fools. I know that you used to think hard that I prohibited you such kind of reading; but, with such an instance of its baneful effects continually under my observation, I was determined that you should be educated in total ignorance of its fascination."

"I did, mama, sometimes, I confess, think both you and my governess unkind; but am now fully convinced of the justice of your proceeding, and thank you, a thousand times, for the prohibition. But what is your real opinion, mama, of this affair between the captain and Dorcasina? do you think he can have any serious thoughts of marrying her?" "I confess, my dear," replied Mrs. Stanly, "that I am rather at a loss what opinion to form of the business. But were I to hazard one on the subject, it would be, that, tempted by the estate to which she is heiress, he has made her some overtures of marriage; but that sickened, disgusted, and embarrassed by her fondness in our presence, he pretended indisposition to be freed from her fulsome attention." "I cannot think as you do, mama," said Harriot. "He appears to be a man of so much good sense, and such delicacy of sentiment, that it is incomprehensible to me, how he can think of marrying a woman so old, and so ridiculous." "Well, well, we shall soon know how it will terminate," said Mrs. Stanly; "for he talks of pursuing his journey next week; and it is probable that, if a connection does take place, the matter will be settled before he leaves them." Harriot then retired to bed, convinced, in her own mind, that the captain would never marry Dorcasina, and wondered her mama could entertain an opinion, which appeared to her so totally unworthy of him.

While Mrs. Stanly and her daughter were thus discussing the matter, captain Barry held a conversation with James upon the same subject. "James," said the former, "what a scrape you have led me into. Dorcasina has been so outrageously loving, that I could not stand it; but pretending indisposition I made a precipitate retreat. I suppose she will follow as soon as the company are gone, and continue to persecute me with her officious tenderness. But do you stand centinel, and if she approch, tell her I have gone indisposed to bed." He had hardly time to settle himself fairly in bed before Dorcasina in fact arrived. James stopped her at the door, "my master, ma'am," said he, in a low voice, "has gone to bed quite sick, he has now fallen into a slumber, and he bid me say that he could not see any company whatever this evening."

Dorcasina withdrew, alarmed, and retired to bed; but could not compose herself to sleep. Anxiety for the captain kept her turning, groaning, or crying during the whole of it.

At length morning arrived, and as soon as Dorcasina heard James leave the chamber, she ran to him and inquired eagerly how his master had passed the night. "He was very restless the first part of it ma'am," replied James, according to his instructions; "and slept but little; about midnight he fell into a sound sleep, which lasted till morning; and he has waked much better, and entirely free from pain, but is rather weak, and desires to remain still and undisturbed through the day." This desire of the captain's was conveyed to Dorcasina, that she need not attempt to bore him with a visit. Though she exceedingly regretted the prohibition, she readily complied with it, and did not attempt to enter the chamber the whole day; but employed herself in making and sending him comforting things, and stepping about on tiptoe to prevent the rest of the family from making a noise to disturb him.

Mr. Sheldon, in the mean time was revolving in his mind the incidents of the preceding day; and was totally unable to form any probable conjecture concerning the intentions of his guest respecting his daughter. He had observed, with pain, her fondness and attention; and, with equal pain, the disgust it appeared to excite in him. That Dorcasina was fixed in the opinion of being soon connected with him, was very evident; and that she should be so void of understanding, as to form that opinion merely upon the civility of the captain he was loth to believe. Sometimes, as he observed him to eye Harriot Stanly with pleased attention, he was tempted to think that her charms had made an impression on his heart, and forced him to repent his engagement with Dorcasina. In short, he was lost in a labyrinth of doubt and perplexity, from which he saw no way of extricating himself but by applying directly to his guest and requiring an explanation of his intentions. But as Barry had never addressed him on the subject, he thought that would be acting with too little delicacy. After revolving the matter for some time in his mind he finally concluded to trust to time, and the honor of the captain, for the developement of all this mystery.

The day following it was reported that the captain was much better; but he dared not again run the hazard of appearing below, for fear of undergoing the same mortifications he had so recently suffered. James now informed him that the only means to prevent a visit from Dorcasina was to send her a message by him, that he would as usual visit her in the evening, and let him as heretofore go in his stead. He was averse at first, from this proposal, but the dread of seeing her again in his chamber (now she had become more disagreeable than ever, since he had seen and conversed with Harriot Stanly) at length overcame every consideration, and he consented on condition that this should be the last visit, and that James would now entirely break with her. To these conditions James objected: "I cannot with decency, sir," said he, "break with her so abruptly; it will require a little management. I will give her some hints of it this evening and make her one visit more, which shall be the last while we stay in the house." "I agree to those conditions," replied the captain, "if you will swear to keep her at a distance from me." James said he would do the best he could, and immediately left the chamber of his master to carry the intelligence to Dorcasina.

That lady was highly gratified by the message, for the three evenings that his visits had been omitted, seemed to her three ages. She therefore had some little delicacies prepared to treat him with, her chamber nicely cleaned, a cheerful fire blazing on the hearth, and her person adorned with uncommon care; for she intended, that evening, to see her lover and be seen by him. After she was thus prepared to receive him, she sat an hour, at least, waiting his arrival, with the utmost impatience, and wondering what could thus prevent it. At length, fearing that something unfortunate had befallen him, she arose and was going to his chamber to inform herself of the cause of the delay, when fortune, who was peculiarly propitious to James while at Mr. Sheldon's, and who raised him aloft on her wheel, for the purpose of afterwards making him descend with the greater celerity, brought him, at that instant, to meet her in the middle of a large, dark chamber, as he was going to her with an apology, of his own framing, from the captain. The thought instantly occurred to him that, as they were in the dark, it would be best for him to personate his master. Therefore, taking her hand, and speaking in a low, and soft voice, he said, "how unfortunate I am, lovely Dorcasina, in being deprived of the happiness of your company this evening. Your father and Mr. Stanly are come to make me a visit. The moment they leave me I will fly to your chamber, and, in your presence, forget the disappointment I now suffer." "Since this is the case," returned she, "I do not see what prevents my going and passing the evening with you." "Oh, no, if you love me do not think of it; perhaps Mr. Stanly would judge it improper, and I should be sorry to have even him suspect my Dorcasina guilty of an impropriety." "Oh," said she, "I am not under the least concern on that score. Mr. Stanly is one of my most intimate acquaintance; and surely one may indulge one's self in a little innocent freedom among friends." So saying, she moved on towards the door; while poor James was at his wit's end how to prevent her entrance; as that would fairly blast all his schemes and ruin him forever in his fortune. For a moment he stood hesitating and irresolute what to do. At length happening to recollect that the key was on the outside of the door, he sprung forward, "I will open the door for you," said he, "pray let me open it." So saying, he began to fumble, pretending he could not open it; till having locked it fast he clapped the key into his pocket. "Blast the door," said he in a low voice, "what is the reason I cannot open it?" "Let me try," said Dorcasina, "I am more acquainted with it than you are." "Oh no," said James, "I shall succeed presently; give yourself no trouble about it."

Luckily the chamber was so large, and the fire place round which the gentlemen were seated was at such a distance from the door, that as they were engaged in conversation, the noise made by James did not attract their attention. But, as his evil genius would have it, he came near being detected on another quarter, when he least expected it. For hearing Betty's voice on the stairs, and apprehending that she was coming that way, with a light, to go to the chamber of her mistress, "I will see," said he, "if Betty has not got a light, by which I may see to open this confounded door." Then gliding quickly out of the chamber, into an entry, through which Betty must necessarily pass, and placing himself behind the door, the moment she entered it, he dashed the candle out of her hand; and, in his hurry to escape, knocking her down, and entangling his foot in her clothes, he was thrown on the floor by her side. "Thieves! murder! fire! robbers!" vociferated Betty. "Confound your yelling," said he, in a grum voice; "utter another sound till I am gone, and I'll cut your throat." This threat sufficiently intimidated poor Betty, who lay more like one dead than alive; while James, inwardly wishing her at the devil, was endeavouring to disengage his foot.

The noise Betty had made was sufficient to alarm the whole house. The sound reached not only the captain's chamber but likewise the kitchen. The three gentlemen finding themselves fastened in, were in the utmost consternation, supposing that some villains had entered the house and were murdering all below. The servants, on the other hand, imagining that some terrible disaster had happened above, were coming, in a body, up the back stairs, with Scipio at their head. James at length making a sudden exertion, freed himself from Betty by carrying off part of her petticoat, just as the gentlemen had forced the door of his master's chamber; and hardly touched the stairs till he got to the bottom, and then went directly out of the house.

Dorcasina, in the midst of this scene of confusion, had thought best to retreat to her chamber and wait the issue, fearing that if the gentlemen caught her at the door of their chamber, they might suppose she had been listening to their conversation.

The gentlemen from the chamber and the squadron from the kitchen met in the entry, at the same moment, where they no sooner beheld Betty sprawling on the floor, and perceiving that it was one of her foolish frights that had alarmed them, than the latter, with one accord, in spite of the presence of the gentlemen, setting up shouts of laughter, inquired whether it was a cat or a dog that occasioned her terror now. Mr. Sheldon, on the contrary, was really angry, and without inquiring the cause of her outcry, told her he hoped that this would be the last time, she would thus, for nothing, alarm them. Poor Betty bore the reproaches of Mr. Sheldon, and the scoffs of the servants, without answering a single word; and when, after the gentlemen had returned to their chamber, the servants inquired into the cause of her exclamations, indignant at their incredulity she kept a profound silence, and retreated to the chamber of Dorcasina, to screen herself from their impertinence, and to relate the disaster she had met with.

"What is the matter, Betty?" said Dorcasina, as soon as she entered. "Matter ma'am," said Betty, "matter enough, I think, I'm almost dead with the fright." "Well, come, sit down and compose yourself, and tell me what has happened." "Why, as I was coming up stairs ma'am, thinking of no harm, to ax you about supper, just as I got into the entry, somebody put out the light, throw'd me down, trampl'd over and over me, and, in a terrible voice, said he'd cut my throat if I spoke a single word. I really thought then I should have lost my senses. But up comes Scipio and the rest from the kitchen, and your father, and Mr. Stanly, and the captain come t'other way; and then he went off down stairs like a spirit; but tugg'd so hard to carry me off with him, that, look here, ma'am, he took off almost half my petticoat. Then, whilst I was in all this fright, comes your father a scolding, Scipio a grinning, and all the rest a laughing, that it was enough to provoke a saint. Don't you think, ma'am, if they had been in my place, they wou'd have been as frighten'd as I was; and don't you think I had reason to be, ma'am?"

Dorcasina, who hardly knew what to make of it, considered some time before she replied; at length, "it is impossible for me Betty," said she, "to form any judgment from your account of the matter; as your terror generally magnifies molehills into mountains, and harmless people into evil spirits. I shall endeavour to find out the truth of the affair, and then I will give you my opinion of it."

Betty was not a little mortified to find she raised no compassion in any quarter; and, after having received orders about supper, she went rather out of humour into the kitchen, Dorcasina, at her request, lighting her quite down to the bottom of the stairs, for she declared she would not go alone for all Mr. Sheldon's estate.

Mr. Sheldon and Mr. Stanly after the alarm occasioned by Betty, soon took their leave of the captain, who immediately undressed himself and went to bed, tortured by a thousand fears, lest James should have been imprudent enough to be with Dorcasina, while the gentlemen were with him. But he was soon relieved from his apprehensions; for James, after walking backwards and forwards, for a short time before the house, finding that the alarm was over and all was still within, went round and entered the kitchen by the back door, as if he had just returned from a walk. The moment he entered half a dozen tongues opened upon him at once to relate the alarm occasioned by Betty, who in the midst of the recital, coming herself to the kitchen, they broke off in the middle of the story in order to attack her.

James finding that the gentlemen had quitted his master's chamber, went directly up to give him an account of the difficulties, in which he had been engaged. "What possessed you, James," said the captain, "to personate me, when there was not the least necessity for it. What uneasiness, and fear and apprehension has not this infamous business cost me! But this night shall end it. I will endure it no longer. Go, in the name of heaven, this once. You got yourself into the present difficulty by your folly; and you may extricate yourself as you can. Go; but remember this is the last visit, to which I shall give my consent."

James did as he was ordered, and groped his way in darkness and silence to the chamber of his mistress, but observing under the door that there was a brisk light in the chamber, he thought best not to enter without knocking. Dorcasina, who as she sat listening had heard her father and Mr. Stanly leave the chamber of the captain, and, expecting him every moment, concluded he had now come. But on opening the door behold it was James with his master's compliments, desiring that the candles might be put out and the fire extinguished; as since his late indisposition his eyes were weaker than ever. "Shall I assist you, ma'am?" added he, and went directly to the fire, while Dorcasina extinguished the candles. Having thus arranged matters to his mind, "I will go and tell him, ma'am, that you are ready for him, and he will be here in an instant."

So saying, he left the chamber, and walked across the next; but came limping back again directly, and assuming his master's voice, "I have at length" said he, "got free from company that was very irksome to me, as it kept me from the presence of my love. But tell me, were you not greatly terrified at the horrid outcry raised by Betty?" "I was at first a little startled," replied Dorcasina, "but as soon as I recognized her voice, my terror subsided. But pray do you know what happened to her?" "Yes, I can explain the whole matter to you. Coming suddenly upon me in the entry, she started, and letting fall the candle it went out as soon as it touched the floor. In turning about to join you again, I ran against her and pushed her down, she then sent forth the cries, which alarmed you. I desired her not to make so much noise, for she would raise the whole house. In endeavouring to step over her, my foot got entangled in her clothes, and it was some time before I extricated myself. As soon as I could I returned to my chamber door, fearing lest you should be alarmed; but not finding you there, I went in, just as your father and Mr. Stanly were coming out to see what had happened; and I joined them to prevent their having any suspicion of the truth."

"It is astonishing," said Dorcasina, "how fear will magnify and alter things. Betty, not knowing you, thought you knocked her down and trampled over her on purpose; and that you threatened to cut her throat."

James, who was glad to be rid of a subject, respecting which he was obliged to use so much equivocation, only laughed at Betty's terror; and directly began upon their intended journey. After informing Dorcasina that he had fixed upon that day week for his departure, "do you still entertain the same sentiments of kindness for me?" said he. "Will you not shrink back, when your affection comes to be put to the severe test of leaving your father's house, in a clandestine manner, to follow me to New England?" Dorcasina, who was a little hurt by these questions as implying a doubt of the strength of her attachment, replied, "did I not imagine that you were well convinced of the regard I have for you, I should think you doubted the sincerity of my professions: be not under any apprehension of my shrinking from the enterprise; my affections are too firmly fixed, and my heart too unchangeably your's, not to think every obstacle trifling, which stands in the way of our union. Nay, so ardent is my love for you, that I even rejoice in the opportunity of giving you this proof of it." "Thank you, my angel," replied James; "this declaration makes me the happiest of men: and now I would inform you that I think we had better not meet again, unless by accident, till the happy time arrives, when I shall carry you off in triumph, to make you forever mine. I cannot help being apprehensive that your father will throw some obstacle in the way of our union; or that some untoward accident will happen to prevent it. Let us therefore not meet, till we meet to part no more. This will diminish the danger of our design being suspected, and perhaps you had better not, before your father, shew me any particular marks of your regard." Dorcasina said she hardly knew how to live in the house a week with him, and forego every opportunity of enjoying his company; but if he thought it most prudent, she would acquiesce, notwithstanding the sacrifice. Having thus gained his point, and settled every particular respecting the elopement, James wished her good night, and left her to her repose.

Thus was this poor lady deceived and led on to take a rash and disgraceful step, by equivocations, misrepresentations and falsehoods. Had she not been rendered deaf as well as blind, by the mischievous little deity, she must, in a thousand instances, have detected the imposture.

Chapter V.

THE next morning, James, to the infinite satisfaction of his master, informed him that he should visit Dorcasina no more. Being now at ease in his mind he rapidly recovered strength, riding out every day, and passing the chief of his time below. He spoke frequently, before Dorcasina, of the near approach of his departure; and as frequently with tears in his eyes, expressed his gratitude both to her and her father, for the kindness and attention they had shewn him.

Mr. Sheldon observing that his daughter appeared rather pleased than otherwise, when the captain spoke of his departure, was still confounded at the mysteriousness of their conduct. But while he saw her so cheerful, and observed no impropriety in her behaviour, he felt no uneasiness. Every thing went on smoothly the remainder of the week, and nothing happened to interrupt the harmony of the family. Mr. Sheldon was the only person who experienced any regret; and this was occasioned by his reluctance at parting with so amiable, so modest, and so well informed a companion as captain Barry. The day before the one appointed for his departure, the captain, led by gratitude to Mr. Stanly for the visits paid him in his confinement, and inclination to see again his charming daughter, went, accompanied by Mr. Sheldon, and passed a most agreeable afternoon and evening. The unaffected ease and sprightliness of Miss Stanly were communicated to the company; and it was with regret that, at a late hour, the captain took leave of this amiable family.

During this visit Dorcasina had employed herself in preparing every thing for her intended departure. She packed up what clothes she thought would be necessary, and wrote a letter to her father, informing him of the reasons of her flight. This she did not intend leaving behind, but clasped it up safely in her pocketbook, with an intention of putting it into the first post office they should pass. While she was thus employed, her mind was agitated by a variety of sensations. She could not but feel some painful emotions, at quitting the house of her father, in so clandestine a manner, and from a consciousness of the uneasiness he must necessarily suffer, before he should receive her letter. Then again, reflecting that the time would be but short, and that its contents would make him full amends, entertaining so high an opinion as he did of the captain; add to this the expectation of being so soon united to the man of her heart, and the charmingly singular and romantic manner in which the business had been and was to be conducted, and the uncommon proof her lover would receive of her regard, all these pleasing considerations overcame the little regrets she experienced; and love, joy, and happiness, finally triumphed in her bosom.

At length, the long expected morn arrived. Captain Barry took a most affectionate leave of both his benevolent friends, and among other things, at parting, he said he was sure nothing would afford his parents so much satisfaction as an acquaintance with two people, from whom he had met such a hospitable reception, and who had laid him under such great obligations. "I hope," added he, "that the time is not far distant, when they will have an opportunity of thanking you in person for the kindness you have shewn me." As Dorcasina had prepossessed her father with the idea that the captain had declared himself her lover, he took this speech for the first intimation of it, supposing he meant, by means of an union with his daughter, to bring about an acquaintance with his parents. Dorcasina, being of the same opinion, looked ineffably delighted; while James stood by, observing with anxious attention every thing which passed.

Soon after they were gone, to the great relief of Mr. Sheldon, who felt a void at the absence of the captain, which he knew not how to fill, Mrs. Stanly and Harriot came to pass the day. The conversation, as was natural, turned upon the departed guest. Mr. Sheldon declared that he had of late been so accustomed to his company, that he hardly knew how to live without him; and that he thought him a most valuable and promising young man. Miss Stanly took the opportunity of Mr. Sheldon's leaving the room to rally Dorcasina upon the departure of her lover. "I shall see him again," replied Dorcasina, "sooner perhaps than you imagine." "Hang him," thought Harriot to herself, looking grave, "if he is going to marry this ridiculous piece of antiquity for money, he is not the man I have taken him for, nor worth throwing away a thought upon." Mr. Stanly came to tea, and, to the inexpressible chagrin of Dorcasina, they all stayed to supper; and it was past ten o'clock, when they took their leave. Twelve was the hour James had appointed for his return; and it wanted now but two hours of the time.

Dorcasina was therefore very impatient for her father to retire to bed, which, to her great joy, he did soon after their guests had departed. She then went into the kitchen, and hurried off the servants, telling Betty she might go with the rest, for she had no further service for her. The coast being thus cleared, she went to her chamber and brought down her trunk, her great coat, her hat, and her muff; and sat down, in anxious expectation of her lover's arrival, where we will leave her and return to him and his master.

It was about nine o'clock when they left Mr. Sheldon's, and having rode twenty miles by two, the captain, when he stopped to dine, found himself so much fatigued that he did not think prudent to proceed any farther. This resolution was very fortunate for James, as it gave him time to look about and procure what he wanted, which was a sleigh and a good fleet horse. These he easily obtained in the neighbourhood of the inn where they stopped. As the village was small, it was soon rumoured about that the gentleman at the inn was an officer just recovered of the wounds he had received in the defeat of St. Clair. James told the man, of whom he hired the horse and sleigh, that he wanted to return about twenty miles for part of his master's baggage, and that he should depart in the evening, in order to be back next day by the time the stage passed, by which he might get it conveyed to New England. This being a plausible story was readily believed, and James, after having seen his master in bed, took a French leave and sat off about nine o'clock, in high expectation of soon becoming a man of fortune.

As the night was cold, the travelling was good, and he arrived at L——, in a little more than three hours. There was not a light to be seen in the village, except a glimmering one in Mr. Sheldon's parlour, a sure indication that his mistress was in readiness. He had taken care to have no bells on the horse, so that he drove up near the house without being heard. Having hitched his horse, he softly approached the house, and observing Dorcasina, who began now to grow impatient, sitting in a listening posture, he advanced and gave three gentle taps against the window; this being the concerted signal, Dorcasina's heart leaped at the sound, and immediately putting on her coat and hat, she stepped cautiously to the outward door, which she succeeded in opening, without alarming the family. James, attaching his mistress to one arm, and taking her trunk under the other, left the house in silent triumph. Having seated Dorcasina in the sleigh, he jumped in himself, and drove off with the rapidity of a courier carrying the news of a victory or defeat.

As soon as they thought they had fairly made their escape, the tongues of this happy couple were loosed, and they gave way to the most rapturous expressions of love and exultation. But, alas, how transitory is every earthly joy! and how is every cup of pleasure, ere we have tasted it, infused with some alloy of bitterness! After travelling, with the utmost steadiness five or six miles, the horse, which carried these enraptured lovers, suddenly took fright at something which lay in his way, and set out upon a full run. James used all his address to coax him, and all his strength to stop his career, but in vain. On he went as if lashed by a thousand furies. Dorcasina was terrified and would have jumped out of the sleigh; but James entreated her to be quiet; assuring her that as the road was good they had nothing to fear. But, while he was endeavouring to encourage his affrighted companion, he was not himself free from apprehension.

At length, what he feared, actually happened. One side of the sleigh rising upon a rock, it was fairly overset, and the lovers thrown out. The horse, however, still kept on, and was out of sight in a moment, leaving them half buried in a deep snow bank. Luckily they were neither of them hurt, but their situation was truly pitiable. There was no house in sight, and they did not recollect having passed one for two or three miles. What was now to be done? If they staid where they were they perished; if they turned back it was doubtful whether Dorcasina could hold out to walk to the nearest house; and if they went forward it was uncertain at what distance they would find one. After deliberating for a few minutes, James thought it most advisable, upon the whole, to go on. "Possibly," he said, "the horse may tire, and stop of his own accord, and we may overtake him; or at any rate it is probable we shall reach a house sooner than by turning back." Dorcasina, shivering with the cold, assented to this proposal, and on they trudged, with spirits as much depressed as they had been elated at their first starting.

They had not proceeded far, before they were convinced of the futility of their first hope, that of overtaking the sleigh; for they found it all dashed to pieces, and the trunk having been thrown, with violence, against a stone wall, was forced open, and its contents strewed upon the snow. After viewing the scene for some time, in silent astonishment, James began to gather up some of the scattered clothes; and Dorcasina, following his example, picked up, as well as she could judge by star light, some of the most valuable; loaded with which, they travelled on in the greatest distress and dejection of mind imaginable.

After walking more than a mile, in the dark and cold, and no house appearing, Dorcasina's strength and courage began to fail. "I can go no farther," said she, "I must lie down here and die." James was in great perplexity; but being a soldier and inured to hardship, his distress was wholly for Dorcasina. He entreated her not to be so soon disheartened, but to persevere a little longer, and he did not doubt but they should reach some house. He then offered to throw away the clothes, with which he was loaded, and to carry her in his arms; but to this she would by no means consent, as she could not bear the idea of burthening him with so heavy a load. This kind offer, however, awakened her almost frozen tenderness, and inspired her with the resolution to persevere a little longer. After walking about half a mile farther, to the inexpressible satisfaction of Dorcasina, they discovered a light, which appeared to be about a quarter of a mile distant. But James was now in as great perplexity, and greater agitation, than when he was left by the horse in the snow bank. They were fast approaching a light, which was to discover his long imposition. His future fortune depended on the present hour.

The nearer they drew to the house the greater was his agitation, as he supposed he should be no longer able to disguise himself. He finally concluded, that a voluntary discovery of his person and views, would not only be more manly and generous, but much more likely to obtain a pardon for him from Dorcasina, than reluctantly submitting to an unavoidable detection.

Resuming, therefore, his own natural voice and manner, he said that he hoped Dorcasina would forgive him, for having assumed those of his master, as love alone was the cause; that it was impossible to live in the same house with her and be insensible of her charms; that though he was bred a gentleman, yet as the humble situation, in which fortune had placed him, made him despair of gaining her without an artifice, he had made use of that of personating his master; and that, since matters had gone thus far, and she had eloped with him from her father's house, he thought the best thing she could do, would be to take him for a husband, in whom, he assured her, she would ever find the utmost attention, affection, and tenderness.

Dorcasina, at these words, was almost petrified with astonishment, and could hardly credit the evidence of her own senses; or believe that she had been for so long time so grossly imposed upon. Making a sudden stop, she stood for some time motionless as a statue. To find, on a sudden, as if awaking from a pleasing dream, that she had left the house of an indulgent father, of whom she was the solace and support, and, in a clandestine manner, eloped with a common soldier, a servant to the gentleman by whom she thought herself courted; what a shock must it have been to her! Penetrated by the cold, and exhausted by fatigue as she was, her distress was almost too great to be borne. But as, in her present situation, she had no alternative in her choice, she was obliged to follow James to the house, in order to avoid perishing by the severity of the weather.

Hurrying along with a quickened pace, she kept a profound silence; reflecting, in bitterness of heart, upon the mortifying situation into which James' cunning, and her own credulity had plunged her; while the former walked by her side, observing as profound a silence, and unable to conjecture what Dorcasina's final resolution would be.

In this cold, comfortless, and silent state they reached the house, in which they had discovered the light. James rapped loudly at the door with the butt end of his whip. The man of the house, who was an honest farmer, got out of bed, and desired to know who was there. James, in a few words, related their disaster, and begged, for heaven's sake, that he would immediately admit them, as the lady was almost perishing with the cold. The man slipping on some clothes and coming directly down, with the lamp in his hand, which had been burning in his chamber, unfastened the door, and admitted the distressed travellers, and soon had a cheerful fire to warm and comfort them. The good woman of the house now made her appearance, and desired to know, if the lady had not better have a warm dish of tea, after the cold she had endured. Dorcasina thanked her for her civility, but said she had no occasion either to eat or drink, and requested only the favour of a warm bed. The woman said she should be accommodated directly, and added, "I suppose you are man and wife, and that one bed will answer for you both." "No," replied Dorcasina, with great quickness and spirit, "we are not, nor never shall be." "I ax pardon, ma'am," said the woman, "I meant no harm, I only wanted to know, because we have but one bed but what is taken up."

This speech of Dorcasina's destroyed all James' towering hopes, and demolished, in a moment, the pleasing fabrick, which he had for more than a month been assiduously labouring to erect. "Let the lady have the bed by all means," said he, in a humble and mortified manner: "I am a soldier, and can sleep on a blanket before the fire." The woman now went to warm the bed for Dorcasina, and while her husband stepped out to get some fuel for the fire, James resolved to make one more attempt to soften the heart of the obdurate fair. He therefore fell on his knees, and begged her to have compassion on his sufferings, and not to kill him by her cruelty, adding, that, since he had aspired to the honor of her hand, he had loved her so ardently, that he could not possibly live without her. In a serious and commanding voice, Dorcasina bid him arise: he obeyed. "James," continued she, in the same tone, "you have conducted towards me in an unmanly, artful, and dishonourable manner, and engaged me to take a step, which will be an eternal disgrace to me; on which account, you have reason to fear the just weight of my father's displeasure. But I will forgive you all, and even screen you from his anger, if you will tell me sincerely whether your master was knowing to your plot."

James, who now saw that Dorcasina was too deeply offended to allow him to entertain any hopes, alarmed too at the idea of her father's displeasure, suddenly came to the resolution of returning to his master, to whom he was strongly attached and from whom nothing but the hopes of making his fortune would have drawn him. It therefore stood him in hand, to save his master's reputation as much as possible, as he justly apprehended that without this protection, he should never obtain forgiveness from him, in case he ever discovered how he had carried on the farce with Dorcasina. Choosing therefore, to confine the "plot" in Dorcasina's question to the incidents of that night, he replied, "no, madam, it was all my own contrivance; and he is totally ignorant of it." "How then—" said Dorcasina, and she was going to question him how and where he had left his master, when the return of the farmer and his wife put an end to further conversation, and Dorcasina retired to bed; but it was in vain she attempted to close her eyes to sleep. She now, for the first time, reflected with extreme distress, on the pain and anxiety the step she had taken would give her father, and upon the disgrace which would unavoidably attach itself to her. She thus continued the remainder of the night, turning from side to side, and weeping tears of the most bitter anguish.

James being accommodated with a blanket, and left to his repose, thought it would be his wisest course to return immediately to captain

Barry. As soon therefore, as he thought the farmer and his wife asleep, with as little noise as possible, he left the house, and taking a cross road to the village where the captain lay, he had the good fortune to arrive next morning before his master was stirring. After helping him to rise and dress, and seeing him seated at his breakfast, he took the opportunity of going to the man of whom he had hired the horse and sleigh, the evening preceding. Here he found, to his great satisfaction, that the horse had arrived before him, and, having settled matters with the man about the sleigh, he returned to the inn to attend the commands of his master. After breakfast, they set forward on their journey, the captain having no suspicion that James had been absent from the inn.

We will now return to the mansion of Mr. Sheldon, and relate what passed there, when it was known that Dorcasina was missing.

Early in the morning, Betty, entering as usual the chamber of her mistress, was surprised to find that she was up before her. Having put things in order in the chamber, she went down into the kitchen and busied herself till breakfast was ready. After waiting for some time, Mr. Sheldon sent her a message, requesting that she would call up Dorcasina. At this, Betty was somewhat alarmed; but supposing Dorcasina might have returned to her chamber before her father came down, she went up again, and not finding her there, she discovered, on casting an eye round the apartment, that a large travelling trunk, and a considerable number of Dorcasina's clothes were missing. Running down to Mr. Sheldon, in a great fright, "as sure as I am alive, sir," said she, "Miss Dorcasina has gone off after the captain." Mr. Sheldon desiring her to explain herself, she informed him that, going into the chamber very early, she found that Miss Dorcasina was not there, and that the bed was made. "I thought it was very strange," continued she, "for Miss Dorcasina would never let nobody make her bed but me, saying as how I suited her better than any body else could. Howsomever, I come down into the kitchen, and was there till Nanny said you wanted me to let Miss Dorcasina know that breakfast was ready. Then I began to be all over in a terrible fluster; but thinks I, I'll go see if she han't gone back to her chamber. But when I came there, not a soul could I see, and looking round in her chamber and closet, I missed her travelling trunk, her great coat, which I saw hang up last night, and a great many other things."

Mr. Sheldon, in a maze, ordered Betty to follow him to his daughter's chamber, in order to ascertain what was missing. As Betty well knew every article of clothing her mistress possessed, she was able to inform him precisely what things she had taken away. They discovered in this search, that her hat, riding dress, and muff were gone, besides some linen, gowns, and a number of other articles of clothing proper for the season; by all which he was convinced that it was on her part a voluntary elopement. This conviction threw him into the utmost perplexity and distress. Why she should have left his house in so clandestine a manner, he could form no probable conjecture. He was loth to entertain so ill an opinion of captain Barry as to suppose he induced her thereto; and yet her going so immediately after him had a very suspicious appearance. But why should either of them wish to carry on the business with so much mystery, when they knew the high opinion he had of the captain, and how readily he should have given his consent to their union, had it been asked in a proper manner. In short, he was lost in doubt, trouble and perplexity; and charging Betty to conceal her elopement from the servants, and to leave them to suppose she was still in her chamber, instead of taking his breakfast, for which he had now no appetite, he went to impart to his friend Mr. Stanly, the cause of his distress, and to consult with him what steps were to be taken in the present embarrassing emergency.

Finding Mr. Stanly, his wife, and daughter assembled at breakfast, and knowing them all to be the friends of Dorcasina, he related to them, without any concealment, every particular of his daughter's flight, with which he was himself acquainted. Mr. Stanly was surprised, his wife astonished, and Harriot amazed. They sat for some moments looking at each other, without uttering a single word. This silence was, at length, broken by Mr. Stanly. "Indeed," said he, "this conduct of Dorcasina's is very extraordinary; and I am totally at a loss how to account for it. Did she leave no letter behind, nothing to afford you any light into the matter?" "Not a line," replied Mr. Sheldon, "and I am lost in darkness, doubt and uncertainty. I came hither to ask your friendly advice, whether I had not better pursue Barry, who cannot be far on his journey, and see if she be not with him." "I think," said Mr. Stanly, "I should not. That would be only making it public; and your first object, till you can gain some intelligence of her, ought to be, if possible, to conceal her imprudence. This may be easily managed between you and Betty, by pretending she is indisposed and confined to her chamber; you can do no more at present without injuring her reputation. I doubt not but you will in a short time hear from her; as it is impossible, with the affection she has ever shewn for you, but that she must soon write, and inform you whither she has gone, or at least of the motives of her flight. You will then have some light to direct you respecting the measures further to be pursued. At present, it is all uncertainty and obscurity; and it will be impossible to determine whether you go right or wrong." "What you say is just and reasonable," returned Mr. Sheldon. "You have given the best possible advice, and I shall without hesitation follow it." After some further conversation on the subject, Mr. Sheldon took his leave, his heart almost bursting with anguish.

We will now return to the infatuated Dorcasina, whom we left turning and tossing, in a state of mind not more to be envied than that of her distressed father. The morning found her in the same disconsolate situation, and she had not closed her eyes, during the time she had been in bed. As soon as she heard the family stirring, she arose; and having dressed herself, went down to the fire. This she would gladly have avoided, to prevent the mortification of seeing James, who she supposed was still there. But as there was no fire place in the room in which she had lodged, she was compelled to go below for the sake of a fire. Descending, therefore, with as much reluctance as a Frenchman to the guillotine, her eye glanced round on entering the room; but to her great relief she did not discover James. The farmer, his wife and children immediately made room for her to approach the fire, and the woman kindly inquired if she had got any sleep, and if she felt well, after her last night's fatigue. Dorcasina answered, in an obliging manner, to these queries; and then requested to know what had become of the soldier, who had accompanied her thither. "I don't know, ma'am," said the man, "I was up by the dawn, and found him missing. I think he must have decamped in the night. He was an honest fellow, however, for he left behind the blanket, which we had lent him." Dorcasina, infinitely relieved at this intelligence, said she thought she heard somebody go out in the night, and supposed it was he. "I suppose he is your servant, ma'am," said the man. "No," replied Dorcasina, hesitatingly; "he belongs to an officer—an acquaintance of mine;" and then, to prevent any further questions about him, she asked how far it was to L——, and was astonished at being informed that it was only ten miles; for it appeared to her that she had walked that distance at least, after being thrown from the sleigh. She then inquired of the farmer if he owned a horse and sleigh; and being answered in the affirmative, she made an immediate agreement with him to carry her to L——, the evening approaching; for she was ashamed to return to the village in the face of day, supposing that, by that time, her elopement was known to every person in it.

After having passed a most uncomfortable day, in the house of these obliging people, and rewarding them liberally for their hospitality, she sat out, just after the sunset, with the farmer, and arrived at 7 o'clock at L——.

Ashamed to appear, fugitive as she was, in the presence of her father, she took the resolution of going directly to Mr. Stanly's. After dismissing the man, she knocked at the door, which being opened by a servant, she requested to speak with Mrs. Stanly. This lady, upon coming to the door, was greatly surprised at seeing her; but she had the delicacy and the prudence to conceal her emotions; and to receive her as if she was totally ignorant of what had passed. "I am happy to see you, Miss Sheldon," said she, "pray walk in." "Have you any company?" asked Dorcasina. "None at all, my dear; there is nobody within but Mr. Stanly and Harriot." So saying she led the way into the room, saying, as she entered, with a significant look, "Here is Miss Sheldon, come to pass the evening with us." Mr. and Miss Stanly took the hint, and received her in their usual polite manner, without taking the least notice of the information they had received from her father. If they had been really ignorant of the rash step she had taken, they would have made many interrogatories upon her wan, distressed and haggard looks; her absence of mind, and her low spirits. Instead of making observations upon any of these, they endeavoured to cheer and comfort her. Harriot, especially, exerted all her gaiety and good humour, which by degrees partly dissipated the gloom, in which her guest was enveloped.

While the females were chatting upon various subjects, Mr. Stanly, anxiously desirous of relieving the distress of Mr. Sheldon, slipped out of the room and sent him a billet, informing him that he might now rest in peace, for his daughter had arrived, apparently in health, though somewhat dejected in spirits. He then advised him not to think of coming to see her; but to let her manage the matter as was most agreeable to her own feelings. Mr. Sheldon, in his answer, said, that by the intelligence he had received, his mind was relieved of a load, which had become almost insupportable. He then thanked him for his friendly advice; which he said he should punctually follow. After pouring forth his gratitude to heaven, for the safe return of his beloved daughter, this excellent man retired to rest, with sensations far different from those with which he had been agitated during the day.

After the family had supped, Dorcasina requesting to speak with Mrs. Stanly in private, that friendly lady took her up into her chamber. As soon as they were seated, "Oh, Mrs. Stanly!" exclaimed Dorcasina, bursting into tears, "what have I not suffered, since I last saw you? and what do I not yet suffer? Oh, my dear father! what must be his distress!" Mrs. Stanly replied that she was sorry to see her thus unhappy, and begged her, in the most soothing and friendly manner, to acquaint her with the cause of her present distress; as perhaps she might think of something to remove, or, at least, to mitigate it. Dorcasina thanked her for her goodness; and after wiping away her tears, gave her a concise though particular account, of her whole connection with James, and the manner in which she had been imposed on by him, from the first time she had received him into her chamber, till the adventure of the last unfortunate night.

Mrs. Stanly was filled with astonishment at the artful manner in which the affair had been conducted; as well as at James' extreme good fortune, in having so long escaped detection, which she thought was little short of a miracle; nor was she without suspicions that the captain must have been in some degree accessory to their private interviews. But these suspicions she prudently kept to herself. After a silence of some minutes, she told Dorcasina, that she could not blame her for being pleased with the addresses of such a man as captain Barry; but that she was extremely imprudent to consent to accompany him, in so clandestine a manner, to New England. "The moment," said she, "that he proposed any such plan, you ought to have suspected his views, and not have taken a single step without consulting your father, who would have been so able and willing to advise you. But I hope, my dear, you will learn wisdom by experience; and that the present mortification will put you upon your guard against the arts of mankind in future." Dorcasina replied that she was confident it would. "But this affair," said she, "is past, it cannot be recalled; and the mortification of being pointed at, for running away with a servant, and of becoming the jest or pity of the whole village, is not to be endured." "You need not distress yourself on that account," returned Mrs. Stanly; "for I can assure you, from good authority, that no person even in your father's house is acquainted with your flight, except your father and the faithful Betty." "You have seen my father, then," exclaimed Dorcasina eagerly. Mrs. Stanly, then, confessed that he had paid them a visit in the morning, as soon as he had discovered her elopement, to request Mr. Stanly's advice in what manner to proceed; and that Mr. Stanly had advised him, for the present, to concealment and secrecy; and moreover that Mr. Stanly had two hours before dispatched a billet to Mr. Sheldon, informing him of her safe arrival. "Thank heaven it is no worse," exclaimed Dorcasina; "and a thousand thanks to you, my dear and valuable friend, and likewise to Mr. Stanly, for the kind, delicate, and obliging manner, in which you have received and treated a runaway, a fugitive, an idiot." Mrs. Stanly rejoiced, with all her heart, to see her so sensible of the impropriety of her conduct; but told her it was now time to go to bed, and to endeavour to obtain some rest, of which she must necessarily stand in great need. Upon this they separated, and Dorcasina went to bed with a heart so lightened, that, in five minutes after her head was upon the pillow, she was burried in a profound sleep, which lasted uninterrupted till morning.

After breakfast, Dorcasina informed Mrs. Stanly that she longed, yet dared not to see her father. "I am sure you need be under no apprehension at seeing so kind, so indulgent, and so affectionate a parent," said Mrs. Stanly. "Shall we invite him to dinner?" Dorcasina hesitated—at length said she, "if you will engage for him that he shall not mention a word of what has passed, I will endeavour to collect resolution to see him." "I think I can engage for him," said Mrs. Stanly. She then went and informed her husband of Dorcasina's desire, and he immediately sat down and imparted it to Mr. Sheldon, as well as the engagement his wife had come under for him; and concluded by requesting the pleasure of his company to dinner. This affectionate parent, longing as impatiently to behold again his darling child, as if she had been absent from him as many months as she had been hours, gladly accepted the invitation.

As dinner time approached, Dorcasina started every time she heard the knocker. At length Mr. Sheldon entered, and simply asked Dorcasina how she did; as if she had been only at Mr. Stanly's ever since she had left home. It was not in her power to answer him. Her words choaked her; and, after vainly attempting to speak, she burst into tears and abruptly left the room. Mr. Sheldon, though pained for the moment at her distress, did not, upon the whole, regret it, as he hoped the greater mortification she suffered now, the less credulous and imprudent she would be in future.

Dorcasina did not return till she was summonned to dinner, by which time she had become pretty well composed. During this repast, Mr. Stanly exerted himself to entertain Mr. Sheldon; Mrs. Stanly, with her easy politeness, to introduce indifferent subjects of conversation; and Harriot, by her sprightliness and good humour to raise and cheer the mortified Dorcasina: in all which they succeeded so well, that by the time dinner was ended, the conversation became general and animated, and the guests easy and happy.

After dinner, Mr. Sheldon took an opportunity of seeing Mr. Stanly alone, in order to inform himself from that gentleman, of the particulars of Dorcasina's elopement, which he had received from Mrs. Stanly. They were both equally lost in astonishment at James' impudence and address, at his good luck in escaping detection, and at the surprising credulity of the unsuspecting Dorcasina. Mr. Sheldon lamented these foibles of his otherwise amiable daughter; and said they laid her so open to the snares of the artful and designing, that he should be in constant apprehension for her; and that it was his only wish on this side the grave, to see her well disposed of in marriage.

After passing a tolerably cheerful afternoon and evening, Mr. Sheldon and his daughter took their leave, and returned home. Being arrived at the house, Mr. Sheldon entered first to see if there was nobody in the way; and, finding the passage clear, advised Dorcasina to go directly to her chamber. She there found a comfortable fire, and the faithful Betty, by Mr. Sheldon's orders, waiting with the utmost impatience to receive her. The moment she beheld her, "dear ma'am," said she, "how glad I am to see you again! I was in a terrible fright when I found you was missing; and was afraid that the captain, with his palavers, had enfeigled you away to nobody knows where; and where we shou'dn't have seen you again for one while."

Dorcasina felt so happy at being again under her father's roof, that she allowed Betty's tongue its full latitude; who gave her an account of every particular that had passed in the family, during the two days she had been absent.

Next morning, Dorcasina went down to breakfast as usual, and the servants are totally ignorant to this day, that she had been out of the house since the captain's departure. Thus ended this most extraordinary affair, without drawing after it any mortifying consequences. Dorcasina again resumed her usual occupations; but the captain had made so deep an impression on her heart, that she could not, for a long time afterwards, think of him without a sigh.

Chapter VI.

FOR four years, after the adventures related in the preceding chapters, Dorcasina conducted herself with the utmost propriety, and her father flattered himself that time and experience had entirely done away all her romantic ideas; and that she had now become as rational a woman in regard to love and marriage, as she was in every other respect. About the end of this term, he one day received a letter from Mr. Cumberland of Philadelphia, requesting permission to pay his addresses to Dorcasina. Mr. Cumberland, who was a merchant engaged in extensive commerce, was turned of fifty, and had been three years a widower. He had five children, who were all of them married. He was a respectable, economical, domestic kind of a man, who loved money, and, next to that his wife (when he had one) and his children; and was what the world calls an excellent husband and father. Having married his two youngest daughters, since the death of their mother, his life became so solitary that he began to think of taking another wife. Having but a very limited acquaintance, and being too deeply immersed in business to have leisure to look round himself, he requested a friend to recommend to him some lady, who he thought would make him a suitable companion. This friend had heard of Dorcasina Sheldon, of her father's estate, and the amiable parts of her character. He therefore recommended her to Mr. Cumberland as a person in every respect suitable to become his wife. Mr. Sheldon, having formerly had dealings with Mr. Cumberland, and knowing him to be a man of integrity and punctuality, was pleased with the application; and thought that, if Dorcasina gave him her hand in marriage, she would be extremely well disposed of. He recollected Mr. Cumberland to be a very well looking man, and wished his daughter might have an opportunity of seeing him. In his answer, therefore, he informed him that if he could make himself agreeable to his daughter he should be happy in the connection.

As soon as it was convenient for Mr. Cumberland to leave his business, he prepared for the journey. Mr. Sheldon, in the mean time, thought it prudent to give his daughter information of this proposed visit, and to prepare her to receive Mr. Cumberland as her lover. Having put that gentleman's letter into her hands, and watched her countenance, while she perused it, he told her that, as he knew Mr. Cumberland to be a worthy man, he hoped that she would find him an agreeable one; adding, that nothing could afford him so much satisfaction as to see her happily settled in marriage. "And do you think, sir," said she, "that I would give my hand to a man, who thus desires to have me for a wife, without ever having seen me?" "And why not, my dear," replied her father, "if he prove agreeable to you after you become acquainted with him?" "That he never can, sir; it is impossible. I shudder at the idea of becoming the wife of a man, who, in a love affair, goes on in the same cold, regular, and systematic manner, in which he transacts all his other business. This letter you see has been written a fortnight. No sir, the man to whom I unite myself in marriage, must first behold me, and at a glance be transfixed to the heart, and I too sir, must conceive at the same time a violent passion for him. In short, our love must be sudden, ardent, violent, and mutual. Matches made upon this foundation can alone be productive of lasting felicity."

Mr. Sheldon was a good deal discomposed at this speech, but not so much surprised as he would have been, had he not, in his early youth, entertained nearly the same sentiments. But his knowledge of the world convinced him of their falsity, long before he attained the age of Dorcasina; and he had hoped, as was before observed, that her's, by this time, were entirely changed. Instead, however, of denying altogether the truth of her assertions, he judged it best to take a middle course. He therefore told her in reply, that though such a passion as she described might be conceived in early life, yet that both she and Mr. Cumberland were now too far advanced to be capable of experiencing such raptures; and that all that was to be expected, was a calm and rational happiness, founded upon esteem and strengthened by habit, and a knowledge of each other's good qualities. "You are very much mistaken, sir," replied Dorcasina. "I am confident that I am as capable of experiencing the tender passion now, as I ever was, at any period of my life; and I never will give my hand to a man, for whom

I do not feel it in the liveliest manner." "Well, suppose you should feel it for Mr. Cumberland, when he arrives?" "I am positive, sir, I never shall." "How is it possible for you to judge before you see him?" "I judge, sir, as I told you before, by the formal manner of his proceeding, and that without having ever seen me." "Well, you have no objection to seeing him I hope, and treating him with politeness." "None in the world, sir; provided you require nothing more of me." "That is all I require at present," said Mr. Sheldon. This conversation was interrupted by the arrival of Mr. Cumberland himself. It was in the dusk of the evening, and they had just ended tea as he entered. Mr. Sheldon received him with pleasure, and introduced him to Dorcasina as an old acquaintance. To please her father she received him with a tolerable grace; but not with all the politeness which was natural to her, and with which she would have treated him had she not known his errand.

The evening passed in conversation between Mr. Sheldon and Mr. Cumberland, in which Dorcasina took very little part: they talked of war and peace, of the expected division in the approaching session of congress; and especially of trade and commerce, those being subjects upon which Mr. Cumberland harrangued most fluently. He did not, however, pass the evening without observing Dorcasina, and examining her person, in a very critical manner. He was not at first greatly pleased with it; but after considering the thousand a year, he looked at her again, and thought her quite tolerable. Her having lived in so retired a manner was another recommendation, as she would not be likely to be so expensive a wife as one bred in the city. He observed, moreover, that she worked all the evening, and he flattered himself, from this circumstance, that she would make him an industrious wife. In short, he went to bed thoroughly satisfied with her; and without any suspicion that he should meet with the least difficulty in obtaining her.

The next day, Mr. Sheldon purposely took an opportunity of leaving together the widower of fifty, and the virgin of forty-five. "I suppose, madam," said he, as soon as Mr. Sheldon had left the room, "your father has informed you of the business which brought me here." Dorcasina turned all colours, and looked all ways. She was so totally disconcerted at this strange, abrupt, and singular commencement of a courtship, that she was wholly at a loss how to reply. At length, in hopes of inducing him to speak in a less mercantile style, "Sir?" said she. "I suppose madam your father has informed you that I came here with the design and hope of rendering myself sufficiently agreeable to obtain you for a wife." This was more explicit, and rather more tolerable. "My father did mention to me something of a letter he received from you, sir." "I hope, madam, you have no objection to receiving me for a husband." "The man, whom I receive for my husband must first be my lover, sir." "O certainly madam, by all means. I do not wish to hurry the ceremony. After we have settled the affair between us (as I flatter myself we shall) I shall of course be your lover until we are married." "I suppose it to be optional with you, sir, whether you will be my lover or not." "Why as to that madam, I will be sincere with you. I should not wish to become very fond of any woman, before I knew whether we were like to make a bargain or not." "Well, sir, to be as plain with you, I must inform you that our sentiments are so widely different, in that respect, that it will be impossible for them ever to harmonise; and you had better provide yourself with a wife elsewhere." "I know not where to look for one, madam, who would suit me so well in every respect as yourself; and since I have come so far on purpose, I should be sorry to return without having accomplished my object." "I am extremely sorry, sir," returned Dorcasina, more and more disgusted, "that you should have taken so much trouble to so little purpose; for, be assured, I can never consent to become your's; and had I been informed in season of your intended journey, I should certainly have taken some method of informing you that it would be fruitless." "Oh! Miss Sheldon, you must not say so. I shall tarry here some days; and, in that time, as you will have opportunity to consider of my proposal, you will, I hope, change your mind in my favour."

The entrance of Mr. Sheldon prevented Dorcasina from making any farther reply; and glad to be relieved, she made a precipitate retreat to her chamber. Mr. Cumberland informed Mr. Sheldon of the conversation he had had with his daughter, and of the little encouragement she had given him; upon which Mr. Sheldon expressed his regret; adding, that he should be perfectly satisfied to see her disposed of to so good a husband as he was sure Mr. Cumberland would make her. The latter thanked him for the good opinion he entertained of him, and begged he would intercede in his favour with Dorcasina. Mr. Sheldon readily gave his promise, but said that, after the refusal she had given, he had but little hopes of success. As soon, however, as an opportunity offered, he began with Dorcasina upon the subject; he told her, he had but one wish ungratified, on this side the grave, and that was to see her united to some worthy man; that he had flattered himself that Mr. Cumberland would prove agreeable to her, as from his knowledge of his character he was sure he would make her an excellent husband. "His children," added he, "are all married; he is a handsome man; his circumstances are affluent, and his character unexceptionable. Now tell me what reasonable objection you can have to him?" "I told you, sir, before I saw him, my objections to him; and that I was sure I should not like him. He has come here to make a bargain, as he calls it, just as if he had come to purchase an estate, without feeling for me any of that tender passion which makes the delight of the married life, or inspiring me with the least of it for him."

"I find I must be plain with you," said Mr. Sheldon, "and repeat that, at your age, you cannot expect either to experience or inspire a passion, which only belongs to youth, and that it is high time for you to give up all ideas of conquests and raptures, which, when they are experienced, are never lasting, and always settle down into the rational kind of happiness which, at your time of life, you ought only to look for." "And I must likewise repeat, sir," returned Dorcasina, "that I by no means despair of both experiencing and inspiring a violent and tender passion; and until I do, sir, allow me, I entreat you, to remain single. I am very happy with you, and do not wish at present to change my situation."

The latter part of this speech was uttered with so much earnestness that Mr. Sheldon found it would be vain to urge the matter any farther. With a sigh, therefore, he gave up his favourite wish; and with a sigh, he reflected upon the further consequences which might follow his daughter's obstinate adherence to those juvenile and romantic ideas, which had already been productive of so much mortification.

As soon as he had quitted her, he went to inform Mr. Cumberland of the ill success of his application; and, at the same time, advised him to give up all thoughts of obtaining his daughter, as he feared, he said, that all further endeavours would prove entirely fruitless. This advice Mr. Cumberland was extremely unwilling to follow. He had walked over Mr. Sheldon's grounds, and found an estate so fine, so large, and every thing about it in such excellent order, that having once set his heart upon it, he was very loth to give it up without making another effort to soften the heart of the obdurate Dorcasina. "I will try once more to move her, sir," said he. "She pleases me so much that I cannot think of quitting her without making another attempt." "I wish you success," said Mr. Sheldon, "but fear you will be disappointed."

We will now go back to the day, upon which Mr. Cumberland arrived at L——. Scipio, in assisting the servant to take care of the horses, learned from him that Mr. Cumberland was a widower, and he immediately suspected that his object was Dorcasina. Being a fellow of a merry humour, he often amused himself with Betty's simplicity, and, unwilling to let slip so favourable an opportunity as the present, the first time he saw her, after Mr. Cumberland's arrival, "well Betty," said he, "dare sweetheart come for you; dare massa Cumberland, a widower from Philadelphia." "Pho," said Betty, "I wish you wou'dn't be so full of your jibes, Scipio. It isn't at all likely he come to see me." "Yes he be, Betty—he wife die, two tree year ago, and he dater all marry. Pose he want sumbody wass he sirt, cook he vittles, make he bed; and so come gette you." Betty, with another pho, pushed by him and left the room; but it did not escape Scipio's penetration that she looked pleased at the bare mention of a sweetheart. Whenever she had occasion to go into the room, which she did several times the first evening of his arrival, she eyed Mr. Cumberland with attention, and thought him the handsomest man she had ever seen. As often would Scipio, when she returned to the kitchen, ask her how she liked him and whether she should not admire to have him for a husband.

It was autumn, and the weather was cool. Mr. Cumberland wishing, therefore, to have his bed warmed after riding, Betty readily undertook the office; and Mr. Cumberland, when he went up to bed, asked her a number of questions, and amongst the rest how old she was. "About as old as Miss Dorcasina, sir," said she. "Aye, and how old may Miss Dorcasina be?" "A little more than forty, sir." This question, joined to Scipio's insinuations, began to inspire even the humble Betty with strange and aspiring ideas. "Who knows," thought she, "but he had come to see me? There has been such things in the world before now, as a gentleman's marrying a servant maid; and I myself knew a pretty girl that a gentleman fell in love with, as she was handing him a dish of tea. He married her, and she is now waited upon by maids herself." These thoughts occupied her as she was going down stairs; and Scipio meeting her at the door, with the pan in her hand, asked her what Mr. Cumberland had said to her. "Why, he wanted to know how old I was," said she, with a simper. "Bery well," said Scipio, "he begin bery well, spose he want to know how old you be first. Besure you warm he bed to-morrow night. He say someting more, nex time he fine you alone; he don't want court you fore ebbery body. Mine wat I say, Betty, don't let Miss Dorcasina know he cum for court you; may be she want him herself." Betty made no answer, but determined in her mind to follow the advice.

In the course of the following day, Mr. Cumberland discovered that Betty was the favourite and confidant of Dorcasina. He therefore conversed with her more freely, while she was warming his bed, than he had done the evening preceding; especially as he found that she was in no haste to quit the chamber. Among other questions he inquired if she ever had any sweethearts. This question quite nonplused poor Betty, as she was equally unwilling to tell a fib, or to acknowledge the truth. At length, however, she made out to say, "I live so out of the way of being seen here, sir, that I never had many." "That is a great pity," said Mr. Cumberland. "If you lived in Philadelphia I dare say you would have many a one."

This compliment served to turn Betty's head completely; and her ideas were now as wild and extravagant as ever those of her mistress had been. Scipio did not fail to interrogate her again, and had the pleasure of observing that he had become her oracle; and that she believed every word he said. He charged her anew not to lisp a syllable of the matter, as Mr. Cumberland, if he should find out that she could not keep her love affairs secret, would think her very silly and not fit to be made a lady. Dorcasina, contrary to her usual custom, had not made Betty acquainted with Mr. Cumberland's business. He had disgusted her so much by his manner of transacting it, that the subject, as well as the man, was extremely disagreeable to her; and this silence greatly helped on Scipio's deception. He soon suspected, from appearances, that Mr. Cumberland was not like to succeed with Dorcasina, and was confirmed in it, by accidentally overhearing the last conversation he had had with Mr. Sheldon, in which he expressed his determination to make one more attempt to gain her. Scipio now thought that if he could but contrive to substitute Betty in her place, when he should again urge his suit, it would make most excellent sport. Knowing that his master had some urgent business, which absolutely required his presence, at the distance of twenty miles, and that he would be two days absent upon it, he was determined to set his wits at work to amuse himself, in his absence. Dorcasina had likewise been informed by her father that he was under the necessity of leaving

Mr. Cumberland to be entertained, for a day or two by her, as business of consequence called him from home. Dorcasina immediately suspected that this was a concerted plan between him and Mr. Cumberland, to give the latter a better opportunity of repeating his addresses. At this supposed stratagem, so totally unworthy of her father, she felt hurt and offended, and determined wholly to disconcert their plan. With this view she, that evening, dispatched a billet to Harriot Stanly, earnestly requesting her company for two or three days, as her father was the next morning going from home upon business; and begged that she would come as early as possible. Miss Stanly, who knew nothing of Mr. Cumberland's being there, and supposing that Dorcasina would be quite alone, returned for answer that she accepted her invitation with pleasure, and would endeavour to be there in season to breakfast with her.

The same evening, as Betty was going as usual with the pan to Mr. Cumberland's chamber, Scipio followed her into the entry, and told her that she ought to give him a better opportunity of conversing with her than the few minutes he had when he went up to bed. "Mine wat I say, Betty, don't tay a minute ater he go up; and when you bid he good night, tell him dat de lady he want to see will be in de back parlour alone at eleben clock morrow ebening." Betty followed her instructions most punctually; and as she was leaving the chamber, "the lady that you want to see, sir," said she, "will be in the back parlour alone to-morrow night at eleven o'clock," and immediately disappeared. Mr. Cumberland taking it for granted that it could be no other than Dorcasina, was pleased with the intelligence, though he thought it somewhat singular, that she should thus appoint him a meeting so late in the evening, when he could see her alone, in her father's absence, at almost any hour of the day. He, however, supposed that she could sometimes be whimsical as well as the rest of her sex; but as he imagined that she had changed her mind in his favour, this suspicion gave him no uneasiness.

The next morning Mr. Sheldon, after apologizing to Mr. Cumberland, and recommending him to Dorcasina, set off on his journey, and at the same time Harriot Stanly arrived. Mr. Cumberland, understanding that she was come to pass some days, now thought he saw the propriety and condescension of Dorcasina's conduct; and was so extremely well satisfied therewith, that he set no bounds to his officiousness and attention, and even shewed no small degree of

fondness. Dorcasina thinking that he was determined to force her to
like him, was so disgusted that she hardly treated him with common
civility; while he, imagining that her reserve was wholly owing to her
modesty, abated nothing of his attention. Harriot Stanly, mean time,
was sufficiently amused by the boyish fondness of the one, and the
stateliness and reserve of the other.

In the evening, after they had supped, Scipio began to fear that his
project would miscarry, as he now, for the first time supposed, that the
ladies would not go to bed before Mr. Cumberland. Here, however,
fortune favoured him. About ten o'clock Mr. Cumberland began to
grow impatient for the interview. Supposing that Dorcasina wished
first to dispose of Miss Stanly, looking very significantly upon Miss
Sheldon, he said that he did not feel disposed to sleep, and should
therefore sit up and read an hour or two, and, as he had no wish to keep
them up, he thought they had better retire. Dorcasina, rejoiced at the
opportunity of escaping from his persecution, immediately started
up, and saying, "come Harriot, let us go," they wished him a good
night.

Betty, who happened at this time to be in the room, was delighted
beyond measure, and went immediately out to communicate her joy
to her friend and counsellor Scipio. This African wag, almost equally
rejoiced at this unexpected proposal of Mr. Cumberland, told Betty to
make haste and warm the ladies' bed, and then go and dress herself in
her best clothes, and be ready in the back parlour to receive him. "But
must I not have a fire this cool evening?" said Betty. "Fire! no, you fool;
no candle nudder. Dark night best for courting, cause den lubber no
see sweetheart blush wen he kiss her, and love keep um warm nuff."
Betty, recollecting that James, whom she thought to be captain Barry,
always went in the dark to her mistress' chamber, thought Scipio was
perfectly right, and understood all about it. "But what in the world
shall I say to him?" said she; "I shall be in such a fluster that I shan't
be able to say a single word." "Say," said Scipio, "why, you muss say
noting but yes and no, and dat muss be in a wisper, dat he may tink you
modest; and you mus'n't tay but half an hour, dat he needn't tink you
forrard."

Away went Betty, quite in an ecstacy, to warm the bed for the two
ladies; but so much was her mind taken up with the coming scene, and
the thoughts of being a lady, that, regardless of what she was doing,
she overturned the pan and spilled all the coals in the bed. "Mercy on

me," cried Dorcasina, smelling the fire, "what's burning?" "The bed," exclaimed Harriot; and tearing off the clothes, they with some difficulty extinguished it. "How came you to be so careless, Betty?" said Dorcasina. "Accidents will happen," replied Betty, intoxicated with the idea of soon becoming Mrs. Cumberland, "and if I don't warm your bed to please you, you may get somebody else." "Betty," said Dorcasina, "this is very strange language, and such as I shall not put up with. I desire, therefore, that you would learn to be a little more respectful." "I don't want you to put up with it," retorted Betty; "for I don't intend to be your drudge much longer." She then bounced out of the chamber, leaving Dorcasina in astonishment at the new language she held, and totally at a loss how to account for this sudden alteration in her conduct.

Betty, more occupied with other concerns than what constructions would be put upon her behaviour, went immediately to her own chamber, and dressed herself in a cast muslin of Dorcasina's, and her best cap and handkerchief, and then went to the place of meeting. After she had sat half an hour, chilled by the cold, the clock struck eleven, and in a few minutes the door opened and Mr. Cumberland entered. He was directed to the place where Betty was seated, by the dim rays of the setting moon, and approaching and placing himself by her side, "How kind is this, madam, thus to give me an opportunity of conversing with you, free from interruption. I hope that you, at length, relent, and will consent to make me happy." "Yes, sir," whispered Betty. "But may I depend upon it? and will you not again change your mind as women are apt to do?" "No, sir." "Thank you madam. And shall I inform Mr. Sheldon when he comes home that you have given your consent?" "Yes, sir." This was followed by a salute from the lover, which so transported poor Betty, that she knew not whether she was in the body or out. A silence of some moments ensued, which was broken by Mr. Cumberland. "I do not," said he, "approve of long courtships; especially as I live at such a distance, and am so much engaged in business that I hardly knew how to spare the time to come now. Since we have closed the bargain I see no necessity of coming again more than once. In about six weeks my ships will all be fitted away; will you not consent to be married then?" "Yes, sir." Another salute followed this consent, and few more questions with the same number of laconic answers filled up the half hour; when Betty, punctual to the instructions she had received, and fearing to be guilty of some impropriety, arose to depart. Mr. Cumberland holding her by the hand said, "must you go so soon, madam?" "Yes sir," said Betty, and after receiving another kiss she left the room, and went immediately to her chamber, where she passed the night without closing her eyes to sleep, in thinking of the new clothes she would have; of the surprise of Mr. Sheldon and Dorcasina, when they should become acquainted with her good fortune, and of the astonishment and envy it would excite among the servants.

As to Mr. Cumberland, he thought it singular that he could get nothing from Dorcasina but monysyllables, and those only in a whisper; but he was so elated with the prospect of adding a thousand a year to his present income, that with the *yes*, which he thought confirmed it his, he was perfectly satisfied; and slept more soundly than he had done before since he had been at L——.

Chapter VII.

IN the morning Betty did not make her appearance in the kitchen, till breakfast time; and then she came dressed out in her Sunday apparel, to the no small astonishment of the white servants, and the inexpressible diversion of Scipio, who did not fail to get out of her every thing which passed in the back parlour. As soon as she had breakfasted, instead of assisting in the kitchen, as usual, she retired again to her chamber, where she passed great part of the forenoon, hoping and expecting to receive a visit from Mr. Cumberland.

Dorcasina was so displeased with the insolence of Betty the evening before, that in order to shew her displeasure, she determined not to employ her in any thing during the day; and observing that she did not appear as usual, and supposing it was from shame and compunction for her last night's behaviour, she inquired of Nanny, who waited on her instead of Betty, what was become of her. "She keeps her chamber to day ma'am," replied Nanny. "What, is she sick then?" "No ma'am, not sick, but bewitched. She came down this morning dress'd out in her changeable lustring, and would hardly give any of us a civil answer; and as soon as she had breakfasted she returned again to her chamber, and I have not seen her since." Dorcasina wondered afresh at her strange conduct, but was totally at a loss how to account for it.

Mr. Cumberland was, this day, more fond, more officious, and more foolish than ever: Dorcasina more stiff, more reserved, and more disgusted; and Miss Stanly more highly entertained and diverted. Mr. Sheldon finished his business so as to get home by three o'clock in the afternoon, to the no small relief of Dorcasina, who was resolved, after that day, to shut herself up in her chamber, and not be seen by Mr. Cumberland, except at meals, while he should continue at L——.

Mr. Sheldon had not been at home half an hour, when Mr. Cumberland, impatient to communicate the joyful intelligence, desired to speak with him in another room; and there he informed him that Dorcasina had given her free and full consent to become his wife. Mr. Sheldon rejoiced almost equally with Mr. Cumberland; but, wondering what had caused so sudden and so total a change in the sentiments of Dorcasina, he desired to know what methods Mr. Cumberland had used to accomplish his purpose. "I made use of no means at all," replied Mr. Cumberland, "but suppose I am indebted for this happiness to you." He then related the message Betty had delivered in the chamber, and every particular of the interview in the parlour. Mr. Sheldon thought the conduct of his daughter rather singular; but, supposing that a little mystery was necessary to make her relish any matrimonial plan, he imputed it entirely to her romantic notions; and said, "well, well, women love to have their own way, and when their freaks hurt nobody it is well enough to indulge them."

During tea, the company, all but Dorcasina, were in high good humour; and she, happy at again seeing her father, and catching a spark of the general conviviality, relaxed considerably of her late reservedness.

After the tea things were removed and the servant withdrawn, Mr. Sheldon entered, in the following manner, upon the subject which most interested him. "I hope my dear," addressing himself to his daughter, "that your delicacy will not be offended if I express before Miss Stanly the pleasure I feel at your late compliance with my wishes: she and her parents are our friends, and I would have nothing concealed from them." Dorcasina, at this speech, looked at him for an explanation; being totally unable to comprehend his meaning, or to conjecture to what particular part of her conduct he alluded. Observing her to be silent, and imputing her silence to her modesty, he proceeded: "Mr. Cumberland will not think I flatter him, after seeing me willing, and even solicitous to entrust to him the charge of my only child, when I say that I think he will make you extremely happy."

Mr. Cumberland bowed, Miss Stanly smiled, and Dorcasina stared with astonishment.

"To see you happily married, as I have often told you," proceeded Mr. Sheldon, "has for some years been my most ardent wish; this wish being now so nearly accomplished, and the choice you have made being so perfectly satisfactory, I can look forward to the end of life, without the smallest degree of anxiety or apprehension."

"What choice do you speak of, sir?" said the astonished Dorcasina, "I am sure I have made none. Be pleased to explain yourself." "Dorcasina," said Mr. Sheldon, "after matters have gone thus far, this trifling does not become you. It is childish; therefore, pray give it over and be serious." "I really, sir, do not understand you, or comprehend what you would have me say. But I certainly never spoke with more seriousness than I now do in declaring that I have yet my choice of a person for a husband to make." The manner in which this speech was uttered, beginning to stagger the faith of Mr. Sheldon, he looked at Mr. Cumberland, and Mr. Cumberland at Dorcasina; while the sparkling and intelligent eyes of Miss Stanly darted from one to the other, as if she wished to develope the mystery.

A silence of some minutes ensued, which was at length broken by Mr. Cumberland. "Surely, madam," said he, "you cannot so soon have forgotten what passed between us last evening." "What passed between us last evening!" repeated Dorcasina, more and more confounded. "Nothing on my part but bare civility I am sure; as Miss Stanly, who was present the whole time, can testify." "She was surely not in the back parlour madam, when I had the pleasure of conversing with you there, between eleven and twelve o'clock." "What do you mean, sir?" said Dorcasina, colouring with resentment. "And what is it you would insinuate? I have not set my foot in the back parlour these three days." "I surely dreamed it, then," said Mr. Cumberland, astonished in his turn at the peremptory manner in which she denied it. "And a most pleasing dream it was." "I imagine you dream still," replied Dorcasina.

A short silence again ensued; at length Mr. Sheldon having revolved the matter in his mind, said: "there must be some mistake in the affair. My daughter, Mr. Cumberland, is not used thus to disavow her actions." Then turning to Dorcasina, "Mr. Cumberland undoubtedly imagines that he had an interview with you last evening, in the back parlour. How to clear up this mystery is now the question." "I am a witness for Miss Sheldon," said Miss Stanly, "that she was not alone with Mr. Cumberland last evening, and that she was in bed half an hour at least before the clock struck eleven." "I am not allowed then," said Mr. Cumberland, "to credit the evidences of my own senses." "Was there a candle, or light of any kind in the room?" asked Mr. Sheldon. "None but the faint beams of the setting moon," replied Mr. Cumberland. "You could not then distinguish by your sight whether it was my daughter you conversed with or not." "Who else could it be?" said Mr. Cumberland. "Had I not every reason to suppose it was she, after Betty had informed me that she wished to see me there." "Astonishment! Betty informed you that I wished to see you in the back parlour?" said Dorcasina, and immediately rang the bell with great violence. "Nanny," said Dorcasina, upon her entrance, "tell Betty that I wish to see her." Nanny carried the message to Betty in her chamber, where, thinking it beneath her to do any more work, or to associate any longer with the servants, she had passed great part of the day; waiting with the utmost impatience to receive some message, or a visit from Mr. Cumberland. "Who is with Dorcasina?" said Betty. "Why her father, and Mr. Cumberland, and Miss Stanly."

Betty, supposing that the matter had all been laid before them, and that she was now summoned to receive their congratulations on the occasion, went down with great alacrity.

"Betty," said Dorcasina, as soon as she entered the room, "did you tell Mr. Cumberland that I wished to see him in the back parlour last evening?" "No ma'am," replied Betty. "Then I do not understand the meaning of words," said Mr. Cumberland. "Can you say Betty, that you did not tell me so, the night before last, as you left the chamber, after warming my bed?" "I told you, sir, that a lady would be in the back parlour, but not Miss Dorcasina." "Who was the lady?" asked three or four voices all at once. Betty at this home question was somewhat confounded, and stood looking this way and that without making any answer. "Speak, answer me directly," said Mr. Sheldon; "tell me who the lady was, or dread my severest displeasure." "It was I, sir," said she, with the most ridiculous grimace, and the most sneaking and mortified tone of voice. Mr. Cumberland frowned; Mr. Sheldon smiled; Dorcasina looked serious, and Harriot tittered. At length, said Mr. Sheldon, "did you expect to pass yourself off for Miss

Dorcasina?" "No, sir," replied Betty, "I had no such a thought." "What, then, was your motive for wishing to see him there?" "Because I thought, sir, he wished to see me." Mr. Cumberland again frowned.

"And what did you think he wanted to see you there for?" "Why, Sir, to——to——speak his mind freely to me about marriage." "And what could have put that strange notion into your head Betty?" "Scipio, sir." "Scipio? a scoundrel! he then is at the bottom of the business?" "Yes, sir, he is; for sartain I never should have had such supreme notions, if he had not kept such a joking, and telling me how that the gentleman liked me, and come on purpose to see me." Betty then almost sinking with shame, mortification and disappointment, made a motion to leave the room. "Stay," said Mr. Sheldon, "I have not yet done with you. I must have you and Scipio face to face." He then rang and ordered Scipio to be called in. He presently thrust in at the door, his black shining face, half serious, half laughing. "Scipio," said Mr. Sheldon, in an angry tone, "how came you to fill Betty's head with the ridiculous idea that Mr. Cumberland's visit was designed for her?" "I ask pardon massa, I no mean treat massa Cumberland ill. I only in fun with Betty, and no tink she fool enough to breve me."

Mr. Sheldon, in his heart, felt more disposed to laugh than to be angry; but observing that Mr. Cumberland was sorely vexed, he lectured Scipio for his impudence, and Betty for her folly; and then dismissed them.

Mr. Cumberland, who, from mortified pride, thought Scipio had come off much too easily, and that he deserved a good horsewhipping, sat swelling with vexation. Mr. Sheldon looked serious, and Dorcasina fretted; Harriot Stanly, finding they were likely to have but an uncomfortable evening, thought it would afford some amusement, to herself at least, to propose that Dorcasina should now consent to make Mr. Cumberland amends for the mortification he had so recently suffered. In quite a serious manner, therefore, she thus addressed her. "I hope, Miss Sheldon, you will not think me impertinent, if I presume to give my opinion upon this business. Your father has honoured me with the appellation of friend; availing myself of that title, I take the liberty of advising, since your father is so solicitous to see you married, that you should now give the promise to Mr. Cumberland which he thought he had obtained; and consent to make him happy." Dorcasina coloured and was silent; but, observing that her father and Mr. Cumberland both regarded her earnestly for an answer, she replied:

"I am sorry, Miss Stanly, that you should think me capable of so suddenly altering my opinion, upon a point, which involves all my worldly happiness. Mr. Cumberland is, I doubt not, a worthy man, and may make some other woman very happy; but he certainly was not designed for me. Our souls are not congenial. I feel for him none of that passion which gives to life its highest joys; and if I mistake not, he is inspired with no great degree of it for me. Let him, therefore, take for a final answer, my serious declaration that I can never be his." "'Tis very well, madam," said Mr. Cumberland, with the utmost sang froid; "since my person is not to your mind, I shall give you no further trouble."

Mr. Cumberland, from the first moment he beheld Miss Stanly, was struck with her youth, her figure, and her vivacity; but hoping to gain with Dorcasina, what with him was the one thing needful, he had paid her but little attention. Being now so flatly rejected by Dorcasina, he turned his thoughts towards Miss Stanly, and had been gratified to hear her plead for him with that lady, and took it as a good omen in his favour. He now compared her imposing form, her sparkling eyes, her blooming cheeks, with the diminutive figure, the faded complexion, and tarnished lustre of the eyes of Dorcasina. The more he observed her, the more he was charmed; and before bed time had really conceived for her as strong a passion as he was capable of feeling; for a proof of which, he had settled it in his mind, that he should be willing to take her without a penny of fortune. When, therefore, she was about to retire, he in a whisper begged the honor of half an hour's conversation with her after Mr. Sheldon and his daughter should have retired. Totally unconscious of the conquest she had made, and supposing he wanted to say something about Dorcasina, she very readily complied with his request; and giving a hint to Dorcasina, she communicated it to her father, and they immediately withdrew.

Being left alone with Miss Stanly, Mr. Cumberland took her hand and squeezing it very hard, "you are a charming young woman, upon my word," said he. "May I presume to ask Miss if you are engaged." Harriot immediately saw his drift, and was greatly surprised; but determining to humour him, she replied, with great modesty and apparent simplicity, "no sir, I am not." "I am very glad to hear it," said he; "I hope to prevail on you to engage yourself to me. Come, shall we make a bargain? I am rich, and you shall ride in your coach."

"How many children have you?" asked the facetious Harriot.

"I have five, Miss, but they are all married." "I fear they would not like so young a mother-in-law." "Oh, never mind that, Miss; if they don't like you they may stay away. I have a right to marry according to my own fancy, without consulting them." "But your time, I suppose, is chiefly taken up in the counting house." "A good deal of it is; but if I have so charming a wife, I shall spend less of it there, and more with her." "Oh, but I shall want to visit a great deal, receive a great deal of company, and attend all the public amusements, and must have a gallant all the time." "Well, I have a cousin who shall wait upon you sometimes." "How old is he," asked Harriot. "About forty." "Oh, hang it, that won't do; I must have a young fellow." "Well, there are young fellows in plenty in the city, who will be proud of attending you, when I am engaged." "Suppose they should take it in their heads to make love to me?" "You must speak to them no more." "Oh! if they really loved me that would be cruel." "They ought not to expect any kindness from a married woman." Harriot now thinking she had carried the farce far enough, said; "Well, if you insist upon my banishing every young fellow from the house, that shall fall in love with me, I have done with you. Like most of my sex at my age, I am very fond of admiration, and expect to make numberless conquests. Instead, therefore, of immuring myself with a husband old enough to be my grandfather, I am resolved to flirt and coquet with every young fellow, that comes in my way." "Bless me, Miss, how extravagantly you talk! Where did you get such strange notions? I did not expect to find them here in the country." "Oh! you will find them, whenever you meet with smart young girls like me; especially when they are going to marry rich old husbands. Why, do you think they marry old men from affection? No such thing, I assure you; it is only to spend their money genteelly for them, to dress, and to be admired." "Why, Miss, you are the strangest—but good night, I must think of you no more." "What, not have me after admiring me so much?" "No, Miss, it won't do, so good night." So saying, he abruptly retired; while she went up and amused Dorcasina with her humourous courtship. "A pretty husband, truly," said Dorcasina, "my father had picked out for me; that could, in the course of one evening, so easily transfer his affections from one object to another. But I did not want this proof to convince me that the man was not capable of loving with ardour."

As to Mr. Cumberland, he was so mortified at his want of success, that, ordering his servant to get up at daybreak, he arose himself soon

after, and set off in a very ill humour, for Philadelphia, before a soul
of the family was stirring.

Mr. Sheldon, at his rising, was not a little surprised to find his guest
had so abruptly left him; but imputing it to the right cause, he
endeavoured to bear it like a philosopher.

The disappointed Betty was seen less on this day than she had been
on the preceding one. Mortification now kept her aloof; and had not
Nanny taken pity on her, she would not have broken her fast for the
day. Dorcasina felt too much for her to require her services on that
day; but the next morning she sent by Nanny, requiring her attendance
in her chamber. On her entrance, she was so much struck with her
mortified and dejected appearance, that her resentment for her late
insolence entirely subsided; and, without taking the least notice of
what had passed, required her assistance as usual; which she gave her
with the utmost alacrity.

But what Betty dreaded as the severest and greatest trial, was going
again below among the servants. Having picked up part only of the
particulars of her affair with Mr. Cumberland, they were ready to
attack her, the first moment she should make her appearance. But
Scipio, who bore her no ill will, thinking that he had had sufficient
amusement, and Betty sufficient mortification, prudently restrained
them; and partly by entreaties, but more by promises of giving them
all the particulars, prevailed on them to spare her further confusion.
For a long time afterwards, however, they could not revenge themselves
upon her, for any little affronts, in a more effectual manner than by
calling her Mrs. Cumberland.

Chapter VIII.

ABOUT three years after Mr. Cumberland's unsuccessful attempt upon
Dorcasina, Harriot Stanly received a pressing invitation from an
intimate boarding school acquaintance, who was lately married, to
pass the winter with her in Philadelphia. As she was fond of the city,
and never had been there, except a few days at a time, since she left
school, the request was highly gratifying to her. Her parents knowing
the lady to be perfectly discreet, amiable and polite, and willing to

gratify their beloved daughter, cheerfully consented to her accepting her friend's invitation; though they were sensible they should severely feel the privation of her company.

Before her departure she paid a visit to Dorcasina, whom she found engaged in, and exceedingly delighted with, a new novel. "Have you read it, Harriot?" asked she eagerly. "No," replied Harriot, "I never have read a single novel in my life." "Never read a novel!" exclaimed Dorcasina, with astonishment. "Poor girl, I really pity you. You know not how much exquisite pleasure you have missed. To read the suspense, the hope, the despair, the distraction, the interesting situations, the joy, the tumult, and the bliss of faithful lovers, according as the little deity was propitious or otherwise, has been the delight of my life; and it has been my supreme wish and expectation to realize the tender and delightful scenes, so well described in these enchanting books."

"If I may be allowed," replied Harriot, "to form an opinion by the little I have observed of life, and by what I have been told of novels, they are seldom natural; but colour every thing much too highly, and represent characters and situations, which never have existed." "Your incredulity, my dear, is not surprising, since it arises from your ignorance. I would advise you, however, to remain in it no longer; but to seek instruction, improvement, and delight, in the perusal of these inestimable volumes. Why, you will be laughed at in Philadelphia, and set down as a person destitute of all taste and refinement, if you let them know, good heavens! that you never read a novel."

"They may set me down for what they please," said Harriot, "I have promised mama that I will never read one without her permission, and I shall, at all events, perform what I have engaged."

Finding it impossible to be serious upon this subject with Dorcasina, Harriot resumed her usual playful manner and continued, "I am pleased with the world as I find it, and hope to get through it as well as those whose sentiments are much more refined. You now, for instance, would not, I suppose, be content with a lover, who was not all perfection; but any decent sort of a man will do for me." "Why then did you not accept of Mr. Cumberland?" "Oh! hang him; he was too old. Besides, you know I was but his second choice; you were his passion: but finding you cruel, he thought, rather than go home without a wife, he would take me. Three years, however, having passed over my head without procuring me another offer, if I find he is not yet married, I rather think I shall set my cap for him." "You cannot surely be in earnest Harriot." "You will think I am perhaps, when you see me return Mrs. Cumberland. Have you any commands to Philadelphia. If I meet there with any swain, who has the same ideas of love that you have, shall I send him to sigh at your feet?" "Oh! no; if you love me do not send him. But if you should meet with an accomplished young gentleman, who entertains right notions of the tender passion, you can mention a friend of yours, whose ideas perfectly coincide with his. Perhaps it will incite in him a curiosity to see me; and seeing me may inspire him with love; and, if I at the same time should be equally susceptible, we may become the happiest human pair."

After some further conversation, Miss Stanly took her leave, unable to determine whether Dorcasina was most an object of ridicule or compassion.

The next day she was carried, by her father, to Philadelphia, where she was received with all that enthusiastic pleasure, so natural to youthful friends, after several years separation. She had been but three days at the house of her friend, when one evening, to her great pleasure and surprise, captain Barry entered. He had some time before quitted the army, and gone into merchandise in Philadelphia. His surprise, at meeting Miss Stanly, was equal to her's, and his pleasure much greater. Since his departure from L——, she was greatly improved in person and manners. A womanly dignity had taken place of youthful levity; and though she retained all her vivacity, it was well corrected by a just sense of propriety and decorum. Although he had been extremely pleased with her when he saw her at L——, seven years absence, during which he had passed through a variety of different scenes, had almost obliterated her from his memory. Being now in a lucrative business, and in a situation to follow his inclination, and meeting with one so greatly improved, who had before so much pleased him, he would have given way to the agreeable sensations, with which she inspired him, had they not been mingled with a fear that she had not remained so long unengaged. The company that evening was numerous and chiefly engaged at cards; but Miss Stanly declined playing, which gave Barry an opportunity of conversing with her, almost unobserved. He inquired after her parents, and whether Mr. Sheldon was still living and his daughter unmarried. "I never shall forget," said he, "the kindness I experienced from them; ever since I have been here, I have intended paying them a visit; but business has hitherto prevented. Mr. Sheldon is one of the worthiest of men; and Miss Sheldon, setting aside some peculiarities, an excellent woman."

In the course of the conversation, Harriot, never suspecting that the captain could be unacquainted with Dorcasina's elopement with his servant, inquired what had become of James. By Miss Stanly's inquiring for James, so immediately after he had mentioned Dorcasina, he naturally supposed that she must be acquainted with the part he had had in the first of the connection, and was not a little embarrassed by the question. Instead, therefore, of giving her a direct answer, "you touch me, Miss Stanly," said he, "in a tender place. I never, in the course of my life, was guilty of any thing I have so much reason to be ashamed of, as of that transaction." "Why, surely," replied Harriot, surprised, "you were not accessory to her elopement?" "What elopement do you speak of," said he, surprised in his turn. This brought on an eclaircissement; and the captain was, for the first time, made acquainted with the particulars of that singular affair. He expressed both indignation at the duplicity, and astonishment at the address of James; and endeavoured in vain to recollect whether he had at any time missed him, after leaving Mr. Sheldon's. He did not think proper, at that time, to explain himself any farther, respecting the part of his conduct which gave him so much compunction; and Harriot, though curious to know, did not think she had any right to interrogate him.

After Miss Stanly became an inmate at Mrs. Morton's, captain Barry's visits at the house were much more frequent than before. This fact did not escape the observation of Mrs. Morton, any more than the marked attention he paid to her amiable friend. She therefore rallied Miss Stanly, upon the conquest she had made; assuring her at the same time, that nothing could afford her greater pleasure than to see her united to so worthy a man, and to have her settled in Philadelphia.

Harriot, whose heart was entirely disengaged, could not but be pleased with captain Barry and his attentions. His character having more in it of solidity than brilliancy, his valuable and amiable qualities did not all at once disclose themselves; but every new interview brought them more and more to light, and consequently raised him higher in her esteem. The youthful heart of Harriot, had been a little touched, when she saw him at L——, under all the disadvantages of ill health, Dorcasina's persecutions, and the consciousness of having acted towards her a disingenuous part. His person was now much improved, although he was turned of thirty; and he appeared more animated and agreeable, as well as more amiable; but still modesty, that general attendant of merit, was the most conspicuous feature of his character.

Harriot, in reply to the raillery of her friend, declared that captain Barry had never addressed her on the subject of love; and that having formerly had some knowledge of each other at L——, she supposed that his attentions were merely those of an old acquaintance. This was literally true; for he had not yet the assurance to declare himself. It was not long however, before the fear of losing her, forced him to an explanation. Another gentleman of large fortune, a genteel person, and happy assurance, swore in a large company, where Barry was present, that Harriot Stanly was the finest girl he had ever beheld, and that he would spare no pains to obtain her. This declaration alarming Barry, he went directly home, and immediately wrote her a letter, wherein he declared the passion with which she had inspired him, and begged the honor of being received by her as a lover. Harriot's heart went pit-a-pat upon perusing the letter; but how muchsoever she was pleased with his request, she very modestly and delicately referred him to her parents.

Delighted with so favourable an answer, capt. Barry immediately wrote to Mr. Stanly upon the interesting subject, informing him of his present situation and prospects, and the desire he had of becoming his son in law. Mr. Stanly replied, that having full confidence in his daughter's taste and discretion, and wishing only for her happiness, he should never oppose any connection that she might think proper to form; and politely added, that if captain Barry were the man of her choice, he knew of no one, on whom he could more cheerfully bestow her.

Transported with pleasure, captain Barry hastened, with the letter, to Mr. Morton's; and requesting an interview with Miss Stanly, he communicated to her the contents. The business between them was soon arranged, and he was thenceforth to be received as a lover.

Chapter IX.

DURING these transactions at Philadelphia, Dorcasina met with a great and real misfortune at L——.

Mr. Sheldon, one day at dinner, was seized with an apoplexy. Dorcasina, like one distracted, dispatched one servant for a physician and another for Mr. Stanly. She wrung her hands in the deepest distress; hung over her senseless father, in speechless agony; then, turning her eyes to heaven, fervently prayed that he might be restored. Her prayers were, in part, answered. He began to recover the use of his senses just as Mr. Stanly arrived; but being extremely weakened by the violence of the shock, he was immediately conveyed to bed. Discovering that her father again knew her, and was again sensible to her cares and attentions, Dorcasina was composed, and conceived strong hopes of his recovery.

The physician arriving, and prescribing for him proper cordials and restoratives, he recruited daily; and finally regained so much strength as to be able to walk about the house, and enjoy the company of his daughter and friends; who were not without some expectations of his recovering a tolerable state of health. In these however they were disappointed. After about a month had elapsed, he one day discovered the symptoms, which his physician had told him would probably precede a second stroke. This circumstance he cautiously communicated to his daughter, and desired that messengers might be sent for the doctor and Mr. Stanly. On the arrival of the latter, Dorcasina was desired by her father to leave the chamber, as he wished for some conversation with their common friend. As soon as she had withdrawn, Mr. Sheldon taking Mr. Stanly's hand and affectionately squeezing it, thus addressed him. "I find, my dear friend, I am fast approaching that country "from whose bourne no traveller returns," and am happily not dismayed at the prospect. I have lived beyond the common age of man, and can look back with satisfaction upon a life spent in the practice of piety and virtue; and forward, through the merits of a Saviour, to a happy immortality. I experience, at this solemn hour, in a peculiar manner, the futility and emptiness of all the writings and arguments (many of which from curiosity I have perused) of athiests, deists, and freethinkers: nothing, I feel most sensibly, but religion and virtue, is capable of supporting the soul on the brink of eternity. These two supports disarm death of its terrors. But, alas! they do not extinguish, in the heart of a fond parent, all anxiety for an only child. My daughter will be left without a guide. You know her weakness, as well as her goodness. To your care I commend her. Watch over, and, if possible, prevent her connecting herself unworthily."

These were the last words of a good man at the hour of death, he was seized with another fit and immediately expired. Mr. Stanly was deeply affected; but not being certain that he was really dead, he left the chamber to call some assistance. Meeting, on the stairs, the physician and Dorcasina, and desiring the former to proceed to Mr. Sheldon's chamber, he took the latter by the hand, and begged her to accompany him to her's. "My dear father is gone then," exclaimed she, in a tone of agony. "I hope not. He is just seized with another fit. Stay with Betty in your chamber, and I will be back in a few minutes." Returning to the chamber of his friend, he found the physician, attended by several of the domestics, making some efforts to bring him back to life. They were, however, ineffectual. He had breathed his last. So died this good man, leaving behind him a character worthy of the highest esteem and closest imitation.

Mr. Stanly was just turning to quit the chamber, when he was met by Dorcasina, who could not be prevailed on, by all Betty's entreaties, to wait his return. She beheld the physician setting in silent melancholy, and the servants shedding tears of unfeigned sorrow for the death of their beloved master. "And is my dear parent then gone?" said she; and sprung forward to embrace the breathless corpse: but she fainted in the effort, and was conveyed senseless to her chamber. To this fit of fainting succeeded a universal weakness, which deprived her of the melancholy satisfaction of following the remains of her beloved parent to the grave. So deeply was she affected by the stroke, that it was succeeded by a long and severe illness, which confined her to her chamber nearly the whole winter; during which time, Mr. and Mrs. Stanly were unremitting in their attentions, and endeavours to soothe and console her.

Chapter X.

THE first symptom which Dorcasina shewed of recovery did not take place till towards spring; which was her calling for some of her favourite authors. This was to her affectionate maid, matter of great consolation, as she had for a long time despaired of her life. The book on which Betty happened to lay her hand was Roderic Random. As this was not so much to Dorcasina's taste, as novels of a more modern date, it had lain untouched in her closet for more than twenty years; but being now in a manner new to her, she perused it with great avidity.

Mr. Sheldon had, just before his death, hired a servant, a hale, robust young fellow from New England, by the name of John Brown. From his first entering the family, Betty had taken a greater fancy to this young man, than she had ever done to any person before. She frequently called him into the parlour, during the confinement of her mistress, and treated him with delicacies, which servants do not often taste. John, in the honesty of his heart, thanked her a thousand times, and loved her as a mother; without ever suspecting that she had cast upon him the eyes of affection. She had likewise frequently taken occasion to mention him to Dorcasina, praising him as a likely, honest, young man, and one that would make "a proper good husband."

Dorcasina finding that Roderic Random, under the name of John Brown, had lived with Narcissa (whom he afterwards married) as a servant, was struck with the name, and immediately concluded, that his namesake, so favourably spoken of by Betty, must likewise be a gentleman in disguise.

Filled with this idea, but without communicating it to Betty, she wished much for an opportunity of seeing him. Her invention at length procured her one. Being now able to sit up the greatest part of the day, "Betty," said she, one morning, when she felt better than usual, "I have a curiosity to see your favourite John Brown. I saw so little of him before my confinement that I have almost forgotten his looks; after I rise, pray send him up with some wood." Betty, pleased with the idea that her favourite should attract the notice of her mistress, gave a ready assent.

Dorcasina, now about rising, was particularly scrupulous (for the first time since the death of her father) in regard to her dress, and with a ray of pleasure on her wobegone countenance, she called for clean linen and a fine cotton robe. Her best cap was put in order, and her hair, which was turned quite white, and grown to a considerable length, was, upon this occasion, cut short, and parted upon her forehead.

Her dress, being at length adjusted to her mind, she fixed herself in her easy chair, in a languishing attitude, and sent Betty down to desire John to bring up some wood. John did as he was desired, without testifying either pleasure or curiosity. He passed by the chair, in which Dorcasina had, with so much care seated herself, cast one glance upon her, and laying his load upon the hearth, was proceeding to put it upon the fire, when Dorcasina, in the gentlest manner imaginable, said: "you need not put it all on now, John." John, who was in the act of stooping to take up a stick of wood, did not perfectly understand her: "ma'am?" said he, turning round and looking her in the face. "There is sufficient for the present, I say." John put the remainder in the corner, and as he turned to go out, Dorcasina purposely dropped her handkerchief. He stooped and picked it up, "I thank you, John," said she, in the same soft voice, accompanied by a languishing smile. "You are quite welcome, ma'am," said John, and immediately left the chamber.

The circumstance of his picking up her handkerchief confirmed Dorcasina in the idea that he was a gentleman; though his manners were uncommonly awkward and his speech boorish. No sooner was he withdrawn than Betty returned; "well, ma'am," said she, "don't you think he is a likely young man?" "You will be surprised, Betty," said Dorcasina, "when I tell you my real sentiments of him." "What is it, ma'am? you didn't see no harm in him I hope." "I saw, Betty, under the disguise of a servant, the appearance and manners of a gentleman. That he is one I am very confident; and I would give a great deal to know his history, and the accidents that have reduced him to his present situation." Betty, who neither believed nor relished the idea of his being a gentleman, was, by this declaration, almost put into a passion. "Why ma'am," said she, "you are quite out in your reckoning. I am sure he has got nothing of the gentleman about him. He is just like one of us; and, besides, he says his father is a tenant upon a farm in New England; and I wou'dn't give him for forty gentlemen." "Ah! Betty, he has invented that story, to conceal his real situation. I no more believe his being the son of a tenant in New England, than that his real name is John Brown." "Goodness! ma'am, are you going to argufy him out of his name too?" "I want no arguments, Betty, to convince me of what I have asserted."

Betty, having had many proofs that her mistress had a spice of obstinacy in her disposition, and finding it increased by age and infirmities, for the present, gave up the contest; which left her mind in no very agreeable situation. She had penetration enough to discover that Dorcasina was getting again into her old vagaries; and she feared, now she was uncontroled, that she would commit greater absurdities than ever. She had, moreover, entertained hopes of obtaining John for a husband herself; and she was not at all pleased with the idea of having her mistress, with her fortune, for a rival. With these cogitations she returned to the kitchen, muttering to herself as she went down stairs, "her reading only one of them there develish books, now, has turned her brain quite topsy-turvy."

The next day, Dorcasina dressed herself with the same care she had the day preceding, and directed that John should again bring up the wood; she being now determined to have some conversation with him, and find out if possible his real name and character. After the wood was placed on the fire, and John had turned to go out, "John," said Dorcasina, "sit down, I want to have a little conversation with you." This request greatly embarrassed John, who, not being accustomed to the company of ladies, stood for a moment, hesitating and irresolute. At length, however, he seated himself upon the edge of a chair. "Have you always lived in Pennsylvania, John?" interrogated Dorcasina. "No ma'am." "Where did you live before you came here?" "In the state of Rhode Island, ma'am." "The state of Rhode Island? That is a great way off. How came you to strole hither John?" "I wanted to see the world, ma'am." "You do not see much of it in this retired village." "I——I seed a good deal of it in my way here, ma'am." "And have you no wish to see any more?" "I am very well contented as I am, ma'am." A silence of some moments ensued; and John's embarrassment, the effect of his diffidence, fixed Dorcasina in her first opinion. "How old are you, John?" said she. "About two and twenty, ma'am." "Were you ever in love?" At this question, John reddened up to the very ears. "I——I don't know as I ever was, ma'am." A short silence again ensued, and John, tired of his situation, arose to depart. Dorcasina, thinking she had said enough for the present, and finding that he had no inclination to discover himself, suffered him to withdraw.

Betty, immediately after, entering the chamber, "well Betty," said she, "it is as I imagined; he is a gentleman in disguise." "Did he tell you so himself, ma'am?" asked Betty alarmed. "Not in so many words," said Dorcasina, "but all his actions evinced it. He hesitated, and seemed uneasy, as not knowing what to say to the questions I put to him, and it was with difficulty I could get even short answers from him; plain proofs that he did not wish me to penetrate too far." "Why, I will lay a wager," said Betty, "that the young man was uneasy because he was bashful, and thinks you so much above him. Why, with me now, he is as free and sociable as any thing, and tells me every thing I wants to know about his father and mother, and brothers and sisters." "Ah, Betty, you are deceived. He tells you such stories only to amuse you. He has, no doubt, some powerful reasons for his concealment, which time perhaps will unfold; mean while, when he is in the house, and I am not in bed, I wish him to bring up all the wood I have occasion for."

Betty went away silent and dissatisfied; resolved, the first opportunity, to inform John of the strange notions Dorcasina entertained of him; and to beg him to undeceive her, the next time she should enter into conversation with him.

As to Dorcasina, after being, by the death of her father, for months deprived of health and happiness, she now again began to enjoy both. Her increased years, instead of destroying her early romantic prejudices, only served to strengthen and confirm them; and she arose from her bed of sickness with ten times more extravagant ideas than she had ever before entertained. The reader will recollect that John blushed, when Dorcasina asked him if he had ever been in love. Now John's feelings being not quite so delicate and refined as hers, he consequently was not so susceptible of that tender passion. He had, however, entertained a sneaking sort of kindness, for a young woman in the place of his nativity, daughter of one of his father's nearest neighbours; but he had never gone so far as to ask her for her company. Dorcasina's question, by recalling Dolly to his mind, called up those blushes in his sun burnt face, which she imputed to so different a cause.

Dorcasina immediately concluded that having somewhere seen her accidentally, he had fallen deeply in love with her; but that his youth, his modesty, or perhaps his situation, had prevented his declaring himself; and that, in order to be near her, and to enjoy the pleasure of her company, he had let himself as a servant to her father. Fired with this idea, she began to entertain for him sentiments of a tender kind, and at the age of forty eight, to indulge again in those golden reveries, in which she had dreamed away the best part of her life.

The evening following, Betty invited John into the parlour; and, after treating him with a piece of tart, and a glass of wine, "John," said she, "I am going to tell you some privacy; and you mus'n't, for your life, ever speak of it to any living soul. Miss Dorcasina is a good soul as ever lived, and I am sure I love her as if she was my own mother; but you knows, John, every body has their failings; and Miss Dorcasina gets strange crotchets into her head sometimes. You must know that she has took it into her noddle now, that you are a gentleman, and have only put on the disguise of a servant; for what reason she cannot tell; and all I can say argufies nothing to the purpose; still she will insist upon it, and that was what she stopped and axed you so many questions for, to-day, to see if she cou'dn't find out who you was. Now, what I wants of you is, the next time she pumps you, to tell her flat and plain, that you are not, nor never was a gentleman."

John was so astonished at this speech, that he could not answer a single word. A variety of confused ideas rushing into his mind, he sat (regardless of Betty) wondering what Dorcasina could mean, and to what her assertions could tend. Betty waited some time expecting an answer; but finding him still silent, "what say you? John," said she. "Will you do as I desire?" "I'll consider of it," said John; and abruptly leaving the room, retired to bed to think without interruption upon the strange and unexpected intelligence he had received. Betty, hurt by the sudden manner in which he had left her, exclaimed, "I'll warrant now he'll stick himself up, and think himself a gentleman in earnest. I wish I hadn't been such a fool as to tell him of it."

John, who though extremely ignorant and illiterate, did not want for understanding, lay awake almost the whole night pondering upon the singular opinion of Dorcasina concerning him; and wondering what she had seen in him to lead to such a conclusion. He was perplexed with a variety of doubts, without being in the least elated; for the idea that so great and rich a lady, as he thought Dorcasina, and one almost old enough to be his grandmother, could have taken a fancy to him, never once entered his head. After more than half the night, spent in wild conjectures, and groundless surmises, he came to a conclusion, that, let the issue be what it would, there could be no harm in suffering her to remain in her error.

Next day, when he went up to the chamber with his wood, Betty was purposely present to inform herself whether he complied with her request. As to John, honest and well meaning as he was, he could not help feeling a little more confidence at the consciousness of being thought a gentleman; and let no one condemn him; perhaps it was not in human nature to avoid it. Dorcasina again requested him to sit down, and he now complied without any hesitation. "How long did my father engage you for, John?" said she. "For no stated time, ma'am; I was to stay as long as we could agree." "What wages was he to give you?" "Ten dollars a month, ma'am." "And are you willing to continue with me, now he is gone?" "Yes, ma'am, very willing." "I am glad of it; I shall increase your wages to fifteen dollars." Here the pleasure of being thought a gentleman fairly overpowered interest, in the bosom of John. "Ten is enough, ma'am," said he; "I don't desire any more." Dorcasina, delighted with this proof of a noble soul, urged the matter no farther, fearing it would offend his delicacy; but she determined that he should do no more work, and have as much money as he wished for. She then consulted him upon the management of her estate, and the work that was necessary to be done in the spring, which was fast approaching. "My dear father," said she, "left a great burthen upon my hands, in leaving me so large an estate to manage. I shall have occasion for some person to assist me in it; and as I think you a very proper one, I shall make you my overseer. I do not wish you to labour another day; but only to direct, and attend to the labourers; and see that the business goes on properly." "I thank you, ma'am, and will use my best endeavours to serve you." He was then dismissed, highly pleased with his promotion.

Betty sat all this time frowning and dissatisfied. She saw her mistress taking rapid strides towards making him her husband, whom she had hoped to obtain for herself. Had not this been the case, Betty was sufficiently concerned for the honor of her mistress, to use all her influence in dissuading her from such an act of self degradation as marrying a person so much beneath her. To have, in addition to this, her dearest hopes blasted, to find a rival of her affections in her mistress, and to have the person, upon whom she had set her heart, thus torn from her, was more than she had philosophy to endure.

"What are you about, ma'am?" said she, as soon as John had withdrawn, "you will just spoil an honest, industrious fellor by setting him up so. He'll soon be proud and lazy enough I'll warrant." "You are totally mistaken in your ideas of him Betty. I only wish to restore him to the level from which he has, perhaps for my sake, descended; and I would do it in as gradual and delicate a manner as possible." "Why, it is enough, ma'am, to drive one distracted to hear you insist on it so, that he is a gentleman. I don't believe you will find a single person in L——— of your opinion." "No matter, Betty; I shall not trouble myself with the opinion of people of no penetration. It is sufficient for me that I am convinced; and I shall pursue what measures I please, in regard to him, without consulting any person whoever." This determined speech, as usual, silenced Betty, and unable to contain herself any longer, she went into an adjoining chamber, and there gave vent to a torrent of tears.

While she remained in this situation, John happened to pass through the chamber in the way to his own. "What is the matter, Betty?" said he, "What do you cry so for?" "To see Miss Dorcasina make such a fool of herself," sobbed out Betty. "Why what has she done?" inquired John. "Why she had taken it into her head, not only that you are a gentleman, but that she is in love with you." "Pho, Betty," said John, "how you talk." "Well, its true, and you'll find it so; but you needn't go for to holding up your head and valuing yourself upon it. She has taken a fancy to others before you, and mayhap she'll see somebody she'll like better and change her mind; and then where will all your fine expectations be? Better stick to your kind, John, and not look so high to be disappointed in the end. I know of one that loves you as she does her eyes, and that would be always constant, kind and true."

At the former part of this intelligence John stood astonished, not having before had the least suspicion of it. As to the latter insinuation, he regarded it so little, as not even to take the hint, though it was so broad a one; and Betty had the mortification of being left by him in the same unfeeling and abrupt manner that she had been before. John, having shut himself up in his chamber, set himself seriously to consider of the information he had received; and from Dorcasina's late treatment of him, he was inclined to believe it true, though he hardly dared flatter himself with such a piece of good fortune. Dorcasina's age was not the least objection; he thought he could like her very well, and live very happy with her. The humble Dolly was entirely forgotten; and the astonishment his family, and their neighbours would be in, when they should hear of his marriage, for some time employed his thoughts: but he did not, like many others, determine in his prosperity to cast off his poor relations. On the contrary, he resolved, like Joseph of old, to send for his father, and fix him upon a farm, which he knew Dorcasina possessed about three miles from L——.

Chapter XI.

It was now April, the trees began to put forth their infant buds, the tender grass began to spring, and numerous birds were heard at early dawn, rejoicing in the rennovated year. Dorcasina, not insensible to the charms of the season, her health now improved by the almighty and irresistible power of love, dressed herself with unusual care, intending, with the assistance of John, to leave her chamber, and visit the house below, a thing she had not done for four months before.

Having given a description of her person, at the age of twenty, it will not be amiss to give a sketch of it, after a lapse of nearly thirty years, and to shew what ravages time, that mortal enemy of all beauty, had made in her appearance. She had, in her late sickness, been deprived of all the flesh her bones were ever clothed with; and her skin was sallow and full of wrinkles. Her front teeth were all gone, and her hair was quite white. In short she looked older than many women of sixty. To appear upon this occasion young and airy, she was dressed in a delicate muslin robe. Her hair, which she had the night before cut short and put in papers, was curled, in imitation of a wig, all over her head; and to conceal its natural whiteness, was loaded with powder.

After employing Betty all the morning, to set her out in this ridiculous manner, John was summoned to attend her. He, at first view, was struck with her appearance, and hardly knew her to be the same woman; so unbecoming was her dress, and so unsuitable to her age and present situation. "Come, John," said she, "give me your arm, to assist me down stairs." John, not being accustomed to gallanting ladies, and hardly knowing what she meant, stood at a good distance and stretched out one of his arms full length towards her. "Come nearer," said she, "and stand by my side." John did as he was commanded, and braced himself up by her side like a statue. She then took hold of his arm and moved forward to the top of the stairs. Having descended a few steps, she unfortunately turned her ankle, and falling, drew John after her, in such a manner, that this pretty couple tumbled together to the bottom of the stairs.

At this unfortunate moment, who should open the door upon them but Miss Stanly. She had, the day before returned from Philadelphia; and knowing the long confinement Dorcasina had suffered, since the death of her father, came now to make her a friendly visit. What a ridiculous scene presented itself to the astonished Harriot! Expecting to find Dorcasina, in her chamber, in a suitable and convenient dress for an invalid, what was her amazement to see her, at the moment of her entrance, come tumbling down stairs, dressed almost like a bride; and a great lubberly country fellow bouncing down with her.

The moment after their fall presented a scene for the pencil of Hogarth. Both feeling themselves hurt, and supposing the injury greater than it was, they lifted up their heads and looked wistfully and wofully at each other, without speaking a single word, or making the least attempt to rise. Harriot, in the mean time, regarding them in silence, apprehension and astonishment.

At length, they all three found the use of speech together. "Are you hurt, ma'am?" said John, getting up and scratching his head. "Oh, dear," said Dorcasina, "my leg is broken." "How came you to fall?" said Harriot. John now, with the assistance of Harriot, raised Dorcasina from her humble posture. "When did you get home Miss Stanly?" said Dorcasina. "Your unexpected appearance would have quite surprised me, if it had not happened at such a moment. Dear John, lift me gently; I cannot set my foot to the floor."

The whole house was, by this time, alarmed, and the servants all collected in the entry to learn the cause of the uproar. Dorcasina, with the assistance of Miss Stanly and John, reascended the stairs, with much more difficulty than she had descended them. As soon as she reached her chamber, her leg, which she supposed to be broken, was examined by Harriot and Betty; who found the skin and bones perfectly sound; but the ankle considerably swelled; from which they judged it to be no more than a sprain. After bathing it, wrapping it in baize, and placing it upon a pillow, her own pain being a little relieved, Dorcasina's concern was directed to John. She sent Betty down and summoned him to attend her. As he entered, "did you receive no injury in the fall, John?" said she, in a tone of apprehension and sympathy. "I fear you did, and I shall blame myself for being the cause." "I hurt my wrist a little, but nothing to speak of," said John. "Oh dear!" said Dorcasina, "was ever any thing so unfortunate? Betty, warm some more brandy quick. Come here, John, and let me look at your wrist." Discovering it to be swelled and discoloured, "Oh dear," said she, "do you call this a trifle?" Then making him pull off his coat, and turn up his sleeve, she bathed and bound up his wrist, in the tenderest manner, with her own hands, weak as she was, and then, with a thousand charges not to use it, she dismissed him.

Dorcasina now turned her attention to Miss Stanly; expressed great pleasure at seeing her, and inquired about all the news, all the fashions, and all the new novels. Harriot answered all her questions, and satisfied all her curiosity.

Dorcasina then began to talk upon the subject nearest her heart, which was John. She praised his fidelity, and attention; and said she thought herself extremely fortunate in having engaged a young man so capable of assisting her, in the management of her business. "And do not you think, Harriot," said she, "that he has very much the air and manners of a gentleman?" "I did not particularly observe him," replied Harriot; "but I do not recollect any thing very striking, in his appearance." "That's just what I've always said," interrupted Betty; "I told Miss Dorcasina that she wou'dn't find a single person to join her, and I hope Miss Harriot, that you will argufy her out of it." "Why, Betty," said Dorcasina, "you are strangely altered. Before I discovered the merit of John, you spoke frequently of him, in the highest terms; but now you cannot bear to hear me say a word in his favour." "I thinks just the same of him, ma'am, as I always did; he is a civil, honest young man; but not half so much of a gentleman as Scipio."

By all she heard and observed, Harriot plainly discovered that Dorcasina was still the same ridiculous woman, and that her affections were now placed upon a servant. This discovery gave her great uneasiness, for she felt for her a real friendship, and had hoped that the severe stroke of her father's death had cured her of all her follies. She, however, passed the whole day, with Miss Sheldon, and when she returned home at night, and was interrogated by her mother, upon the state of Dorcasina's health, she related in a lively and humourous manner, the scene she had witnessed, at her first arrival, the conversation which had passed respecting John; and her apprehensions of Dorcasina's inclinations towards him. At this recital, Mrs. Stanly was both diverted and astonished; and said that she hoped Harriot was out in her conjectures; though she confessed that the indications of a passion for the fellow were rather too obvious. "We must not suffer this match to take place, mama," said Harriot. "We are all the friends she has who are capable of advising her. Let us consult papa, and try if we cannot hit upon some method to arrest the business in its present stage." "It is possible, my dear that you may be mistaken. Let us wait, till our suspicions are fully confirmed, and not represent her as guilty of such a weakness before we are well assured of the fact. It will give your papa great uneasiness. Mr. Sheldon, on his death-bed, begged him to watch over and be a friend to his daughter. We will therefore not trouble him unnecessarily." Harriot readily assented to the justness of her mama's ideas, and they agreed to wait for further proof of her insanity, before they should mention to him their suspicions.

Mrs. Stanly, about this time, caught a violent cold, which, confining her to her chamber, prevented Harriot for some time from making further observations upon the love affair of Dorcasina. The latter lady was likewise confined by the sprain in her ankle, it being nearly a fortnight before she was able to put her foot to the floor. During all this time, John was constantly in her chamber two or three hours every day, where Dorcasina gave him all the encouragement a man could wish for, to declare himself her lover. But John, thinking the matter went on very well, and judging that the declaration ought to come from her, as being in every respect so much his superior, did not make her any formal avowal of his passion. This, in her conversation with Betty, she constantly imputed to his great modesty, as she had before done the backwardness of captain Barry.

Tired, at length, of waiting for an explanation, she determined to begin upon the subject herself. For this purpose she one evening desired his company in her chamber, and ordered Betty to prevent every interruption. John having seated himself at his usual respectful distance, "John," said Dorcasina, "you must, before this, have perceived by my conduct, that I am far from being insensible of your merit." "Yes, ma'am," said John. Dorcasina a little confused, was, for a few moments silent. At length she proceeded, "neither am I so blind as not to have discovered that the character of a servant does not belong to you; but that you have assumed it for particular reasons, with which I hope in time to be made acquainted." She was now again silent; and John, unwilling either to confess the truth or be guilty of a falsehood, made no reply, but appeared much confused. This embarrassment would have been a full confirmation in Dorcasina's mind (if confirmation she had needed) of the truth of her conjectures. She therefore went on; "I likewise very plainly perceive the passion with which I have inspired you, and which your modesty prevents you from declaring." Here she stopped again and waited an answer. John, observing that she had done speaking, and thinking that it was time now for him to say something, mustered up all his resolution and replied, "Yes ma'am, you are right. I do indeed feel a great regard for you." "Regard! John," returned Dorcasina, looking languishingly upon him; "that is a cold expression, compared with the passion with which you have inspired me for you." John really wished to express himself so as to please her; but he was too ignorant of polite language, and especially of that of novels, to do it readily to her satisfaction. He therefore endeavoured to recollect some of the terms made use of by his old acquaintance, in Rhode Island, and at length hit upon one which he thought would exactly suit. "I have a great kindness for you, ma'am," said he. "Ah! John," said Dorcasina, bursting into tears, "I fear I have been deceived, and that you do not love me." John, greatly concerned at her tears, and wishing sincerely to relieve her from her distress, caught eagerly at her last expression, and therefore went to her, and taking her by the hand, said, with real concern, in his countenance, "don't take on so ma'am, pray don't. I do love you dearly. I loves you better than I do any body in the world." Dorcasina, comforted by these words, made a motion for him to sit down by her side, which he complied with, without letting go her hand. To convince her of his affection, he even ventured to salute her.

Matters being thus settled to their mutual satisfaction, they very sociably passed together the remainder of the evening.

After John had retired, Dorcasina rung up her faithful confidant. "Ah! Betty," said she, as soon as she entered, "I am now superlatively happy. John—Mr. Brown I mean, has at length declared his passion for me; and in such a modest, engaging manner, as could not have failed of winning my heart, even if he had made no strong impression on it before." Thus much, in the joy of her heart, she communicated to Betty; but concealed from her the circumstance that she herself had made the first advances, and fairly drawn out of him, the few sentences he had uttered. She, moreover, acquainted her that as he was the supreme lord of her affections, and would shortly possess both her person and estate, it was her desire that all the family should call him Mr. Brown, and treat him with all the respect due to a person, who would shortly become their master.

This intelligence, though long expected, was too much for poor Betty. She answered not a word; and after seeing Dorcasina in bed, and performing all the little offices required, she withdrew to her own chamber, and there gave a free vent to her tears. Having thus, in some measure, relieved herself, she dried her eyes and went below to communicate to the servants the orders she had received.

The first person she encountered was Scipio, whom she drew aside, and informed of the determination of their mistress. The servants had long noticed with wonder and envy, the peculiar favour shewn by Dorcasina to John; but Scipio alone had any suspicions of her real motive, and these he hardly dared entertain, because he could not realize that his mistress would bestow herself thus unworthily. This negro was purchased by Mr. Sheldon, when very young, and had lived in the family full fifty years; had grown grey in its service, and was, like Betty, strongly attached to Dorcasina. These two alone remained of the original domestics of the family; all the rest had been changed. Scipio, besides an acute penetration, possessed a great share of that pride so frequently found in persons of his complexion. He now felt for the honor of the family, and could not bear the idea of Dorcasina's degradation. "Debil!" said he, "what you tell me, Betty? Missy lub John? John go marry missy? Den he be massa, pose. No, Betty; dis muss not be; dis sall not be. Massa Brown, ha! No, no Betty. John Brown no be massa here, I send him to debil fuss. Massa Brown, ha!"

This resentment of Scipio's greatly comforted Betty; for having a high opinion of his understanding and spirit, she flattered herself that he would contrive some means to break the match. They now proceeded together to the kitchen, Scipio requesting her to let him communicate Dorcasina's commands to their fellow servants.

John having gone to bed, the other domestics were in the kitchen. "So," said Scipio, addressing them, "John muss be call John no longer; noting but massa Brown, besure; but he sall have enough of massa Brown to make he sick. You all, Mary, Susan, Dabid, morrow morning, say, good morning massa Brown? How you do, massa Brown, and call him massa Brown at ebery other word." They all relished highly the joke, and promised to do as Scipio desired.

Next morning, as soon as John made his appearance, he had such a torrent of "Mr. Brown's" let loose upon him that it quite overpowered him; and he could not hold up his head or say a single word all breakfast time; and he was glad to take refuge from their persecutions in Dorcasina's chamber, where he was soon after summoned to attend her. She now told him it was not proper that he should any longer associate with the servants; and that she should give orders for him to eat, in future, with her. She then gave him the key of her father's chamber, which she said should thenceforth be his, together with all the wearing apparel, which he would find in that apartment, adding, "as you are very near my father's stature, the clothes, I presume, will suit you tolerably well. You will, therefore, do me a singular pleasure, to dress yourself, in a handsome suit, and come and drink tea and pass the evening with me."

John took the key; and, after thanking her a dozen times, and making as many awkward bows, went away, blessing his stars for his good fortune; and immediately entered the chamber, to contemplate his newly acquired treasure. Having locked himself in, he passed the whole forenoon in overhauling his wardrobe. On examining and counting the superfine coats, the handsome underclothes, the silk stockings, the holland shirts, and other smaller articles of dress, his joy was boundless. Spreading them upon the bed and viewing them separately and collectively, "and all these," he exclaimed, "are mine." He then, in his prosperity, not forgetting his humble relations, chose some a little out of fashion, and laid them by for his father; others that were partly worn he destined for the use of his brothers; thus passing the whole morning in greater happiness than ever a monarch experienced at ascending a throne.

As Dorcasina had invited him particularly to tea, and had mentioned nothing of his dining with her, on that day, he thought best not to appear before her till the appointed hour. At dinner time, therefore, he ventured again into the kitchen, where, as soon as he appeared, "Mr. Brown" was again vociferated by every tongue. He bore their jokes with patience, and dined in silence; comforting himself that it would be the last time he should eat in their company.

After swallowing a hasty dinner, he again retired to his chamber, where he amused himself with trying on some of the clothes. Finding, as Dorcasina had imagined, that they fitted him very well, he chose a suit, which Mr. Sheldon had procured but a short time before his death; and, by the middle of the afternoon, was completely equipped. He passed the remainder of it, in walking the chamber, in admiring himself in the glass, and in wishing for the hour at which he was to present himself before his mistress.

It was now after sunset, and he had opened the door to go to Dorcasina's chamber; but stepped back to take one more look in the glass. Betty, who knew nothing of his being there, unfortunately, at that moment, passed the door in her way down stairs. His back being towards her, she saw only the stature and the clothes. Such an apparition, in such a place, and at such an hour, was too much for poor Betty. She darted, like lightning, down stairs, rushed into the kitchen, where there happened at that time to be no person but Scipio, with her hair standing on end, and her face pale as ashes. She could only exclaim, "Oh Scipio! I have seen him, I have seen him!" "Seen who? what you mean? what ail you?" interrogated Scipio. "Mr. Sheldon; I have seen his apparition." "Pho! what nonsense! where you see im?" "In his chamber; mercy on me, in his chamber; in the self same clothes he had made not two months before he died." Some of the other servants now coming in, "holl you tongue, Betty," said he, "don't be fool; I go see what foolish ting scare you now." So saying he went directly up to the chamber of his late master, which Mr. Brown had not yet quitted; for on stepping back to examine himself in the glass, he had found something amiss in his dress, which he was still engaged in rectifying.

Having adjusted his dress, to his satisfaction, he was again approaching the door to issue forth, when Scipio, darting a look of indignation upon him, threw it hastily to, locked him in, put the key in his pocket, and walked deliberately down stairs.

Betty, hearing him approach, ran hastily to meet him, to inquire whether he had not seen the ghost. "Yes, Betty," replied he, "I see same apparison you see, dress sure enough in massa bess croase; and I lock him in he chamber, dat he need not come scare us." "Mercy on me," cried Betty, "how had you the courage to go so near? And besides, do you think you can keep in a spirit, by locking the door? why it can come under the door, or through the key-hole, in the twinkling of an eye. Oh! dear, I shall be afraid to move about the house, and shall expect to see it behind me, at every step." "Pho, Betty, don't be fool, and mine what I say; pend upon it ghos can't come out. Here de key; while I keep um, you see no ghos. Now mine, Betty; don't go for trouble Missy Dorcasina about ghos, but holl you tongue." Betty, perfectly satisfied with the truth of what Scipio had asserted, felt her terrors somewhat abated, and promising not to mention the affair to Dorcasina, they parted.

We will now return to John, who was astonished to find himself treated so cavalierly by Scipio. He first attempted to open the door; then called, knocked and stamped, but all to no purpose; and was finally compelled to sit down contented, and remain a prisoner.

Dorcasina, mean time, sat wondering, why neither John nor Betty made their appearance. After waiting a considerable time, she rang for the latter. Betty hearing the bell, and knowing she must attend, began to tremble from head to foot, and, in a whisper, begged Scipio to accompany her up stairs. To this he assented, and by the way charged her anew not to mention to Dorcasina the apparition they had seen.

As she entered the chamber, "Betty," said Dorcasina, "where is Mr. Brown?" "I don't know ma'am." "Is not he below?" "No, ma'am; they say he hasn't been seen there since dinner." "He must then be in his chamber; go to the chamber that was my father's, and tell him that tea is waiting, and that I am impatient for the pleasure of his company." Betty, at this command, began to tremble anew. "It isn't likely he's there, ma'am; the door was open and I look'd into the chamber, and Scipio has been up since, and locked the door, and he wasn't there." "This is astonishing," said Dorcasina, "where can he be?" "I can't tell ma'am."

Dorcasina waited above an hour, with the greatest impatience, totally unable to account for John's non-appearance. At length, said she, "I will seek some intelligence of him, by inquiring of the other servants." Luckily for Betty, instead of sending her down, she rang up another of the maids. "Do you know anything of Mr. Brown, Susan?" "No, ma'am." "When did you see him last?" "At dinner." "Which way did he go?" "I can't tell, ma'am." Susan was then desired to send up the other servant, and they all but Scipio attended the summons. He had purposely taken himself out of the way for the evening, to avoid answering any queries that might be made respecting John. Dorcasina put the same questions to each of them, that she had done to Susan, and received the same answers. She then inquired for Scipio, and being informed that he was not at home, she dismissed them. She now began to be seriously uneasy, lest her beloved had met with some misfortune. She walked the chamber; the clock struck ten, and her uneasiness was changed almost to agony.

John, mean time, finding he was not likely to be liberated, about nine o'clock very peaceably undressed himself and went to bed; and while his mistress was half distracted between doubt, fear, apprehension, and love, he was sleeping as soundly as if nothing had happened.

Dorcasina's terrors continuing to increase, she would not suffer Betty to leave her. This, for the latter, was a fortunate circumstance; for the appearance of the ghost so ran in her head, that she had not the least inclination to quit the chamber of her mistress. At length, about twelve, unable longer to endure this state of suspense, she was determined to go and examine the chamber she had assigned to John, to see whether he had changed his clothes, and endeavour, by that means, to gain some insight into his mysterious absence. She communicated her design to Betty and desired her to accompany her. This greatly alarmed her; but she hoped to dissuade her mistress from it, by informing her that Scipio had the key. "Then," said Dorcasina, "you must go to his chamber, and get it, for I am determined to visit the apartment, and satisfy myself." Betty's terrors now returned with increased violence, "Oh! dear, ma'am," said she, "I would not go to Scipio's chamber alone, at this time of night, for all the world." "Don't be such a simpleton, Betty; but go and do what I require." "You must excuse me, ma'am," said Betty; "I sartainly can't go; I shall sartainly think I see your father at every step." "I find, Betty, you will never be cured of your foolish fears," said Dorcasina; and taking up the candle, "follow me," said she, "see if you are afraid to go now." Scipio slept in an upper chamber, and Betty followed in an agony of fear. When they had got about half way up stairs, her terrors overcame every other consideration; and, making a full stop, "I beseech of you, ma'am," said she, "not to go to your father's chamber; I see his spirit there to night, as plain as I see you; and Scipio seed it too and locked it in." "Pho!" said Dorcasina, "what ridiculous nonsense!" Thus saying she proceeded on to the chamber door, and insisted on Betty's going in and getting the key, while she waited without. The noise they made awaked Scipio; who, hearing their voices, expected a storm was coming. "Scipio," said Betty, "are you awake?" "Yes," returned he, in a grum voice; "what plague you want dis time night?" "I want the key of Mr. Sheldon's chamber. Miss Dorcasina will go there to look for John, though I told her that you and I had both seen a spirit there." "She better not go," said Scipio, raising his voice, for Dorcasina to hear; "she be frighted, I neber see such sight before." "Scipio," said Dorcasina, "you did not use to be so childish, send me the key, and do not trouble yourself about me." "I no truss you dare lone, ma'am; if you go, I go too. Get out Betty, and leave candle for me see dress me."

Betty, overjoyed that they were to be accompanied by Scipio, very readily obeyed his orders; while Dorcasina, in spite of her uneasiness, was out of all patience at their folly. Scipio was a long time in dressing himself, that he might consider how he should act in the present emergency. He, at length, made his appearance, and again endeavoured to dissuade Dorcasina from visiting the chamber, but in vain; she commanded him to follow her. The three being arrived at the door of the fatal chamber, "if you will go in, ma'am," said Scipio, "let me make noise fuss, for fright away ghos." So saying, he set up a yell, which could only be exceeded by the warhoop of the Indians. Betty screamed, and Dorcasina herself was startled. Every person in the house was awaked and alarmed; each thought the house beset by thieves and murderers; the maids sprung from their beds, and run for protection to the chambers of the men.

As for the person, about whom all this bustle was made, being waked out of a sound sleep by the tremendous yelling, and the screams which immediately succeeded, at his chamber door, he was, upon this occasion, though not naturally timid, greatly terrified. The roof of the kitchen, which was of one story, was directly under one of the windows of his chamber. Upon the first alarm, therefore, without consideration, or hesitation, he sprung out of bed, drew a blanket after him, in which he hastily wrapped himself; then opening the window, he leaped out upon this roof, from which, by means of a ladder, he reached the ground in safety.

The noise he made, in thus quitting the chamber, being distinctly heard by Dorcasina and her attendants, Betty again screamed, "the ghost! the ghost!" and her strength failing her, through excessive terror, she dropped almost senseless upon the floor, and in her fall extinguished their light. They were now in utter darkness, Dorcasina's grief and anger both lost in amazement; Betty upon the floor half dead with apprehension; and Scipio grinning and rejoicing in the success of his plan. They remained, for some moments in silence and suspense, but soon heard a noise approaching from another quarter. The two men servants, in an upper chamber, having their suspicions of murder and robbers confirmed, by Betty's second outcry, whose voice they recognized, they determined to go to her assistance, and sell their lives, if necessary, as dear as possible. One of them, being armed with a large jack knife he had in his pocket, and the other with a cane, which happened to be in the chamber, they sallied forth, followed by the maids, who were afraid to stay behind. Directing their steps to the chamber, from which the noise proceeded, they had reached the door, when they were heard by those within. Scipio, readily comprehending who they were, was not in the least daunted; but Dorcasina, being, as was before observed, lost in amazement, now began, for the first time, to feel some apprehensions. Thinking the house was haunted, in good earnest, she moved up close to Scipio, and stood profoundly silent. The door now opened, and the men listened for some further noise to direct them; but finding all still, "we are mistaken," said David; "there is nobody here; let us go to the chamber of Miss Dorcasina." Dorcasina knowing his voice was relieved from her fears, and readily comprehended what had brought them hither. "David," said she, "you need not be alarmed; I am safe; but go down and get a candle immediately, that we may see whether Betty be dead or alive."

Betty who had lain all this time almost senseless, now revived, and said she was not quite dead, but was almost. David, having groped his way down into the kitchen, soon returned with a light, and discovered the two groups, who were mutually astonished at each other. At one extremity of the chamber, which was large, stood Dorcasina and Scipio, one at the head and the other at the feet of Betty; at the other the two maids wrapped in blankets, holding fast by Robert, who himself was but half dressed. They stood for some moments gazing at each other in silence. Scipio could hardly contain himself; and Dorcasina could scarcely refrain from laughter, at seeing the whole family thus strangely collected. Recollecting, however, that John, her dear John, alone was missing, a sigh succeeded the smile on her countenance, and she thus dismissed them. "You may all retire again to bed; the alarm which called you up was a false one; it was only one of Betty's foolish frights. Come Betty, I have indulged you long enough in your folly; rise and follow me. And you, Scipio, come likewise to my chamber; I want to have some conversation with you."

Scipio did as he was commanded, and followed his mistress, in no small uneasiness, lest he should be forced to acknowledge the trick he had played John, and thereby incur her displeasure.

"Scipio," said Dorcasina, as soon as she was seated, "tell me seriously what gave rise to the ridiculous idea of your having seen my father's spirit." This was a home question; and Scipio, who wished to avoid telling his mistress downright falsehoods, would have been embarrassed for an answer, had not Betty, who firmly believed she had seen a spirit, now put in her oar. "La, ma'am," said she, "I seed it first, a little after sunset, as I was going down to bring up the tea urn. The chamber door was open and I seed your father as plain as I see you this minute. His back was towards me, and he had on the very coat he had made a little before his death. I run down and told Scipio, and he went up and seed it too, and locked the door that it need not get out."

The truth now for the first time flashed upon Dorcasina's mind. "What have you done, Scipio?" said she, "it was Mr. Brown whom you saw, and Mr. Brown that you locked in. How could you be so deceived?" "Why, how cou'd I tink, ma'am, it was John, in massa chamber, and in massa crose?" Dorcasina was not without some suspicion that Scipio's ignorance was all affected, knowing him to have an understanding superior to superstition; but she was so overjoyed at finding out the mystery, and at having reason to think that her beloved John was safe, that she let it pass merely as a piece of waggery. "Here, take the key again," said she, "and go in softly; if he is asleep, though that is not probable after the monstrous noise you made at his door, you need not awake him. Go quickly, and come and inform me whether he is there."

Scipio, taking the candle, went to the chamber; where he found not Mr. Brown, but his clothes, as well as those of Mr. Sheldon, in which he had been dressed, lying about the floor, and the bed in disorder. He found also a window open, which left him at no loss to conjecture which way the affrighted John had escaped. Delighted with the success of his plots, he pulled down the window, gathered up the clothes that were scattered about and put them out of sight into a closet; then hastily beat up and smoothed the bed, that it might not be discovered that any person had occupied it. Having thus put the chamber in tolerable order, he returned to that of his mistress. "I hope ma'am," said he, as soon as he entered, "you now be convince it was no John we see. I hunt ebery corner, under bed, in de croset, and no John dare." "Good heavens! Scipio, what do you tell me? You plunge me again into despair. I will go myself, as I first intended, and see if I can discover nothing that will serve for a clue to clear up this strange mystery."

Thus saying, she glided quickly to the chamber in question; she throws her eyes around; she calls upon John, her beloved John; but no answer is returned; all is still and silent as the chambers of death. She returned to her own, lost in perplexity and despair. "What could that noise mean, Scipio," said she, "that we heard at the chamber door?" "What, sure nuff, Misse," said Scipio, pretending to look amazed. "Good heavens!" cried Dorcasina, "I shall go distracted. Some dreadful accident must have happened to my dear Mr. Brown! I shall not go to bed this night, but you may go Scipio; and pray, as soon as ever it is light, get up and muster David and Robert, and make inquiries all over the village, and if possible, bring me some tidings of him." Scipio thinking himself very fortunate to come off so, retired to bed; while Dorcasina passed the remainder of the night, in the greatest distress imaginable.

It is now time to see what became of poor John, after his descent from the chamber window.

The nearest dwelling to Mr. Sheldon's house was the miserable hut of a poor labourer, with whom John had contracted a considerable intimacy. Thither, upon this terrible occasion, he took his way. Having reached the door almost breathless with terror and running, and to his great joy finding it unfastened, he entered without ceremony. The man being waked by his entrance started on end, and asked who was there. "It is I, John Brown," said John, "Our doors are all fastened, and I wish you to lend me a rug, and let me lay down on your floor." The man supposing, that having upon some occasion stayed out too late, he had got fastened out, readily granted his request, and told him he would find one on a chest at the head of the bed. John, rolling himself in the rug, couched down by the fire, and endeavoured to get to sleep; but the unaccountable noise he had heard so ran in his head, that it was a long time before he was sufficiently composed. At length, however, he fell asleep; but waked again with the first dawn of morning.

He now began to consider, and be ashamed of his situation. An hour or two of sound sleep had chased from his imagination all those frightful ideas, with which it had, the preceding night, been filled. But how he could return home, in his present plight, or how appear before

Dorcasina after his cowardly flight, were considerations which gave him great uneasiness. A sudden thought entered his head. He raised himself up, and observing that the man and his wife were still buried in a profound sleep, he softly opened the door, and quitted the house without disturbing them. His intention was to mount the ladder, and enter his chamber by the same window, through which he had escaped from it; praying ardently that none of the family might be stirring, and if he should chance to meet any person on the way, that he might be taken for an Indian, some of whom, now and then, passed through the village. With this view he wrapped himself, head and all, in his blanket, and began to retrace his steps to the mansion of Dorcasina, with almost as much speed as he had quitted it.

Scipio, mean time, punctual to the commands of his mistress, and expecting to find John skulking in some of the out-houses, had raised his fellow servants, and examined every place, in which he thought there was a probability of finding him. Having failed of success here, they next set out for the very cottage, in which John had taken shelter. They had proceeded about half way, when on turning a short corner they unexpectedly met him. John endeavoured to pass them undiscovered; but Scipio's eagle eyes instantly recognized him, and running up, and taking him by the hand, "Ha, John!" said he, "you here? grad to see you gin. We been look ebery where, and no fine you. Run, Robbut, and tell Missey we found him; she be very grad." Robert did as he was desired, while poor John, almost sinking with shame, wished them all to the d——l. With Scipio, especially, he was quite outrageous, for having, by locking him in, been the cause of all his mortification: but he did not think this a proper time to shew his resentment. He walked on, therefore, sullen and slow, without deigning to answer one of their interrogations.

Robert, mean time, had communicated the joyful tidings to Dorcasina. "Is he indeed found?" exclaimed she. "Where, where is he, Robert? Conduct me to him that I may once more behold him in safety." "Coming along the road, ma'am; he will be here directly." Dorcasina, revivified by this intelligence, flew down stairs (Betty following close behind) and opening the door to be ready to receive him, what a dismal spectacle presented itself to her view! Her beloved John, wrapped in a blanket like an Indian Sachem, without shoes or stockings, approached her "with solemn steps, and slow," while Scipio and David marched on each side, with as much solemnity, as if they were attending a funeral. "John, my dear John," exclaimed Dorcasina, reaching out her hand, as soon as she saw him, "how happy I am to see you again. But where have you been, and how came you in this situation?" John, vexed, indignant, and mortified, without lifting his eyes from the ground, made her the following reply. "Ax me no questions, and I'll tell you no lies. I've got home again with a whole skin; let that suffice; let nobody trouble themselves to inquire any further, if they do they will only lose their labour."

To all present, except Scipio, these circumstances relating to John, were very mysterious; and he, judging that his mortification, for this time, had been sufficient, was resolved not to expose him. Dorcasina, pitying his situation, and making allowance for his ill humour, only desired him to go to his chamber, and dress himself, and then come and breakfast with her. Although John was very indifferent about the honor of breaking his fast with Dorcasina, he was ready enough to exchange his present dress for one more convenient. He, therefore, soon equipped himself in the suit in which he had been dressed the night before. His vanity, however, had been so severely humbled that he did not feel quite so much exultation as he had done the evening preceding; and it was with the deepest humiliation, that he presented himself before his mistress. But she appeared so happy at beholding him again, and seeing him dressed in so handsome a manner; and her reception of him was so endearing and affectionate, that he was soon inspired with a little confidence. Dorcasina, observing after breakfast that he had recovered his usual temper, again expressed a wish to know what had befallen him. "I hop'd, after what I said at the door," said he, "that you wou'dn't trouble yourself no more about it. I can't tell you, and so pray, ma'am, don't never ask me again." Dorcasina finding how grating the subject was to him, though she burned with curiosity to know the particulars, thought best to desist; and in order to amuse him, and make him forget his own mortifications, she related every particular of what had happened during the night to herself.

During the recital he was silent; nor, at the conclusion of it, did he make a single comment, or express the least degree of wonder; as he thought he knew how it all had happened, and from whom had proceeded those dreadful sounds, which had caused him so much alarm. He was in fact convinced that Scipio was at the bottom of the whole business; and felt equally mortified and indignant at having been made the object of his impertinent humour. He could not, however, complain of him to Dorcasina, without acquainting her with the whole scene; and to do this he at present felt no disposition. He, therefore, determined to conceal his resentment till he should become the master of Scipio, and then he resolved to take his full revenge.

Chapter XII.

BETTY, seeing how matters were going on between Dorcasina and John, and that he was more caressed than ever, was quite in despair that Scipio was not likely, with all his stratagems, to prevent this connection, a connection so degrading to her mistress, and so painful to herself; and was resolved to make one effort more to break it off. With this view, a few evenings after the night, on which the events related in the preceding chapter had happened, without communicating her intention to any one, not even to Scipio, she directed her steps to the house of Mr. Stanly. On inquiring for Mrs. Stanly, she was informed that she was in the parlour, with no other company than Miss Harriot. She presented herself before them, they received her with kindness, and after many inquiries about the health of Miss Dorcasina, whom neither of them had seen since the day after Harriot's return from Philadelphia, on account of Mrs. Stanly's indisposition, Betty informed them that she had come to entreat their advice and assistance. She then opened before them her whole budget of trouble. She told them that Miss Dorcasina had taken John for a gentleman; that she had fallen in love with him; that he slept in her father's chamber, and dressed in his clothes; that Miss Dorcasina called him Mr. Brown, and made all the servants call him so; that he eat, and passed most of his time with her; and finally, that she was resolved very soon to marry him.

Mrs. Stanly and her daughter were grieved, but not greatly surprised at this intelligence, as it was what they had some reason, from Harriot's observations, to expect. They praised Betty for this mark of attachment to her mistress; endeavoured to comfort her; and promised her that they would enter seriously into the business, and exert themselves, to the utmost of their power, to prevent the match.

Betty, encouraged by these promises, and placing great dependance upon their exertions, returned home much relieved of the burden, by which she had for some time, been oppressed.

After Betty had departed, this amiable mother and daughter held a consultation upon the case of their friend. Mr. Stanly was gone to Virginia upon business, which would detain him a month. This they regretted exceedingly, as Dorcasina might be married before he would return. In this situation, they were at a loss what course to pursue. At length, however, it was determined that Mrs. Stanly, who was now much better, should go and talk seriously with her, and represent to her, in a forcible manner, the impropriety of her conduct, and the disgrace she would bring upon herself by marrying a fellow whom nobody knew; one so much younger than herself; one so perfectly clownish in his manners, and so totally illiterate.

After they had come to this conclusion, they retired to bed; but Miss Stanly could not sleep. Her head was filled with Dorcasina's amour. She feared that all her mother's representations and arguments would have no effect upon one, who, in all the love matters in which she had ever been engaged, had acted as if she were totally devoid of reason. After pondering a long time upon it, a sudden thought struck her mind, and a plan presented itself to her imagination, which she thought would be much more likely to succeed with Dorcasina, than all the representations, arguments, and remonstrances her mother could use.

Mr. Stanly was an officer in the militia, and a man of a small size; and Harriot, as was before observed, a young lady of a large stature. Her plan therefore, was to dress herself in her father's uniform; to visit Dorcasina in the evening; to pretend to be violently in love with her; and, by these means, to endeavour to disengage her affections from Brown. The idea of this courtship delighted her sprightly imagination exceedingly. She thought she could act the swaggering young officer to perfection; and she calculated not only upon doing Dorcasina an essential service by this stratagem; but upon drawing from it a copious fund of amusement for herself. She therefore resolved to obtain her mother's consent to her plan, and put it in execution, without delay.

During breakfast next morning, "mama," said Harriot, "I do not believe that, with all your eloquence, and all your arguments, you will succeed in convincing Dorcasina of the impropriety of her present connection. You had better let me undertake it. I think I can manage her best." "Upon my word, my dear," replied Mrs. Stanly, "you discover no small degree of vanity in thinking yourself more capable of managing this affair than your mother." "Aye but, mama, I shall take quite a different method; one much more to Dorcasina's taste; and upon that circumstance I should build my hopes of success, more than upon my own abilities." "Well, let me hear your plan, and if I think there is a probability of your succeeding, I shall very willingly give up the task." "I am afraid you will not consent to it, mama." "I begin to suspect beforehand that I ought not; but come, let me hear it." "Why mama, it is to dress myself in papa's regimentals, visit Dorcasina two or three evenings in a week, and pretend to be a young officer violently in love with her." "I am not surprised that you doubted my approbation; consider, my dear, for a moment, the impropriety of the thing." "In Philadelphia, I grant you, mama, it would be not only an impropriety, but a scandal. Here, in this obscure village, the case is quite different; and beside, I am sure I can do it without danger of detection." "But what will your papa, and what will captain Barry say to it, my dear?" "You need not tell papa of it, mama; and as for captain Barry, perhaps I shall never tell him; and perhaps I may; it will be just as the humour takes me. If he looks grave I shall laugh; and if he laughs, which I think is most probable, I shall tell him he is a man after my own heart." "Admirably settled upon my word; but suppose you should succeed, in robbing John of Dorcasina's affections, how will you come off? It will be cruel to deprive her of one lover, and disappoint her in her expectations of another." "Trust my invention for that, mama. I dare say I shall be able to extricate myself handsomely. I do not believe there is much danger of her breaking her heart for any lover, at her time of life."

Here they were both silent; Mrs. Stanly revolving the matter in her mind; and Harriot looking earnestly at her, to endeavour to read her thoughts; so eager was she to put her proposed plan in execution. The silence was first broken by Mrs. Stanly. "I will first endeavour, my dear, to move her by reason and arguments. If I do not succeed, I will consider afterwards of your wild scheme." Harriot, taking this for her mama's consent, was greatly overjoyed, and begged her to go and make her attempt without delay. "But I know, mama," added she, "that I shall have to turn wooer after all." "Well, well, we shall see, my dear," said Mrs. Stanly, and they dropped the subject.

In about an hour after this conversation, they heard the rattling of a carriage, and looking out at the window, whom should they see taking an airing in the coach, but Mr. Brown and Dorcasina. "This is too much!" exclaimed Mrs. Stanly. "I could not have thought she would have published her own disgrace so soon." "You see, from this mama," replied Harriot, "the necessity of expedition. I dare say, if we cannot prevent it, that the banns will be published next Sunday." "I will go this very afternoon," said Mrs. Stanly, "but I am extremely sorry she has thus exposed herself, even if we succeed in preventing the match."

Towards evening Mrs. Stanly got into her chaise, and was driven to Miss Sheldon's. Upon her entrance she found that lady and John, tête à tête in the parlour. After an exchange of civilities, and congratulations upon the recovery of each other's health, "Mrs. Stanly," said Dorcasina, "shall I introduce to you Mr. Brown?" John arose and made his awkward bow: Mrs. Stanly assuming a haughty air, which was by no means natural to her, cast upon him a look of contempt, without even nodding her head, or uttering a single word. John shrunk into his native insignificance, and Dorcasina was sensibly mortified. Mrs. Stanly, soon after, began to converse with Dorcasina, upon indifferent subjects, and John, finding himself but a cypher, very wisely left the room, and retired to his chamber.

Tea was brought in soon afterwards. "Inform Mr. Brown," said Dorcasina to Betty, "that tea is ready." "Miss Sheldon," said Mrs. Stanly, "I am not used to eating with servants, and if John Brown is to drink tea with you, I must wish you a good evening." Dorcasina coloured, and knew not what to reply, feeling a degree both of vexation and mortification. She was unwilling to offend so good, and so esteemed a friend as Mrs. Stanly; and her pride was much hurt, at seeing so much contempt thrown on her beloved John. After musing a short time, "go," said she to Betty, "and see if Mr. Brown is in his chamber." Betty went, and returned with the report that he was. Dorcasina then sent up his tea, and the two ladies drank theirs by themselves.

As soon as tea was over, and Betty withdrawn, "pray tell me," said Mrs. Stanly, "with the confidence of a friend, whether the reports that you are going to marry that fellow be true." "Pray, madam," said Dorcasina, "speak of him with a little less contempt; you may depend upon it, he is a gentleman born and bred." "How can you be sure of that?" asked Mrs. Stanly. "I know it by his air, his manner, and his

whole deportment." "It is strange that people should see so differently,"
replied Mrs. Stanly. "To me he appears in every thing the very reverse
of a gentleman. But if he be such, why should he let himself as a
servant?" "Oh a number of reasons might induce him to do it; he
might have been reduced in his circumstances; and I have read of
gentlemen who have disguised themselves as servants for the sake of
being near a beloved object."

"Miss Sheldon," said Mrs. Stanly, "depend upon it, you are grossly
deceived. This fellow is no other than a common ignorant labourer,
without manners, and without education; and, if he pretend to any
thing more, he is an arrant impostor." "He makes no pretentions to
any thing above the character he has assumed, and this proof of his
modesty raises him more highly in my opinion." "Oh Miss Sheldon,
I am sorry to see you thus blinded! Let me beg of you to dismiss him
from your family, and think no more of him." "What! dismiss him,
who is the darling of my fondest affections? You know not, madam,
what you require. My whole happiness, nay even my existence,
depends upon him." "Depend upon it Miss Sheldon, that this is only
an extravagant whim, and believe me, you will be much happier
without him, and that you will find him to be a low, ignorant, vulgar,
fellow. You must consider that you will not, by marrying, raise him
to your level; on the contrary, you will degrade yourself to his; and,
after the few first weeks of passion are over, you will begin to see him
in the same light with other people; you will tremble every time he
opens his mouth for the vulgarisms he will utter, and the ignorance he
will discover. Where then will be your happiness? Besides, how
infinitely more respectable will you be, to live single as you are, than
to marry a man so much younger, even supposing him to be your
equal in rank and character. What would your venerable father say,
were he now alive, and a witness of the folly you are going to commit?"

At the mention of her father, Dorcasina's eyes filled with tears, and
she remained for some time silent. At length, she replied, "I take your
advice in a friendly part, madam, because I know it to proceed from
friendly motives: but permit me to observe that it is you who are
deceived; you are not sufficiently acquainted with Mr. Brown duly to
appreciate his merit. My attachment to him is pure and ardent; and his
is no less so to me. I must be the best judge of what will promote my
own happiness, and I expect to find it, in a supreme degree, in a
connection with Mr. Brown; and no power on earth shall force me to

forego that happiness, or to drive the dear youth to despair by refusing him my hand." "I have only then to regret," replied Mrs. Stanly, "that you are so fixed in your determination; but having discharged the duty of a friend towards you, by forewarning you of the disgrace and unhappiness that will be the inevitable consequence of this connection, I can do no more, and must leave you to follow your own inclination." So saying she arose to depart, and not being pressed by Dorcasina to lengthen her visit, she wished her a good evening, and returned directly home.

Harriot, who had been impatiently waiting her return, eagerly inquired how she had succeeded. "Just as you foresaw," replied her mother. "I could not make the least impression upon her." She then related every particular of the conversation which had passed between them. Harriot listened to her attentively, and as soon as she had done speaking, asked whether she might not now put *her* plan in execution. "If it were not for your papa," replied Mrs. Stanly, "I would, after what I have done, leave her to her own folly; but his regard to the memory of Mr. Sheldon is so great, and the manner, in which he recommended Dorcasina to his care, so solemn, that if this match takes place it will render him, for a while, extremely unhappy. For his sake, therefore, I must wink at what still appears to me a great impropriety." "Oh mama, never think of that, it will never be known; and, if it should happen to get abroad, it will not be considered as an impropriety here."

Thus saying, she ran directly up stairs, and equipped herself a la militaire, to try how the clothes would suit. She found them indeed rather too large; but not thinking that a matter of much consequence, she tripped down again, and entering the parlour with a sober countenance, made her mother a very low bow. Mrs. Stanly started, and was struck with the resemblance between Harriot's present appearance, and that of Mr. Stanly when he was of her age. "Well mama, how do you like me?" cried Harriot. "Like you, my dear, why you are the exact resemblance of your father's youth; and Dorcasina, if she recollects his appearance then, will certainly recognize you the moment she beholds you." "Never fear, mama, I intend to disguise my face a little, so that she will not know me so easily." "But you do not think of beginning your attack this evening," said Mrs. Stanly. "It is too late to go thither at this hour." "No, mama; I only wanted to see how the clothes would suit. I shall not commence lover untill tomorrow evening." So saying, she returned to the chamber, and in a short time was dressed in her female habit again.

Harriot, next morning, thought she would pay Dorcasina one visit more, in her own proper person, before she commenced her intended attack, in the character of a military beau. She, therefore, went to the house, but had not the pleasure of finding her at home; she had ridden out on horseback, accompanied by John. After some conversation with Betty, Miss Stanly asked if Scipio were at home, and being answered in the affirmative, she desired Betty to go into the kitchen and send him to her. "Well Scipio," said she, as soon as he entered the room, "your mistress is going to be married, is she?" "Ah missy! so de tory go, but I tink she better be sleep." "So I think, Scipio; and moreover that something must be done to break up this connection." "Ah missy! I fear it no do, she doat so on the lubber, she muss hab him." "Well, it is but trying: I know you are an honest man, Scipio, and that you can keep a secret; therefore I think I may safely trust you." "Try me, missy, and if I tell, call me wat you please." "Well, then, Scipio, if there should come a young officer a courting to your mistress, and you should think you know him, keep your suspicions to yourself; and above all prevent, if possible, any of your men from following him, to endeavour to find him out." Scipio instantly understood her meaning, and engaged to do as she desired.

At this instant they were alarmed at the appearance of Dorcasina, in a very singular situation.

In order to account for this we must go a little back in our history. Having been informed that wigs were all the rage, among the ladies of Philadelphia, Miss Sheldon had the week before sent thither, and purchased one of a light flaxen colour, and had her own grey hair close shaved, hoping that the next growth would be darker. She had at the same time purchased a small black hat, with two enormous high feathers. Having dressed herself in a new riding dress, this hat, this wig, and these feathers, she mounted a mettlesome horse, and cantered off, with John by her side, with the air and spirit of a girl of eighteen.

They rode five miles out without meeting any accident, but having got about two miles on their return home, Dorcasina's horse, taking a sudden start, set off upon the full run. Finding herself unable, in any degree, to check his career, she confined her efforts to the sole object of keeping her seat. John, being but indifferently mounted, was soon distanced in the race.

> "Away went" Dorcas, "and away
> Went Dorcas' "hat and wig."

The wind blowing fresh, and Dorcasina's hands being both engaged, she could not avoid leaving her head-dress behind her. Her hat and feathers went first, and John, seeing them, wisely dismounted and picked them up. The wig soon followed; but it was its fate to fall into more brutish hands. A great hog happening to pass, at the instant it was blown off, seized it for his prey, and turning down another road, avoided the observation of John, and secured it.

Dorcasina, meantime, kept on Jehu-like, her head undecked even by a single hair; to the no small astonishment of the people whom she passed. Her person had been well known to all the people, who lived on that road; but so much was she altered, by her late sickness, and by her present evil plight, that not a single person who now beheld her, though the number was not small, recollected to have ever seen her before. The doors and windows were filled with women and children, as she passed, and all that saw her stood amazed at the singularity of the phenomenon. Some stared, some hallooed, and some were frightened. Some, more ignorant and superstitious than the rest, thought the appearance supernatural, and, having heard of witches riding through the air on broomsticks, concluded that this was one, who chose to be conveyed in a less elevated manner.

The horse at length reached home without having thrown his rider; but as he suddenly stopped at the gate, overcome as she was with fear and fatigue, she was thrown from him speechless upon the ground.

It was at this instant that Dorcasina was observed by Miss Stanly and Scipio; and they immediately hastened, much alarmed, to her assistance.

Being carried into the house, she soon recovered from her consternation, and the first words she uttered were, "Mr. Brown, where is my dear Mr. Brown?" But Mr. Brown had not yet arrived, and Harriot inquired where she had left him. "In the road," said Dorcasina; "my horse took fright, and run, and"—suddenly recollecting her hat and wig, she clapped her hands to her head, "run, Betty, run," said she, "bring me cap quick, before Mr. Brown arrives; I would not have him see me with my head bare for all the world."

Before she had time to get her cap handsomely adjusted, Mr. Brown entered the room. He bowed stiffly to Harriot, and then addressing himself to his mistress, "why what the gallows got into your horse?" said he, "to run so tarnation fast? I coud'n't come up with you, though I made my horse go as fast as he could lay legs to the ground." "Something frightened him," replied Dorcasina, "but I could not tell what, and it was with the greatest difficulty I could keep my seat. You have got my hat I see, did you not find my wig too?" "Tarnation! is that gone? no, I never seed nothing of it." "I am sorry for that," said Dorcasina. "I gave thirty dollars for it, but last week," (to Miss Stanly.) "You must advertise it" said Harriot. "A good thought, so I will. Mr. Brown will you write an advertisement?" This request non-plussed John. He could hardly write his name legibly, and an advertisement was quite beyond his abilities. Being unwilling however to expose his ignorance before the ladies, he said he would write one in the afternoon.

Miss Stanly, more and more astonished, the more she saw of John, at Dorcasina's infatuation, passed with her the rest of the morning, and then went home to give her mother an account of her visit.

After dinner Dorcasina again reminded John of the advertisement, and he promised to go immediately and write it. Having retired to his chamber, he sat down and scratched his head, not knowing how to extricate himself from his present embarrassment. A happy thought at length occurred. He knew that Robert, one of the hired men, could write, he called him in therefore from the field, carried him up into his chamber, locked the door and bribed him to secrecy. Matters being thus adjusted, Robert set down to write, and John to indite; between them they produced the following advertisement.

"NO al men by thes presants, whereas Miss dorcasina Sheldon Wil giv five dolars to any Body that wil find her wig. she lost it last Thusday riden a horsebak.

P.S. said wig Was frizled al over afore and Behind like negurs owl."

This curious production was carried by Robert and posted up in the very tavern which had formerly had the honor of entertaining Mr. O'Connor. Being on the following days read by numbers, it fully cleared up the mystery of the strange apparition, which had been seen on Thursday. "Who could have thought," said one, "that it was Miss Sheldon? how sadly she has altered since she lost her loving father."

"Poor lady," said another, "how unfortunate, to lose all her hair and be obliged to wear a wig." We will now return to the history of this unfortunate wig. The hog which had seized upon it in its fall, ran shaking it nearly a quarter of a mile, and then dropped it in the middle of his wallowing place. Some boys, passing that way, soon after, observed it, and with a stick extricated it from its filthy and degraded situation, and, being ignorant of its value, agreed to hang it up for a mark to throw at. Having satisfied themselves with throwing, and torn the poor thing in a dreadful manner, they desisted, and one of the boys, thinking the hair might be of use for some purpose or other, carried it home, where it caused a variety of speculations; none of the family being able to conjecture what it could have been. Two days after, the father of the family, happening to be at the tavern, saw the advertisement; and, though the present appearance of the wig was not precisely such as had been described, he immediately concluded that it must be the same. He went, therefore, directly home, tied the wig in a handkerchief, and presented himself with it before Miss Sheldon. Alas, how great was her mortification at seeing this ornament, which she had two days before adjusted to her head with so much satisfaction, now brought home in such an altered and miserable condition, torn almost to pieces, filled with dirt and clay, part of the hair gone, and what remained hanging as straight as so much flax. She however, paid the man his money and dismissed him. She and Betty then applied themselves assiduously to sewing up and cleansing it. The poor thing underwent anew all the tortures of papering, pinching, boiling and baking; but, after all their labour, and all their anxiety, it never regained its pristine elegance.

Chapter XIII.

On the day of this direful disaster, Miss Stanly waited, with the utmost impatience, for evening. "Twilight grey," at length "clad all things in its sober livery," and this charming girl hastened to her chamber, and clad herself in the military livery of her country. Her coat was blue, faced with buff, and her underclothes of the latter colour. She turned back her hair; her eyebrows, which were regular and arched, as if drawn by a pencil, she altered and enlarged with a burnt cork, and adding a little rouge to her native red, her appearance became quite masculine; and seldom have mortal eyes beheld a more beautiful young fellow than she appeared to be. Hanging a sword by her side, and throwing over the whole a broadcloth cloak, she set out, in high spirits, for the mansion of Dorcasina.

Being arrived at the door, she gave a thundering knock; on its being opened by a servant, she altered her voice and inquired for Miss Sheldon. Leaving her cloak in the entry, she followed the servant to the parlour, where, according to her custom in the evening, Dorcasina was tête à tête with Brown. Harriot entered, and gracefully bowing, addressed Miss Sheldon in the usual salutation. That lady, greatly struck with her appearance, arose, and begged her to be seated. After a few common-place compliments had passed, "you have the advantage of me, sir," said Dorcasina; "I have not the pleasure of recollecting you." "My name is Montague," replied Harriot, "and I have the honor of bearing a captain's commission in the service of my country." Miss Sheldon then introduced Mr. Brown to captain Montague, and, after a little further chat upon indifferent subjects, he requested the honor of a few minutes private conversation. Dorcasina whispering John, he silently and sullenly withdrew, not at all pleased with the intrusion, the assurance, or the beauty of this young officer.

"I am a blunt, honest fellow, madam," said Harriot, as soon as John had left the room, "and shall therefore acquaint you with my business without apology or circumlocution. I have once seen you before, but was so situated that you could not see me. That once was sufficient, and did the business for me. With one glance I was transfixed through and through. In short, madam, I am deeply enamoured with you, and I have come to see whether I can have the happiness of being looked upon in the same favourable light by you." "A blunt fellow, sure enough," thought Dorcasina; but she was by no means displeased at having made a conquest of so charming a young officer, though her affection for John was too firmly fixed to be shaken by all his attacks. She continued some moments silent, in order to frame a suitable reply; but before she had time to frame and deliver it, our impetuous young hero again addressed her. "Am I to construe your silence as it is commonly taken, madam, into an approbation of my address?" "Sir," replied Dorcasina, with great gravity, "I should be sorry to have you deceive yourself. It is my invariable maxim never to keep a lover in suspense, or to give unnecessary pain. I must, therefore, inform you that it is impossible for me to listen to your addresses, as my heart is engaged to another amiable youth, to whom I have also promised my hand, and he expects from me very shortly a performance of my engagement." "What! have I a rival then?" said Harriot. "I would fain know who he is, that shall dare presume to rival me." "The gentleman, sir, who just left the room, is the one to whom I expect to be shortly united; but permit me sir, to observe, that it is you who want to rival him, instead of his rivaling you." "It amounts to the same thing," said Harriot, "I will not bear to be rivaled by any man. But is it possible that so lovely a woman as you are, can have placed your affections on so awkward a booby as he is?"

"Be pleased, sir," said Dorcasina, "to season your language with a little more civility, when you are speaking of Mr. Brown." "Pardon me, madam," cried Harriot, "my passion transports me beyond all bounds, and that must plead my excuse. But will you not, Miss Sheldon, give me a fair chance? Will you not suffer me to visit you, and endeavour to make an impression on your heart, before the indissoluble knot is tied, which will fix my doom forever?" "All your endeavours, sir, will be fruitless. I am not so light and inconstant as to change one object for another, when my heart is once fixed." "Promise me only that you will wait one month." "I cannot break the promise I have given Mr. Brown, sir, which is that I will give him my hand within that time." "Cruel, barbarous, unfeeling woman!" exclaimed Harriot. "Will nothing move you to grant me a reprieve of one month? Know then that I have one way left, if that Brown dare still to be my rival, I will run him through the body; at least I will cut off both his ears." This she said with so furious an air, at the same time laying her hand on her sword, that Dorcasina was greatly alarmed. "You are so passionate," replied she, "that you quite terrify me; with a little more moderation you would be quite as likely to gain your point." "Oh, my dear, I'll be any thing, I'll be gentle as a lamb, and spare poor Brown's life, and his ears into the bargain, if you will promise not to have the banns published under a month from this time, and will allow me occasionally to visit you, and plead my passion." Dorcasina trembling, at his threat, for the life of her beloved, half surprised, half terrified, and half pleased, consented to defer the matter to the time that was desired. Harriot having gained this point became more rational; John returned; and they conversed, the remainder of the evening, upon indifferent subjects.

While they were thus engaged, Betty had occasion to enter the room, and being greatly struck with the appearance of Harriot, reported, on her return to the kitchen, that there was the handsomest, the most beautifullest, and completest young gentleman in the parlour, that she ever laid her eyes on. This engaged the attention of all present, more especially of Scipio, who remembered the hint given him, in the morning, by Miss Stanly, and taking the water out of Betty's hand, which she had been directed to bring, begged that he might carry it in order to have a sight of this charming youth. On entering the parlour he was struck with astonishment. Having known Mr. Stanly when a youth, he could hardly help expressing his admiration, at the striking likeness of him which he now beheld; he had, however, the prudence to refrain from speaking; but, at leaving the room, he gave Harriot a significant glance, by which she understood that he recognized her.

After passing another half hour, Harriot arose and took her leave in the same graceful manner she had entered; whispering to Dorcasina, "remember your promise, madam, or let Brown tremble for the consequences."

Harriot had got but a little way from the house, when, on looking behind, she observed a man following her. As this gave her some uneasiness she quickened her pace, and he quickened his; she slackened again, and again he slackened. She began now to be seriously alarmed, and thought, if he meant nothing worse, he would follow her home and discover who she was. Agitated by a variety of disagreeable ideas, she kept on till she got opposite to a house, with the inhabitants of which she had some acquaintance. Here she faced about and made a full stop, determining to wait till the person should come up, and then endeavour to discover why he followed her. The man observing her to stop, stopped also a few moments himself. At length he advances, Harriot's courage fails, and she wishes she never had engaged in the adventure. On the man's nearer approach, who should he be but honest Scipio. He had followed her, he said, to see that no harm befell her. She was greatly relieved, and thanked him sincerely for his attention, "but Scipio," added she, "you frightened me so sadly, before I knew who you were, that I shall always in future be afraid to go home without you." "Berry well, missy, I follow you home ebery night, when you come courting. How you make out? I hope you make missy Dorcasina send away dat John Brown." "I cannot tell yet, Scipio, how I shall finally succeed; but she has promised me to defer publishing the banns for a month, and in that time I shall use my utmost endeavours to prevent their being published at all." "Bery well, bery good, for the fuss visit, missy; all come right in good time." "I hope so, Scipio."

He now walked behind again till Harriot reached home, where she gave an account to her mother of every thing that had passed, excepting only her being frightened by Scipio. She only observed that he had followed her home, and engaged to do so, as long as she should continue her nocturnal visits.

As soon as Harriot had taken her leave, Dorcasina acquainted John with the purport of captain Montague's visit, and with the promise she had been compelled to make him. John hardly knew whether to be dissatisfied or not. He was by no means pleased with the idea of having so formidable a rival, and greatly feared, that in the course of the month, his mistress would be induced to change her mind. On the other hand, he had not any greater relish for having either his life or his ears at the mercy of the sword of his rival. After some hesitation, therefore, he delivered his sentiments as follows. "If he would take it out in boxing, I shou'dn't be a morsel afeard but what I should be more than his match; but them there plaguy sords I don't want to meddle with, for I don't know nothing about 'em. But I hope now that you will prove true to me, and not go for to be taken in by his feathers, his shoulder knots, and his follol." "My dear Mr. Brown," replied Dorcasina, "you do me great injustice by such an insinuation: No—my affection for you is fixed on too strong a basis to be shaken by any of his efforts. But he is a fiery blade, and we must manage him the best we can. He will probably afford us no inconsiderable degree of diversion; for he makes love in the strangest manner imaginable." John, being pretty well satisfied with these assurances, retired at an early hour, and in a deep sleep soon buried all his jealousies, and all his apprehensions.

Dorcasina did not think proper to inform him of all the pleasure she experienced at this new conquest. Not that she had the least inclination to be inconstant; but the sudden conquest of so charming a young man gave her a high idea of the power of her charms, and raised her vanity to the highest pitch. Besides, the having two lovers at once, their being rivals, and jealous of each other, was so pleasing and so romantic, that she could hardly contain her satisfaction, till she could unbosom herself to Betty.

"Well, Betty," said she, "was not that a perfect Adonis who visited me this evening?" "I don't know who you means by Handonis, ma'am! but he was the most perfectest beauty of a man that my eyes ever beheld; but who is he, ma'am? what is his name, and where did he come from?" "He is called captain Montague, Betty; he did not inform me from whence he came—and what do you imagine was his business?" "I am sure I cannot tell, ma'am." "Cannot you guess, Betty?" "No, ma'am, I cannot." "It is strange, Betty, you should be so much at a loss; why he has declared himself my lover." "Is it possible?" exclaimed Betty, in a tone of surprise. "Why is there any thing so very surprising in it?" asked Dorcasina peevishly. Betty finding she had committed an error, and wishing to retrieve it, said, "why, ma'am, as you are just going to be married I did'nt know as any body would think it worth while to come a courting now." "You see, Betty, that makes no difference, I continue to make conquests, whether I am engaged or not; this young man was violently smitten, only upon having one view of me. He does not appear to be a whining, pining lover; but is all fire and spirit, and for killing every body that opposes him." "Why had you not better take up with him, ma'am?" "Ah, Betty, you know not what you say. Do you think me so fickle as to quit my dear Mr. Brown? However I may be amused with this new amour, depend upon it, I love him too well, ever to look upon it in a serious light." This speech damped Betty's hopes, which had begun to revive; and she spoke not another word while she continued in the chamber.

Dorcasina's ideas were pleasing, her dreams agreeable, and she awoke next morning, in perfect good humour with herself and all the world.

A few evenings afterwards, captain Montague again presented himself before Dorcasina. She was alone. "What a lucky fellow am I to find you thus alone, my dear," said Harriot. "I am determined to secure my advantage, and to prevent all interruption by the intrusion of that sneaking fellow of a Brown." So saying, she locked both doors without further ceremony. Dorcasina, startled and displeased with the freedom of his address, and the boldness of his action, said, with great spirit, "I do not chuse to be made a prisoner in my own house, sir; and I insist upon having the doors unfastened again immediately." She then arose and unlocked one, and was approaching the other, near which Harriot stood, who seizing her by both hands, partly by force, and partly by entreaty, led her back again to her seat. "I will accommodate matters with you, my dear," said Harriot. "I will have one door locked, and you shall have the other open." Dorcasina, not knowing what to think of such a strange procedure, was silent and vexed. Harriot placed herself by her side, and looking up in her face with a most bewitching smile, "well, my dear," said she, "I flatter myself you have by this time come to a resolution in my favour, and intend to make me forever happy by blessing me with your love." "Indeed, sir," said Dorcasina, "you are greatly mistaken, and I must again repeat what I told you at your former visit; my heart is unalterably fixed upon another object." "Why it is surprising now that you should prefer Brown to me; am I not much handsomer, and vastly more genteel?" "I am not going to make any comparison between his person and yours; it is sufficient that my affections were placed upon him, long before I ever saw you." "Well, but, my dear," said Harriot, "I expect to supplant him in your affections, and that, upon a further acquaintance, you will find me absolutely irresistible." "If vanity could make you irresistible, you would certainly become so," said Dorcasina, laughing. "I acknowledge I have a spice of vanity in my composition, but I do not like myself the less for it; and if you would confess the truth, I do not believe that you do—but this is wide of our subject, do not you intend to try to love me? You cannot imagine what a fond attentive husband I should make. If you would only drive this fellow of a Brown out of your head we should soon be as loving and as happy as two turtle doves." "If I should succeed in driving him, for a short time from my head, his image is so deeply engraven on my heart, that his idea would very soon return." "Pho! my dear, only make the effort, and I am confident you may dislodge him from you heart also, and place me there in his stead." "And what should I gain by such an exchange, pray?" "Gain? why every thing. A handsome well-bred fellow, for an awkward, ungenteel booby; an ardent lover for a lukewarm one, a gentleman for a clown, and the applauses of all good people for your choice."

Before Dorcasina had time to reply, somebody was heard approaching the door, which she had unlocked, and which led through a narrow passage into the kitchen. Harriot sprung towards it, and having opened it a little way, perceived that it was John. "So, Brown, is it you?" said she. "You must be content my lad, to tarry without; there is no admittance for you here." John then making a slight effort to open the door, "stand," cried Harriot; "approach no farther, at your peril," and she half unsheathed her sword. "For heaven's sake my dear Mr. Brown," exclaimed Dorcasina, "if you value my life, or your own, come no further." John desisted, and Harriot went on, "now you are quiet I will reason the case with you a little. You and I, Brown, both have pretentions to this lady, and I suppose are equally enamoured with her; now you living under the same roof have daily opportunities of urging your suit; I think it therefore but just, that when I come, you should quit the ground, and leave me to try my fortune. I will leave it to the lady herself, whether this be not a fair and equitable proposal; what say you to it Miss Sheldon?" "That all your endeavours will be vain, sir." "That will be better known hereafter, my dear." "Come what say you, Brown, to my proposal?" John muttered something about the lady's being promised to him, and that nobody had any right to try to rob him of her. "Very well," said Harriot, "our swords, I find then, must decide the contest. When and where will you meet me?" "Retire, Mr. Brown, I beseech you for my sake," exclaimed Dorcasina, "and do not engage with this hot-headed young man." "As to your sords," said John, (whose choler by this time was pretty well raised, though, fearful of the sword, he dared not discover how much he was vexed) "I knows nothing about em, but if you dares to strip and box it out, I am your man." "Good heavens! fellow, do you think I would degrade myself and my profession so much as to go to boxing? Know that it is beneath a gentleman to use any other weapon than sword or pistol, and of these you may take your choice." "Merciful heavens!" said Dorcasina, approaching the door, "deliver me from this madman. Mr. Brown retire, pray do, and not, by engaging with him, drive me distracted." John, not feeling the least inclination either to have his brains blown out, or to be run through the body, did as he was desired, and sullenly marched off, leaving Harriot complete master of the field.

The servants, collected into a group, had been listening to this scene with great delight, especially Scipio, who could not sufficiently admire Miss Stanly's spirit and humour.

As soon as John had left the door, Harriot again addressed herself to Dorcasina. "Now," said she, "you are mine for this evening, by right of conquest; I have fairly driven the enemy off the ground." "And do you think," said Dorcasina, who had been much alarmed, and was now really angry, "to recommend yourself by such conduct as this?" Harriot, finding that she had carried matters too far, and that Dorcasina was seriously offended, got down upon her knees before her, took first one hand and kissed it, then the other; begged, prayed and entreated to be forgiven. In a word, she said so many *handsome* things, so many *witty* things, and looked such *bewitching* things, that Dorcasina could no longer hold out against her, and graciously held out her hand, in token of reconciliation. Harriot instantly started up, and again seating herself by the side of Dorcasina, entertained her, for half an hour, in the most agreeable and sprightly manner imaginable. She then took her leave, saying, "I shall soon visit you again, and hope, my dear, you won't forget me in my absence."

She was again escorted by the faithful Scipio, who extolled her to the skies, for her conduct in the management of Brown.

Chapter XIV.

"THAT Montague," said John, next morning at breakfast, "is the most impudentest fellor I ever heard of. Why, if you suffer him to go on at this rate, he'll draw his sord and turn us all out o-doors before long." Dorcasina, gratified, as was before observed, with the conquest, and greatly amused with her new lover's vanity, vivacity, and singular manner of making love, replied, "Oh, we must in compliance with my promise, bear with his freaks for a short time. He is young, impetuous, and vain, and I do not think he is worth being seriously offended with."

It now became a matter of curiosity whence he came, and with whom he resided, as they never had seen him except at those two visits, nor ever heard that there was such an officer in the village. It was agreed, therefore, that, at his next visit, Dorcasina should endeavour to find out these particulars; for they had both an equal curiosity to be informed of them.

Accordingly, the next time Harriot came, Dorcasina expressed a wish to know her native place, and how long she had been in the village. "I am an inhabitant of the world," replied she, "and have been in this place three weeks; when you will be so good as to give me some encouragement, you shall be informed of every thing you wish." Dorcasina, finding she was not likely, in this way, to gain any intelligence, dropped the subject, and nothing material occurred during the remainder of the visit.

After Harriot was gone, "I burn with impatience," said Dorcasina to John, "to find out where this fellow inhabits. It is very strange that nobody has seen him in the day-time. Can you not, Mr. Brown, hit upon some method of gratifying both my curiosity and your own, by discovering his place of concealment?" John, after a little consideration, replied: "I thinks you an't obliged to see him every time he comes, tho' it be never so often; and if you'll promise not to keep him company, next time he comes, I'll promise to follow him when he goes away, and see where he lives." This proposal was accepted by Dorcasina, and it was agreed that as soon as they heard his knock, which, by its loudness, could be distinguished from that of every other person, she should retire to her chamber, and not appear till the visit was ended.

Betty was luckily in the room when this discourse passed, and as luckily communicated it to Scipio. After a little deliberation Scipio formed a plan in his mind, by which he hoped, not only to prevent John from following Miss Stanly in future, but likewise to draw from it some entertainment for himself. Going, therefore, to Mr. Stanly's, and requesting to see Miss Harriot alone, he communicated to her John's intention, and his own plan to frustrate it. She, approving it, concluded to make another visit that very evening.

Evening being arrived, Harriot announced herself as usual by a thundering knock. This visit so immediately following the last was unexpected. John and Dorcasina were sitting lovingly together; John started, and claiming from his mistress the performance of her promise, she retired immediately to her chamber. Harriot, by this time was ushered in by a servant. "Brown," said she, in an imperious tone, "where's your mistress, where is Miss Sheldon?" "That's none of your business, as I know on," replied John. Harriot, upon this, became apparently quite furious. "What, fellow! scoundrel!" said she, "do you dare give me such an answer? Where is Miss Dorcasina? Answer me directly, I say." John was now mute, and answered not a word; upon which Harriot drawing her sword, brandished it over his head, and ordered him directly into the kitchen, telling him that was the fittest place for such a pitiful fellow as he was. John, at the sight of the formidable weapon, dared not make any resistance, but retreated sullenly into the kitchen, and collecting all the servants together, desired their assistance in disarming Montague. "It's very strange if we four can't master him, and get away that tarnation sord. You, Scipio, go behind him, and clasp him fast in your arms; Robert, do you give him a good dowse in the chops; David shall seize him by the legs, and I'll take the sord." Scipio was the first who replied, "Gor bresse your soul, John, wat you mean? Why he kill us all, one after toder, jus as easy as we kill chicken."

Harriot, having taken a turn or two across the parlour, to consider what step she should next take to amuse herself, to frighten John, and to bring down Dorcasina, at this moment entered the kitchen, apparently in a violent rage. Scipio, fearing John would attempt something against her, went behind him, seized him by the arms, and held him fast, exclaiming at the same time, "don't touch him, musn't touch him, he kille you, he kill us all." Harriot now acted, with a theatrical air, all the violence she had ever seen exhibited on the stage. She brandished her sword, stamped upon the floor, and called aloud upon the name of Dorcasina. Scipio still continued to hold John; the two maids skulked trembling behind the men, and Betty, in the greatest possible consternation, ran up to her mistress, and informed her that they should all be murdered, if she did not hasten down and prevent it.

Dorcasina alarmed, descends the stairs, and presents herself before Harriot, in the midst of this counterfeited passion. The moment she appears, the storm is calmed, and the winds are hushed. Harriot sheathed her sword, the maids emerge, and John is released. "Captain Montague," said Dorcasina, "what do you mean, by all these mad pranks? You turn my house into a bedlam; I will bear it no longer; and if you cannot conduct yourself in a more peaceable manner, my doors shall henceforward be shut against you." Harriot stood listening in a most graceful attitude; and as soon as Dorcasina had finished speaking, making a low bow, replied as follows: "All this, my dear, is but the product of love, and the effect of your fascinating beauty. When I entered the house, I saw not my life, my adorable Dorcasina. I inquire for her, and can gain no satisfaction; this puts me into a passion, and I rave like a madman; but behold you appear, and I am calm, gentle, submissive, and ready to do whatever you command me." Saying this she took Dorcasina by the hand, and led her back to the parlour. Then seating her in a chair, and placing herself by her side, "will you not," said she, "bestow upon me a small portion of your love, in return for all that I lavish so profusely upon you?"

Dorcasina, who had come down fully determined to be seriously angry, could not find it in her heart to hold her resolution. When, looking upon Harriot, she considered her youth, her beauty, and the violence of her love, she felt more disposed to be pleased with having inspired so ardent a passion, than to be angry at any violence which she supposed to be its consequences. "You are a strange, unaccountable, persevering man," said she. "I do not know how to give a refusal in more positive terms than I have done, and yet you will not take it for an answer." "Upon that perseverance I build all my hopes of success," replied Harriot.   "It is an excellent quality, and seldom fails of obtaining its end." "You will find in this instance, at least, it will fail," said Dorcasina; "and you had better not place upon it such implicit confidence." "Well, well," said Harriot, "we shall see. How could you be so cruel as to run away, and conceal yourself when you knew that I was coming?" "Why, how was it possible I should be informed of it?" asked Dorcasina. "Oh! you know by my knock when I am coming as well as if you saw me. Was it kindly done to leave me for company none but your servants?" "Here was Mr. Brown, surely, to entertain you." "Oh yes, Brown, I forgot him, I ask his pardon. He is tarnation good company. But was it not he that put you upon running away from me? Come, confess now that it was more to gratify him, than to follow your own inclination."

Dorcasina knew not what to say; she was embarrassed at being thus closely questioned, and surprised at Harriot's guessing (as she thought) exactly the truth. "You are troublesome, captain Montague," said she, at length. "I am not obliged to answer all your impertinent questions." "There, now, I told you it was so; I want no further proof of the truth, than your evading my question. This one step gained gives me great pleasure, and I have now no doubt of completely succeeding; I shall sleep sweetly to night upon the consciousness of not being wholly indifferent to my adorable Dorcasina. I will now bid you good night and leave you to your repose."

She then, before Dorcasina had time to reply, started up, saluted her, and was out of the house in an instant; leaving Dorcasina in a state of pleasure, surprise and wonder, at the insinuating and agreeable singularity of her conduct.

John, all this time had been listening in the passage, and had heard, to his astonishment, every thing that had passed. He went out of the house soon after Harriot, and observing the way she took, followed her at a little distance. This was not unobserved by Harriot, who had been prepared by Scipio to expect it. She quickened her pace and walked with hurried steps, till she got about half way to her father's house, then suddenly turning a corner into a bye road which had long had the reputation of being haunted, Scipio instantly emerged from his hiding place, wrapped in a sheet, with a white handkerchief, in the form of a turban, upon his head. In less than a minute he stood before John, who, beholding such a frightful apparition in such a place, thwarting his way, turned back and ran as fast as his legs could carry him. Scipio followed close at his heels, nor quitted him till they reached the door of their residence. Then entering at a back door, he slipped off his sheet and handkerchief, and seated himself as composedly in the kitchen as if nothing had happened.

John, mean time, entered the parlour of his mistress, pale, panting, and almost speechless. "Good heavens!" exclaimed Dorcasina, the moment she saw him, "what is the matter? what has happened to you, that you return in this condition?" John threw himself into a chair, and remained horribly silent. Dorcasina, alarmed greatly, and thinking that Montague had done him a mischief, conjured him, with tears in her eyes, to tell her if he was wounded, and to conceal nothing from her. "I beg of you," at length, said he, "never to let that Montague come here again, for you may depend upon it he is the devil incarnate." "What do you mean?" said Dorcasina; "pray explain yourself." He then related, in as concise a manner as he was able, how he had listened in the passage, and heard the conversation; how he had followed Montague out of the house; how he had walked faster than a spirit; how just as he had got to the corner of the haunted lane, he turned suddenly upon him, and was changed into a great white monster, taller than a steeple, and that it had followed him close at his heels, quite to the door.

Dorcasina, upon this relation, bursting into a laugh, "is that all?" said she; "Why I was apprehensive that the fellow had half murdered you." John was not at all pleased at Dorcasina's making so light of what appeared to him to be so serious, and endeavoured to convince her that her pretended lover was no other than the evil one in disguise. "Why, who but him could know," said he, "that you went up stairs to night to please me? And besides, if he has been in the village three weeks, as he pretends, and ben't the devil, some body besides us wou'd sartainly have seen him; and I have axed all the servants and numbers of others, and they all agree that they have never seed no such parson."

"Oh! Mr. Brown," said Dorcasina, "this is a ridiculous and unfounded idea, and I am sorry to see you thus give way to superstition. I dare say, if the truth were known, that the monster, which followed you, was no other than a cat or dog, or some such harmless animal, which your imagination exalted to the height of a steeple." She then related the fright Betty had met with, some years before, in returning from the grove, suppressing, however, some of the previous circumstances. This story had no effect upon John; he could not be convinced that what he had seen was not supernatural.

Dorcasina did not fail of relating to Betty, what had happened to John, and lamented seriously that she could not reason him out of the idea, with which he was possessed. Betty, from similar ignorance, was disposed to be of a similar opinion, and next day related the whole affair to Scipio, and requested to know what he thought of it. Scipio was entirely of the opinion of John, and said that nobody but the "old Nick," could come and go, and change themselves into such strange shapes as he did. This wag, highly delighted that his plan had succeeded so far beyond his expectations, took an early opportunity of going to Mr. Stanly's, and diverting Harriot with an account of it.

This lively lady immediately paid Dorcasina another visit. It was a warm evening in June, and the doors and windows being open, she descried John alone in the parlour. Stepping over the carpet on tiptoe, Harriot got close behind him unperceived, and clapping him suddenly upon the shoulder, "ha! Brown," said she, "what, alone again? What have you done with Miss Sheldon now?" John started up in a fright. "I—I have done nothing with her, sir; please to sit down, and I'll go and call her." "So," thought Harriot, "my new character procures me great respect, I find." John went immediately up stairs in quest of Dorcasina. He met her half way, descending, and informed her, in great agitation, that the gentleman was below, and begged her for heaven's sake to dismiss him as soon as possible. Dorcasina smiled, and passed on without answering. At her entrance into the parlour, she found Harriot laughing heartily at the idea John had conceived of her. Dorcasina inquired the cause of her mirth. At this question, instead of returning an answer, Harriot redoubled her laughter. Dorcasina, thinking her mad, several times repeated her question. At length, after Harriot was a little composed, "I cannot help laughing," said she, "to think how foolish Brown will look when he comes to find that I have supplanted him." "You are almost—a fool, I had like to have said." "Oh, out with it my dear," replied Harriot. "Call me fool, idiot, any thing; the more hard names the better, provided you do but love me." "If I had any thoughts of loving you," said Dorcasina, "I should not call you names." "I know better," replied Harriot, "I know you entertain thoughts of loving me, at this moment. I read it in your countenance, and it will be vain for you to deny it." "You are the strangest, the vainest fellow that ever existed." "Very well, be it so," said Harriot, "since I am so fortunate as to please you." She continued thus to rattle away in her usual lively manner, and Dorcasina could do nothing but laugh, contradict, and be pleased, as usual.

After Harriot had taken her leave, John had a long and serious conversation with Dorcasina upon the diabolical character of her visitor, who, he asserted had, that very evening, appeared all at once by his side, without entering either at the door, or the window. Dorcasina laughed, argued, and reasoned, but all to no purpose; the idea was so strongly fixed that it could not be eradicated.

After she had retired to her chamber, she began to question herself, in a very serious manner. Her constancy to John began to be somewhat shaken. The youth, the beauty, the engaging sprightliness, and even vanity of her new lover, had, in spite of herself, began to make some impression on her heart. She would not however acknowledge it to herself, till this evening, when Harriot accidentally and wildly asserted it. She now felt that it was but too true, and that she was guilty of a breach of that constancy, which she had so fondly cherished, and so warmly defended. Angry with herself at this discovery, she determined to act as honor required, and fulfil her first engagement. Her passion for Montague had not yet arrived at that pitch, as that she had experienced for Brown, and she determined to keep over it a strict guard, and to prevent, if possible, its further progress. Satisfied, after taking this resolution, with the rectitude of her intentions, her mind became composed, and she soon fell asleep.

Next morning, during breakfast, John was uncommonly thoughtful, and Dorcasina in vain endeavoured to get out of him the cause of his uneasiness. She had paid so little regard to the idea he had conceived of her new lover, that he did not feel disposed to contest the point any longer.

As soon as breakfast was ended, he mounted a horse, and rode off, without communicating to any person a design which he had the night before formed. He frequently made excursions on horseback, for pleasure, though Dorcasina could never, since the unfortunate accident which befel her wig, be prevailed on to accompany him. His going now, therefore, excited in her no surprise.

John never stopped till he arrived at the house of a clergyman, ten miles distant, in a neighbouring parish, that of L——, happening at this time to be vacant. Requesting to speak with the minister, in private, he was shewn to the study, and there acquainted him with the particulars of his strange situation. He informed him of his being hired by Sheldon, of the favour he had found in the sight of his daughter, of the devil's coming to thwart him in the character of an officer, and, in conclusion, he earnestly begged the minister to go, and, by his prayers, and his learning, rid the house of this infernal visitor. The clergyman was a man of sense, and at first endeavoured to convince him of the improbability and absurdity of the idea he entertained; but finding all his arguments vain, and that John was strongly impressed with the idea that his presence would set all matters right, he finally consented to accompany him.

They did not arrive at the mansion of Dorcasina till near three o'clock; and, as two was her usual hour of dining, she had suffered no small degree of apprehension, on account of Mr. Brown; nor was it lessened by the recollection of the melancholy mood, in which he had left her. She was, therefore, rejoiced at his safe return, and surprised at seeing him thus accompanied. Her first idea was, that John, fearful of losing her, intended being immediately married. This occasioned her a momentary agitation, but upon second thoughts, recollecting that the banns were not published, her agitation immediately subsided. She was well acquainted with the character of the reverend gentleman, nor was his person wholly unknown to her; as he had been once or twice at the house, during the life of her father. She therefore received him with much politeness, and they dined together with great cordiality.

After the cloth was removed, and the servants withdrawn, "I have brought this gentleman here, ma'am," said John, "hoping he will drive away the devil, and set all to rights between us again." Dorcasina was sensibly hurt at this proof of her lover's weakness; she coloured, hesitated, and knew not what to reply. The clergyman smiled, and was the first to break the silence. "This gentleman," said he, "has given me a strange account of a person, whom he supposes to be supernatural. Will you be so good, madam, as to let me know your opinion of him?" "That he is a mere mortal, a gay, volatile, impetuous young man, and that there is nothing supernatural about him."

The clergyman had, from John's first acquainting him with his situation, been greatly astonished at the choice of Dorcasina, and now that he was in her company, was strongly inclined to represent to her its impropriety; but considering that his acquaintance with her was hardly sufficient to justify his meddling in so delicate a business, and that advice, unasked, is seldom followed, he wisely forbore, and confined himself to the affair, upon which alone he had been consulted. "I am fully in sentiment with you, madam," said he, "and I wish we could succeed in convincing Mr. Brown of his error." "I have laboured to do it, Sir; but hitherto unsuccessfully. I flatter myself however, that, as soon as the captain withdraws his attentions, he will be undeceived." "If it be not an impertinent question, madam, I would ask why, as you are engaged to this gentleman, his attentions are admitted?"

Dorcasina then gravely related the ardent passion of Montague, his fiery disposition, and the engagement she had been drawn into, to prevent his doing Mr. Brown a violence. The good gentleman could with difficulty restrain his risibility to hear a person of Dorcasina's age and appearance describing the transports of her youthful lover; but being able, happily, to command himself, he as gravely replied: "If that be the case, madam, it is best, in order to prevent mischief, to keep your engagement; and I would advise you, sir," said he, turning to John, "to divest yourself of the idea you have conceived, and wait patiently till the month is expired, when you will be richly rewarded for your present disappointment, by the possession of this amiable lady." He then took his leave, and was invited, at parting, to repeat his visit, as he was the person upon whom Dorcasina had pitched to crown her happiness, by uniting her with the object of her love.

"I am sorry, Mr. Brown," said Dorcasina, as soon as they were alone, "that you did not inform me of your intention, as I should certainly have endeavoured to dissuade you from it." "I know'd that well enough," replied John, "and that was the very reason I didn't tell you." "Well, now you see that he agrees with me in opinion, respecting captain Montague, I hope you will be induced to change yours." "When I sees reason to, I shall; and not before." Dorcasina, finding that nothing could undeceive him, dropped the subject, and entertained him with other conversation.

Chapter XV.

A FORTNIGHT of the month was now elapsed and Harriot had not been able to draw from Dorcasina any concessions in her favour, although she plainly perceived that her visits were far from being disagreeable. Encouraged by this discovery, she made them more frequent, urged her suit with greater earnestness, and more seriously than she had hitherto done. But Dorcasina, true to her resolution, and to her first engagement, conscientiously avoided affording the smallest encouragement.

She made serious reflections on the singularity of her situation, and would have been much perplexed had she not been resolutely determined to act an honourable part. She confessed to Betty the impression Montague had made upon her heart. "Here," said she, "are two amiable youths, who both adore me. In taking one I shall drive the other to despair. But honor requires that I should fulfil my engagements to Mr. Brown. I wish, alas! it may not prove fatal to the unfortunate Montague. I am exactly in the situation of Sir Charles Grandison. They are both, in my opinion, the first of men; I love them both, but mine is a double, not a divided love."

Harriot was a little mortified that, at the expiration of the month, and the return of her father, she had made no further progress. She had, however, the satisfaction of reflecting, that she had made an extraordinary effort to save Dorcasina from unavailing repentance; and though she had not succeeded, according to her wishes, it had afforded her a fund of innocent amusement.

The day after Mr. Stanly's return, his lady detailed to him the whole of the business, concealing nothing from him which Harriot had communicated to her. He did not fully approve the part his daughter had acted, and, had he been at home, he would not have consented to it; but as Mrs. Stanly's compliance was from the best of motives, her tenderness for him, and regard for Dorcasina, he very delicately concealed his opinion. "I will go," said he, "and reason with this infatuated woman." "It will be all in vain," replied Mrs. Stanly. "Dorcasina certainly labours under a species of derangement, which renders her incapable of listening to reason. I tried it without effect. Some other means must be employed, if we resolve to break the match." "We must take a little time to consider what is to be done," said Mr. Stanly, "and I wish, my dear, you would assist me with your invention and advice."

Mr. Stanly possessed a farm forty miles distant from L——, very obscurely situated in the interior of the country. His lady suggested the idea of sending Dorcasina thither. "We must separate her from this fellow," said she; "and I think, if she were kept, a twelvemonth, where she could have no access to the books, which have deranged her ideas, it might possibly be the means of restoring her senses." Mr. Stanly approved the idea; "but how," said he, "shall we get her there? She will never go voluntarily; and it would be very difficult to force her." "Oh! we must leave that to Harriot. I dare say her lively imagination will contrive some method of conveying her." "Well, do you two concert the means, and I will see that they are employed." Mrs. Stanly, in fact, had the plan already in her head, and, upon communicating it to Harriot, she readily approved it. It was as follows. Harriot was to pay Dorcasina another visit, in the character of captain Montague. She was to pretend to be in despair at her ill success; to declare that the match between her and Brown should never take place; and that she was determined to concert the methods of preventing it. This sketch, and the rest of the plan, being submitted to Mr. Stanly, met his approbation. Once more he said Harriot might visit her, in her assumed character, but it would be the last time he should consent to her going out, in the habit of a man. Availing herself of this permission, Harriot prepared to make her last visit, that very evening; and her father himself accompanied her almost to the house, to prevent any accident which might befal her.

The last visit she had paid Dorcasina was five evenings before. She had never so long intermitted her attentions, since she first assumed the military character. Dorcasina was uneasy in her absence, but concealed it from John, and even from Betty. "The best thing that can happen," thought she, "is for me never more to see him. I shall soon be united to one, who deserves all my tenderness. I will drive this intruder from my heart, and Mr. Brown shall again become its sole possessor." Notwithstanding these good resolutions, her heart danced in her bosom, when Harriot appeared, and they vanished like mist before the noon day sun.

John and Dorcasina had just returned from a walk in the grove, where they had concluded to have the banns published on the following Sunday. John immediately retired as had been his invariable practice, since he had discovered the quality of this intruder.

"Well my dear," said Harriot, "are you not glad to see me?" "How should I," replied Dorcasina, "when you constantly drive Mr. Brown from my presence." "That name," said Harriot, "is hateful to me; that man is the bane of all my happiness." She then arose; and after walking several times across the room, with hurried steps, laid her hand upon her sword, "why should not I chastise him as he deserves?— but no, I should draw upon myself the detestation of the loveliest of women." She then turned suddenly, and throwing herself upon her knees before Dorcasina, "will you not, lovely, adorable, charming Miss Sheldon, afford me one ray, one gleam of hope?" Dorcasina was softened even to tears. She had never before seen Harriot so humble, so touching, so despairing. She held out her hand, which Harriot almost devoured with kisses. "Rise, pray rise," said she, "You distress me, indeed you do. Were it in my power, I would relieve, and make you happy; but you came too late, my heart was engaged, and I can now only pity, and feel for you the tenderest friendship." Harriot again arose, and again changed her language from despair to passion. She raved, and stamped; "cruel, hard hearted woman," said she, "as if I were not more deserving of your love than that yankee, clown, booby; but know you shall never be his; my detested rival shall never triumph in his victory. This is the last time I will trouble you with my presence. I shall go and employ myself with the means of preventing this ill-sorted union."

She then threw her arms round Dorcasina's neck, and almost stopped her breath with kisses, and concluded by biting her cheek so hard as to make her scream aloud; and then darted out of the house without uttering another syllable.

Dorcasina retired immediately to her chamber, agitated by a contrariety of different feelings. She there gave a free vent to those tears which had before began to flow. "Ill fated, unhappy youth," she exclaimed. "Unfortunate in having beheld these charms which you are doomed not to possess! Why has heaven made me so fair, and given me so tender a heart? Had I fewer charms I should not make such ravages among mankind; or had I less sensibility, their sufferings would not thus distress me."

Betty now making her appearance was desired by Dorcasina to inform Mr. Brown that she was not very well, and could not see him that evening, as she was going immediately to bed.

Dorcasina devoted that night to mourning, for the despair of Montague. The idea of never seeing him again affecting her more than she had thought possible, considering the place John still retained in her affections.

The next day Mr. Stanly sent for Scipio, and conferred with him on the present crisis of his mistress' affairs. Knowing his fidelity and attachment to her, he imparted to him the plan he had laid to save her from the disgrace and unhappiness she was so eager to encounter. "Your mistress frequently walks late in the grove, Scipio; the next evening she spends there, you must give me immediate notice, and have the coach in readiness. Betty also, to whom you must impart the affair, must be ready to accompany her mistress."

Scipio, who was now in despair, concluding that the match was unavoidable, since Harriot's plan to prevent it had failed of success, was overjoyed at the proposal and the commands he had received. In addition to the repugnance he felt, at seeing his mistress thus degrade herself, he was conscious of having played Brown too many tricks, and treated him with too much insolence, ever to be forgiven. He was fearful, therefore, if this match took place, of leading in future an uncomfortable life, or having in his old age to seek another habitation. "I tanke you, massa Tanly," said he, "for take so much trouble about my good misse. Ebery thing sall be done jus as you say." "She will probably be gone some months, Scipio, and I trust that, under your care, her business will not suffer." "Get rid of Brown, sar, and no fear Scipio." "We will send your mistress out of the way first, Scipio, and then we shall see what can be done with Brown. Betty must have in readiness a trunk of clothing for Miss Dorcasina. The key she may keep in her pocket, but the trunk must be sent by another conveyance. " "Yes, sar." "Betty will be seized by two men to be carried to the coach, and she must make some shew of resistance." "Yes, sar." "You see Scipio the necessity of keeping the affair a profound secret, both before, and after it takes place, you must, therefore, if interrogated, appear entirely ignorant." "Yes sar, certainly, sar."

Scipio now went home in high spirits to communicate the business to Betty. But first he made her swear not to reveal it. The joy of Betty was somewhat allayed, by the apprehension that she should see John no more; for, notwithstanding the late unpromising appearances, she still retained a passion for him, and a latent hope of obtaining him. She, however, comforted herself that she should rather never behold him more, than to have the mortification of seeing him the husband of another. She, therefore, immediately set herself at work to make preparations for the intended journey, by packing up her own clothes, and such of Dorcasina's as she would be least likely to miss; for, as the evenings were remarkably fine, she knew it would not be long before she would again walk in the grove.

Mr. Stanly, mean time, dispatched a letter to his tenant, informing him that he should send to his house a lady, who was a little deranged, and her maid to attend upon her; desiring him to accommodate them, in the best manner he could, to supply them with whatever they wanted; but, by no means, to suffer the lady to have it in her power to make her escape. In conclusion, he assured him he should be well rewarded. He next engaged, beside one of his own servants, who was a stranger to Dorcasina, another person, in whom he could place the fullest confidence. They were to have the care of conveying her away, and to them he likewise imparted his instructions. Every thing being thus arranged, they waited only an opportunity of putting their design in execution.

On the following Sunday, to the astonishment of the whole parish, except the family of Mr. Stanly, the banns of marriage were published between John Brown and Dorcasina Sheldon.

The Tuesday evening following was remarkably fine; the moon was at the full, and the sky clear and serene. Dorcasina, according to a resolution she had taken, the morning after Montague's last visit, to think of him no more, had turned all her attention to, and endeavoured to center all her affections in, the man, who was so soon to become her husband. In this commendable resolution she succeeded even beyond her expectations. Triumphing in the conquest she had gained over what she esteemed an unlawful passion, she proposed, during tea, a walk in the grove. Betty being present heard the proposal, and communicated it to Scipio, who, as soon as the lovers had quitted the house, hastened with the intelligence to Mr. Stanly.

The charms of the evening, and the beauty of the images around, the gently flowing Delaware, reflecting from its glassy surface the moon's softened lustre, that beautiful luminary tracing its way silently, and majestically, through the heavens, alternately concealing herself behind clumps of trees, whose thick foliage was impervious to her rays, and stealing cautiously into full view; these delightful objects, added to the presence of one whom she almost adored, and to whom she was so soon to be united, all conspired to raise the happiness of Dorcasina almost to ecstacy. She gazed on her lover with looks of unutterable delight, she pressed his hand, as they walked beneath the wide spreading trees, and fondly imagined that this delirium of joy could end only with their lives. But alas, poor lady, she built upon a foundation of sand. Little did she think she was so soon to experience the vanity of human expectations, and the extreme instability of all human enjoyment. A coach, rattling through the avenue, awoke her from this dream of happiness. They stood still, surprised, to observe it. It stopped opposite to them, and two men jumping out of it, laid violent hands upon Dorcasina. She screamed and John endeavoured to protect her; but what could he do against so superior a force? One of them, who was Mr. Stanly in disguise, drew a sword, and brandishing it over the heads of the lovers, in an altered and harsh tone thus addressed them: "Resistance is vain, Miss Sheldon must go with us. The orders of captain Montague must be obeyed." At this name, and at the sight of the formidable weapon, John quitted his hold of Dorcasina and would have resigned her to her fate; but throwing her arms round his neck in an agony of grief, she exclaimed, "my dear lover! my husband! must we then be parted? parted, at the moment, when we were so near being united forever! No! it cannot, it must not be. Sooner shall my soul be parted from my body!" But the unfeeling mortals, who had seized upon her, without any remorse, or the least regard to her distress, unclasped her arms from the neck of her lover, and tying a handkerchief over her mouth, forced her into coach, and, two of them jumping in after her, they wished John a good night. Then, ordering the coachman to drive on, they were in a few minutes out of the grove; leaving John almost petrified with consternation and astonishment.

Dorcasina, being seated in the coach, found by her side another female, whom, she soon recognized, by the light of the moon, to be her faithful Betty, with her mouth tied up, and her hands apparently fastened behind her. This discovery somewhat alleviated her distress;

and as the coach rolled rapidly along, and the two men kept a profound silence, she began to reflect, with some degree of calmness, upon the vicissitudes of fortune, and the strangeness of her situation. This was the second time she had been thus forcibly carried off. The first had proved to be a mere sham, the trick of a wicked scholar, for his amusement; but manner of this conveyance, so much more honourable than the former, the passion, the impetuosity, and despair of captain Montague; his threats, likewise, which she had before disregarded, now struck her very forcibly, and all conspired to prove in the most incontestable manner, that this second seizure was in good earnest, and an effect of the violent passion, with which Montague was inspired.

She then began to consider in what manner she should conduct towards him; and she first resolved, if any opportunity should present, to endeavour to regain her liberty. If she should not succeed in that attempt, she determined to discourage all his addresses, to be faithful to her dear John, and by her constancy deserve to be again restored to him.

The coach, having now reached the confines of L——, suddenly stopped, where there was not a house to be seen. Mr. Stanly, after delivering a letter to Dorcasina, quitted the coach without being discovered, and walked home to give his wife and daughter an account of his success.

We will now leave them, rapidly pursuing their route, and return to the bereaved Brown, whom we left standing motionless in the grove.

After recovering a little from his first astonishment he walked in a melancholy mood towards the house, being unable to determine whether they were demons or mortals, who had robbed him of Dorcasina.

Scipio, who had watched his return, inquired what he had done with his mistress. "Some men, or devils," said John, "carried her off in a coach." "Carry her off?" exclaimed Scipio, "and you tan by and let em take her?" "What could I do? there was two on em beside the driver, and one had a sord." "Do? I kill one and murder toder. But where, which way dey gone?" John having satisfied him in that respect, Scipio upbraided him, in the severest terms, for suffering the ruffians to carry off his mistress, and poured on him such a torrent of abuse, that John, being no longer able patiently to endure it, doubled his fist and gave him a blow. This was what Scipio desired, knowing himself to be the best man, though so much his senior. Not wishing to hurt the booby, he took him in his arms, and, without any difficulty, thrust him out into the street; then fastening the door upon him, bid him seek a lodging elsewhere, for he should never again enter that house. A striking instance of the instability of fortune! This poor man, who, only a few hours before, thought himself master of Dorcasina and all her possessions, was, in a short space of time, robbed of his mistress, stripped of all his fancied possessions, and by a negro servant turned out of doors. Having no remedy but patience, he hastened to the inn, called for a lodging, and, in no very agreeable frame of mind, retired to rest.

Next morning Mr. Stanly went to the house of Dorcasina, to endeavour to prevail on Brown to quit it; but finding him already gone, he inquired of Scipio what had become of him. Scipio then, in high spirits, related all the particulars of the last night's affair. "You were rather too precipitate with him, Scipio; you should, in consideration of his disappointment, have suffered him to remain here one night, at least—But which way did he go? where do you suppose he slept?" "Oh, I pose he go to de tavern, sar." Mr. Stanly, following him thither, found him much dejected, and taking him aside, asked him if he could conjecture whither Dorcasina was conveyed. "No, sir, it is onpossible for me to guess." "It is a strange affair," said Mr. Stanly. "What do you propose doing with yourself?" "I don't know, sir, I han't resolved." "Mr. Sheldon," said Stanly, "upon his death bed, recommended his daughter to my care and protection, and I shall endeavour to discover who has thus spirited her away; but as it is uncertain when I shall discover whither she is carried, I shall take upon myself the care of her interest. Now as women are sometimes fickle, and it is uncertain when, or whether you will ever see her again, I would advise you to give up all thoughts of her, and return home to your friends." John unwilling to resign his splendid expectations, was silent. "In consideration of your great disappointment," resumed Mr. Stanly, "I will give you a hundred pounds out of Miss Sheldon's property, and her father's clothes are yours already, she having, as I am informed, made you a present of them." "She did, sir." "Those you will also be allowed to take." John revolved the matter for a few moments in silence. If Dorcasina did not return, he should be deprived of all; he thought best, therefore, considering the uncertainty of that event, to take up with Mr. Stanly's offer. They then proceeded together to the house of Dorcasina, where the money and clothes being delivered to him, he returned to Rhode Island, purchased a small farm, forgot Dorcasina, married Dolly, and sat down contented and happy, in the sphere of life for which nature had designed him.

Mr. Stanly then engaged a sober discreet woman to take charge of Dorcasina's household affairs; and Scipio superintending the work without doors, things went on prosperously. He then caused a report to be spread that Dorcasina, sick of her match, had taken a tour to the northward to avoid it.

We will now return to the adventurers in the coach. After having driven for three hours, at the rate of seven or eight miles an hour, they arrived about twelve o'clock at an obscure tavern, in a retired situation. Here, as directed by Mr. Stanly, they stopped to bait. The people were in bed, but the driver knocked them up, and, after informing them that he was conveying a lady into the country, who was deranged, the man in the coach liberated the hands and tongues of the two prisoners, and told them that if they chose they might alight. Dorcasina, constantly intent upon making her escape, availed herself of this permission, and, to her great satisfaction, she and Betty were allowed to have a room by themselves. "Was ever any body so persecuted and unfortunate?" said Dorcasina, as soon as they were alone. "And my dear Mr. Brown, how great will be his despair! Tell me, Betty, how did they get you into the coach? Did not the men servants endeavour to prevent it?" "No ma'am, there wasn't one soul of 'em in the house, and these here men, without so much as knocking, come bolt into the kitchen where I was, and, without more ado, clapped a handkerchief over my mouth, and lugged me out to the coach, which stood at the gate, and then hoisted me into it." "Well, we must not waste this precious time in talking, Betty, but must resolve to act. Here is a favourable opportunity of making our escape, as we can easily get out at this window." "La, ma'am, what shou'd we do then, so far from home, in the night, and no other house hereabouts?" "We can easily hide ourselves among the trees, till morning; and then walk till we find a house." "Oh dear! why I wou'dn't do it for all the world. I'd rather go where they are a mind to carry us. Why the very thoughts of staying so long in the woods, in the night, makes my hair stand on end." "Very well," said Dorcasina, coldly, "I shall certainly improve the present opportunity; and, if you do not choose to follow me, you may tarry behind." Upon this she shoved up the window, and had got one foot out, when the man, who had accompanied them, entered the room with some refreshment.

"Where are you going, Miss Sheldon?" said he, as he seized and pulled her back.

She sat down without answering a single word, greatly mortified at her disappointment. She was then offered some cake and wine, with which they had been supplied by the provident care of Mrs. Stanly, but she refused to accept any, and in a spirited manner, demanded to know by what authority he detained her a prisoner. "By the authority of captain Montague, madam." "Captain Montague has no authority over me, and I require you to set me at liberty." "I do not know how much he has over you, madam; but his authority is very great over me, and I dare not disobey him."

Dorcasina was again silent. She walked the room in agitation, determined to endeavour to move the family in her favour. In about a half an hour from their first arrival, the horses being refreshed, the two men seized Dorcasina, and carried her to the door, where the coach was close drawn up, and the man of the house standing by the horses. As soon as she saw him, Dorcasina, in a loud voice exclaimed, "Mr.—good man—what is your name? for heaven's sake, have pity upon me, and rescue me from these men, who, at the instigation of a young officer, whom I refused to marry, are forcibly conveying me I know not whither." The man stared, and as the moon shone full in Dorcasina's face, the idea which her companions had intimated of her insanity was fully confirmed by her appearance, and the reason she gave for her present removal. The man making no efforts in her favour, Dorcasina was soon placed in the coach, with her companion by her side. The coachman then went back, and returned with Betty, who made not the least resistance, declaring, after she was seated, that she would follow her mistress to the end of the world.

It was half after twelve when they left the inn; and they drove on rapidly and without any accident till near three. The face of the sky which had hitherto been so bright and serene, began now to be overcast with black and angry clouds; the moon was suddenly obscured; the wind blew; the lightning flashed, and the thunder rolled over their heads. In short they were threatened with a violent shower, and no friendly cottage appeared to afford them a shelter. Betty, terrified almost out of her senses, screamed at every flash, and the men were somewhat disconcerted; but Dorcasina sat perfectly composed, reflecting that this was a trifling evil to her, compared with the separation from the man of her affections.

The clouds were so black and thick as to occasion a considerable degree of darkness, immediately after the flashes of lightning especially. As it was very dry the wind brought the dust directly into the coachman's eyes so that he could not see his way before him. In this confusion of the elements, he drove against a large rock, and the coach was overturned. Here was "confusion worse confounded." Dorcasina screamed aloud, and Betty much louder. Fortunately, however the horses stood still, no person was hurt, and the door of the coach was on the upper side. The man, who was uppermost, by the assistance of the coachman soon disengaged himself. He then helped out Dorcasina, whose head, (though her unfortunate wig was again fallen off) was not quite as bare as when she lost it before, her hair having grown about an inch in length, and standing quite erect. The attention of the two men was next turned to Betty, who being undermost was the last to be extricated. While they were engaged in helping her out of the coach, Dorcasina thought it a favourable opportunity to make her escape. She therefore directed her steps towards the fence, which was at a small distance from the coach, and beyond which, by the flashes of lightning, she observed a thick wood.

As soon as Betty found herself safe and unhurt, observing only the men, she inquired for her mistress. The two men, who had not before missed her, began now to look around them; and, by a fortunate flash of lightning, they saw her just clambering over the fence. The one, who had been her companion in the coach ran towards her; but before he reached the fence she was fairly on the other side, and even gotten a few yards beyond it. The man again descrying her, by the lightning, hastened to the spot where he saw her. On reaching it, however he found her still a head of him, endeavouring to gain the wood. But happening to step one foot into a hole she fell upon the ground. In this situation her pursuer observed her, and thinking himself now sure of his prey, he advanced, with rapid strides, towards the place. Dorcasina hearing his near approach, and fearing she should not be able to rise soon enough to get out of his way, especially as she had left a shoe in the hole, suddenly rolled over and over to a considerable distance, and thus evaded him. She had now regained her feet and was pursuing her course towards the wood, when the lightning gave the man an opportunity of observing that he was very near her. He therefore again darted towards her in order to seize her; but she as suddenly darted off in a tangent and eluded his grasp.

Thus, by the favour of the darkness, which succeeded every flash of lightning, she, like an ignis fatuus, constantly had changed her position and escaped her pursuer, till fairly gaining the wood, she was immediately, and wholly concealed from his view. Finding he had entirely lost sight of her, he gave up the chace and returned to his companions to give an account of his ill success.

Betty wept bitterly at being separated from her mistress, and thought she would see a thousand frightful spectres, in that dark and lonely wood.

They now held a consultation upon the method of procedure to be adopted, in the present emergency. Betty was for sitting in the coach upon the spot till morning, and then endeavouring to find her mistress. But the men agreeing, if the coach were not broken, to proceed slowly to the next house, and to return and search for Dorcasina in the morning, she was obliged to submit.

They now with some difficulty righted the carriage, and finding it, to appearance, uninjured, Betty and the man seated themselves within, and the coachman cautiously and slowly moved onward in quest of a house. They had not proceeded far before the clouds began to disperse, without having afforded any rain; and, to their great satisfaction they discovered that the gates of light in the east were unbarred.

The morning's dawn found Dorcasina sitting at the foot of a tree in the middle of the wood. As soon as there was light sufficient for the purpose, she drew from her pocket the letter which Mr. Stanly had placed on her lap, the evening before, and which she had not yet had an opportunity of reading. It was composed by Harriot, and copied in a disguised hand by her father. The contents were as follows:

"Beautiful, cruel, charming, Miss Sheldon,

"AFTER the warning I had given you, could you possibly imagine that I should tamely submit to see you married to my rival? to that low, pitiful Brown? to a fellow not worthy of being a shoe-black to a gentleman, who should deserve your heart. In order to prevent such a shameful instance of self degradation, I shall have you conveyed beyond his reach, and concealed from his knowledge. You shall be well accommodated and treated with all possible respect. Whenever you are inclined to take the exercise of riding, a horse properly caparisoned will always be at your command, but to prevent your escape the man of the house will accompany you. It is my present intention to keep you a prisoner, till your affections shall be thoroughly weaned from my despicable rival, and fixed on me. I shall not presume to approach you myself, but shall have your motions so carefully watched as to render an escape altogether impracticable.

"Such articles of clothing as may be necessary for you in your retreat shall be forwarded, together with a number of books of history and travels, to enable you to pass your time agreeably and usefully.

"In the course of a few months, I flatter myself, my dear Miss Sheldon, that such a revolution, in my favour, will take place in your susceptible mind, as will enable me to restore you to your family and connections at L——, and from thence, in due season, to remove you to a place where it shall be the business of my life to render you happy.

"In the mean time, I remain,

"Your eternally devoted,

"H. Montague."

"P. S. Having no coach of my own, I shall make use of yours to convey you from L——."

Dorcasina had just finished reading this epistle, when she saw a little boy, about ten years old, coming towards her. He was the only child of a widow, who lived in a small neat cottage, near the wood. One of her two cows was missing the night before, and the boy was sent into the wood thus early in search of her. Dorcasina, highly gratified at the sight of a human being, in that lonely place, rose up at his approach. The boy no sooner beheld her meagre form, clothed in white, and her head in the situation before described, than he turned back affrighted and ran, with all speed, out of the wood. Dorcasina ran after him hallooing, begging him to stop, and promising she would do him no harm: but her entreaties were vain; the boy redoubled his pace; and she followed, till, quitting the wood, she perceived the cottage. Finding that it would be impossible to overtake him she gave over the chace.

The terrified boy continued his flight, without once looking behind, till he reached the cottage, where entering pale and breathless, his mother alarmed, inquired what had happened. "Oh, dear mother, I have seen a witch, and she chased me quite out of the wood." His mother, who had more understanding and less superstition than most people in her humble situation, desiring him to explain himself, he began by describing an ugly old woman, clothed in white, with her hair standing on end, and sitting in the middle of the wood. He had got thus far, when he was interrupted by a knocking at the door. "Walk in," said the woman. The door opened and Dorcasina entered. The boy, running up to his mother, and throwing his arms round her waist, exclaimed, "Oh, mother! the witch! the witch!" The woman herself was a little startled at the strange figure that stood before her; but Dorcasina addressing her in gentle accents, soon removed her fears, and raised her compassion. She informed her that, by the overturning of her coach, in the obscurity of the night, she had lost her head dress, and taken shelter in the wood. She then begged for some breakfast, saying she was weary and hungry, having ridden all night without taking any refreshment. The good woman, who had her tea-kittle boiling, and a coarse wheaten cake baking by the fire, set out a little table covered with a cloth as white as snow, and she and Dorcasina were soon seated to a dish of bohea, warm cake, and sweet butter. The fare was homely, but Dorcasina has repeatedly said, it was the sweetest meal she had ever made.

The boy hearing Dorcasina's account, and finding her gentle and inoffensive, was relieved from his fears, and set off again in pursuit of the cow. Dorcasina, finding herself alone with her kind hostess, began to inquire the name of the village, and how far it was from L——. "Oh, dear ma'am," said the woman, "L——, is a great way off; it is almost thirty miles. I remember I passed through it once, when my poor husband was alive." "Thirty miles," repeated Dorcasina, "I did not think it had been so far; I left it last evening, at nine o'clock." She then began to give the woman a more particular account of herself, telling her who she was, how she was upon the point of marriage to a charming youth, and how another young man who was violently in love with her, had conveyed her away by force, to prevent the match. "By the greatest good fortune," added she, "the coach overturned, and I have escaped. If you can contrive any method of conveying me back to L——, and of restoring me to my dear Mr. Brown, you may depend upon being handsomely rewarded." The woman viewed her in silence, and considering her lean withered form, sallow complexion, and toothless mouth, knew not what degree of credit was due to her. Dorcasina perceiving her silence and embarrassment, "if money be wanting," said she, "to procure my conveyance, I will supply you with whatever is necessary, happening to have a considerable sum in my pocket, at the time I was seized."

They had, by this time, finished their breakfast, and the woman observing that Dorcasina must stand in need of rest, advised her to lie down and endeavour to sleep; and she would, in the mean time, consider what could be done. Dorcasina cordially thanked her, and taking her kind advice, was shewn into a little neat bed-room, where, throwing herself upon the bed, her cares were soon buried in a most profound sleep.

The two men, the companions of Betty, were, in the mean time, enjoying themselves over a hot breakfast, about a mile from the place where the coach was overturned. But the affectionate Betty was otherwise employed. Her distress, lest some disaster had befallen Dorcasina, destroying her appetite, she walked the room, sobbing and entreating the men to dispatch their meal, and hasten back in search of her mistress. At length, to her great joy, they arose from the table, and the coach at Betty's desire, being already at the door, they were in a few minutes conveyed back to the spot where the disaster had befallen them. Here the men agreed to scour the wood, which was not extensive, while Betty staid to watch the horses. They left no part of it unexplored, when, to the great grief of Betty, she saw them return without her mistress. They now determined to inquire at all the cottages, which they observed on the other side of the wood. Having driven down the road which led to them, they inquired at the first house, if they had seen a lady, who they said was distracted, and whom they accurately described. Unsuccessful, but not discouraged in their first inquiry, they proceeded to two other houses, with the same ill success; but upon entering the fourth they fortunately discovered the object of their search; who, unconscious of the impending evil, still lay buried in a profound sleep. Upon their interrogating the widow concerning her, she desired them to speak softly, for that the lady in question was asleep, in her bed room. Betty upon this intelligence was transported with joy, and thanked the woman over and over again, for having afforded her mistress a shelter. They then requested to know how long Dorcasina had been her guest; upon which she related every circumstance of the terror of her son, of Dorcasina's following him into the house, and of the account, which she had given of herself. "I thought," added she "that the poor lady talked wildly, when she told about her sweet-hearts, and her being carried off for love." "She discovers her distraction in nothing else," replied the man, "her mind runs entirely upon love."

They now desired that she might be waked, in order to continue her journey; but to this Betty would not agree. "You must not go for to disturb her now," said she; "for she has been jolting all night, and not had a wink of sleep. It is as much as ever I can do to bear it, and I am sure she will be sick, if you do not let her have her nap out." The men consenting to this proposition, Betty softly entered the bed room, and seating herself by the bed side of her mistress, was soon buried in as profound a sleep.

Dorcasina waked first, and upon opening her eyes, did not immediately comprehend where she was. In a few moments, however, her recollection returned, and she was pleased and surprised to find Betty so near her. Her stirring roused Betty, and she eagerly inquired how she had effected her escape, and what fortunate chance directed her thither.

The men had waited, with much impatience, as it was now ten o'clock, and perceiving, by the voices of the females, that they were awake, they, without ceremony, entered the bed room. At this unexpected sight, Dorcasina screamed aloud; but the unfeeling men, regardless of her cries, told her she must prepare to continue her journey. "Whither do you carry me?" cried she. "How much farther, thus against my will, am I to be conveyed?" "Only ten miles, madam; you will then be delivered into other hands." "To none more unfeeling than yours, I am confident," replied Dorcasina. She then went into the other room followed by her companions. There, with tears in her eyes, she thanked her hostess for her kindness, rewarded her with money, and bade her adieu. "You see I am forced from you," said she; "but I shall never forget you." The good woman dropped a tear of pity for her disordered intellects, shook her kindly by the hand, and looked after the coach till the intervening trees concealed it from her view.

In about two hours our travellers reached the farm of Mr. Stanly. It was a retired romantic spot; the house, which had been built by the present proprietor, was small, but neat and commodious. It was nearly a mile distant from any other dwelling, and tenanted by an honest, industrious man, by the name of Giles; whose wife was a neat, discreet, and prudent woman. They received Dorcasina with attention, and conducted her to the apartment designed for her; which, from its extreme neatness, was highly pleasing to her.

The men, as well to refresh themselves as their horses, tarried till the next morning; and then, long ere Dorcasina had unclosed her eyes, set out on their return to L——.

Dorcasina, finding herself freed from their disagreeable company, experienced a momentary satisfaction. The morning being fine, the house pleasant, the prospect delightful, and the people respectful and attentive, she declared to Betty that, had she but the company of her dear Mr. Brown, she could pass the summer there, with the greatest pleasure imaginable.

Thus comfortably settled in her new habitation, where her clothes and books soon arrived, we will leave her, and return to the family of Mr. Stanly.

Chapter XVI.

THE time was now come when Harriot, with the consent of her parents, had agreed to become the wife of captain Barry. He had written to Mr. Stanly to have the banns published, in due form, and arrived at L—— the very next week after Dorcasina, as before related, had left it.

The first evening he was too much taken up with his beloved Harriot, to interest himself about any other person, till she, in her sprightly manner, rallied him upon his ingratitude, and the unsuitable return he made for the affection Dorcasina had formerly lavished upon him. "You do not even inquire," said she, "whether she be dead or alive." "I am ungrateful I confess," replied he, "and ask the lady's pardon. When did you see her? I hope she is well." Harriot then gave him a particular account of all her late transactions; informing him how she had visited Dorcasina, in the character of a young officer, in the hope of detaching her from Brown; her ill success in the affair; and, finally, the plan they had concerted, and put in execution for conveying her out of the reach of both Brown and the books that had so wretchedly perverted her understanding.

After the imposition, which James had formerly practised on Dorcasina, captain Barry could not be surprised, at any extravagance she could commit; but he was greatly diverted with the account Harriot gave of her courtship, and he approved highly of the plan of her removal; saying, if any thing could cure her strange infatuation, it would be a twelvemonth's seclusion from the books, which had corrupted her, and from every person whom she could possibly mistake for a lover.

The second evening after captain Barry's arrival at L——, he was united to the charming Harriot; and the next morning, after taking an affectionate leave of her beloved parents, many tears being shed on both sides, she was conveyed, by her husband, to a house provided for her at Philadelphia.

Mrs. Stanly, though she was much better, had never entirely recovered from the violent cold she had taken in the spring; a disagreeable cough still remaining. Another cold, taken about the time of her daughter's marriage, in a few weeks confirmed her in a consumption. The nature of this disorder is so flattering, and we so easily believe what we ardently wish, that Mr. Stanly did not wholly despair of the recovery of his wife, till two months after she had been given over by every other person. In the mean time, that he need not embitter the first days of his daughter's matrimonial life, he had, several times, informed her that her mother was afflicted with a violent cold, which he hoped she would soon get rid of, and once or twice, when he flattered himself that it was really the case, he wrote her, that she was apparently convalescent. These assurances quieted the uneasiness of the affectionate Mrs. Barry, and suffered her to enjoy, for a short time, the happiness of her new situation.

But, alas, this is a chequered scene, made up of good and ill, and it is sometimes difficult to determine which preponderates. It is the part of the wise to be thankful for present blessings, "to use this world as not abusing it," and, by a virtuous conduct, to endeavour to deserve their continuance. When misfortunes assail us, we should look for relief to that great Being who is the dispenser of both good and ill; and consider that, in this mutable state, the lenient hand of time will mitigate our severest sorrows.

By the last of August, Mrs. Stanly's disorder had increased to so alarming a degree, that her husband dared no longer even to hope. At the desire of his wife he wrote his daughter a true account of her situation, and desired her presence immediately at L——. Mrs. Barry, at this news, was overwhelmed with anguish. Her husband endeavoured by participating, to lessen it. She prepared for her journey, and he accompanied her. Her sensations, so different from what they were, when she last travelled the road, may be easily conceived by those who have, like her, hastened to attend the death bed of a beloved relative.

The meeting, on both sides, was tender and affectionate; the pleasure of once more beholding her beloved daughter, gave to the pallid countenance of Mrs. Stanly a new animation, and a new spring to her almost exhausted spirits. This momentary glow of the dim taper of life was, by Mrs. Barry, eagerly caught at; and, as soon as she had left the chamber, she gave it as her opinion to her father that her dear mama might yet recover. He shook his head in silent sorrow, having been too much flattered, and too often deceived, to indulge further expectations. Harriot's hopes were of short continuance. Mrs. Stanly's agitation, at seeing her daughter, exhausted her strength, and she was the next day weaker than before her arrival. Harriot now despaired. Her husband's business requiring his presence, he left her on the third day, to attend, with her father, the last days of the best of wives and mothers. Mrs. Stanly languished for a month after Harriot's arrival. She then expired, affording, by the well grounded hope she entertained of exchanging present ills for future bliss, the only consolation that bereaved friends can experience.

Harriot's grief was lively and violent; Mr. Stanly's deep and dignified. He had lost her, who for thirty years, had rejoiced when he rejoiced, and grieved when he was afflicted. She was the beloved wife of his youth, and the revered, esteemed companion of his maturer age.

Captain Barry was summoned to attend the funeral, and, a week afterwards, Mr. Stanly was left with no other companions than a son of twelve, and a daughter of ten years of age. He felt his loss more sensibly every day; his house appeared a perfect desert; he walked out to find relief, and again returned, still more depressed. Unable any longer to endure his situation, he meditated in his mind a removal to Philadelphia. The more he considered the scheme, the more eligible it appeared. He could there enjoy the greatest pleasure, of which he was capable, the company of his daughter, and of a son in law, who was extremely dear to him. He could there educate his younger children, and keep them under his own paternal eye. He communicated to captain Barry his ideas on the subject, requesting his opinion, and that of his wife. This unexpected proposal was extremely agreeable to this amiable couple. They highly approved the plan, and urged its immediate execution. Thus encouraged, Mr. Stanly soon came to a resolution to remove. Having settled his affairs at L——, he left it about the first of December, to the no small regret of the inhabitants, who in him, and Mr. Sheldon, had lost their two most useful and respectable citizens.

Chapter XVII.

DORCASINA had been now nearly six months a prisoner, without having once attempted to make her escape, being so narrowly watched by Giles, that she saw no probability of accomplishing it. The summer, had she been accompanied by her dear Brown, would have passed not unpleasantly. When the weather was fine, she rode, attended by Giles, or walked, accompanied by Betty. When it would not admit of either of these diversions, the well chosen books, with which she had been supplied, amused her within doors. She more than once attempted to learn from Giles and his wife, where the person belonged, by whose means she had been brought thither: but their constant answer was that they were engaged to secrecy. Betty, at her first arrival, had privately intimated that her mistress believed she owed her present confinement to a young officer, who pretended a violent passion for her. They were, therefore, not surprised at her interrogations respecting Montague, supposing the mistake, under which she laboured, was a consequence of her derangement.

On the arrival of the gloomy month of November, when the earth was no longer clothed with verdure, when the trees were stripped of their leaves, and their feathered inhabitants had winged their way to warmer climes; in short, when walking and riding were no longer pleasurable, Dorcasina began to be discontented and melancholy. She was not in the least surprised that Montague's passion had carried him so far; but she was astonished that she heard nothing from him; and that he could live so long without seeing her. He had, indeed, informed her, that he should detain her till her sentiments should change in his favour; but, should that ever be the case; where should she find him, or how inform him of it.

Revolving daily all these things in her mind, she determined to apply to Giles, to know whether, in such a case, he had settled any plan of communication. The first time, therefore, that she was alone with her landlord, she inquired, if he had heard lately from captain Montague. "Not very lately, ma'am." "You sometimes undoubtedly hear from him." The man was at a loss what to reply; concluding, however, that it was best to humour her, he answered, "Yes ma'am, once in a while." "Could you not convey a letter to him from me?" The man was again at a loss, but at length replied, "I will endeavour to, ma'am." Here the conversation ended, and Dorcasina, after further consideration, and much deliberation, wrote as follows:

"SIR,

"YOUR threats with regard to me were but too punctually executed; and you have but too well succeeded in separating me from my love. I have now, by your orders, been detained here nearly six months; and my heart has not yet declared in your favour, but remains firmly attached to my dearest Brown; nor while it continues to beat will it ever acknowledge another master. Let me ask you then what you expect to gain by my further detention? You have made the experiment, and have found me constant. And now, I entreat you, sir, to grant me my liberty, and suffer me to return where I alone can be happy, to my dear native village; to my home; and my dearest Mr. Brown."

Having sealed this letter, and directed it to captain H. Montague, she delivered it to Giles, and desired him immediately to forward it.

Giles took the letter; but was greatly embarrassed, not knowing how to dispose of it, or in what part of America captain Montague resided. He consulted, upon the occasion, his wife, and Betty, who both advised him to forward it to Mr. Stanly. He followed their advice, and sent it to L——, enclosed in one to that gentleman, just after he had removed to Philadelphia. It was entrusted to careless hands to be conveyed from thence, and finally lost without ever reaching him.

Dorcasina waited impatiently, a long time, for an answer; but none arriving, she became still more unhappy; and there is no calculating how far her despair would have carried her, had not a new acquaintance, which she contracted about this time, turned her thoughts into a new channel, and given her a set of new feelings.

The township, where she now resided, was large and thinly inhabited, and the farm of Mr. Stanly was situated in a remote corner.

At the distance of five miles was a meeting house, near which were the parsonage, and a public school-house. About the time that Dorcasina, against her will, had become an inhabitant, there had arrived a stranger, a good looking man, of about fifty, who, finding the inhabitants in want of a school-master, offered to undertake the instruction of their children. They at first hesitated, being unwilling to employ a stranger without recommendation; but his age, the decency of his deportment, and their being at a loss where to seek for another, at length induced them to make trial of his abilities.

He boarded with the clergyman; went regularly to meeting; and punctually and successfully discharged the duties of his station, so that the parents of the children under his care, thought themselves extremely fortunate in obtaining so good an instructor; especially as their minister declared him to be a man of piety. Such was his external appearance; but within dwelt all manner of vice and hypocrisy. This worthy instructor, this exact observer of the sabbath, this pious man belonged to Charleston, South Carolina. He had been a man of fortune; and, some business calling him to France, he had there thoroughly imbibed all the demoralizing, and atheistical principles of that corrupt people; and after his return, had squandered his time and money in gaming houses and brothels, though he had an amiable wife and several fine children. By these means, he in a short time contrived not only to dissipate his own property, but to get deeply into the debt of others. To avoid a prison, he was obliged to flee, leaving his family overwhelmed with distress. He wandered from town to town, and from village to village, till he arrived, pennyless, at the place where he was fortunate enough, as before related, to obtain a school, to supply his present necessities.

In the course of the summer, he heard Dorcasina frequently mentioned as a deranged lady of considerable fortune, whom her friends had sent to a remote situation, with a hope that retirement and quiet might restore her intellects. He, at first, regarded it no more than other passing news; but, at length, in autumn, growing weary of the confinement of a school, and of the labour of supporting a character so foreign to his nature, the thought struck him, as he lay ruminating on his bed, to visit Dorcasina, and endeavour to obtain her consent to marry him. To this, his having a wife living was no obstacle, as having changed his name, he now passed for a widower. Dorcasina's supposed derangement was a pleasing circumstance; because, if, in the lucid intervals which he was informed she had, he could gain her consent to become his wife, he could afterwards keep her confined, and enjoy her property.

He deliberated, for some time, on the means of putting his plan in execution; but as no good opportunity of becoming acquainted with her presented, he concluded to defer it till the middle of January, when he expected a week's vacation.

The time being arrived, he engaged a horse for a tour of a week, informing his landlord, that his close confinement had injured his health, and that exercise had become absolutely necessary. Setting off, one evening about sunset, he rode two miles, and then stopped at a house where he was acquainted, drank tea, and remained till near ten o'clock. He then mounted his horse, and proceeding slowly, arrived between ten and eleven, at the house of farmer Giles; the heavens being overcast, and threatening a storm. Rapping loudly at the door, Mr. Giles started out of his sleep, opened the window, and demanded to know who was there. "I reside in this place," said Mr. Seymore (that being his assumed name) "and keep a school five miles from here. Returning from a journey through a road I have never before travelled, I have got benighted, and have lost my way. I shall, therefore, take it very kindly of you, if you will give me a shelter for the night." "What! is it Mr. Seymore?" said Giles. "My name is Seymore, sir." Giles having frequently seen, as well as heard the character of the worthy school-master, hesitated not a moment, but instantly admitted him, and conducted him to bed. Then, putting his horse in the stable, returned to bed himself, well pleased at having an opportunity of entertaining so respectable a guest.

The weather, in the morning, favoured the views of our modern philosopher. It blew and snowed violently; so that when he made a shew of departing, he was so strongly opposed by his host and hostess, that he could not decently refuse their solicitations to tarry with them till fair weather.

Dorcasina had been waked by the knocking in the night; and, by what she heard, was satisfied that some person not belonging to the family was lodged in the house; but, supposing it to be one of their acquaintance, she composed herself to sleep, and thought no more of it. In the morning, Betty, coming as usual to kindle the fire, informed her that the person, who had waked them in the night, by his rapping, was a gentleman, who kept a school, a few miles distant, and had lost his way in returning from a journey. The term gentleman, immediately excited Dorcasina's curiosity. No person of that description had entered the house, since she had inhabited it. "Have you seen the gentleman, Betty?" interrogated she. "Yes, ma'am; he is in Mrs. Giles' bed room, where there is a fire, and I made an excuse to go in, on purpose to see him." "What kind of a looking man is he, Betty? old or young, handsome or otherwise." "He is about as old as you, I guess, ma'am; and is a parsonable looking man enough, tho' I did'nt like him, he looks so sly, as if he wou'd look a body through, with his little sharp black eyes."

Dorcasina had, all winter, breakfasted in her own apartment, so that she could not, with any propriety, go out to breakfast with the family upon this occasion; but she dressed herself with peculiar care, intending after breakfast to contrive some method of seeing the gentleman; not as usual, however, with an idea of conquest; for she still held that she was as firmly bound to John, as if the parson had joined their hands. Her desire of seeing him arose merely from curiosity, and she was actuated in dressing herself with care, only by the laudable ambition of appearing agreeable in the eyes of the stranger.

Seymore, mean time, was breakfasting with the family, in the course of which he made many inquiries respecting Dorcasina. Among other questions he asked if she were ever outrageous. "No, sir," replied Giles, "nor has she shewed the least marks of being crazy above three times, since she has been here; and that was, when she talked about sweethearts." "Ha! that is the string then upon which her madness vibrates?" "Yes, sir, at all other times, and in all other respects, she is as rational and agreeable as any person in the world; and so clever, kind, and obliging, that my wife and I loves her as if she was our sister." "Does she frequently leave her room?" "Every day, sir, and when my wife isn't busy about her household affairs, she sits whole hours, and talks as free with her as if she was her equal."

Had Dorcasina followed her inclination, she would, immediately after breakfast, have sought the company of Seymore; but delicacy withheld her, and she sat, for some time, undetermined how to proceed. Seymore, meanwhile, was racking his invention to get access to her. Being informed by Giles that she had a variety of books, he bethought himself of sending to borrow one, hoping it might lead to an interview. One of the children was, therefore, dispatched with Mr.

Seymore's compliments to Miss Sheldon, requesting the loan of a book for his amusement. She sent immediately a volume of the travels of Anacharsis, with her compliments, and a message that, if it were not agreeable he was welcome to come and take his choice of her whole collection. Availing himself of this permission, he entered her apartment to return the book. As soon as he saw her he stood motionless, and stared at her for some moments with affected surprise. At length, pretending to recover himself, "I have recently read this work, madam," said he, "a volume of which you were so obliging as to send me; and availing myself of your proffered politeness, I have taken the liberty of coming to choose one for myself." "You are very welcome, sir," returned Dorcasina. Then conducting him to the case, which contained her books, "here they are, sir," said she, "take your choice."

Seymore first took down one book, then another; and, by making several observations upon them, led Dorcasina insensibly into conversation. After standing at the bookcase for some time, she requested him to be seated; as this was what he aimed at, he immediately complied. He exerted himself to entertain her, informing her how he had lost his way, and expressing his satisfaction at finding such agreeable company, where he so little expected it. Dorcasina, gratified with the compliment, replied that it was so long since she had an opportunity of conversing with any person of information, that he might readily suppose her satisfaction would be equal with his. The time passed agreeably on both sides, till they were summoned to dinner. Dorcasina dined sometimes alone, sometimes with the family; but her hostess thinking it would gratify her guest, to have her at the table, did not upon this occasion consult her.

This arrangement was not altogether agreeable to Seymore, as he had calculated upon dining in Dorcasina's apartment, and conversing with her uninterruptedly, the remainder of the day. He, therefore, inwardly fretted at Mrs. Giles' officiousness, when, after dinner, she requested Dorcasina not to return. The latter readily complied, nor did she retire till nine o'clock in the evening. During this time Giles and his wife constantly kept them company, and joined occasionally in the conversation, Seymore all the while wishing them both at the d——l. He was, however, tolerably satisfied upon receiving an invitation to breakfast next morning with Dorcasina. As soon as she had withdrawn, Seymore gave it as his opinion that she was no more distracted than he was; and that the person, who removed her upon that pretence, must have been influenced by some sinister motive.

Seymore's surprise, when he first beheld her, did not pass unobserved by Dorcasina. She was sometimes inclined to think it the effect of a sudden passion, with which she had inspired him; but not having heard of his passing for a widower, she checked the presumption. "He probably has a wife," thought she, "and has no right to love any but her. But as marriages are sometimes unhappy, he may not have an affection for his wife, and may have been struck involuntarily with me. But am I not also engaged? I cannot, therefore, return this sudden passion; and, if he is married, he will be criminal to indulge it." Thus reasoned with herself this extravagant lady, who thought it almost impossible for any man to behold her with indifference.

Seymore did not fail, next morning, of visiting, according to invitation, Dorcasina's apartment. As soon as the breakfast things were removed, "you must have thought me a strange being, Miss Sheldon," said he, "to see me stand like a statue, the first moment I had the pleasure of seeing you." Dorcasina's heart palpitated, her colour changed, expecting, after this beginning, nothing less than an immediate declaration of love. She hesitated, not knowing what to answer, and in her confusion stammered out a falsehood. "I——I——I didn't observe any thing particular, sir." "The d——l!" thought he; "I have touched upon the right string. Here is proof enough of her madness if she thinks I have fallen in love with her. However, so much the better. I will go on with my plan." "In order," said he, "to apologize for my sudden surprise, I must beg your indulgence, while I give you a short account of myself." Dorcasina, observing an attentive silence, he proceeded. "I am a native of Charleston, South Carolina; I once possessed riches, and, what was infinitely more necessary to my happiness, a wife, whom I adored. What felicity did I not enjoy while possessed of her! But Providence saw fit, as a punishment for my idolatry, to remove her to a world of happiness." Here, pretending to be deeply affected, he drew forth his handkerchief, put it to his eyes, and was for some moments unable to proceed. At length, "it is now seven years," said he, "since all my happiness was entombed with her. My affliction was so great that I neglected my affairs, and they fell into the greatest disorder. I quitted Charleston, with what money I could collect, and have ever since led a wandering life, careless of the present, and uncertain of the future. My money being at length exhausted, I engaged in this place as a school-master. My employment gives me bread, and takes my attention from the cause of my misery. Yesterday, when I first entered your apartment, I beheld in you the perfect counterpart of my angel wife. No two beings ever resembled each other more strongly; and it was impossible for me to conceal my surprise." Dorcasina listened attentively, and wept freely at this fictitious tale of woe. "It is very singular, sir," said she, when he had ended, "that you should find me here, and that I should so much resemble your departed wife." "It is, indeed, madam. There is a strange coincidence in the little events, (as well as in the great ones) of this world: for what is still more singular, not only your face, but your voice, your manner, your air, in short, every thing about you reminds me so sensibly of her, that I almost imagine I see her before me; and, never since the fatal day of her death, have I enjoyed a moment's pleasure, until I had the happiness of beholding you."

Dorcasina pondered in silence upon the strangeness of the incident; and Seymore, hoping to engage her to grant him her confidence, began by wondering that a lady, so eminently calculated to adorn society, should thus immure herself in an obscure corner. "Ah! sir," said she, "it is not my choice. I was brought hither by compulsion, and here I am obliged to remain." "By compulsion, madam? who has a right in this land of freedom, thus to compel you?" "My story, sir, is singular, but it would be trespassing too much on your patience to relate it." "Nothing could give me more pleasure than to hear it madam; and you will gratify me exceedingly by the recital."

Dorcasina then began and gave a short account of herself and her situation to the time of her father's death. She then related, more particularly, her illness which followed it; her acquaintance with Brown; their mutual passion; the visits of Montague; his passion, his extravagance, his threats, his despair; and, finally, the manner of her being by his agents conveyed thither.

Seymore had never, in his life, been so undecided in his opinion. He knew not what to think of Dorcasina's account of herself. Was she mad, or was she not? was the question. He could easily imagine that a young fellow might conceive such a passion for her property as Montague had pretended for her person; but was it possible, or probable that he could thus force her away, and confine her for such a length of time, and no inquiries be made about her? In short, he was lost in doubt and perplexity. The affair was involved in a mystery, which he knew not how to unveil. "Your adventures are very surprising and uncommon, madam," said he; "and the conduct of Montague very unaccountable. Have you received any visits from him, since you were brought hither?" "No, sir, I have neither seen him, nor heard a single word from him, in the whole term of my confinement." "Astonishing! what can be the fellow's intention? You mentioned, in the course of your story, a letter which you received from him, on the night of your being seized. Will you be so obliging as to gratify me with a perusal of it?" "Most willingly, sir," said Dorcasina. She then immediately produced the letter, which being a confirmation of all she had related, served to render the mystery still more inexplicable; especially since he was, by this time, convinced that the idea of her madness was wholly unfounded.

It was now near noon, and the weather having cleared up, Seymore had no longer any pretext for prolonging his visit. "After dinner," said he, "I must pursue my journey. I leave you, Miss Sheldon, with a heart penetrated with gratitude for the confidence, with which you have honoured me. You have interested me more than I can express, in your welfare, not only by the resemblance you bear to a person who was once so dear to me, but also by the extreme singularity of your present situation, and the unworthy treatment which you have received. I reside only five miles from here. You must have the goodness to permit me sometimes to visit you; as your company alone can soothe the sorrows, with which my lacerated heart has so long been afflicted." Dorcasina, who really felt that interest for him, which he pretended for her, told him she should be happy, at any time, to see him. His account of himself was romantic and extravagant, and of consequence, exactly suited to her taste. She found realized in him that constancy, of which she had so often read; and his company had become extremely agreeable.

It being near dinner time, Seymore quitted the apartment of Dorcasina, and went to seek his friendly host. "Mr. Giles," said he, "I feel myself under great obligations to you, for your hospitality, especially since it has been the means of bringing me acquainted with one of the first of women. She had condescendingly allowed me to repeat my visits; but, unless you will take pay for my entertainment, I cannot avail myself of that permission. But if, whenever I come, (which will probably be on Sundays, as I have no other time I can call my own) you will charge so much a day for myself and horse, I shall feel myself at perfect liberty to follow my inclination." "Well, sir," said Giles, "if we cannot have the pleasure of your company, on no other conditions; if you will not insist on my taking any thing now, I will, in future, receive pay for your board."

Matters being thus arranged, they dined all together, and, after dinner, Seymore took his leave, and pursued his journey, extremely pleased with the success of his project.

Dorcasina, at his departure, felt a void which nothing could fill, and she found her greatest pleasure in relating to Betty what she had learned from him. "What strange events daily take place in this world, Betty," said she, "Who could have thought, that after living so long in this retired place, without seeing a single person superior to the honest inhabitants of the house, I should at last meet with a gentleman so agreeable, so interesting, and that I should so strongly recal to his memory the wife, for whom he has so long mourned?" Betty, who was not so easily imposed on as her mistress, feared that he was not what he pretended; and that he had, at bottom, some knavish design. She feared also that her mistress, forgetting John, was going to relapse into all her former fondness and folly for this stranger, to whom she had conceived the greatest aversion. "I hope, ma'am," said she, "that you are not going to forget Mr. Brown, nor what you have often, and often declared, that you thought yourself as much his wife as if the parson had joined your hands." The reader must not imagine that Betty's inclinations were changed, or that she really wished her mistress and Brown united: that was a distant and uncertain evil; a greater and impending one was what she now wished to avert.

Dorcasina smiled at Betty's apprehensions. "You need be under no uneasiness on that account," said she; "I cannot so easily forget the dear youth, nor the ties which bind me to him." Here she was for a few moments silent, fetched a deep sigh, and then proceeded. "Neither do I think that Mr. Seymore will ever so far forget his first love as to enter into a second engagement; and this is the ground upon which my admiration of him is chiefly founded. Were he to act so much like common mortals as to forget his wife and solicit another, my opinion of him would be wholly changed." These assurances, in some measure, quieted Betty's apprehensions; but the Gileses could not be prevailed upon to think that it would not be a match, and a very suitable one too, if Mr. Seymore could overlook the slight derangement, with which they still thought Dorcasina was at times afflicted.

Seymore, after rambling the country for the remainder of the week, returned on Saturday night, to the house of the clergyman, and immediately gave him an account of his week's peregrination. He informed him of his stopping at the house of farmer Giles (concealing however the time of night, and his pretending to have lost the way or his being detained there during the storm,) and of his acquaintance with Dorcasina. He enlarged upon the particulars of that lady's story, affirming that she was not mad, but perfectly rational, and very agreeable. He thought fit, however, to conceal and alter some part of the account, fearing that the story of her being forced away, by a young lover, would never be believed by a person of Mr. H's understanding, when he should come to see how destitute she was of personal charms: but he wished to convince him that her intellects were sound, that he need not himself be deemed a madman for marrying her.

The Saturday following he again visited Dorcasina, and she received him with a satisfaction, which did not pass unobserved. He tarried till Monday morning, conversing on various subjects, and pretending to be all that was tender, sentimental, and affectionate, but dropped not a syllable of love; his plan being not yet ripe for execution. He intended first artfully to insinuate himself so far into Dorcasina's favour, as to make her wish for his visits, and even to render himself necessary to her happiness. His plan then was to pretend that her resemblance of his wife had rendered her necessary to his, and, by degrees, to drive Brown out of her head, and to substitute himself in his room. This scheme was exactly calculated to take in the unsuspecting Dorcasina; for by an abrupt declaration he would have disgusted her, and thus have defeated his own plan. But, by this artful management, he thought he could not fail of finally gaining her.

He continued his visits, for three successive Sundays, and at every visit rendered himself more and more agreeable. The fourth he thought best to tarry at home and attend meeting. In this he had two designs in view; one to please Mr. H. who did not wholly approve the manner, in which he spent that holy day, and the other to make Dorcasina regret his absence, and be impatient for his return. This consummate hypocrite thoroughly understood human nature. His not appearing on Saturday night, as usual, had the desired effect. Dorcasina passed the whole of the next day in impatience and alarms, and when he made his appearance the week after, she could not conceal the joy his presence occasioned.

Continuing thus his weekly visits, Seymore became insensibly dear to Dorcasina. She counted the intervening days of the week, and waited with the utmost impatience the return of Saturday. She then took from her grey locks (which by this time were tolerably grown) fifty papers; curled them over her head, in imitation of her unfortunate wig; filled them with powder, and ornamented the rest of her person with the utmost attention.

Matters went on thus regularly until the beginning of April, when, one Saturday, Seymore failing in his accustomed visit, Dorcasina's disappointment was so great that she could not refrain from tears. Betty, observing her mistress weeping, requested to know the cause of her trouble. This Dorcasina was ashamed to acknowledge, and turned it off upon the hardship of her situation. Being left by herself she began to make a scrutiny into the state of her heart. "What am I about?" queried she with herself. "Here am I weeping at the absence of one man, while I am as good as married to another. This must be wrong, as conscious guilt withheld me from acknowledging it to Betty. Mr. Brown and I have been, for a long time, separated; perhaps he has forgotten me; perhaps I shall never see him more. Chance has in this, my solitary confinement, thrown in my way one of the most amiable and accomplished of men; he has become infinitely agreeable to me; he is all the company I have it in my power to enjoy: And must I then deprive myself of this satisfaction? Must I refuse to see him, lest he should become too dear to me? Yes, rigid virtue demands the sacrifice. I will act as conscience dictates, and trust in heaven to restore me to my lover. I will write to Mr. Seymore, informing him that I can see him no more. He is my friend, he shall be likewise my confidant. I will lay before him all my reasons. He is delicacy itself, and he will approve my motives, applaud my resolution, and I shall be raised higher than ever in his esteem. But I will see him once more; as he has failed to day of his customary visit, he may think me actuated by peevishness and resentment should I refuse. When he pays me another visit, I will lay open to him all my heart." Having formed this resolution she became more composed; but, at the same time, more dejected.

The week soon passed away; and Saturday again returning, Dorcasina dressed herself with much care, and waited with impatience the arrival of Seymore.

"I am extremely happy at seeing you again, Miss Sheldon," said he, as soon as he entered. "I was prevented, by an accident, from paying you my respects last week; and the time has appeared very long to me." They then fell into conversation upon indifferent subjects, in the course of which, Seymore appeared so tender, and so animated, that Dorcasina entirely forgot the resolution she had formed. He more than once took hold of her hand, pressed it to his lips, and languished fondly in her face. At length, "Miss Sheldon," said he, with much apparent hesitation, "I have made a discovery, by being last week prevented from seeing you, which I wish, but hardly dare to communicate." Dorcasina readily divined what was coming. She trembled, she blushed, notwithstanding her wrinkles, like a girl of eighteen; and her whole frame was greatly agitated. After much hesitation, she at length stammered out, "I do not imagine—I cannot see, sir, why you should be fearful of communicating any thing which concerns you, if it be nothing improper for me to hear." "Ah! that is what deters me; thence arise my fears. But Miss Sheldon is as generous as she is lovely; and I will hope for her forgiveness while I declare to her that she has become infinitely dear to me; that I am miserable when absent from her; and that, in short, I cannot exist without her."

Seymore examined her, with scrutinizing eyes, to examine the effects which this declaration produced. Dorcasina was, for some minutes, silent. At length, assuming all her dignity, "you forget, sir," said she, "the engagements I am under, and that I am not at liberty to listen to your addresses." Seymore then, in a long and studied speech, endeavoured, with all his art, to remove an objection, which he foresaw would be raised. He represented that the time, allowed by law for such engagements to continue binding, was within two months of expiring, and that she would then be at liberty to make a new choice; that, if Brown had loved her as well as he pretended, he would long ere this have sought her out: that the probability was, that having given up all thoughts of ever seeing her more, he had entirely forgotten her, and perhaps formed for himself another connection. These arguments were not without their weight upon the mind of Dorcasina; especially as they accorded with her present inclination; but she did not wish to act precipitately, or pursue any line of conduct, which should hereafter occasion remorse.

After some consideration, "I am at a loss," said she, "how to answer you. Could I be assured that Mr. Brown did not still remain constant, and still entertain the hope of the reward of his constancy, I would not scruple to acknowledge that I am not insensible of your merit, nor of the ardent passion, with which I have inspired you: but, uncertain as I am of any alteration in his sentiments, I ought not, in honor, to enter into any new engagement." Seymore, resolved at all events to carry his point, replied; "You have frequently, when speaking of L——, mentioned a Mr. Stanly as one of your friends. I had formerly some slight acquaintance with that gentleman. With your permission, and as by your desire, I will write to him, and request him to inform me what he knows of Mr. Brown's situation, prospects, and present expectations." Dorcasina consented to this proposal, and Seymore, after prevailing on her to grant him her promise that she would marry him as soon as the year expired, left her in the full assurance of certain success.

Here again we behold Dorcasina suspended between her hopes and fears, and indulging in all the agreeable reveries, and pleasing agitations, which a susceptible heart, upon such occasions, generally experiences.

Chapter XVIII.

SEYMORE, who knew not that there was such a man in existence as Mr. Stanly, till he heard him mentioned by Dorcasina, wishing to ascertain the amount of her property, and, if possible, to develope the mystery of her being forced away from L——, employed a person, in whom he could confide, to go thither, and gain what information there was to be obtained, on the subject. The man thus employed being arrived at L——, took lodgings at the only inn in the place; the landlord of which we have frequently before noticed, as a very loquacious and communicative fellow. The man soon found that he need go no further for the desired intelligence. He here learned that Dorcasina's income was a clear thousand pounds per annum; that, about ten months before, to the surprise of every body, she was published to one of her own servants, an awkward, ignorant, illiterate fellow; but that, just before the marriage was to take place, she was, one night, by three men forcibly conveyed away, and had never been heard of since; that a Mr. Stanly, who had since removed to Philadelphia, and was one of her most intimate friends, was supposed to be at the bottom of the affair, to prevent her disgracing herself by matching so unequally, especially as he had hired Brown to go off, and taken upon himself the management of her property; and never had made any stir about her disappearance. Satisfied with this intelligence, the man immediately returned, and communicated it to Seymore, just in time for him to pay his accustomed visit to Dorcasina.

He thought it his best policy not to mortify that lady, by informing her of the part, which Mr. Stanly was supposed to have taken to prevent her marriage with Brown. He only informed her that the person he had dispatched with the letter to that gentleman, found he had removed to Philadelphia, and that Brown had left L—— the day after she did. He then added, from his own invention, that he had been three months married to a lady in Maryland. The account of Mr. Stanly's removal grieved and surprised Dorcasina; and the marriage of Brown caused her a momentary mortification: but it was soon succeeded by the pleasing reflection that she was now at full liberty to follow her inclination.

Matters were now easily arranged between her and Seymore. It was agreed that she should remain in her present situation, till the time required by law was expired; that they should then be united by Mr. H——; that, Dorcasina being under the protection of a husband, whose authority none would dare dispute, they should proceed immediately to L——, there to enjoy the sweets of domestic tranquillity.

Mr. Stanly, in all his own trouble, had never lost sight of the interest of Dorcasina. He wrote to Giles, from time to time, respecting her welfare, charging him anew, in every letter, by no means to mention his name before her. Giles had frequently in return informed Mr. Stanly that she was well, and apparently reconciled to her situation. He knew, months before Dorcasina was informed of it by Seymore, that Mr. Stanly had quitted L——, but he dared not disoblige that gentleman so much as to let Dorcasina even suspect that he had the least knowledge of him.

Finding that preliminaries were all adjusted between Dorcasina and Mr. Seymore, Giles, his wife, and Betty were unanimous in their opinion that Mr. Stanly ought to be informed of it. Giles, therefore, wrote immediately to that gentleman, acquainting him with every particular, but not having an immediate conveyance, it was a month before Mr. Stanly received the letter. He had, for some time, been meditating Dorcasina's return to L——, and, upon the receipt of this letter, he determined immediately to visit his farm, and satisfy himself whether Seymore was a man of worth, or merely a needy adventurer. In consequence of this determination, he informed Giles that he should soon be with him, but cautioned him still to conceal from Dorcasina his having any knowledge of him. Betty, rejoiced at this intelligence, flattered herself not only that they should speedily return to L——, but that the match, by Mr. Stanly's influence, would be prevented.

While Seymore and Dorcasina waited, with the utmost impatience, the expiration of the year; while Betty, with no less impatience, waited the arrival of Mr. Stanly, an unexpected incident occurred, which entirely disconcerted all their plans, and rendered the interference of Mr. Stanly wholly unnecessary.

By some means or other, Seymore's creditors in Charleston had got intelligence of his place of residence, and his having assumed a borrowed name. One person, who had been entirely ruined by him, and of consequence was irritated against him to a high degree, determined to be in some measure revenged, by arresting and causing him to languish in prison. Having business as far northward as Virginia, he travelled from thence to Pennsylvania for this sole purpose. Coming suddenly upon Seymore with an officer, just as he had dismissed his afternoon school, to the great astonishment of his scholars, by whom he was surrounded, and almost adored, they carried him, for the night, to the nearest public house, his creditor intending to have him conveyed in the morning to the county gaol. The story of his being a married man and a villain rapidly circulated. "A married man," exclaimed one old woman, her eyes turned to heaven, "and a courting another woman! Lack a day! who would have thought it?" "I am sure, with that sanctified look," cries another, "I shou'd sartainly as soon have thought of calling Mr. H. a hypocrite." "As for my part" cried a third, "tho' I didn't love to say nothing about him, I thought he was no better than he shou'd be, since he kept our Sal one day after school and kiss'd her, cause he said her sum wasn't addition'd right. Thinks says I to myself that's a queer sort of a punishment, and Sal hasn't never been to school since."

Seymore, now strictly guarded, was left to his own disagreeable reflections. He cursed his fate, a thousand times; but finding that of no avail, he cast about him for the means of making his escape. In the evening he effected it; and, mounting a horse which happened to stand at the door, took his way towards Dorcasina, whipping the poor beast most unmercifully. On the way he concerted his plan; and, having arrived within a small distance of the house, he alighted, led the horse into a thick grove of trees, tied him there, and approached the house with hurried steps, and a mind ill at ease. Wishing to enter the apartment of Dorcasina, unperceived by the family, he opened the door softly and approached it without noise; but, before he reached it, fortune so ordered it, that he met Betty, who had just quitted it. "Betty," said he, in great trepidation, "I must have your gown." "My gown, sir? What is't you mean, what gown do you want?" "This gown you have on," said he, "deliver it instantly and ask no questions." "A mighty pretty request, truly!" replied she; "I guess I an't a going for to strip myself for you, nor nobody else." "Good heavens! give me the gown, I say; the next moment may be too late." Betty, who never liked him, and now thought him mad, replied, "I won't pull off my gown, I say for you; so now let me pass." Seymore, whose apprehensions every moment increased, finding her obstinate in her refusal, began to take from her by force, what she would not yield to his entreaties. Betty, alarmed at such treatment, had recourse to her usual method, her lungs. "Thieves! murder! help!" vociferated she. "Confound your yelling," exclaimed Seymore, "I shall be ruined." He then stopped her mouth with one hand while he endeavoured to strip off her gown with the other. Dorcasina hearing the outcry, ran out to know the cause. Her amazement at seeing her lover so unexpectedly, and finding him in the act of tearing Betty's clothes from her back, was inexpressible, and she immediately retreated into her apartment, overcome by astonishment, surprise, and resentment. This uncommon noise having reached the other part of the house, Giles and his wife hastened also to the spot. Seymore hearing their approach, and solicitous to accomplish his purpose, renewed his efforts, and stripped Betty of her gown before they arrived. "Dear good Betty," said he, as soon as he had obtained it, "I am not mad, but persecuted by my enemies, and to conceal myself have need of women's apparel. Run quickly, and fetch me a petticoat, cap, and handkerchief; and, for your life do not let the Giles' know I am here." He then rushed into Dorcasina's apartment, and fastening the door, "Forgive my apparently unaccountable conduct, Miss Sheldon," said he, in great agitation, "I have enemies, whom I never injured, they pursue me; from your goodness alone I expect protection; I must disguise myself in the garb of your sex, they will soon be here; but give no ear to what their malice will suggest. I am innocent, and will prove myself so to your satisfaction. Conceal me but this night, and we shall yet be happy." Dorcasina, alarmed for her lover, demanded eagerly to know what she could do. "I have requested Betty," replied he, "to bring me some of her clothes. Go, I beg of you, and hasten her return."

Betty, highly indignant at the treatment she had received, but considerably mollified at hearing the danger, which impelled Seymore to use her so roughly, stood undetermined what to do, when Giles and his wife arrived to learn the cause of the outcry. "What is the matter, Betty?" exclaimed they both in a breath. "I was a little flustered, just now," said she, "that was all;" and, being ashamed of her situation, she hastened up stairs, without any farther explanation. Having put on another gown, she was very deliberately mustering up the things, which had been requested, when Dorcasina, in great agitation, entered the chamber. "Come, Betty," said she, "make haste; be quick, for heaven's sake; or my dear Mr. Seymore will fall into the hands of his enemies." Thus saying, she caught up the things, and darting down quicker than lightning, helped Seymore to disguise himself in them. He pulled off his coat, and put on Betty's petticoat, gown, cap, and handkerchief. The clothes reaching but half way down his legs, he make a most grotesque appearance. But this he concealed by placing himself in an obscure corner of the room. He then requested Betty to lend him her knitting work, and pretending to make use of it, with only a dim light in the room, none but a close observer would have taken him for any other, than a coarse, awkward, masculine woman.

It was not long before Seymore was missed; and, as he had foreseen, his creditor, and those who had guarded him, were advised to search the house of Mr. Giles. They proceeded thither with all possible haste, and Seymore had not been seated, with his knitting work, ten minutes, before the trampling of horses were heard, and a thundering knock immediately succeeded. Betty looked wild, Dorcasina trembled, and Seymore himself was greatly disconcerted. Giles, being interrogated concerning Seymore, declared, and he thought with truth, that he had not been there since Monday morning. This declaration not satisfying the catchpoles, they proceeded to search the house. Having entered Dorcasina's apartment they civilly informed her that they came thither in search for a villain, who called himself Seymore, but whose real name was Wheaton. Dorcasina was silent, and they continued their search. Seymore's chair happening to be placed near the door of a closet, "come Goody," said one of the men, "get up, I must have a peep into this closet." "Take my word for it, sir," said Dorcasina, "you will find nobody there. That poor woman is lame and cannot move without pain; pray do not disturb her." The perturbed manner, in which Dorcasina, unused to falsehood, now delivered herself, served only to raise suspicions; and they peremptorily insisted on searching the closet. Seymore, finding them resolute, rose half way out of his chair, apparently with great difficulty; fearing to stand upright; not solely on account of the shortness of his clothes, but lest he should be betrayed by his stature. He had reached out his hand to move his chair, when Betty who was near him, and pitied him now she saw him in danger, though she did not comprehend its nature, took hold of the chair and moved it for him. Seymore, without looking behind, or observing at what distance the chair was removed, missed his aim, and reaching only a corner of it, came down with violence upon the floor. He groaned aloud, pretending to be greatly hurt, hoping by that means to avoid discovering himself by rising. But the most artful sometimes make wrong calculations. The men present, taking compassion upon one whom they supposed to be an infirm old woman, offered their aid to assist him in rising. The Carolinian, more forward than the rest, stooped and took hold of his arm. This condescension was fatal to Seymore; his creditor Williamson, in examining him so nearly, instantly recognized him. "Ha, villain! have I then caught you?" he exclaimed. Seymore, at these words, started up in a fury, and catching up the chair aimed it at Betty's head, though it fortunately missed her. "Had it not been for your d——d officiousness," he exclaimed, "I should not have been detected. Fool, idiot, that I was to trust my liberty to two such c——d simpletons." They were now endeavouring to force him out of the apartment. He struggled; Betty screamed; and Dorcasina fainted. Seymore, at length finding resistance vain, and submitting sullenly to his fate, was led out, and obliged to endure a variety of coarse jests upon his grotesque appearance.

Mr. Williamson, compassionating Dorcasina's situation, requested Mrs. Giles to hasten to her assistance. Some minutes elapsed before she recovered her senses, and the first use she made of them was to inquire what was become of her dear Mr. Seymore. "He is in the other room; make yourself easy, ma'am; they won't injure him." "I must see him," exclaimed Dorcasina, wildly, and rushed towards the door.

Mrs. Giles, who, as was before observed, was a discreet woman, placed herself against it, and entreated her to be easy, and remain where she was. "Ah!" exclaimed Dorcasina, "the monsters are murdering him, and you will not let me go to his rescue." "They are not, indeed, ma'am; they are only pulling off his borrowed clothes; and will do him no farther harm. But to make you easy, I will go myself and inquire, and immediately bring you intelligence." "So do, my dear, good Mrs. Giles; and pray return quickly, I cannot endure this suspense."

Mrs. Giles then went out, and beckoning Mr. Williamson from the croud, took him aside, and informed him that the lady in the other room, with whom Seymore was upon the point of marriage, was in the utmost distress, and wished to be informed of his crime, and what was to be his fate. Williamson had, while Mrs. Giles was with Dorcasina, learned from her husband some particulars of that lady, and now expressed a wish to return and converse with her himself. He found her, as Mrs. Giles had described, in the greatest possible distress. He first apologized for his intrusion, and then observed that he understood she was interested in Mr. Seymore, and solicitous to know what would be his fate. "He is indeed, very dear to me," replied Dorcasina. "The more is the pity then," said Williamson; "for, believe me madam, he is a wretch wholly unworthy your regard, and my arresting him was for you a most fortunate escape. He has a wife in Carolina, a most amiable woman, and five fine children."

Dorcasina having once before been imposed upon by a villain, did not now, as formerly, and as Betty expected, disbelieve the account; but having learnt wisdom by experience, she exclaimed, in a mingled accent of surprise and agony; "Good heavens, can there be so much deceit in man!" Mr. Williamson assured her, in a manner that left her no room to doubt the fact, that what he told her was strictly true. He further informed her that Seymore was only an assumed name; that his real name was Wheaton; that he was a villain, in every sense of the word; that, after squandering his own, and his wife's property, he had lived, for some time, by cheating others; and that he himself was one of his victims, having been taken in, by him, in an important mercantile transaction, and totally ruined. At this account Dorcasina shuddered with horror, and thanked heaven most fervently for saving her from a danger so imminent. Mr. Williamson now left her, and, as it was now late in the evening, prevailed on Giles to suffer him, with the officers and their prisoner, to pass the night in his house.

The rest of the family having retired to bed, and the house become still, Dorcasina expressed a strong desire to see Wheaton once more, and to upbraid him with his unparalleled villany. Betty endeavoured at first to dissuade her; but finding her inflexible, she went first to see if it were practicable, and to prepare the way for her admission. She spoke at the door with one of the guards, and, asking whether Wheaton was in bed, was told that he had thrown himself upon a bed in his clothes. She then inquired inquired whether her mistress could be admitted to see him. "By all means," said the man, "but we must be present." Betty returning with this answer, Dorcasina felt some repugnance at having two strangers to witness their interview; but, after a short deliberation, her desire of once more seeing him, and of hearing what he could possibly urge in his vindication, overcame every objection; and requesting Betty to follow, she directed her steps to his apartment.

"So, madam," said Seymore, as soon as he saw her, "what has procured me the honor of this visit?" Dorcasina could not refrain her tears at beholding him. "I come," said she, "to ask how you could so basely deceive me; how you could invent so many falsehoods; and pretend so much affection?" "I can very easily answer your questions," replied the shameless wretch; and, adding insult to injury, "it was your money, and my necessities that induced me to deceive you; and you, credulous old fool, so greedily swallowed the grossest flattery, that it would have been difficult to avoid imposing on you. Ridiculous vanity, at your age, with those grey locks, to set out to make conquests! I have really so much regard for you, as to advise you to give up all thoughts of that kind, and to assure you that any man would be distracted to think of marrying you except for your money."

Dorcasina was thunderstruck at this rudeness, and, hastening out of the apartment, hurried to her own, where throwing herself upon the bed, she lay a long time without speaking; while Betty sat patiently by her side, waiting to see what would be the effect of the disagreeable truths, which Seymore had uttered.

Dorcasina at length broke silence, "I begin to think, Betty," said she, "that all men are alike false, perfidious, and deceitful; and that there is no confidence to be put in any of them." "You have been acquainted with some bad ones, besure, ma'am; but they a'n't all so; for consider, ma'am, how good your father was, and how good Mr. Stanly is. But as for this here creature I never could endure him; and I heared Mr.

Williamson a saying how that he was one of the new fangled sort, an athest, a jacobite, and an illumbenator. I am but a poor ignorant creature, but I am sure these religions cannot be good because they have made so bad a man of Mr. M. of our village." "You surprise me, Betty; Mr. M. a bad man? it cannot be; he has always been esteemed a man of the best moral principles, though he was rather unsettled in his religious ones." "It is, however, strictly true, ma'am; and he has become the talk of the whole village; every body is scandalized that a man of his years, who has children grown up, and who has been one of the best of fathers and husbands, should, all at once behave in so unbecoming a manner. They say it is partly owing to a book he is very fond of, writ by one Tom Paine, who I am sure deserves the gallows for leading men astray from their wives and families." "What do you mean, Betty? What has he done?" "Why he keeps a Madam, and boards her out about a mile from his house, and passes great part of his time with her. He supplies her also with money for all her extravagancies, and she goes drest like any queen; while he hardly allows his wife and daughters enough to keep them decent. Besides, he has grown so cross at home, that his family takes no comfort, while he is in the house, and his wife, as good a woman as ever lived, takes on at such a rate in secret, (though she will not hear a word against her husband) that she is a mere otomy, and her daughters are afeard she will go into a consumption."

"I am greatly shocked with your account, Betty; and do not wonder you quarrel with his religions as you call them. But you quite mistake the matter, Betty; it is because he has no religion that he thus wantonly sports with his own reputation, and the health and happiness of an amiable family. Those pernicious sentiments, the growth of other climes, have found their way to this once happy country, so justly celebrated for the domestic felicity of its inhabitants. May heaven prevent the further progress of Jacobinism, atheism, and illuminatism; they all seem to be links of the same chain." "Amen, say I," answered Betty.

Dorcasina's chagrin at the late discovery kept her awake great part of the night. Towards morning, however, she fell into a slumber, and before she again opened her eyes, Seymore was conveyed where she never saw him more.

Upon the following day, Dorcasina was thoughtful and silent. The danger she had so recently escaped, the imposition which had been practised, and the disagreeable truths she had heard from Seymore, had upon her a surprising effect. Her eyes seemed to be opened, and the romantic spell, by which she had been so many years bound, all at once broken. She reflected, with extreme disgust, upon many parts of her past life, and wondered how she could have been so blind to the merits of Lysander; how she could have been so deceived by O'Connor, Philander, and James; and how she could have doated, with such extravagant fondness, upon so vulgar a fellow as Brown. One thing more than the rest appeared to her an inexplicable mystery, the conduct of Montague. Who could he be? where could he reside? why did he still continue to confine her, and why did she hear nothing from him? She began to think of his passion, as she had formerly thought of Philander's, that it was all a pretence, and that he only amused himself with her credulity. But why then should he carry the joke so far?

In this state of doubt and perplexity, she applied to Giles, conjuring him to inform her who Montague was, when he heard from him, and how long he intended keeping her a prisoner. Giles repeated the old story of his being under engagements to secrecy; he added, moreover, that he had not lately heard from Montague; but expected it would not be long before he should; and hoped he should then have it in his power to inform her that she would soon be liberated. Dorcasina then urged him to connive at her having an opportunity to escape, offering him more money than he could possibly get by detaining her. Giles was somewhat embarrassed; but finally told her that, if he did not hear from Montague within a fortnight, he would contrive some method of conveying her to L——. This he thought he might with safety engage, as, within that time, Mr. Stanly would undoubtedly arrive. Dorcasina was rejoiced at obtaining this promise, and thanked him, with tears in her eyes, for so unexpected a favour. She immediately communicated to Betty the pleasing intelligence, who appeared as much elated as if she had not been apprised of Mr. Stanly's expected arrival.

About three days afterwards, as Dorcasina was sitting disconsolate at a window, Mr. Stanly, on horseback, suddenly made his appearance. She could not at first credit the evidence of her senses; but upon his nearer approach her doubts all vanished. She flew to the door, and seized him by the hand, but was unable to articulate a single syllable. He appeared equally surprised, but was the first to break the silence. "Miss Sheldon," said he, "is it possible? can it be you?" "Indeed it is," said she, greatly affected, "but pray come in. I thank heaven for having at last sent me a friend." He followed to her apartment; and inquiring by whom and by what means she had been conveyed thither, she recounted all the particulars of that mysterious transaction, with which before he was perfectly acquainted. She then related the principal incidents of her life, during her residence with the Giles', excepting indeed the most important part, her connection with Seymore. This her mortification would not suffer her to mention.

Dorcasina now inquired concerning the family of Mr. Stanly; her own; and whether he had lately been at L——. The severe stroke Mr. Stanly had experienced since he had last seen Dorcasina, and with which she was yet unacquainted, came so forcibly to his recollection that it almost unmanned him. He, however, collected sufficient fortitude to inform her of all the changes which had taken place in his family, and concluded with some account of that of captain Barry. Mrs. Barry had, about six weeks before, been delivered of a son, who lived but three weeks. His death had affected her to such a degree that it brought on a fever. Captain Barry had likewise been very ill with the colic. "I, however," continued he, "left them both much recovered." During this recital, Dorcasina was variously affected. She shed tears of unfeigned sorrow for the death of Mrs. Stanly; and Harriot's marriage with captain Barry excited mingled sensations of surprise, pleasure, and regret.

Enquiring, at length, what had brought him into so retired a place, he informed her that he was upon a visit to a farm which he owned not far distant; and that her appearance at the window, attracting his attention, had induced him to stop. She then earnestly entreated him to exert his influence in procuring her a release from her present confinement. This he readily promised, and assured her that he should not return to Philadelphia, till she could accompany him. Then inquiring for Giles, and being informed that he was at work in the field, he said he would go and talk with him alone and endeavour to bring him to terms. Having conversed with Giles upon his own business, he inquired how matters stood between Seymore and Dorcasina. Being satisfied with the particulars of the termination of that connection, he commended Giles for his attention to Dorcasina, and his fidelity to him in keeping his secret. It was then agreed upon between them, that Giles, appearing fearful of the authority which Mr. Stanly might employ, should consent to Dorcasina's departure. Matters being thus arranged Mr. Stanly returned to the house, and communicated to Dorcasina his success. Her pleasure at the sudden prospect of returning to L——, was somewhat damped by the consideration of the loss of almost the only family with which she associated, and her dear and valued friends. Upon her mentioning to Mr. Stanly this painful circumstance, he proposed that she should go first to Philadelphia, and make Harriot a visit, who he said, he was sure would rejoice to see her.

A recollection of past scenes caused her at first to hesitate; but reflecting that giving up Harriot's acquaintance would be depriving herself of great satisfaction, she resolved that she would endeavour to forget what was passed, to think only of the present, and indulge in the pleasure of visiting the only intimate female acquaintance she had left in the world.

Mr. Stanly remained at his farm three days, during which time he provided a means of conveying Dorcasina and Betty to Philadelphia. On the fourth morning, the last week in May, after nearly a twelvemonth's residence in the family, they took leave, not without some emotion, of the honest people, from whom they had experienced the kindest treatment, and most unremitted attention.

The second day after their departure, they beheld the setting sun gild the distant spires of Philadelphia. They entered it in the evening, Dorcasina's apprehensions at the idea of meeting captain Barry, every moment increasing.

The chaise at length stopped at a handsome house, in Chestnut-street. Entering it without ceremony and desiring Dorcasina to be seated, Mr. Stanly rang for a servant. He first inquired, with some anxiety, after the health of Mr. and Mrs. Barry, and being informed that they still continued convalescent, "let Mrs. Barry, know," said he, "that Miss Sheldon has arrived." When this intelligence was communicated to that lady she was sitting, with her husband, in her own chamber. "I shall feel a little awkwardly at seeing her," said he, "and perhaps she too will be embarrassed; I therefore bid you good night, my dear." Miss Sheldon was then requested to walk up stairs. She dreaded the first interview with captain Barry; but it was too late to retreat. She followed Mr. Stanly, and was greatly relieved at finding Mrs. Barry alone.

The pleasure experienced by these two ladies, after so long a separation, may be more easily imagined than described. They recounted to each other all that had happened in that period; they talked of L——, of its inhabitants, and of the attachment to it, which they preserved. Mrs. Barry said that, since the city was so subject to that severe scourge, the yellow fever, she should, during the summer, make her residence at L——. This intelligence was highly gratifying to Dorcasina, and she yet flattered herself with enjoying much of the company of her beloved young friend.

On the following morning, captain Barry had a severe return of his illness, which lasted nearly the whole day; this rendered Mrs. Barry perfectly miserable, and prevented Dorcasina from seeing him, as it confined him to his chamber. On the next, however, he was so far recovered, as to pay a visit to his wife. Dorcasina was present when he entered. The paleness of his countenance was so similar to what it had been eight years before, when he was received into her father's house, that she was greatly struck by his appearance, and did not behold him without some degree of emotion. His easy politeness, however, notwithstanding his weakness, soon quieted her agitated mind. Not a hint was dropped that could call up the recollection of past scenes. Mrs. Barry's spirits returned with the returning health of her husband, and they passed the day, in a very agreeable manner.

A few mornings afterwards, intelligence was brought to Mrs. Barry that her principal female servant, one in whom she put the greatest confidence, and upon whom she depended as a housekeeper in her confinement, had disappeared, and taken with her several articles of considerable value. In the present weak state of both heads of the family, this was a disagreeable and even distressing incident. Mr. Stanly being sent for, sought the girl but in vain; she was not to be found. A person to supply her place was immediately procured; but proving unfaithful, she caused Mrs. Barry great uneasiness.

Dorcasina observed all these things with an attentive eye; and one day, when she was with Mrs. Barry, in her chamber, and no other person present, she thus addressed her. "I find that, in my ideas of matrimony, I have been totally wrong. I imagined that, in a happy union, all was transport, joy, and felicity; but in you I find a demonstration that the most agreeable connection is not unattended with cares and anxieties." "Indeed, Miss Sheldon," replied Mrs. Barry, "your observation is just. I have been married a twelvemonth, to the man whom of all the world I should have chosen. He is every thing I wish him to be; and in the connection I have enjoyed great felicity. Yet, strange to tell, I have suffered more that I ever did before, in the whole course of my life. The first shock after my marriage, was from losing my dear mama, a loss that can never be repaired. I then suffered severely in bringing into the world a son. This, however, was soon forgotten in the delightful care of nursing my dear infant. But, alas! of that satisfaction I was soon deprived, he was carried off in a fit, before he had compleated his fourth week. This loss threw me into a fever, from which I had not entirely recovered, when Mr. Barry was severely attacked, and his life endangered by a colic. These are the serious evils I have suffered. Among the less may be named considerable loss of property by sea, and the vexation I have recently suffered by the conduct of my domestics; but I do not repine. The great disposer of all events knows what is best for us to suffer; and I was taught, by my dear mama, not to look for uninterrupted felicity in this transitory world. I am thankful for the blessings I have remaining, and look forward with hope to the re-establishment of my own health, and that of my dear Mr. Barry, when I doubt not we shall again enjoy a reasonable portion of felicity."

During this address Dorcasina was silent; and marvelled much to see the sprightly Harriot Stanly, metamorphosed, by one year's matrimony, into a serious moralizer. But it was a season of affliction, and she did not doubt but returning health, would in some measure restore her charming vivacity.

She remained a fortnight with her friends, conducting, during the whole time, and conversing with so much propriety, and good sense, unmixed with any of her former extravagance, that they were extremely delighted with her, and thought her a most valuable and agreeable companion. Mr. Stanly rendered her an account of her pecuniary affairs, which he said he had taken upon himself in her absence to manage; for which mark of his attention, she paid him her grateful acknowledgments. Finding her friends rapidly recovering, and her inclination to see L—— daily increasing, she took an affectionate leave of them, and was accompanied by Mr. Stanly, to her dear native village.

Scipio had been apprised of her coming, but was, notwithstanding, so overjoyed at seeing her, that he could not refrain from tears. "Gor bress you, missee," said he, wiping his eyes, "you ben gone great while. How grad old Scipio be to see you gin." Dorcasina shook him by the hand, inquired of his health, and that of the other domestics; and experienced that pleasure so dear to all uncorrupted minds (to which she had so long been a stranger) of revisiting the place of her nativity.

Mr. Stanly, having business to transact at L——, passed a week there; during which time the idea of being again at home, added to the enjoyment of his company, and the affectionate attention and assiduities of her servants, rendered Dorcasina extremely happy. But, no sooner was he gone, than she began to experience a sensation before unknown. Her dearest friends being separated from her by death or removal, she found herself alone, as it were, on the earth. The pleasing delusion which she had all her life fondly cherished, of experiencing the sweets of connubial love, had now entirely vanished, and she became pensive, silent and melancholy.

Betty observed this change with concern; and endeavoured to amuse her, by talking of the times that were passed. "Betty," said she, "my own conduct will not bear reflecting upon; I cannot look back without blushing for my follies." "I am sure, ma'am," replied Betty, "I don't know whose conduct will bear reflection, if yours won't; so good, and kind and charitable, and dutiful as you have always been." "In the moral duties, Betty, I cannot indeed accuse myself of any neglect; but in my connection with the other sex, how miserably have I been duped." "Oh, never worry about that now, ma'am; you may yet get a good husband, and live as happy as the days are long." "Never, Betty; I shall never be married. I have not charms sufficient to engage the heart of any man; and I never will consent that any man shall marry me, merely for the sake of my property. But tell me Betty, who do you think that Montague could be? Have you heard any thing of him since our return?" At this unexpected question, Betty hesitated. She wished to gratify the curiosity of her mistress, and clear up a mystery which had long perplexed her, but was a little apprehensive of the consequences. She at length, however, ventured to mention Harriot Stanly, and the motives for which the deception had been practised. The moment she heard her name, the truth flashed upon her mind; and she was astonished that she had not before discovered it. She was a long time silent, reflecting upon the adventure, and a hundred circumstances corroborating the truth of what Betty had told her, she wondered she was so blinded, at the time, as never to have suspected her. She now, for the first time, felt the full force of her obligations to that excellent family, and more strongly regretted the distance to which they were removed.

She now turned all that enthusiasm, which love formerly inspired, to acts of benevolence and charity. In the exercise of these heavenly virtues, she became more cheerful, and more resigned. In this state of mind she yet continues. A letter, which she has lately written to Mrs. Barry will give the best idea of her present situation, and show, moreover, that, notwithstanding the evils she has suffered from her attachment to novels, she cannot yet dispense with them.

"MY DEAR MRS. BARRY,

"TILL very lately, I was ignorant of the extent of my obligations to you and Mrs. Stanly. Betty has informed me to whom I am indebted for my preservation from a connection, on which I cannot reflect without extreme mortification. What exertions did you not make to save me from rendering myself despicable and miserable! Heaven be praised that they were successful.

"My fate is singular; and I sincerely wish it may serve as a beacon to assist others, of similar dispositions, to avoid the rock on which I have been wrecked.

"My dear father—But I will cast no reflections on his memory. Attached to novels himself, as a source of amusement, from which he had received no injury, he did not foresee, or suspect the mischiefs they might produce, in a young girl like me, ignorant of the world, and of a turn of mind naturally romantic. I was therefore left to gratify my taste for this kind of reading, without restraint; and this imprudent indulgence has been the cause of my ruin. I now find that I have passed my life in a dream, or rather a delirium; and have grown grey in chasing a shadow, which has always been fleeing from me, in pursuit of an imaginary happiness, which, in this life, can never be realized. The spell is now broken; the pleasing illusion has vanished. Having long been a dupe no less to my own vanity and credulity, than to the artifices of those, who chose to seek their interest or their amusement, in playing upon them, I now find, and most sensibly feel the consequences of my ridiculously romantic and absurd conduct.

"However unjust and indelicate may be the opinion, that matrimony is essential to happiness, it is perhaps the first that a romantic girl forms. For myself, I candidly acknowledge that it has governed all the actions of my life. My parentage, my fortune, and I may add, my moral character, gave me the fairest prospect of forming an advantageous connubial connection; and such a connection was once in my power. Heaven forgive me if I am sometimes half tempted to wish its curse on the authors of the writings, which had so far perverted my judgment, and depraved my taste, as to induce me to reject it. To their fascinating influence on my young and unexperienced mind it is owing that, instead of being a matron, rendering a worthy man happy, surrounded by a train of amiable children, educated in virtuous principles, and formed by our mutual cares and examples to virtuous habits, and of promoting and participating the happiness of the social circle, in which we might be placed, I am now, in the midst of the wide world, solitary, neglected, and despised.

"In this situation, in order to avoid becoming a female cynic, or sinking into a state of total apathy, I have sketched out for myself a plan, from which I expect to derive happiness, sufficient to prevent life from being a burden. My income is considerable, and my expenses comparatively small. Having no dependants nor needy relations, that accumulation of property, which in most cases is prudent and commendable, would in me be ridiculous. It is, therefore, my intention to seek out proper objects of charity, principally among those who, by misfortunes, and without any blameable misconduct of their own, have been reduced from opulent or easy circumstances to indigence; and to bestow on them what I have no occasion to use myself. This will be my serious employment: but it will leave me many leisure hours, for which I must have some amusement; and this is most readily found in books.

"And here I encounter another wretched effect of that course of reading, in which I was so injudiciously indulged. A strong relish for novels, if unchecked in its operation, naturally prevents the formation, in young minds, of a taste for books of real instruction and utility. Even history and travels, unless they wear the extravagant garb of fiction, are too dull and uninteresting to engage the attention. This is precisely my case. The library left me by my father (who possessed a truly classical taste) consists of a well-judged selection of modern books. But it is in vain that I seek amusement in it, except in the class of works of the imagination. I am obliged, therefore, to take it in those very books, which, by perverting my judgment, and filling my fancy with visionary expectations, have occasioned most of the serious evils of a very eventful life. They now amuse without the power of injuring me, for, in that respect, they have already done their utmost. I read them with the same relish, the same enthusiasm as ever; but, instead of expecting to realize scenes and situations so charmingly pourtrayed, I only regret that such unallayed felicity is, in this life, unattainable.

"Permit me to mention one more ill effect of my course of reading, which, were I differently situated, would be a source of much mortification. I think I possess a mind, which was originally capable of considerable improvement by cultivation. Had my education been properly directed (I speak it without meaning to convey any reflection on my dear departed parent) I believe I might have made acquirements, which would have enabled me to bear a part, perhaps to shine, when thrown among people of general information. Instead of this, however talkative I may be among those, who, like me, find amusement only in novels, in such company I am obliged to be shamefully silent.

"And now, my dear Mrs. Barry, if you should ever be blessed with daughters, let me urge you, by all the regard you must feel for their best interest and happiness, to copy in their education, the plan pursued by your excellent mother. Withhold from their eye the pernicious volumes, which, while they convey false ideas of life, and inspire illusory expectations, will tend to keep them ignorant of every thing really worth knowing; and which, if they do not eventually render them miserable, may at least prevent their becoming respectable. Suffer not their imaginations to be filled with ideas of happiness, particularly in the connubial state, which can never be realized. Describe life to them as it really is, and as you have yourself found it, chequered with good and evil. Teach them that a considerable proportion of human misery proceeds from human imprudence; and that, although the most exemplary virtue will not secure its possessors from the common calamities of life, it will enable them to bear, with equanimity and resignation, the portion of evil which the wisdom of providence shall see fit to allot them.

"With a high sense of the obligations I am under to you, and the most cordial wishes for the happiness of yourself and family, I am, my dear Mrs. Barry, most sincerely, and affectionately yours,

DORCAS SHELDON."

L—, July 8th, 1800.

NOTES

epigraph *"felix quem faciunt aliena pericula cautum"*: a commonly cited Latin proverb. See, for example, Benjamin Franklin's version in "The Way to Wealth": *"Wise men . . . learn by others' harms, fools scarcely by their own."*

5.11 "'tempers the wind to the shorn lamb'": proverbial; a common eighteenth-century sentiment found, for example, in Laurence Sterne's *A Sentimental Journey Through France and Italy* (1768): *"God tempers the wind,* said Maria, *to the shorn lamb"* ("Maria").

7.4 "Lysander": the use of pastoral pseudonyms was a common romantic convention. Lysander is one of the true lovers in Shakespeare's *A Midsummer Night's Dream.*

8.36-37 "'disguise thyself as thou wilt, slavery, thou art a bitter pill'": Laurence Sterne, *A Sentimental Journey,* "The Passport. The Hotel at Paris." Sterne's novel was one of the most popular of the type of eighteenth century sentimental novels that Tenney ridicules.

15.5-6 "'open as day to melting charity'": William Shakespeare, *Henry the Fourth, Second Part,* IV. iv. 31-32: "He hath a tear for pity and a hand / Open as day for melting charity."

15.34 "Harriet Caroline Clementina": Harriet Byron, Caroline Grandison, and Clementina della Porretta, the three central women characters in Samuel Richardson's novel *Sir Charles Grandison* (1753-54) noted respectively for great delicacy, dutifulness, and piety.

18.6 "dulcinea": any idealized woman longed for by a lover, after "Dulcinea del Toboso," the peasant woman that Don Quixote imagines to be a lady whom he falls in love with.

19.10 "'who whistled as he went for want of thought'": John Dryden, "Cymon and Iphigenia," l. 85: "And whistled as he went, for want of Thought." In Dryden's poem (a translation of the first tale of the Fifth Day in Boccaccio's *Decameron*), the phrase refers to Cymon, the brutish son of a Cyprian lord whose reason is awakened after falling in love with Iphigenia.

27.7   "Thetis": a Nereid or sea-nymph in Greek mythology, the mother of Achilles.

28.6   "Sir Charles Grandison": the hero of Samuel Richardson's 1753-54 novel of the same name, intended by Richardson to portray "a Man of TRUE HONOUR."

36.28   "Scipio": Scipio Africanus the younger, or Scipio Æmelianus, known for his self-control.

38.2   "'gracious, mild and good'": Jonathan Swift, "Verses on the Death of Dr. Swift, 1731," l. 181. The poem is a satire anticipating the self-congratulatory responses to the announcement of Swift's death, including the "gracious, mild, and good" Queen's comment, "'Is he gone? 'Tis time he shou'd'" (l. 182).

44.18-20 "The ensuing scene can be easily imagined by the feeling heart; and to those devoid of sensibility, the description would be insipid; we, therefore, pass it over in silence'": an allusion to the eighteenth-century cult of sensibility, popularized in novels such as *A Sentimental Journey* and Henry Mackenzie's *Man of Feeling*.

60.2   "rencounter": an encounter between two adversaries; a battle or skirmish.

74.19   "touched the string of my sorrow": see note for 85.15-16.

79.5   "papish": an adherent of the pope, a member of the Roman Catholic church.

80.10-11 "'How blessings brighten as they take their flight'": Edward Young, *Night Thoughts* "Night the Second," l. 602. Young's *Night Thoughts* was a popular devotional work that combined elements of sensibility, sublimity, and melancholy.

82.11-18 "'Heav'n first taught letters ...'": Alexander Pope, "Eloisa to Abelard," ll. 51-58.

85.15-16 "'touch the string upon which vibrated all her sorrows.'": Laurence Sterne, *A Sentimental Journey*, "I touch'd the string on which hung all her sorrows. . . . The string I had touch'd ceased to vibrate" ("Maria").

85.37 "Richardson": Samuel Richardson, author of the popular, highly emotional novels *Pamela* (1740-42), *Clarissa Harlowe* (1747-48), and *Sir Charles Grandison* (1753).

92.14 "took a French leave": derogatory colloquialism for leaving or doing anything without notice or permission. Originally, a neutral term for the eighteenth-century custom common in France (and imitated in England) of leaving a reception without notifying the host or hostess.

97.19 "hallow": variant spelling of ho*llow*.

98.8 "small clothes": knee breeches.

106.13-14 "'louder and yet louder strain'": John Dryden, "Alexander's Feast," l. 124: "A lower yet, and yet a lower strain." In Dryden's poem, the line describes music, which is portrayed as having the power to manipulate the emotions.

107.27 "Momus": the Greek god of mirth.

108.6 "Philander": a trifling lover. A character in Beaumont and Fletcher's play *Laws of Candy*; the occasion for Young's "Night the Second" (see note for 99.13-14) is the death of a "Philander."

118.11 "tippee": in the height of fashion.

122.2 "'stood collected in her might'": John Dryden's translation of the third book of Virgil's Ge*orgics*, l. 363: "When he stands collected in his might, / He roars, and promises a more successful Fight." The *Georgics* are a panegyric on rural life, with the third book celebrating the power of "Love"—the "secret joys of sweet Coition" (l. 376)—over all the farm animals.

128.29 "dishabille": in a state of undress, or dressed informally, probably with the careful appearance of negligence.

133.28-29 "'None without hope . . . '": Lord George Lyttelton, "Epigram," from *The Works of Lord George Lyttelton* (London: J. Dodsley, 1774), 623. Lyttelton participated in many of the popular forms of aesthetic expression, constructing "ruins," a Doric temple, and a pastoral "sheep-walk" on his grounds at Hagley Park and writing a romantic account of his travels to North Wales.

136.12-13   "Madame Sevignie": (Marie de Rabutin-Chantal, Marquise de Sévigné) a Frenchwoman (1626-96) famous for her letters to her daughter.

140.24   "Harriot Byron": Harriet, the female protagonist of *Sir Charles Grandison*.

141.11   "canns": vessels for holding liquid.

142.10   "jehu-like": driving fast and recklessly. Jehu was the tenth king of Israel in the Old Testament, noted as a fast, reckless chariot driver. See 2 Kings 9:20.

151.3   "eclaircissements": solutions, clarifications, explanations (French).

152.10   "the defeat of St. Clair by the Indians": General Arthur St. Clair was the governor of the Northwest Territories. He, with an army of miltiamen and irregular soldiers, was surprised by Indians in a camp on the Wabash River (near the present Ohio-Indiana border) and routed with only half of his men unharmed. (November 4, 1791)

156.15   "gracious, kind, and good": see note for 38.2

158.6   "trig": spruce, smart, neatly dressed.

159.29   "guess": used here as an attributive adjective, meaning *kind of*.

168.2   "taking a trip to Scotland": colloquialism for eloping. English couples in the latter half of the eighteenth century would often elope to Gretna Green, a village on the southern border of Scotland, where the village blacksmith performed irregular marriages without a minimum age requirement or the publication of banns required by the Anglican Church.

212.16   "cast muslin": a cast-off or second-hand dress.

213.37   "changeable lustring": a glossy silk fabric that changes colors under different aspects.

225.28-29   "that country 'from whose bourne no traveller returns'": Shakespeare, Haml*et* III.i, ll. 79-80: "The undiscover'd country from whose bourn / No traveller returns."

227.5   "Roderic Random": Tobias Smollet's 1748 novel, *The Adventures of Roderick Random*. *Roderick Random* is a picaresque rather than a sentimental novel, but still has the sentimental ending of the hero's long-thwarted marriage.

235.16-17 "a scene for the pencil of Hogarth": William Hogarth (1697-1764), a British artist renowned for creating groups of paintings that told a story in scenes, such as *The Rake's Progress* (1735) and *Marriage à la Mode* (1745).

235.38 "baize": a coarse woolen material with a fuzzy surface.

248.38 "'with solemn steps, and slow'": cf. Oliver Goldsmith, "The Deserted Village," l. 115: "careless steps and slow;" Alexander Pope, "Dunciad," IV l. 465: "timid step, and slow;" John Milton, *Paradise Lost*, XII l. 648: "wandring steps and slow."

257.4-5 "'Away went' Dorcas . . . ": William Cowper, "John Gilpin": "Away went Gilpin, neck or nought, / Away went hat and wig." A mock-heroic ballad about a "linen-draper bold" (l. 21) whose horse, like Dorcasina's, ran away with him.

259.35-36 "'Twilight grey . . . 'clad all things in its sober livery'": John Milton, *Paradise Lost*, IV ll. 598-9: "Twilight grey / Had in her sober livery all things clad."

276.24-26 "'Sir Charles Grandison . . . double, not a divided love'": The plot of *Sir Charles Grandison* revolves around his courtship first of Clementina della Porretta and subsequently, after Clementina's refusal of him for religious reasons, of Harriet Byron, who raises questions about his "divided" love.

286.9 "'confusion worse confounded'": John Milton, *Paradise Lost*, II l. 996.

289.21 "bohea": Bohea tea, then considered a low-quality black tea from China.

297.18-20 "France . . . demoralizing, and atheistical principles of that corrupt people": during the eighteenth century, Paris was the center for a group of *philosophes* who denied the existence of a God and searched for mechanistic explanations for human phenomena.

312.37 "catchpoles": warrant officers who usually arrest for bad debts; a contemptuous term.

316.2 "jacobite": a Jacobin is a follower of the French political society dedicated to the propagation and maintenance of extreme democracy and absolute equality.

316.2 "illumbenator": "Illuminator" is a contemptuous name for the Illuminati, a term used by extension from the German *Illuminaten* for atheistic or free-thinking groups like the French Encyclopædists.

316.11-12 "a book ... writ by one Tom Paine": *The Age of Reason* (1794-95), a controversial book attacking the Bible and propounding a deistic view of revealed religion, for which Paine was condemned in the United States as an atheist.